Elizabeth Falconer lives in Gloucestershire and spends part of the year in the south of France. *A Barefoot Wedding* is her fifth novel; her first four novels, *The Golden Year*, *The Love of Women*, *The Counter-Tenor's Daughter* and *Wings of the Morning*, are also published by Black Swan.

A BAREFOOT
WEDDING

Elizabeth Falconer

BLACK SWAN

A BAREFOOT WEDDING
A BLACK SWAN BOOK : 0 552 99756 0

First publication in Great Britain

Black Swan edition published 1999

1 3 5 7 9 10 8 6 4 2

Set in 11pt Melior by
County Typesetters, Margate, Kent

Black Swan Books are published by Transworld Publishers Ltd,
61–63 Uxbridge Road, London W5 5SA,
in Australia by Transworld Publishers,
c/o Random House Australia Pty Ltd,
20 Alfred Street, Milsons Point, NSW 2061,
in New Zealand by Transworld Publishers,
c/o Random House New Zealand,
18 Poland Road, Glenfield, Auckland
and in South Africa by Transworld Publishers,
c/o Random House (Pty Ltd),
Endulini, 5a Jubilee Road, Parktown 2193.

Reproduced, printed and bound in Great Britain by
Cox & Wyman Ltd, Reading, Berks.

To Jutta

I must dance bare-foot on her wedding day,
And, for your love to her, lead apes in hell.

William Shakespeare
The Taming of the Shrew

Chapter One

The day began badly, and got worse. Waking reluctantly from a deep and dream-haunted sleep, Rachel lay for a moment, blinking at the pale square of cold light that was the curtained window of the bedroom she shared with her husband. Slowly, she became aware of the sound of dripping water. She switched on her bedside lamp, and peered about her, trying to locate the source of the sinister little sound. She got out of bed and saw at once the large dark stain on the carpet, and then the drops of water falling, plop, plop, in a steady stream. She looked up at the ceiling and her eyes widened in horror at the sight of the swollen bulging plaster, like a great white pregnant belly. She ran back to the bed and shook her husband's shoulder. 'Wake up, Stanley! *Please*, Stanley, wake up! Something horrible is about to happen!'

Stanley Madoc opened his eyes and sat up, immediately alert, but before he could ask Rachel what it was that she found so alarming, the ceiling came down with a frightening roar, and it seemed that a cloudburst had broken over the major part of the room. Rachel shrieked, and burst into tears.

'Don't be idiotic, my dear. It's only a burst pipe. Didn't you get the lagging checked in the summer?' Stanley got out of bed, and, finding a path through the sodden debris scattered over the carpet, led the way up to the second floor, where their three children slept. A large puddle was seeping under the door of the bathroom, and he opened it and went in. The floor was awash. Water ran in a steady stream from the radiator pipe, and could be seen disappearing through the gaps between the floorboards. Stanley's and Rachel's bedroom was immediately below; it was perfectly clear what had happened.

'Rachel, didn't you get the plumber to come and check everything, as I told you?' Stanley, who knew what the answer would be, sounded seriously displeased.

'I'm sorry, Stanley. I forgot.'

'Pointless leaving things like that to Mum, Dad. You should know that by now.' Adam, a supercilious fifteen-year-old, stood in the doorway, pyjama-clad, grinning, while his twin brother Ned, and their younger sister Ciaran, both bursting with curiosity, brought up the rear.

'The water must be turned off, *at once*!' ordered Stanley. 'Where is the stopcock, Rachel?'

'I'm sorry, I've no idea.'

'*I* know where it is,' said Adam, importantly; 'I'll go.' Without waiting for a reply, he turned and ran downstairs.

'Get dressed, all of you.' Stanley spoke briskly. 'We're up now. We might as well use the extra time to make sure you get to school punctually, for a change.'

'Oh, Dad, it's only twenty to seven.' Ciaran assumed her pleading expression, looking at her father through her eyelashes.

'Don't argue.'

Breakfast was a glum affair. The twins and their sister sat at the table, noisily munching cornflakes, while Stanley, the kitchen telephone cradled beneath his chin, his face taut with irritation, his small dark eyes angry behind the modish black metal frames of his spectacles, did his considerable best to persuade a series of local plumbers to come and deal with his domestic crisis. He was having an extremely frustrating time – it seemed that there were a great many burst pipes in Oxford that morning. 'It's no good, you'll just have to keep on ringing round until you find someone, Rachel.' He replaced the phone with unnecessary force. 'I have a lecture at eleven. I must get my notes in order.'

Luckily, there had been enough water in the kettle to make coffee. Silently, Rachel poured some for her husband, and he drank it swiftly, standing up. He looked at her accusingly. 'You will *do* it, won't you, now? Just work through the Yellow Pages; it's not a problem.'

'Yes, dear, I'll try.'

'Not *try*, Rachel. *Do*.'

'Yes, Stanley, I will.'

The two boys exchanged sly grins and got up from the table, ready to cycle to school. They were clones of their father, not very tall but powerfully built, with Stanley's dark intelligent eyes and black hair. The younger child, Ciaran, was twelve and although she had inherited her mother's wispy fair hair, her eyes were a luminous flecked hazel, like those of a fox. She was not yet considered old enough to cycle to school on her own, so Stanley usually dropped her off on his way to college, and Rachel met her at the end of the afternoon and walked home with her. Seeing her father preparing to leave, she, too, swallowed her last spoonful of cornflakes and stood up. 'Dinner money, Mum?' she asked.

'Oh, God,' said Rachel; 'I forgot. Is it Friday already?'

Ciaran did not bother to continue this routine conversation. She turned confidently towards Stanley. 'All right, all right, don't fuss. Get in the car; we'll sort it out on the way.'

11

Rachel went with them to the door, and watched the bicycles and the car make their way down the short drive and turn into Lovelace Road. She waved, but no-one noticed. She sighed, tightened the belt of her dressing-gown, and went back into the house, closing the door and retrieving the mail from the wire basket fixed to its inner side. It was quite cold in the hall, and she hurried back to the kitchen, poured herself the remains of the coffee, sat down at the kitchen table and began to censor the contents of the basket. It was her particular self-imposed duty to do this, in order to circumvent Stanley's angry reaction to the volume of junk mail that flowed like a colourful tide through their front door on a daily basis. She gathered up the pile of rejects, resisting the temptation to break the seals of the ones that ordered her to open them immediately, or risk losing several million pounds or a holiday in the Seychelles. I wish, she thought, as she stuffed the offending bundle into the bin under the sink.

She sat down again, took another sip of her cooling coffee and examined the remaining half-dozen letters. Five of them were addressed to Stanley, and four of these were obviously bills. Last year, Stanley had decided to pay the monthly accounts himself, after a string of red reminders and one actual disconnection of the electricity supply. This had involved him in an expensive reconnection, and a good deal of personal humiliation and embarrassment in the face of the snide remarks of their neighbours. Rachel herself had thought the whole episode quite amusing, and had rather enjoyed the two evenings spent without television, by candlelight, and with take-away food for supper. Stanley and the children, unfortunately, had failed to see the funny side of it.

The sixth letter was addressed to Rachel herself, and had a Cambridge postmark. Frowning, suddenly alert, she turned the envelope over, and saw that the flap was sealed with a small personal sticker, printed with the words *The Rev. G.S. Lovell, The Rectory, Deeping St Cuthbert, near Ely, Cambs*. The postcode was so small that one would have needed a magnifying glass to read it. Father Lovell, thought Rachel, I'd forgotten all about him; he must be really old by now; eighty, at least. She slid a knife under the flap to open the envelope, took out the single sheet of paper and unfolded it.

My dear Rachel, she read,
It is many years now since our paths crossed, but I was able to ascertain your present whereabouts with little difficulty through the University network. Fortunately, I had remembered your married name.
I feel it my duty to inform you that your father is now extremely infirm, and very ill indeed. I gather from the District Nurse that it can only be a matter of weeks before the poor man passes on, and I felt that you might wish to know this, before it is too late. I am sincerely sorry to be the bearer of these unhappy tidings, and trust that you will forgive the intrusion, if such it be, my dear.
Yours in †
G. S. Lovell

Rachel stared at the handwritten page, and noticed that her hand was shaking. A goose walked over her grave, and she placed the letter on the table in front of her, smoothing it out carefully. She read it again, twice, her heart beating rapidly, her mind full of questions, as well as acute feelings of disquiet, and of guilt. Was her father at home, or in hospital? Was he all alone, with only the rector and the district nurse to care for him?

A vivid picture of the bleak little fenland farmhouse, her childhood home, rose before her eyes. Around the ugly Victorian house, an uneasy combination of raw red Fletton bricks and black creosoted timber weatherboarding, under a concrete pantiled roof, clustered its brick barns and timber outhouses, surrounding a permanently wet and muddy yard, with its foul-smelling smoking central dunghill. The flat fields, fens and reedbeds stretched for miles on every side, under a huge windswept sky, sometimes blue as a bird's egg in summer, more often a sullen grey, cross-hatched with sleety driving rain, carried on the relentless east wind which blew, salt-laden, straight off the North Sea. I must go to him, of course, said Rachel to herself, numbly, and the very idea of returning to that cold, loveless house, especially in January, filled her with dread.

The back door opened and Madge came in on a blast of cold air, bringing with her the blue plastic milk-bottle carrier with its four fresh pints. Madge, dear, kind, slatternly Madge, Rachel's cleaning-lady and greatest friend, came three mornings a week to help her keep some sort of control in the losing battle with the domestic challenges of her life, as mother of three and mistress of the huge Edwardian house that Stanley considered a quintessential part of the successful career of an ambitious Oxford don. He did not expect to have to wait very long for his Chair, in spite of his wife's inadequacy in the important business of their social life. This failure on Rachel's part to emulate the good example of other University wives, in the giving and receiving of dinners and drinks parties, was an ongoing source of disappointment and frustration to Stanley, and of embarrassment to herself.

After one more than usually disastrous dinner party, when the food had been either raw or burned, Stanley had lost his temper completely. 'I suppose that coming from a background that was little better than a slum, Rachel, one can hardly expect you to take seriously the importance of a more civilized and elegant lifestyle.'

Rachel had not responded to these unkind remarks, but had secretly asked herself whether Stanley's own background, as the son of a Welsh coalminer, had been so very different from her own. Not that she had anything at all against coalminers. On their few visits to Stanley's ageing parents, she had found them delightful, utterly unpretentious, still living in the tiny terraced house in which their only child had been born and raised. They were both touchingly proud of Stanley's success. Sitting at their tea-table, eating cold ham, laver bread, and a salad of cucumber and tomatoes, she had envied them their modest, orderly and loving home, knowing how much she herself would have preferred their way of life to that of the residents of the grandiose Lovelace Road. She could never understand why it was that the possession of a superior intellect should necessitate a negation of one's own culture, together with a burning desire to be elevated into another, presumably superior class.

'It'll have to be hoovering this morning, Madge. The water's off, so we can't do the washing.'

'Is that a fact?' Madge dumped her shopping bag and the milk on the table. 'What's up then? Burst pipe, is it?' She pulled off her red woolly cap and shook out her glossy black curls.

'Oh, God! I've forgotten to keep phoning for a plumber – Stanley will kill me if I don't get someone to fix it before he gets home.' Rachel leapt to her feet and grabbed the phone book, leafing through the Yellow Pages until she found 'Plumbers'. She dialled the first number, but there was no answer; then several more without success, while Madge, enjoying the drama, put the breakfast things in the dishwasher.

After seven abortive attempts at locating a plumber, Rachel hung up, and stared out of the kitchen window at the long frost-bitten garden, with its large but far from immaculate lawn and overgrown horse chestnuts. 'Madge,' she said quietly, 'it's not just the bloody plumber. It's my dad. He's ill, I've got to go to him. I must.' Returning to the table she sat down heavily, and Madge, full of concern, sat down beside her.

Rachel pushed Father Lovell's letter towards her, and Madge read it carefully, tracing the words with her finger. 'Poor old sod,' she said. 'Your dad, I mean.' She put her hand on Rachel's arm. 'You find out about trains, and get packed, love. I'll take care of everything here, I will; don't you fret.'

'What, could you come every day?'

'Nights, too, if you want. Babysitting, and that.'

'What about Danny and Mike?'

'I'll bring them with me. They can bunk in with yours, can't they?'

'I suppose they could, yes,' said Rachel, though she doubted whether Stanley would approve of such an arrangement.

'Well, don't hang about, get on with it, then. Ring up the station right away. I can do the plumber after you've gone.'

An hour later, Rachel was in a taxi on her way to the station, frantically trying to remember whether she had forgotten to carry out some vital task before her departure. She had left a short note for Stanley, fastened with a paper-clip to Father Lovell's letter. *I will call you in a day or two, and let you know how things are. Love, R.* Then, as an afterthought, she had added: *P.S. There's no phone, so I'll have to go to the phone box. I suppose you could always ring Father Lovell.*

At the station, she bought a second-class return to Ely.

'Day return?'

'No. I don't know how long I'll be away.'

'Right.' The clerk told her the cost of the ticket, and Rachel presented her Visa card, astonished at the enormity of the price, and wondering how much money she actually had in her account at the moment.

The journey was very long, and very tedious, and it was a quarter to ten when she arrived at her destination. A bone-chilling wind blew through the station, and Rachel pulled her muffler over her head and round her neck, tucking the ends into her coat. She took the solitary waiting taxi out to Deeping St Cuthbert, and on through the dark, icy, reed-fringed lanes to St Cuthbert's Fen, where she found her father's house in darkness, except for a dim light burning in the kitchen. She paid the driver, and watched as his rear lights retreated into the darkness, taking her last point of safe human contact with them. She turned, and carrying her small canvas grip, picked her way carefully across the frozen yard to the kitchen door. She lifted the latch, and was not at all surprised when the shabby old door opened. It had never in her memory been locked; nothing worth stealing, her father had always said.

She closed the door quietly, put down her bag and looked round the dim, smoke-blackened, low-ceilinged kitchen of her childhood. Nothing had changed since she had left the place to go to university, eighteen years ago. The same brass oil-lamp, with its white milk-glass shade, cast its feeble light over the greasy, ring-marked table, a makeshift affair of elm planks resting on a pair of wooden trestles.The same set of ill-matched beechwood bodger's chairs stood round the table, and the same black dresser held the familiar willow-pattern china. On a deal washstand beneath one of the windows was an enamel basin, and underneath was the bucket in which water was drawn from the well in the yard, for the farm was not connected to the mains. Beasts and humans alike depended for every drop on the supply hauled up daily from the well.

In the shadows, near the Dover stove fitted into the chimney-breast on the far side of the room, an unfamiliar object caught Rachel's eye. It was a bed, and in it, under an old-fashioned Paisley eiderdown quilt, lay her father, apparently asleep. She took a deep breath and crossed the room as quietly as she could on the bare flagstones of the floor, and sat down on the chair that stood beside the sick man's bed. After a while, he coughed and turned his face towards her. He opened his eyes: unfocused, glazed, pain-filled and angry. He stared at her. 'Amy?' he croaked, half-raising his head.

'Hello, Pa.'

'Who the hell are you?'

'It's me, Pa; Rachel. I've come to see you.'

'Bugger off, gel, you'll get nowt out of me.'

He turned his face away, and Rachel saw in the lamplight how sharp was his nose and how prominent his cheekbones, the yellow skin taut over the skull.

Stanley had had a satisfactory day, by his standards. His lecture had gone well, the hall had been packed, his young audience alert, well-informed and responsive. In today's world, which seemed to him to be unduly dependent on instant access to and manipulation of information by means of technology, he found it rather gratifying that philosophy remained a popular subject with the intelligent young. He had lunched with friends at a fashionable Oxford brasserie, given a tutorial in the afternoon, and drunk a glass of sherry with the Master before driving home. As he turned off the Woodstock Road and entered Lovelace Road, its pavements already sparkling with hoar-frost under the original Edwardian street-lamps, he recollected the boring affair of the burst pipe, and fervently hoped that the matter had now been dealt with, that the house would be functioning normally, with a half-way decent meal in preparation. He turned into his driveway, and observed with displeasure that every single light in the house appeared to be switched on, and none of the curtains drawn. A strange van stood in the drive.

As soon as Stanley entered his house, he knew that something was amiss. He heard the loud blare of the radio, and his nose detected a strong odour of frying onions. He hung up his coat and went to the kitchen. At the stove stood Madge, she of the glossy hair but imperfect cleaning skills, shaking a large frying-pan of chopped onion, potato and mince. Her two children, fair-haired Danny, aged about ten Stanley thought, and coal-black Mike, a couple of years younger, sat at the table. Mike was an engagingly attractive little boy with a huge smile and a head covered with minute tight black curls, like tiny coiled springs. 'Hi, man!' he said, grinning at Stanley.

'Hi,' said Stanley. 'Good evening, Madge. Where's Rachel? Is she with the plumber?'

Madge turned from the stove. 'Plumber's upstairs with the kids, he is. Could you give them a shout? Supper's ready.'

Stanley went to the foot of the stairs and called his children's names, with a request to come down at once. They failed to respond, and he returned to the kitchen and despatched Danny upstairs in search of them.

'There's a letter for you on the table, Dr Madoc, sir. Poor Rachel, she had to rush off to her old dad, she did. Seems he's on the blink, poor old chap; dying, or something, very likely, he is.'

Mystified, but with the dreadful foreboding that his already chaotic domestic life was about to go seriously wrong, Stanley picked up Rachel's letter and read it carefully, along with that of the Reverend Father Lovell.

'It's ever so far away, to wherever it is she's gone, poor soul. She probably hasn't even got there yet.' Madge, scooping her fry-up into a brown earthenware

19

dish and popping it into the oven, spoke with a kind of sympathetic relish, as if Rachel's long, arduous journey to Cambridgeshire was some event she might have witnessed on the telly.

What a bloody nuisance, thought Stanley, I can't even telephone her for an assessment of the situation. I suppose I could always phone the clergyman fellow, get him to tell me what the form is. Somehow this idea had little appeal for him, being Welsh himself, and if anything at all nowadays, a chapel man. He was not particularly into the Anglican faith, and felt little inclination to becoming involved with this Father Lovell, a neo-Papist by the sound of things. 'Well,' he said, 'how very unfortunate.' He almost said inconvenient.

'Still,' said Madge cheerfully, 'it's an ill wind. I've told her I'll come every day while she's gone. Nights, too, if you like. I could use the dosh, I could.'

Stanley shot a startled glance in Madge's direction, but could detect no hidden agenda in her remarks or demeanour. The children, accompanied by the plumber, a tired-looking middle-aged man, came thunderously down the stairs and into the kitchen.

'Pipe's mended, Dad,' said Adam. 'You can turn on the water now.'

'You do it, since you know where everything is, Adam.' Stanley turned his attention to the plumber. 'What do I owe you?'

'Seventy-five quid, sir. Forty for the call-out; the rest materials and labour. Plus VAT, sir.'

Stanley took out his cheque-book, with a strong feeling that he was being taken for a ride, but an equally strong feeling of relief that the water was now running. 'How much does that amount to?' he asked.

'VAT at seventeen and a half per cent?' The plumber took out his calculator. 'That's eighty-eight quid, near as makes no odds, sir.'

Stanley wrote the cheque and handed it over.

'Pipes need lagging, sir, and no mistake, or it'll very likely happen again.'

'Perhaps you'd like to give me a quote for the job?'

'Much obliged, sir. I'll do that. I'll get back to you presently.'

'Make it soon, please.' Stanley accompanied the plumber to the door, then returned to the kitchen. Madge and all five children stood at the sink, admiring the stream of water that flowed from the tap.

'Water's on, Dad,' said Adam, as if he were the sole perpetrator of this miracle.

'So I see, Adam,' replied his father dryly. 'Now Madge, what about some supper? It's long past the usual time.'

By ten o'clock supper was finished and washed up, Madge had departed with her boys, and Stanley's children were reluctantly obeying his orders to finish their homework and then go to bed. Feeling quite tired and very nearly ready for bed himself, he decided not to bother lighting the fire in the sitting-room. He poured himself a whisky, sat down on the sofa in front of the empty fireplace and unfolded the *Guardian*.

Soft footsteps on the carpet announced the arrival of a child, and he looked over the top of his spectacles at Ciaran, standing timidly beside the sofa in her dressing-gown. Her feet were bare.

'Where are your slippers, Ciaran?'

'I can't find them.'

Stanley shook his head, and smiled at his daughter, so like Rachel as a young woman, with the same apologetic, diffident air, as if she expected to be found wanting. 'What's the trouble, *cariad*? Is your bed cold?'

'No, it's OK.'

'What, then?'

'It's Mum. I don't like her not being here.'

Stanley sighed. He held out a hand, and Ciaran sat down beside him on the sofa. He put his arm round her and gave her a hug. 'We'll just have to manage as best we can,' he said. 'Madge'll be here; it'll be OK, you'll see.'

Ciaran snuggled against him, tucking her feet underneath her dressing-gown. Carefully, Stanley reopened his newspaper and found his place.

'Madge is a slut, Adam says.'

'Really, Ciaran, that's a rather sweeping character analysis, don't you think?'

'What's it actually mean, "slut"?'

'It means someone, usually a woman, of less than impeccable habits of cleanliness.'

'Oh. You mean like Mum?'

'No, Ciaran, I do *not* mean like Mum. Your mother may be disorganized, but she is not a slut.'

'Adam says Madge is a whore, too.'

'And on what premise does Adam base his argument, Ciaran?'

'He says her kids don't match, so she must be.'

Unable to challenge the logic of this, Stanley decided to terminate the conversation. 'Come on,' he said. 'It's time we were all in bed.'

He turned off the lights, leaving one on in the hall, then accompanied his daughter to the second floor, and tucked her into her bed. He switched off her lamp and said good night.

'Leave the door open a crack, please, Dad.'

'OK.'

Wearily, he descended the stairs and made his way to his and Rachel's room. He opened the door, switched on the lights, and saw to his horror that the place was still in a state of absolute chaos, with shards of sodden plaster scattered everywhere. The air was filled with the foul smell of wet carpet, a small erratic drip still falling from the gaping hole in the ceiling. The bed was unmade, and it was obvious that Madge had not even entered the room, for she had made no attempt whatsoever to clear up the mess, let alone change the ruined bedlinen. Stanley uttered a string of Welsh obscenities, a half-forgotten litany of blasphemous phrases, part of the culture of his schooldays and still deeply rooted in his consciousness.

He retrieved his pyjamas from the back of the bathroom door and took himself to sleep in the spare room. 'Adam's right,' he muttered angrily, 'the bloody woman is a slut. She'll have to go. I'll speak to Rachel as soon as she gets back.'

He got between the cold sheets of the guest-room bed, and stared bleakly at the ceiling, chilled to the bone, missing the comfort of Rachel's warm body beside him. I'd better telephone the Reverend Thing tomorrow, he thought glumly. I must find out how long she's likely to be away. I need to know where I stand.

Rachel woke at dawn, roused by the alarm clock of her childhood, a vile-tempered rooster, crowing loudly from his position of authority on top of the midden. Her own bed having been taken down to the kitchen to make the task of nursing her father easier, Rachel had chosen to sleep in her parents' room rather than occupy the small and dank-smelling third bedroom. Recovering from the initial surprise at finding herself in her father's brass-framed double bed, she rolled back the covers and went to the window, pushing back the thin cotton curtain. The pale disc of the sun was barely visible through layers of pearly mist, low on the horizon, but she could just make out the frosted ridges of the flat surrounding fields and the distant silvery lakes of flooded fenland. Rachel could not remember a year in which the winter rains had not burst through the banks of the dikes, bringing disruption to the farming families and frequent devastation to their crops.

Below her, in the farmyard, brown hens pecked and scratched around the foot of the dunghill. The rooster flapped his wings angrily, then shook his scarlet crest and descended from his perch, scattering his harem of hens from his path as he did so. Horrid thing, thought Rachel; he always was a brute. How stupid, she reminded herself, the old one must have died years ago. Anyway, they're all the same, it makes no difference. She opened her grip and took out the thick trousers, wool tights and heavy sweater she had had the good sense to bring with her, and dressed rapidly. There was no question of a wash first; she would have to make some sort of arrangement later. Not having eaten anything since she had bought herself a sandwich and a coffee on the train, she was ravenously hungry, and this pressing need for food exercised her mind almost as much as her concern for her father.

She found him still asleep, and, putting on her coat, went quietly out to the well to haul up a bucket of water. She filled the kettle, and put it on the stove to boil, having first removed the heavy iron disc over the firebox. The fire itself was very low, and Rachel added half a shovelful of anthracite nuts to the smouldering embers. Carefully, she closed the door of the firebox, picked up the empty kindling basket and went out in search of wood, in order to bring the stove quickly up to its proper temperature. She found the woodpile without difficulty; it was exactly where it had always been, stacked neatly in the woodshed behind the barn.

As she snapped the dead frozen branches across her knee and filled the basket, she could hear the hungry complaining squeals of the pigs inside the barn. They had heard her in the woodshed, and were demanding immediate attention. She left her full, heavy basket outside the door of the barn and went to look at the pigs. The moment they caught sight of her, their squeals rose to a frantic cacophony, compounded of distress and anticipation in equal parts. Rachel observed the froth that dripped from their pink snouts as they did their best to mount the walls of their pens in a state of near-hysteria. My God, she thought, they're probably starving. She looked wildly round, saw the bins in which the feed was stored, and, grabbing a bucket and filling it, ran from pen to pen, beating the pigs on the nose in order to make enough space to pour the feed into the troughs. In five minutes there was silence, broken only by the munching and slurping of sixteen famished pigs.

Rachel replaced the feed-bucket, picked up her wood-basket and staggered across the icy yard to the house. I must remember to give them water later, she said to herself. She kicked open the kitchen door, humped the basket to the stove, and knelt down in order to poke the kindling into the firebox. The flames crept through the wood and began to crackle, and this optimistic sound was followed almost at once by a faint hum from the black iron kettle. She closed the door of the firebox, wiped her hands on her trouser legs, and stood up.

'Fed the bloody swine, gel?'

'Yes, Pa.' Rachel smiled at her father. 'I'll get you some tea in a minute.' She sat down on the side of the bed and took his thin hand in hers. 'Did you sleep at all? Would you like an egg for your breakfast?'

Ernest Cropthorne shook his head. 'Just the tea. Bloody egg'd come straight back up. There's bugger all left inside, gel.'

There was a tap on the door, and it opened, admitting the square, navy-blue-clad figure of the district nurse. 'Ah, Mrs Madoc, there you are. Rector said you might come.' She put her medical case and a loaf of bread on the table. 'I thought you might not have had time to go down to the shop, so I brought this for your breakfast.'

'Thank you, how very kind of you,' said Rachel

gratefully, getting up from the bed. She held out her hand. 'My name's Rachel, how do you do?'

'Brenda,' said the nurse, shaking hands. She took off her coat, and went to the bedside. 'Hello, Mr Cropthorne, how are we today, then?'

Ernest Cropthorne's answer was inaudible as far as Rachel was concerned, but she felt pretty sure that it was abusive, or inappropriate at the very least. A thin jet of steam was issuing from the spout of the kettle. She found the teapot, warmed it, spooned tea into it and poured on the boiling water. While it brewed, she took an egg from the bowl on the dresser and carefully lowered it into the remains of the water in the kettle, to boil for four minutes. She cut a couple of thick slices of bread and ate one of them. She looked in the larder for butter and milk. There was no butter, or even margarine, and no fresh milk. There were two cans of Carnation milk, one of them already opened, the top roughly pierced. Rachel chose the unopened one, and, finding a can-opener in the dresser drawer, opened it and poured the contents into a jug. She covered the jug with a round muslin cloth edged with blue beads, a relic of her childhood. Then she took the two cans and put them in the plastic bucket under the washstand. Thank God it's not summertime, she thought, or the place'd be full of flies.

While she set the table for her breakfast, she watched unobtrusively as the nurse attended to her patient. After giving him an injection, Brenda had pulled back the sheet and quilt, rolled the sick man onto his side, and pushed aside his pyjamas to examine his extensive bedsores. One in particular, on the base of Ernest's bony spine, was a large and severely inflamed ulcer the size of a golf ball, and gave off a deeply offensive smell when the dressing was removed. Wearing a mask and surgical gloves, Brenda applied a thick white ointment to the sores, and covered the worst one with a fresh

26

dressing. 'There you are. You'll be a lot more comfortable now, won't you?'

'Bloody won't.'

'Now, now, that's not very nice, is it, when I've come all the way out here to look after you, Mr Cropthorne?'

'Don't bother coming then, gel. My Rachel's here now; she'll see to me.'

Brenda remade the bed, turning over the two thin pillows, and carefully tucking in the coverlet.

'Let it be, woman! Can't move me bloody legs if you do that, can I?'

Patiently, Brenda loosened the bedclothes over his feet. 'OK now?' she asked, but all she got for her pains was a resentful grunt.

Rachel approached the bedside with a mug of tea. 'Can you manage, Pa? Or shall I hold the cup for you?'

'Not fuckin' dead yet,' said Ernest, taking the blue mug in his trembling hands.

Brenda packed up her case, put the soiled dressings and gloves into a paper bag and disposed of it in the firebox. Rachel offered her tea and she sat down at the table and drank it, while Rachel ate her egg and the soft white butterless bread. 'Thanks for bringing the bread, you must tell me what I owe you,' she said. 'There's nothing in the larder at all, except a flitch of bacon, and some eggs and potatoes in the barn. I must go to the shop. I hope my bike's still here.'

Rachel went out to the freezing, windswept yard with Brenda, and they stood for a moment beside the nurse's very ancient pale blue A30. 'It won't be long now, dear,' said Brenda gently, putting her hand on Rachel's arm. 'But it's good that you've come, poor old man. He can't eat anything now; it's just cups of tea, and whisky if he asks for it. He doesn't need the bedpan any more, just the bottle now and then, and that's only a trickle. I'll come again tomorrow, and give him a wash and another injection. Pretty soon it'll be time to put in a line, and give him a morphine pump, then he can press the button when the pain gets too bad; it'll make it easier for him. The doctor will come out with me, and he'll explain it all to you.'

'I understand,' said Rachel. 'Thank you.'

'It's nothing,' said Brenda. 'I'm glad to be able to help, my dear.' She dumped her medical case on the rear seat of her car, and installed herself behind the wheel.

'By the way,' said Rachel. 'Someone must have been feeding the pigs for my father. Do you know who it is?'

Brenda smiled. 'It was my young lad did it for him, Rachel. He'll be that glad you're here now. Billy's not overly into pigs, if the truth were told.' She laughed. 'Specially that ole devil boar!'

'Oh, dear, I'm so sorry,' said Rachel, and laughed, too. 'Please tell him thank you, won't you?'

Brenda drove away, and Rachel watched her little car bumping along the track between the bare brown fields. Beyond a far clump of leafless trees she could see the stone tower of St Cuthbert's church. I must go to the shop, she thought, and call on Father Lovell. Then I'd better send a card to Stanley and tell him what's happening. He's never home until after dark, and I really don't want to cycle to the phone box at night.

As she stood shivering in the inhospitable yard, surrounded by the uncompromising emptiness of the Fens, Rachel experienced a curious sensation of unreality, as if this entire episode of her father's illness and her own homecoming was a figment of her imagination, or a long-drawn-out and disturbing dream. It seemed forever since she had left Lovelace Road, an age since she had seen the ceiling burst over her bedroom, a very long time since she had opened Father Lovell's letter. Was it really only yesterday?

The wind whipped her fine fair hair round her face,

stinging her eyes, and she went to the barn to look for her bike. She found it, suspended on two six-inch nails, high on the wall. She fetched the short wooden stepladder, then climbed up it, unhooked the bicycle and lowered it to the ground, scraping her knuckles against the rough bricks as she did so. Sucking her bleeding fingers, she wheeled the bike to the house, and propped it beside the kitchen door. Then she got the bucket and took water to the pigs, six pails in all.

She went back to the house, and stoked up the stove. Then she removed the empty cup from her father's bedside table. 'I've got to do the shopping, Pa. I won't be very long. You'll be OK, won't you?'

Ernest did not reply, but stared at Rachel vacantly, as if he had forgotten who she was. She put on her coat, and wound her woolly scarf round her neck. She picked up her bag. 'I've found the bike, Pa. I won't be long.'

Chapter Two

On the Wednesday morning following Rachel's departure for Deeping St Cuthbert, Stanley received a postcard from her.

Sorry I dashed off in such a hurry. Poor old Dad is very ill; they don't think he'll live for very long now. I'm glad I'm here with him – I'm sure you would feel the same, Stanley. I can't say when I'll be back, but Madge will cope, I'm sure. Love to all, Rachel. XXXX

That settles it, said Stanley to himself, spooning marmalade onto the piece of burnt toast prepared by Ciaran for his breakfast: Madge will have to go. I can't endure her, even for one more week.

The five days of Rachel's absence had produced plenty of evidence of Madge's inadequacies, in Stanley's view. On the fourth day he had managed to engage a plasterer to come and repair his bedroom ceiling, and had then telephoned Madge from his room in college.

She had answered the phone at once. 'Hello?'

'Madge, this is Dr Madoc here.'

'Oh. Hello.'

'I've arranged for a plasterer to come to the house this afternoon, at four-thirty, to mend the bedroom ceiling.'

'That's good.'

'Please ensure that you put down plenty of news-papers, dust-sheets, any suitable protective covering, on the carpet and over the furniture, in case he makes a mess.'

'Yes, OK.' Madge cast an eye on the kitchen clock. 'It's nearly half-past three, I'll have to run and get the kids right away. It's two different schools they're at, Dr Madoc, don't forget.'

'Yes, yes. Well, you'd better hurry. Don't on any account miss the plasterer, will you?'

'No, I won't, don't worry.' That's if the buses don't play up, she added to herself, hanging up.

It was after half-past four when she came hurrying back with Ciaran and her own children, none of whom had enjoyed being forced to run all the way from the bus-stop, scolded and urged on by the panicking Madge.

As it happened, Adam and Ned had arrived home early, and were just admitting the plasterer as she hurried up the drive. 'Glory be, man,' she gasped, 'I thought I'd missed you.' They all trooped into the house, and walked across the hall, leaving muddy foot-prints on the checkerboard tiled floor. Adam, Ned and the younger children headed for the kitchen to raid the fridge, and Madge took the plasterer upstairs to the bed-room. He examined the hole in the ceiling, and said he reckoned that would need a fair old bit of plaster. He enquired of Madge where he could obtain water, and she showed him the bathroom, with its art nouveau decorations and large Edwardian bath, complete with elegant swan's neck taps.

'Very tasty,' the plasterer remarked, turning on a bath-tap. 'Right. I'll bring up my buckets and stuff, and mix up in here.'

Madge carried out Stanley's instructions to the letter. With the help of Adam and Ciaran, she made sure that the still-damp carpet and the furniture in the master bedroom were suitably protected, and watched the plasterer as he erected his stepladder, in case he should disturb the carefully laid-out dust-sheets and newspapers. All seemed well; he fetched his bucket of plaster and set to work.

Madge and the children returned to the kitchen to relax around the table, enjoying their tea of Marmite sandwiches and orange juice. Madge made herself a cup of tea, and rested her throbbing feet on a spare chair. Running was not an exercise in which she took any pleasure.

The children, their eyes glued to the kitchen telly, munched their way through the thick soft white bread of their sandwiches in silence, as they watched a noisy animated cartoon. The film came to an end, and Madge got to her feet reluctantly and switched off the TV.

'Leave it on, Madge,' ordered Adam.

'Not on your nelly,' said Madge. 'You've got your homework to do, Master Adam. You know your father's rules, don't you? Ned, too.'

'Another half-hour won't matter,' said Adam stubbornly. 'I want to watch a bit of the snooker. We all do, don't we?'

'Please, Madge, Dad'll never know.' Ciaran got down from her chair, and put her arms round Madge's solid hips. '*Please*, darling Madge.'

All the children joined in a chorus of 'Please, Madge!'

'No way, it'd be more than my job's worth, it would.' Madge loosened Ciaran's arms from their grip, and began to clear the table. 'Come on now, settle down, the both of you. The rest of you go upstairs to Ciaran's room, and play quietly.' Ciaran, Danny and Mike trooped off cheerfully, acknowledging defeat quite gracefully. 'Go on, you two. Get your books out and get on with it.' Madge removed the remaining mugs from the table, and gave it a swift wipe with a wet dishcloth.

Adam and Ned, their faces taut with annoyance, got their schoolbags from the hall and thumped them down on the table as violently as they could to express their displeasure.

'That's enough,' said Madge equably, rinsing milk bottles at the sink. She listened, half-amused, as books were placed on the table, and the boys sat down with much scraping of their chairs on the floor.

After a pause, Adam spoke quietly. 'You're a fucking cow, Madge, and I hate you.'

'What did you say?' Astonished, Madge turned towards them, her hands dripping.

'I said, you're a FUCKING COW, and I HATE YOU!' Adam stood up and glared insolently at Madge, his fists clenched. Madge stepped forward, her eyes blazing, raised her wet hand and slapped him across the face as hard as she could. Adam yelped, clutched at his ear, and swore at her again, raising his right arm in a threatening manner.

'Don't you *dare*, young man!' Angrily, Madge faced up to Adam, challenging him to try anything.

Ned, white-faced, leapt to his feet. 'You leave my brother alone! I'll tell my father on you. You're not allowed to strike a child! It's illegal, you'll go to prison!'

'HO!' shouted Madge. 'I'd rather be in prison than have to look after some people, I would.'

'Bloody sow bitch!' muttered Adam, retreating behind his chair.

'Do you want another?'

'NO! Don't you touch me!'

'You're a dirty slut, too!' shrieked Ned, from the safety of the far side of the table. 'Dad says so, so there!'

'Does he indeed?' said Madge, looking grim. 'We'll see about that!'

'And a *whore*, too, Dad says!' Ned, unable to stop

33

himself, blundered on. 'Else why is Danny a white boy and Mike black?'

Madge, shattered, utterly disbelieving that the sons of her closest friend could speak to her in such a way, held onto the back of a chair and stared at them as though they were aliens. Adam and Ned stared back at her, pale, nervous and unsure of themselves. Tears filled Madge's eyes and rolled down her cheeks. Silently, she turned her back on them and carried on with the milk bottles. Silently, with anxious glances at each other, the two boys sat down and opened their books. The red imprint of Madge's large hand showed clearly across Adam's cheek.

The plasterer came downstairs, leaving white footprints on the stair-carpet. He carried his stepladder over his shoulder, and his bucket and tools in his free hand. He handed Madge the empty paper bag that had contained the dry plaster. 'Bin this for me, love, will you?'

Madge took the bag, and put it in the bin. 'All done?' she said.

'All done,' replied the plasterer, 'and a smashing job it is too, though I say so myself. There's not a lot of these old plaster ceilings around these days; it's a pleasure to do the work. Lovely cornice, too, innit?'

'Yes, it is,' agreed Madge, although she did not know what a cornice was. 'Can I get you a cupper, then?'

'No, ta, it's nearly my teatime. I'll be off now. Tell the gent I'll come back tomorrow and check whether it needs a final coat, OK?'

'Yes, fine, I'll tell him.' Madge saw the plasterer off and returned to the kitchen. Without speaking to the boys, she began to prepare supper. She had planned to make chicken paprika, a favourite dish of her own children, but now she felt sad and depressed, and disinclined to undertake creative cookery. She looked in the fridge for a substitute, and found four cooked sausages and some leftover boiled potatoes. She got a large can of baked beans from the cupboard, poured the contents into a pie-dish, sliced the sausages and potatoes into the beans, and sprinkled a thick layer of crushed Weetabix over the top. She looked at the kitchen clock: twenty-five past six. Dr Madoc would be back by seven. She added a few dabs of butter to the surface of the dish, and put it into the oven, setting it at medium. Ignoring Adam and Ned, she went to the foot of the stairs and summoned the other children. She told them to go into the sitting-room and read comics until supper-time, then got out the Hoover and cleaned the powdery footsteps off the stairs. She peered into the master bedroom, saw that the ceiling looked OK, and decided to leave the dust-sheets where they were, in case they were needed again tomorrow. Dr Madoc was still sleeping in the guest-room, so he wouldn't need the room tidying just yet. She went downstairs, put away the Hoover, checked that the supper was browning nicely, and put four plates in the warming drawer. She heard Dr Madoc's key in the door, and the footsteps of Ciaran running to greet her father, followed at a little distance by Danny and Mike.

'Hi, kids. How's things?' Stanley, in cheerful mood, ruffled the children's hair and hung up his coat. He came into the kitchen, looking benevolent. 'Everything OK, Madge? Did the plasterer come?'

'Yes, he did, and he'll come back tomorrow, to check.' Madge put on her coat, and took down the anoraks of Danny and Mike from the hooks on the garden door. 'I'll have to be off now, Dr Madoc,' she said quietly. 'I'll be here in the morning, just as I promised Rachel. I'll not let her down.'

'Aren't we staying for supper, Mum?' Mike looked at his mother, his enormous brown eyes anxious. 'Have we been naughty?'

'No, darling, *you* haven't been naughty.' Madge

looked meaningfully at Adam and Ned, as they sat, heads down, furiously scribbling. She zipped up her sons' anoraks, and crammed their bright woolly caps onto their heads. 'We'll be off home then, Dr Madoc. Good night.'

'What's eating her?' asked Stanley, as the back door closed on Madge and her little boys.

Adam looked up from his geography homework. 'Dunno,' he said. 'Does it matter?'

'I suppose not, really. Supper's in the oven, is it?'

'Yes,' said Ciaran. 'Can't you smell it?' She pulled a face. 'It's burnt again.'

'Dad,' said Adam, steering the subject away from Madge. 'Homework would be a lot easier and much more fun if we had a CD-ROM, like at school.'

'Would it really?' Stanley sat down at the table and examined his son's paperwork. 'You seem to be managing quite well with the use of your own intelligence,' he said.

'Yes, but it would be *better*, and a lot *quicker* if we had our own computer, Dad. It's how everything's done now, I'm not kidding. Absolutely everybody has one at home nowadays.'

'Well, we shall have to see,' said Stanley. 'These things cost money, you know. Hurry up and finish your work, both of you, and we'll have supper.'

He went upstairs to the bedroom to inspect the repair to the ceiling, and was pleased to see that the chap had done a good job.

After the children had gone to bed, Stanley put the dirty plates into the dishwasher, poured himself a whisky, and worked peacefully in his study until eleven o'clock. Taking his evening paper and the *New Statesman* with him he went up to his temporary bedroom and turned down the bed. He got into his pyjamas and, needing a pee, went along the corridor to his old room. As soon as he switched on the light in

36

the bathroom he saw the carnage that had struck his much-admired original Edwardian fittings. The green linoleum floor was heavily bespattered with splodges of white plaster, which, upon investigation, appeared to be stuck fast to the floor. Even worse was the state of the precious bathtub itself. A good deal of wet plaster had solidified in the waste pipe, and the enamel had been badly scratched by the plasterer's bucket. The elegant brass taps were disfigured with solid streaks of plaster, doubtless left by the plasterer's hands. Full of dismay, appalled at the carelessness and damage, Stanley turned towards the lavatory and lifted the lid, half-anticipating some further disaster. Evidently the man, having found the bath already blocked, had decided to empty the remains of his plaster down the lavatory pan, with predictable results. Stanley closed his eyes, too upset and angry to do or say anything for the moment. He went upstairs to the children's bathroom and used their loo.

The next morning, before taking his daughter to school, and himself to his college, Stanley read Rachel's card, and found her news far from reassuring. Damn it, he said to himself, this is getting to be beyond a joke. It's no good, Madge will definitely have to go. If Rachel's going to be away for some time, I'll have to employ a professional housekeeper.

Ernest Cropthorne clung to life for another three weeks. During this time, Rachel cleaned the house as best she could with the inadequate domestic equipment at her disposal, and did her best to keep her father warm and comfortable. One night, near the end of the second week, she lay awake listening to the poor man groaning with pain, and when the nurse came as usual the following morning, Rachel reported this new development to her.

'Right,' said Brenda. 'It's time for the morphine.'

She returned that afternoon with the doctor, and they set up the small green plastic box, and put a line into the back of Ernest's hand. Carefully, the doctor pointed out to him which button to press in order to deliver more pain relief if required. Ernest nodded, without much interest.

The doctor picked up his bag, ready to depart. Rachel saw him and Brenda to the door. 'When he can't press the button for himself, Mrs Madoc, you'll have to do it for him, when you think he seems to need it.'

'I understand; thank you.'

'I'll be over tomorrow, as usual, to see him,' said Brenda.

'Yes,' said Rachel. 'Thanks.'

They drove away.

For the next week, her father seemed more comfortable, and slept a good deal. She was running short of money, and since there was no cashpoint in Deeping St Cuthbert, and she did not like to ask the village shopkeeper to cash a cheque for her, she decided to cycle into Ely and go to the bank. The cashpoint there obliged her with fifty pounds, much to her relief. Not being at all sure how much money she had in her account, she decided to telephone Stanley and ask him to pay in next month's housekeeping right away, just to be on the safe side. Stanley did not like Rachel to phone him in college unless it was an emergency, but she dialled the number anyway, and he answered at once.

'Yes?'

'Stanley. It's me.'

'Oh. Hello, dear. How's your father?'

'Not good, I'm afraid. He's on morphine now.'

'Poor old chap.'

'Yes.' After a suitable pause, she continued. 'Stanley, I'm in Ely now. I had to get some cash. I'm not very sure about my bank balance, so I was wondering whether you could pay in my next month's money now? I don't want a cheque to bounce, or anything.'

Stanley gave an audible sigh. 'Very well, Rachel, I'll do that. Please try to keep a record of your expenditure, my dear.'

'Yes, Stanley, I will. I'm sorry.'

'Never mind.'

'Is everything all right at home, darling?'

'Yes, everything's fine.' He hesitated briefly, then went on. 'Poor Madge couldn't cope on her own, so I've had to engage a temporary housekeeper.'

'*Really*?' Rachel sounded startled. 'Is that wise, Stanley? How did the children react to that?'

'Splendidly. They like her very much. She seems to be a very nice person, excellent with children.'

'Oh. Well, I suppose that's good. It's only till I get back, anyway.'

'Of course.'

'I've no more change,' said Rachel. 'I'll have to hang up. Don't forget the money, will you?'

'I won't,' said Stanley. 'Goodbye, dear.'

When Rachel returned to the farm, her bicycle basket crammed with groceries, and an extra plastic bag dangling from the handlebars, it was nearly five o'clock and beginning to get dark. She propped the bike beside the door, gathered up her shopping and went into the kitchen. She dumped the bags on the table, turned up the lamp and went over to the bed to see how her father was feeling. He lay motionless, so deeply asleep that he seemed hardly to be breathing. Rachel sat down on the chair at the side of the bed, and then suddenly realized that the line for the morphine was no longer attached to the back of her father's hand. The plastic tube dangled over the edge of the bedside table and a small puddle, presumably of the morphine solution, had stained the floor beneath. She looked at her father more closely and saw that his face was as white as alabaster, and, when she put a hand on his forehead, felt as cold. Oh God, she thought, he's dead, and I wasn't here when he needed me most. Poor Pa, how awful for him, to die all alone.

For an hour she sat beside him, holding his cold stiff hand. She felt terribly sad, as if the very last link of her real roots had finally been severed. Equally, she felt relieved, even glad, that her father's tormented life had ended, and prayed that he was now at peace with whatever kind of god he believed in. One thing's for sure, she thought, carefully extricating her hand from his, he isn't here any more. She straightened the coverlet and the pillows under his head, then, worried that his mouth was slightly open, fetched a clean tea towel and folded it into a long, narrow band. She slipped it carefully beneath his chin, and tied the ends on top of his head. She remembered seeing a movie long ago in which this small ritual had been performed. It's a good idea, she said to herself; no-one would want to be buried with their mouth open, especially Pa.

Rachel put away the shopping, and, lighting the lantern, went out to the barn to feed and water the pigs. After she had humped the last heavy bucket of water from the well and poured it into the stone trough from which the pigs drank, she stood for a moment, breathing heavily, pondering the hard, sad, lonely life her father had led since the loss of his young wife, thirty-seven years ago. Amy Cropthorne had suffered a fatal haemorrhage immediately after giving birth to Rachel at home. I expect having a baby at home was the natural thing for them, she thought, just like calving or lambing, or farrowing pigs. Her own childhood, alone with her father on that silent fen, had inevitably been a difficult process for them both. For him, her presence must have been a constant ghostly reminder of the strong, fair-haired young woman he had loved, and who had been to him so much more than a wife. She had been friend, partner and workmate on the little farm. She had been far better educated than he, and knew how to manage accounts, and bargain aggressively for the best price for their pigs, potatoes and sugar beet. Together, they had made a formidable team; without her, he was nothing. Rachel had always known that she could never be any kind of consolation to him, and that he regretted that she had not been a boy. He could at least have trained up a son to help him with the farm, and ultimately inherit it, for what it was worth. As it was, he felt awkward and out of his depth with the little girl, and got her into the village school as soon as they would take her. By this one decisive act he had shaped Rachel's future, and she took to education like a duck to water.

In the fullness of time she had gone on to the local high school, but here she had encountered the cruelty, intolerance and snobbery of girls from less humble backgrounds than her own. They had ridiculed her shabby, second-hand uniform, rubbished her old-fashioned black bike, and, worst of all, mimicked the way she spoke. Deeply wounded by their unkindness, and with her confidence seriously undermined, the eleven-year-old Rachel had avoided her tormentors as best she could, and, aided by the total absence of any kind of social life, had worked hard throughout her years at the school. This endeavour had resulted, without any particular conscious effort on her part, in the winning of an exhibition at Cambridge, to read History. Her headmistress, a perspicacious and kindly woman, who had observed Rachel's difficulties with some concern, had congratulated her warmly. 'At Cambridge, Rachel, I am sure you will find a more sympathetic environment in which to develop your undoubted gifts,' she had said. 'It will be an opportunity for you to spread your wings.' Her father, too, had managed to raise a smile. 'Good on yer, gel,' he said. 'You'll be a teacher. Yer mum would've bin pleased.'

Rachel sighed, picked up the lantern, cast a careful eye over the pigs once more, and walked back to the house. She stood at the door for a moment, looking around her at the dark buildings huddled together in that lonely wasteland of dikes and ditches, of willow-fringed small streams and fields of sugar beet. The sky was black and full of stars; the frost already on the ground, and silvering the rooftops. What happens now? she asked herself. Is this all mine, or is it mortgaged to the hilt?

Inside the house, it felt warm and peaceful. The lamp burned steadily, shining on the battered table beneath it, and the logs in the stove glowed red through the peephole in the firebox. Rachel looked at the clock: twenty past six. She had not eaten since breakfast; now, she felt ravenously hungry and at the same time incredibly tired. She went to the larder and got a couple of potatoes from the sack, and put them in the oven to bake. She cut a thick slice of bacon from the flitch, and put it in the frying-pan, ready to cook when the potatoes were done. On a stone shelf stood a large glazed brown pot, with a spigot protruding from its side. She got a cup and held it under the spigot, while she turned the tap to see whether the pot contained anything. A trickle of amber-coloured fluid slowly filled the cup. She held it to her nose: elderberry wine. Cautiously, she took a sip. Hm, not bad, she thought, remembering the summer holidays, the hours of toiling in the hot sun, harvesting the ripe black fruits from the hedgerows, for her father's annual winemaking. She took the cup of wine to the kitchen and set it down on the table, then she found a fresh, unused candle and stuck it in a glass tumbler. She cleared all the paraphernalia of sickness from her father's bedside table, and spread it with a threadbare but clean linen napkin. She lit the candle and put it carefully on the table, where it burned steadily in the still air, casting its small light on Ernest's peaceful face, pale, emaciated, but no longer distorted with pain.

Rachel set the table, ready for her supper. Then she sat down and raised her cup of wine. 'Here's to you, Pa,' she said aloud. 'I wish I'd got to know you better.'

Early next morning, although it was raining heavily, Rachel cycled into Deeping St Cuthbert to inform the doctor of her father's demise. He arranged to drive out to the farm as soon as his morning surgery was over. 'What about the undertaker, Mrs Madoc? Have you spoken to anyone yet, or the rector, about funeral arrangements?'

'No, I haven't. We're not on the phone, I'm afraid.'

'Oh, I see. Well, perhaps you'd like me to get someone from town to come out and see you? Perhaps this afternoon? I'm sure you'll be glad to have the body removed from the house?'

'Er, yes, I suppose so.' If she felt a twinge of surprise at this brisk disposal of her father's remains, Rachel did not show it. 'Thank you,' she said. 'That would be kind.'

She bought a loaf of bread and cycled back to the farm. She fed and mucked out the pigs, then, with the instinctive wish that her father's home should look as neat and clean as possible before the advent of the professional organizers of his last rite of passage, she heated a bucket of water on the stove. On her knees, she scrubbed the floor from end to end of the kitchen. She worked backwards, finishing up at the door. Thankfully, she got to her feet, squeezed out the floor-cloth, and slung the filthy contents of the bucket onto the midden.

Inside the house, the damp floor had reduced the temperature by several degrees and the air smelt of carbolic soap. Rachel sighed. How stupid I am, she thought; it doesn't look any better and it smells a bloody sight worse. She wiped down the table, cleared away the used cups and plates, and added wood to the stove. Then she put on her coat, and sat down on the chair beside her father's bed.

The district nurse arrived at eleven-thirty. 'Poor man,' she said, eyeing the corpse. 'It was a merciful release, really. Cancer is a terrible thing, isn't it?'

Rachel, wondering whether this was a professional visit, or in fact one of condolence, offered Brenda a cup of tea.

'Thanks, dear, but I won't. I've just come to collect the drugs and that. There's others need the morphine pump; there's never enough equipment to go round.'

'Yes, of course; go ahead,' said Rachel.

At that moment the doctor drove into the yard. A man of about forty, he wore a bright red scarf and a thick Norfolk jacket. He got out of his brand-new Range Rover and entered the house, carrying his important-looking black medical case. I wonder why? Rachel asked herself; there's no-one here needing treatment. Without removing his scarf, the doctor briefly examined Ernest Cropthorne's withered corpse, then, opening his bag, took out a pack containing death certificates. Of course, thought Rachel, smiling faintly, her question answered. The doctor sat at the table to fill up and sign the death certificate. 'There you are, Mrs Madoc,' he said, handing it to her. 'I'm really very sorry,' he added, perfunctorily, 'but it was a merciful release for him, to be honest.'

Rachel felt like saying 'How the hell do you know that?' Instead, she made a murmur of assent, took the piece of paper from him, folded it carefully and put it in her pocket.

There was a commotion in the yard, and through the window Rachel saw a large black limousine coming to a halt. A short man in a long black coat got out and advanced towards the house. Rachel went to the door and let him in.

'Ah, Ollerenshaw, you got here all right, then?' The doctor closed his bag and prepared to leave, his part of the job done. 'How's business? Pretty brisk, I dare say?'

The undertaker looked pained, and glanced furtively at Rachel, expecting signs of distress at this insensitive question. 'We're always busy at the turn of the year, Doctor,' he said in a sepulchral tone. 'February's the real killer, though. It's the damp, you see. It gets in everywhere.' Rachel waited for him to say that it was often a merciful release for all concerned, but he did not.

'Well, I'll be off now,' said the doctor briskly. 'Goodbye, Mrs Madoc, it was nice meeting you.'

'Goodbye,' said Rachel, and went to the door with him. He jumped into his green Range Rover and drove away, scattering hens in his path.

Inside the house, the district nurse was busying herself collecting and packing all Ernest's medication and equipment. The undertaker had seated himself at the table and was laying out a series of printed brochures illustrating the various types of coffin available, together with a tariff of his charges for a full bereavement service, including the installation of the deceased in a chapel of rest prior to the burial ceremony. Feeling extremely unwilling to take part in what seemed to her the grim and slightly farcical commercialization of her father's death, Rachel interrupted the man's well-honed sales pitch and bluntly asked him how much he charged for the full service.

'Two thousand five hundred pounds.'

Rachel gasped involuntarily at this astonishing piece

of information, and she swallowed. 'What is the price of the least expensive coffin?'

'This simple but dignified light oak casket would be five hundred pounds; say four seven five for cash. Up front, of course.'

Rachel stood up, instantly making up her mind. 'No, thank you. I don't intend to avail myself of your services, Mr Ollerenshaw. Thank you for coming. Good morning.'

The man, startled at this assertive behaviour on the part of the bereaved, stared at her, his small pink mouth hanging open. It was his experience that in the first hours of their loss people would agree to pay almost any price, just to get the body out of the house and the whole burial thing taken out of their hands. He stood up, facing her across the table. 'May one enquire the reason?' he asked, with as much dignity as he could muster.

'One may,' said Rachel crisply. 'It's a rip-off, that's why.'

'I see.' Red-faced, the man gathered up his brochures and put them carefully back into his black leather folder.

'Thank you for coming,' said Rachel again. 'Goodbye.'

'Goodbye.' Looking rather crestfallen, the undertaker had no choice but to leave. At the door he turned, rallying a little, and loosed off a parting shot. 'I knew you Cropthornes were a tacky lot of tight-fisted bastards, but you're the first person I've met who wouldn't give their dad a decent burial.'

'You're entitled to an opinion,' said Rachel calmly.

The man left.

The district nurse laughed. 'Good on you, Rachel. He's nowt but a vulture, that one, preying on the dead.'

'It's a simple matter of cash, Brenda. I haven't got

that sort of money. I'll have to go and have a word with Father Lovell; see what he can suggest.'

'Would you like me to help you lay your dad out, dear?'

'Yes, I would, very much, Brenda. Thank you.'

Carefully, they washed the dead man's body and shaved his face. Then, with some difficulty, they dressed him in his one decent cream flannel shirt, his black market-day suit, and his brown boots, meticulously polished. At last the job was done, and Rachel combed his sparse grey hair, parting it neatly.

'We'd best put him on the table,' said Brenda. 'That way, he'll be easier to move, later on.'

'Yes, OK.'

Together, they transferred Ernest to the table. He felt as light as a feather, scarcely weighing more than a child. 'His boots are the heaviest bit of him, now,' said Brenda, and Rachel laughed, for she knew the nurse meant to be kind. They straightened his jacket and tie, combed his hair once more, and then, as an afterthought, his bushy grey eyebrows.

Brenda, her mission completed, drove away, and Rachel, after eating a sandwich, got on her bike and rode into Deeping St Cuthbert to call on the rector.

Father Lovell was at home, having a well-earned nap after his lunch, but he roused himself and invited Rachel into his study. She sat down on the chair provided for visitors, facing the rector across his desk. She took the death certificate from her pocket-book. 'My father died yesterday,' she said, proffering the certificate as evidence of this fact. 'The undertaker came and told me it would cost two thousand five hundred pounds to bury him, but I can't afford so much money, Father, and I doubt that my dad had anything to speak of in the kitty.'

'This is sad news, Rachel, but not altogether unexpected?' The old priest took the certificate and read it, then smiled at Rachel sympathetically. 'What can I do to help, my dear?'

'Well, I want to bury him, naturally.'

'Of course.'

'I don't think my mother was buried in Deeping, was she?'

'No, she wasn't,' said the rector. 'It's quite possible the funeral took place in her home village, but I've no idea where that was, have you?'

'None at all,' said Rachel. She sighed. 'My father could never bring himself to talk about her, ever. She was a closed book, between him and me. I did have a vague feeling that it would have been nice to bury him with her, but I don't suppose it matters at all, really, does it?' She smiled bleakly. 'It's burying him that's important, now. The question is, what is the cheapest way?'

'What about your husband, Rachel? Won't he pay the expenses?'

'Yes, I expect he would, but I don't want to ask him. He never had much respect for Pa while he was alive. I daresay he'd have even less if he saw the state the farm's in now. In any case, it's my business, isn't it, burying my own family?' She looked steadily at the old priest, her grey eyes bright and intense in her pale face, her untidy fair hair pulled back into a rubber band. She is the image of her mother, Father Lovell said to himself, his thoughts flying back more than thirty years.

'The thing is,' said Rachel flatly, 'I haven't even told Stanley that Pa's dead, I don't know why. I expect it's because I feel bad about neglecting him myself, feeling a bit ashamed of him, all these years. I don't know whether you knew about it, but Stanley and my father had a frightful row before we got married, and they've never spoken since. Neither have I, really, until now,' she added sadly. 'So you see, I need to do this on my own, Father; give him all my attention, if you understand?'

'Of course, I understand perfectly, Rachel.' He pondered for a few moments, frowning, then suggested that he should ask the local carpenter to knock up a simple box, and instruct the sexton to dig the grave. 'Fortunately,' he said, 'after the heavy rain we've been having, the ground will be quite soft, so the digging shouldn't be too difficult.'

Rachel nodded. 'How much will all this cost?' she asked.

'I think fifty pounds would cover it.'

'Well, good, I think I can manage that.' She took out her cheque-book and wrote the cheque. She smiled apologetically as she handed it to Father Lovell. 'Sorry if I seem rather penny-pinching,' she said. 'I don't mean to be.'

'Of course you don't.'

Two days later the carpenter drove out to the farm in his small van, with the box roped to the roof-rack. Rachel helped him to unload the coffin, which smelt sweetly of woodshavings, and carry it into the house. Carefully, they lifted the dead man into his simple casket, and Rachel put a pillow under his head. Swiftly, and skilfully, the carpenter nailed down the lid. Then Rachel brought the tractor and trailer to the door, and together they carried the box outside and lifted it onto the trailer.

Followed by the carpenter in his van, Rachel drove the tractor to the graveyard. Father Lovell, dressed in his vestments, met the little procession at the gate, and Rachel and the carpenter carried the coffin to the grave-side. Then, aided by the sexton with his set of long leather burial straps, they lowered it carefully into the ground. Father Lovell offered Rachel a small bunch of flowering thorn, and she took it with a pleased smile, and dropped it onto the lid of the coffin.

After the short ceremony, she shook hands with them all and thanked them for their help. 'It was a lovely funeral,' she said. 'Pa would be pleased.' Then she climbed onto the tractor again, and drove back to St Cuthbert's Fen.

Chapter Three

Una-Mary Tanqueray's funeral in Florizel was a far cry from the low-key obsequies of Ernest Cropthorne. After her peaceful death at the age of eighty-three in the London home of her daughter Nelly Turnbull, her ashes were scattered over the sea off Florizel, in accordance with her wishes. Nelly, her husband Hugo, and their three teenage daughters, Phyllida, Sophie and Gertrude, flew to Guernsey with the casket, then took the launch to Una-Mary's island, and her family home, *Les Romarins*. They were accompanied, somewhat churlishly, by Henry, Nelly's older brother, and heir to the property.

The weather was mild, as it often is on Florizel in February, and the sea calm, breaking softly on the sand of the rocky cove below *Les Romarins*. The next day, at dawn, Nelly and Hugo, with their daughters, rowed out into the bay to carry out the last rites. Hugo rowed the boat, Nelly scattered her mother's ashes, and the girls threw fistfuls of daffodil heads in yellow drifts over the peaceful glassy waters of the bay. They sang 'He who would valiant be', Una-Mary's favourite hymn, making as much noise as they could, and then rowed back to the shore. After pulling the boat above the tideline, they stood silently for a few minutes looking out across the sea to the other islands,

Sark, Herm, Jethou, misty in the dawn light, and watching the yellow flowers bobbing on the pale grey water.

They climbed the cliff path to the house, and Hugo took a bottle of champagne from the shabby old fridge. He opened it, and poured five glasses, while Nelly fried eggs and bacon on her mother's vast Victorian kitchen range. Elsie, Una-Mary's faithful cleaning-lady, anticipating Nelly's homecoming, had had the foresight to light the stove the day before. This had been a thoughtful action on her part, for in February the old granite house was damp and not very warm. The antiquated range provided not only the usual means of cooking, but all the hot water and a few slightly warm radiators downstairs. Upstairs, conditions were pretty spartan.

Sophie set out knives, forks and plates on the kitchen table, and Phyllida made coffee. Gertrude, the youngest of the sisters, stood at the sink gazing at her grandmother's collection of dusty cacti, ranged in little pots on a glass shelf in the window. They looked well past their sell-by date, withered and dry and cobwebby. Like Granny, she thought sadly, and tears filled her almond-shaped eyes and misted her thick goldrimmed spectacles.

As little children, all three girls had seemed to be clones of their mother, small, fine-boned, with identically cut copper-coloured hair and hazel eyes, but now the resemblance was much less striking. Phyllida, aged eighteen, had paid a great deal of money to have her beautiful hair shorn to practically nothing, and what remained stuck up in waxed spikes all over her head. As a further act of self-mutilation, she had had a small gold stud inserted in her nose, and a tattoo of a snake encircled her right upper arm. If her parents were appalled at her appearance, they took extremely good care not to show it.

The younger sisters, Sophie and Gertrude, aged sixteen and fifteen respectively, were currently doing their best to look scarily intellectual and as unhip as possible. Both wore their hair long and scraped severely back into a single thick plait, and their skirts were ankle-length and shapeless, in the style of Virginia Woolf, or so they imagined. Unlike Mrs Woolf, however, they rejected the elegant footwear of the Thirties in favour of hefty black leather biker's boots, their only concession to adolescent fashion. Gertrude, from necessity, wore her thick, unflattering spectacles, and Sophie, though potentially as good-looking as her mother and her older sister, wore ugly metal braces on her teeth and her forehead was temporarily disfigured with acne.

Nelly herself, at forty-two, still had the looks and manner of a much younger woman. She was now a consultant paediatric physician, her work divided between a London hospital and her partnership in a private practice. 'Right, it's ready,' she said, carrying the frying-pan to the table. She shared out the bacon and eggs, and they all sat down.

Solemnly, Hugo raised his glass. 'Granny,' he said.

'Granny.' Nelly and the girls raised their glasses, and they all drank, then hungrily attacked the food.

'I'm glad it's such a lovely day,' said Nelly, with her mouth full. 'She always was lucky with the weather.' She looked up, her eyes bright. 'It's how I'll always remember her: the sun shining, the seagulls, the beach. If she's in heaven, she won't have had far to go, will she?'

'It's weird, being here without her, isn't it?' Sophie scraped up egg-yolk with a piece of bread.

'What makes you think she's not here, darling?' Hugo smiled at his middle daughter, his blue eyes gentle behind his spectacles.

'What? Do you mean she'll be *haunting* us all?'

Phyllida laughed and drained her glass. 'Bizarre thought, Papa, Granny creeping about the house in her nightie, rattling the door-handles!' Of the three girls, Phyllida was the most problematical, and Hugo's favourite child. Now, provocatively, she pushed her glass towards him, silently requesting a refill.

Ignoring this gesture, Hugo frowned. 'You know quite well that's *not* what I mean, Phylly.'

'Papa means she'll always be here, as long as the people who loved her are still around,' Nelly suggested quietly.

'Oh, good,' said Gertrude cheerfully. 'Years and years, then?'

'Yes,' agreed her mother, smiling. 'Years and years.'

'Cool,' said Sophie. 'Will she be here at Christmas?'

'I expect so, darling.'

Phyllida tapped her empty glass with her fork. 'Any more in the bottle, Papa?'

'If there is, Phylly, your mother and I will share it.'

'You are foul. I hate you.'

'I know you do. It's a pain, isn't it?' Father and daughter smiled at each other without rancour, and, to Nelly's relief, Phyllida let the subject drop.

The kitchen door opened and Henry came in, red-faced, bleary with sleep, wrapped in his Jaeger dressing-gown. 'Any chance of tea, Nelly?' he asked rather peevishly. He eyed the champagne bottle and the plates of breakfast. 'Why didn't you wake me? You've done the deed, haven't you?' The words 'it's not fair' hung in the air, accusingly.

'Yes, Henry,' said Nelly, 'we have. I'm sorry. I didn't think you wanted to come out in the boat.'

'Poor old girl, last respects,' mumbled Henry. 'Feel rather cheated.'

'What a bloody stupid load of crap!' exclaimed Phyllida loudly, her cheeks pink. 'Last night you said quite clearly that you thought it a gross idea, scattering Granny's ashes on the sea.'

Henry drew himself up, affronted. 'I'm sure I said no such thing!'

'Yes, you did, Henry, as a matter of fact.' Nelly poured a cup of coffee. 'Come on, sit down and have some breakfast. We'll go down together to the cove, later on. She'll still be there, won't she?'

Henry looked slightly mollified and sat down at the table. He glared at Phyllida, his eyes hard. 'As for you, Miss, I'll thank you to keep a civil tongue in your head while you're here. This is *my* house now, don't forget.' He turned to Hugo. 'Where on earth do your girls pick up such filthy language, Hugo?'

'From us, I imagine.'

Nelly fried eggs and bacon for her brother, and Sophie made more toast. While Henry consumed his breakfast, Hugo and the girls excused themselves, leaving Nelly to cope with him alone. She poured herself more coffee and waited for him to speak.

'I'll have to get Higgins over from Guernsey to do the valuation as soon as possible. Sooner the place is sold, the better. You'll have to make arrangements to ship the furniture and books and stuff you want to go to London, and sell the rest, Nelly. I'd like it all out of here in a month's time. Shouldn't be difficult.'

Nelly looked at her brother coldly and did her best to stay cool, not to allow him to make her angry. 'Hold on, Henry, there's no great rush, is there? It's not as if you need the money urgently, surely? In any case, I think it takes a bit of time to obtain probate.'

'Nevertheless, the sooner it's all dealt with, the better. Bloody place is falling down, needs a thorough overhaul.'

'In that case it probably won't fetch much, will it?'

Henry shot her a sharp glance. 'Rubbish! A pigsty on

55

this island would fetch a bomb, as well you know.'

'Yes, I expect you're right.' Nelly sighed, then decided to put her cards on the table. 'As you probably know, Hugo and I would like to buy *Les Romarins* from you, if we can arrange our finances to make that possible.' She looked at him levelly. 'Ma knew you hated the house, Henry. She would have left it to me, if it weren't for the laws of inheritance here. She would have left the house to me, and the money to you. As it is, it's the other way round, more's the pity.'

'Hm,' grunted Henry. 'She didn't just leave you the money, Nelly. She left you every bloody thing she possessed, except the buildings and land.' He stared at her, his sense of being somehow swindled clearly evident. 'How much *is* the cash, anyway'?'

'About a quarter of a million, I understand.'

'Not enough, is it? House will fetch more than that.'

'Probably.' Nelly got up, and leaving Henry sitting at the table, went in search of her family.

She found Hugo in the summer-house, sitting in a disintegrating rattan armchair, reading. 'Where are the girls, Hugo?'

He looked up from his book, marking the place with a finger. 'Gone to see Elsie, I think, and bring the dogs home.'

'Oh, good. I'd forgotten about the dogs.' She sat down, looking tense and worried. 'Henry wants everything out of the place in a month, Hugo. Can you *believe* the insensitivity?'

'Easily,' said Hugo. 'Nothing your brother does surprises me any longer. In the current parlance, he is a nerd.'

Nelly laughed, ruefully. 'What can we do, darling? I really do terribly want us to keep the house, if we possibly can.'

'So do I, more than anything. In different circumstances, I'd love to live here permanently. It's a perfect place for a writer; silence and no social life.'

'If that's how you really feel, why don't we just sell the London house, and move?'

'You know why not, my love. Your job, and the girls' education. It would be criminal to take them away from where they are and send them off to some snooty boarding-school. If we lived here, that's what we'd have to do, isn't it?'

'Phylly doesn't go to school just now, anyway.'

'I know, but Sophie and Gertie do, darling.'

'Yes, of course; you're right.'

Hugo looked at his wife and smiled tenderly, as she sat nervously picking at her fingernails, doing her best to pluck a solution to their problems out of the ether. After twenty-one years of an occasionally volatile marriage, they had reached a plateau of mutual love and respect, which had brought much happiness to them both. 'Apart from the girls, darling Nelly, there's your work. There's no way you could give that up. You'd go off your trolley in six months.'

'Do you really think so?'

'Yes, I do. You'd be unbearable. I'd have to divorce you.'

She laughed, and so did he. 'What to do, then?' she asked, and heaved a sigh. 'We haven't enough money to keep both houses, that's for sure.'

'I suppose we could sell some of the furniture? I imagine it's quite valuable?'

'I don't know,' said Nelly. 'I'd hate that, I think. Wouldn't you?'

'Well, yes. Obviously it would be much nicer if it all stayed exactly as it's always been. After all, it's taken a couple of hundred years to acquire its special magic. You can't buy that kind of thing, can you?'

'But if Henry flogs the place, that's exactly what will happen to it. The house will be stripped of everything that makes it what it is.' She looked at Hugo, and smiled faintly. 'If that happens, I expect poor Ma *will* go round the place rattling the door-handles.'

The solution to their problem arrived swiftly and in an entirely unexpected manner. They spent the afternoon wandering through the rooms of Una-Mary's beautiful but shabby old Georgian house, trying to decide what, if anything, they could bear to part with in order to raise the necessary cash, but without very much success.

In the drawing-room, Nelly stared morosely at the carpet. 'I have a feeling this is Aubusson,' she said. 'I suppose that might fetch a bob or two?'

'No chance,' said Hugo. 'Look at all the dog-pee marks.'

'God, you're right.'

Hugo looked at his watch. 'What are you planning for supper, darling? Shouldn't we be doing something about it? It's nearly half-past six.'

'I think Elsie left a chicken in the fridge. I'll get it out now, and stoke up the range.'

'I'll light the fire in here, and then go and see what I can find to drink with the chicken. Where's the cellar key?'

'Hanging on its hook on the dresser, unless someone's moved it.'

Nelly departed to the kitchen, where she found the girls playing poker at the table, while Una-Mary's elderly King Charles spaniels lolled against the warm range. When the dogs saw Nelly, they staggered to their feet and gave her a rapturous, if wheezy welcome. 'Have they been fed?' she asked.

'Yes,' said Sophie, without looking up from the cards. 'Elsie fed them at lunch-time. They just have a biscuit in the evening, Mum.'

'Oh. Right.' Nelly took the chicken from the fridge. It was a large maize-fed affair, to judge by the colour of its skin, and she put it on the draining-board to warm up a bit before attempting to roast it. She stoked up the range, opening the damper at the back, then went in search of potatoes in the larder. As well as potatoes, she found strings of large red onions and garlic. Great, she thought, I'll roast some of those, too. Damn, I should have thought about picking some sprouts from the garden, while it was still light. Never mind, I expect there's frozen peas or something in the freezer. She filled a bowl with potatoes, onions and a head of garlic and returned to the kitchen.

'Fire's lit.' Hugo was washing his hands at the sink. He looked at the dresser. 'Good, there's the key.' He took the big hunter torch and went along the passage to the heavy cellar door, unlocked it and pushed it open. He shone the light over the narrow stone stairway, and went down to the cool underground cellar, brushing aside the cobwebs that fell in festoons from the lime-washed joists above his head, hindering his passage. A switch at the bottom of the steps produced a faint and inadequate illumination from two twenty-five-watt light-bulbs.

Slowly, Hugo made his way along the rows of brick bins that housed the wine collection of his late father-in-law. Hugo had never met him, since the old man had died some time before his daughter's marriage, but as Hugo shone the torch on the rows of dusty bottles, some with famous labels, he began to realize that Nelly's father must either have known a great deal about wine, or else had had a very good wine-merchant.

He chose two bottles of St Emilion, then, out of interest, continued down the avenue of bins to inspect the rest of the Tanqueray clarets. Halfway down, his eye fell on a parchment-yellow label. It was edged with a black engraved border depicting vines growing on an elaborate iron framework, and bearing a vignette portrait of a saint carrying a key. Beneath the saint, Hugo saw the words, in large scarlet letters: *Pétrus, Grand Vin*, and a fat red seal with a yellow P on it. Carefully, Hugo put down his bottles of St Emilion, and, taking out his handkerchief, wiped the dust from the label. Above the word Pétrus he saw the date in black, 1970, and also in black, below, the word Pomerol. Beside the red seal was printed in black *Mme Edmond Loubat, Propriétaire à Pomerol-Gironde. Mis en bouteilles au Château. Appellation Pomerol Controlée.*

Hugo gazed at the bottle, and a *frisson* of pleasure and excitement ran through him. He counted the bottles in the bin: eighteen. I don't believe this, he thought; I must be dreaming. He counted them again, to be sure. Then he picked up the St Emilion and returned to the kitchen, closing the cellar door behind him. He put the wine on the table. 'If you girls aren't going to help with preparing the dinner,' he said, 'perhaps you'd better remove yourselves to the drawing-room, so that your mother and I can cook in peace.'

Phyllida gathered up the cards, looking mutinous, quite a usual occurrence with her. 'What a drag, Papa. It's cold in there.'

'No, it isn't. The fire's lit. By *me*, I might add.'

'Well, then, boring old Uncle Henry's there.'

'That's your personal misfortune, my dear.'

'Oh, all right.' The girls took themselves off, accompanied by the dogs, and left the door open on purpose, so that their remarks could be clearly overheard by their parents. 'What's eating him, then?'

'Male menopause, I expect,' said Phyllida loudly.

'Don't be daft,' said Gertrude, 'it can't be. He's only forty-two.'

'OK. Premature senility, then? Or even *impotence*? It can happen. Schubert died from syphilis, at the age of *thirty-one*, you know!'

Manic giggling was Phyllida's reward for this piece of undistinguished adolescent wit, followed by the crash of the drawing-room door being slammed.

Nelly looked at Hugo. 'Fiends!' she said. 'What have we done to deserve such vile children?'

'Nelly, my darling, put down that knife and come with me.'

'Why? What's happened?'

'Just come.'

Nelly wiped her hands, and, mystified, followed Hugo down the cellar steps. He led the way to the clarets, and shone the torch on the precious bottles. 'There, take a look at that.'

Nelly looked, frowning. 'Pétrus? So?'

'Don't you know about Pétrus, Nelly?'

'Presumably it's a wine.'

'Darling, it's probably the most sought-after and expensive wine in the world. You have eighteen bottles of it.'

'How expensive?' asked Nelly quietly.

Hugo told her, give or take a few thousand.

'No shit!' said Nelly, and covered her mouth with her hand.

Hugo took her arm. 'This is just the beginning.' He led her along the rows of bins, shining the torch to reveal the labels of other famous vintages. 'This is why I chased the girls away. If Henry finds out about it, I'm pretty sure he'd cut up rough in one way or another.'

'How could he, if it's mine?'

'Well, he could refuse to sell you the house, out of spite, however much you offered, couldn't he?'

'Yes, I see what you mean. So, what must we do?'

'We must tell him that we'll raise a mortgage on the London house in order to meet his asking price. Then we'll go quietly back to London, talk to the bank, and buy the house. Then, once the contract is completed, we'll arrange for the wine to be sold at auction. With any luck, Henry will never even know about it. He's not a wine man, is he? Whisky's more his thing.'

'Is that really OK, Hugo? It sounds a bit sneaky, doesn't it?'

'Certainly not. The stuff belongs to you, Nelly, and nobody else.'

In the very early morning Phyllida woke, disturbed by the low shaft of moonlight that shone through her open casement. She got out of bed, and leaned over the window-sill. As it dropped towards the western horizon, the moon lit up the cabbages and sprouts in the kitchen garden below, turning the apple trees with their limewashed trunks into pale ghosts, and making a shining path across the silvery sea beyond. The night air was mild and balmy, and quite unlike the acrid atmosphere of London. She looked at her watch: six-forty. Quite soon the day would break; the dark peaceful hours of night would be over, and the daily battle against the boredom of existence would begin again.

Phyllida took off her nightdress, and stood for a moment or two, taking a sensuous pleasure in the slight chill that caressed her naked body, enveloped in the draught flowing from the open window. She picked up her jeans and sweater from the floor, and got dressed. She checked that her roll-up kit was in her pocket, picked up her big, heavy Reeboks, then stole silently down the main staircase of the house, and left it by the garden door. Outside, she sat down on the step and put on her trainers. Then she ran across the dew-drenched lawn, through the gate in the high granite wall and into the field beyond. The meadow was full of drowsy sheep, some of them with lambs at foot, so she closed the gate carefully and walked unhurriedly through the peaceful flock to avoid disturbing them. Once over the wire on the far side of the field she began to run, going straight down the steep, bramble-fringed, stony path that led to the beach below. Sure-footed as a goat, she raced down the bumpy track, gathering speed for the last few metres and leaping from rock to rock until she emerged from the tunnel onto the pale, smooth, tide-washed sand of the cove she had known from a little girl. She stood for a long moment, gazing at her most treasured haven, the one place that in all her eighteen years had always had the power to soothe and comfort her, however difficult life was, or however foolishly she had behaved.

A few bedraggled daffodil heads were strewn among the sea-wrack, left behind by the outgoing tide. Tears filled Phyllida's eyes, for she had loved her grandmother dearly and was missing her badly. Slowly, she walked along the beach until she reached her own particular rock at the far end. She climbed up its smooth side and crouched on the top, looking out over the sea to the dim far shapes of Herm, Jethou and Sark, like grey whales dozing in the early light. She pulled her tin of rolling tobacco from her pocket. As well as the tobacco, the tin contained a pack of cigarette papers and a screw of foil containing some small green twigs of marijuana. Taking her time, Phyllida made herself a joint.

As she smoked it, inhaling the scented smoke deep into her lungs, she thought about Una-Mary, wondering if her grandmother could actually see her now, and if so, what she would have had to say about her using drugs. Probably not much; that had been the comforting thing about their relationship. She might not entirely approve of your actions, but she didn't utterly condemn you for them, either. Like the time I got done for drinking and driving, she thought, wincing at the memory of that nightmare experience.

She had gone to a party, and because she was late,

had nicked the keys and taken Nelly's car to get there. The party was only a few blocks away, and she had only been slightly hammered when she left at three-thirty, intending to go home, park the car, and go quietly in at the door to the basement kitchen, leaving her mother's keys on the table, and no harm done. Everything would have gone according to plan, if that flaky cow Serena Fairbrother had not cadged a lift from her. 'Please, Phylly, be a duck. There's this bloody man trying to grope me. You'll save my life if you can drop me off, it's not far out of your way, is it?'

'OK, get in,' Phyllida had agreed grudgingly, half annoyed, half quite eager to display her driving skills. She had been taught to drive during the previous summer holidays, when she had spent the whole of August on the estate of a friend's rather grand parents, in Scotland. Speeding round the private roads of the Fort Tullaigh acres, with the mad but glamorous Kit by her side, she had taken to driving like the proverbial duck to water, and thought the whole thing a doddle. From Kit, too, she had learned the pleasures to be derived from alcohol, sex and soft drugs, and the combination of all these elements had led her into the mistaken conviction that she was now an adult, and in charge of her own life. From that moment, everything had seemed to be turned on its head. School, and in particular her A levels, had become a monumental bore, and she had ceased to do any work at all.

Serena, glad to escape unmolested from her admirer, had jumped into the passenger's seat and Phyllida had driven off. She drove skilfully and sensibly through the empty streets to Serena's house, and dropped her off. She did a neat three-point turn and drove back down the street to the main road, then, forgetting to check that the road was clear, turned left in the direction of home. Suddenly, there was a blare of lights, a screech of brakes, a terrific impact on the rear end of

Nelly's precious BMW, and a tinkle of smashed glass. Stunned, Phyllida sat there, shaking, then her door was wrenched open and a man's hand switched off her engine and removed the key. 'Are you OK? You're not hurt?'

'No, I'm not hurt. Are you?'

'No, more by good luck than your moronic driving, young lady. Have you been drinking?'

Phyllida had burst into tears, the police had arrived, sirens wailing, and she had spent the rest of the night in a police cell, to be collected early in the morning by a distraught and furious Hugo.

To say that this unfortunate episode had caused consternation in the Turnbull household would be a monumental understatement. Phyllida was a clever girl, much had been expected of her A levels and a bright academic future had been forecast for her. Then, in October, one of the teachers at her school had read the brief report of Phyllida's appearance in court in her evening paper, and in due time Nelly had been summoned by the headmistress and asked to remove her eldest daughter from the school forthwith.

It had been a great comfort to Phyllida that Una-Mary was at that time staying with them for quite long periods, since her age and infirmity caused Nelly much anxiety and she did not like her mother living alone on Florizel. Her grandmother had been the only member of the family to sympathize at all with Phyllida in her troubles, the only one who did not express rage and astonishment at her behaviour, and Phylly spent many hours at her bedside, chatting. Even her younger sisters had treated her with a certain scornful coldness. Now, three months later, a school had still not been found that wished to take her, a fact that she found somewhat humiliating, to say the least. Worst of all, her best friend and uncritical ally had died and left her all alone, or so she felt in her heart sometimes.

Phyllida finished her joint, and shoved the stub down a crack in the rock. Looking out over the sea, now a limpid green in the light of early morning, it seemed to her that London, her grotesque behaviour, the problems of school and her A levels, were suddenly very far away, and quite unimportant. I wish I could stay here always, she thought; live here, where Granny was.

It was then that she saw the boat, a dark-blue-painted fishing smack, moored to an orange marker buoy at a little distance from the shore. In the boat were two men, wearing navy blue Guernsey sweaters, pulling up lobster-pots. One was middle-aged, small and dark, with a deeply tanned face, clearly an islander. The other was young, with short blond hair, and when he stood up in the boat appeared to be very tall. At that distance Phyllida could not see the colour of his eyes, but she knew that they would be blue.

Chapter Four

On the day following her father's funeral Rachel got up early, fed the pigs, and returned to the house to have breakfast. As she sat at the table, drinking her hot strong tea, she decided that she must make a list of all the things she would have to do before she could return to Oxford. She thought of Stanley and the children at home, probably still snug in their beds. Is it Saturday today, she asked herself, or only Friday? A fly-spotted calendar hung from a nail beside the window, and she crossed the room to consult it. She tried to work out how many days she had been in St Cuthbert's Fen, but could not be absolutely sure. How weird, she said to herself, I haven't seen a newspaper, or listened to the radio, or watched television, since I left home.

Her father's calendar had the saints' days marked in red on the pages of each month, and she wondered how such a thing had come into his possession. Religion had never been a priority with Ernest, as far as she could remember, and she felt slightly curious, as well as surprised by the calendar's being there at all. Equally, in passing, she felt astonished that there appeared to be a saint for every day of the year. Each name occupied the entire space allocated for the day, leaving no room for the writing down of appointments, and suchlike. Obviously her father had not objected to this inconvenient fact, for the pages of the calendar were completely unmarked with notes of any kind. Not a single name or telephone number marred the red printing of the saints' days. Thinking of telephones, Rachel said to herself, I must go at once, and phone Stanley. If it *is* Saturday, he'll probably be at home anyway.

She washed her cup and plate, then fetched her bicycle from the barn and pedalled into the village to use the telephone box outside the post office.

'Hello?'

'Stanley. It's me, Rachel.'

'Oh, hello, dear. How's your father?'

'He died a couple of days ago, Stanley. I buried him yesterday.'

'Why didn't you call me, Rachel?'

'I didn't think you'd want to drag the children over here in the middle of winter. Not a lot of point, really, was there? It's not as if you and Pa had anything in common, and he'd never seen the children, not even when they were born.'

'That's all true, up to a point, Rachel. But respect for the dead is important; I wouldn't want anyone to think that his family was lacking in duty to the deceased.'

'Who's "anyone", Stanley? Father Lovell? There's no-one else here who knows about you, so you needn't lose sleep over that.'

Stanley chose to ignore this implied criticism. 'What's the position over the farm, and the land, Rachel? Is there a will?'

'I don't know. I'll have to look. That's why I've phoned, Stanley. I'll have to stay here for a bit and try to sort everything out. Will you be able to manage on your own?'

'Yes, of course, don't worry about it. Antonia is looking after us extremely well; the children like her.'

'Well, good, that's all right then. I'll hang up now, Stanley. I'll ring in a couple of days.' She replaced the phone. *Antonia*? she thought, frowning, then dismissed the slight sense of unease from her mind. She left the phone box, bought a loaf from the shop, and cycled back to the farm.

The first thing to do, she decided, was to get rid of the pigs as soon as possible. She had no real idea of how much the in-pig gilts would fetch at auction these days, but gauged that Ernest's small herd should be worth four or five hundred pounds, plus extra for the boar. Against the far wall of the barn was a stack of straw bales, and a dozen bags of feed. That should raise another couple of hundred, she calculated. The rector had told her that her nearest neighbour kept pigs, and might be prepared to buy her father's from her. I'll go over and see him this afternoon, she said to herself, but first, I must look in Pa's desk; go through his things, see what I can find. As far as she knew she was her father's only living relative, so, in all probability, the little farm was now hers. Though I expect it's mortgaged, or worse, heavily in debt, she told herself, with a twinge of anxiety.

Feeling like a trespasser, and extremely reluctant to pry into her father's most private affairs, she went slowly up the narrow staircase and opened the bedroom door. Apart from the bed in which she had been sleeping, there was little furniture. Beside the bed stood a small night-table, and on it was a green metal candlestick holding a stump of candle, with a box of England's Glory matches beside it. At the foot of the bed, a painted wooden chest stored sheets and blankets. Beneath the window stood a small knee-hole desk, with drawers on either side. Rachel sat down on the chair that served the desk, and attempted to lift the lid. It was locked, and she looked around her, trying to guess where her father had hidden the key. The drawers of the desk were not locked, and she opened them one by one. Carefully, she examined each drawer, and found farming pamphlets, a herd-book, boxes of bills, a ball of twine, a magnifying glass, a set of false teeth (whose? Her father had kept his own all his life), and a clipping from a local paper showing a very young Ernest with his prize-winning pig at Ely show. There was no sign of a key, and patiently Rachel went through each drawer again, pulling them out as far as possible, and running her fingers into each corner. Suddenly there was a gentle click, as a secret panel was released, and opened, revealing a small canvas bag. Inside the bag was a bunch of keys and Rachel found the one to the desk without difficulty. She opened the lid, and folded it down carefully onto the supports which she pulled out from the sides.

The lid was lined with moth-eaten green baize, edged with a strip of faded brown leather, and she put her hands on the fabric, stroking it gently, conjuring up the image of her father toiling over his accounts, trying to do the work originally undertaken so much more efficiently by his young wife.

Facing Rachel was a row of pigeon-holes containing a variety of documents, carefully filed, each according to its classification. For the next two hours she worked steadily through all the papers, and discovered that Ernest had not had a bank account, but kept all his money in the Post Office Savings, and had a credit balance of a little over seven hundred pounds. His tax returns appeared to be in impeccable order, his very small taxes paid to date. The title deeds of the property were there, and the place appeared to be unencumbered, though not worth very much, she imagined, with the buildings in a near-derelict state and the land liable to flooding.

Rachel sighed, her spirits subdued by the depressing evidence of her father's harsh and unrewarding life. I suppose I'd better go to Ely and find a solicitor, she said to herself; let him see all this, and apply for probate, or whatever it's called. She closed the desk, and locked it. She looked at her watch: one-twenty. I'd better have something to eat, and then go and see what's-his-name, Jarvis, about the pigs. She put the bunch of keys into her pocket and went down to the kitchen. As she fried a slice of bacon, and an egg, she looked across the room at the bleak spectacle of her father's empty bed, and realized that she would have to find a way of dismantling it, and getting it back upstairs to her old bedroom. Oh God, I really should wash his sheets and blankets, she thought, shovelling her bacon and egg onto a plate, and sitting down to eat.

After lunch she put on her coat and cycled across the fen, brown and soggily dejected under a lowering grey sky, to Jarvis's farm, a distance of some three miles. She found George Jarvis, a man in his mid-forties, in his large modern pig-house, dosing piglets with an out-sized plastic drench. 'Good afternoon,' said Rachel, and introduced herself.

'Sorry to hear about your dad, Mrs Madoc. He'd been ill for some time, I believe?'

Rachel smiled, but said nothing, and waited for him to say that it must be a merciful release, but he did not. 'Is there something you wanted?' he asked, continuing to ram the drench down the throats of his squealing piglets.

'I wondered whether you'd want to buy my father's boar, and some in-pig gilts?'

'Ah, I see.' He glanced at her, calculatingly. 'How near are they to farrowing, then?'

'Couldn't say for sure – they look pretty near it, but I don't know the exact dates, Mr Jarvis.'

He looked at his watch. 'It'll start getting dark in an hour. I'll come over now, and take a look at them, if you like.'

71

'Thanks. I'd like to get them dealt with.'

'OK. I'll just get this lot finished, then I'll give you a lift back.'

They drove to St Cuthbert's Fen, having stowed Rachel's bike in the horsebox coupled to the Land Rover. In the yard she retrieved her cycle, then led the way to the barn. Predictably, George Jarvis was exceedingly scornful of the pregnant pigs, even more dismissive of the boar. 'Twenty quid apiece, that's all they're worth,' he said, brusquely.

'Fifty,' responded Rachel, stubbornly.

'Forty, then?'

'Cash?'

'OK, done.' He got a fat wad of notes from the inside pocket of his jacket, and counted out six hundred pounds.

Rachel took the money, recounted it, and put it in her pocket. 'What about the boar? How much will you offer for him?'

'I don't really need another boar.' Jarvis went over to the boar's pen, and dug his strong fingers into the animal's back and loins. 'I'll give you a hundred for him, as a favour, really.'

'OK.'

'Got any feed?'

'Yes, a few bags, and some straw.'

'Let's have a look.'

She showed him the feed bags and the straw, and he examined them carefully. 'Fifty quid, to take it all off your hands, Mrs Madoc?'

'Get real, Mr Jarvis. It's worth a lot more than that.'

'How much do you want?'

'A hundred.'

'Eighty?' He tapped his foot impatiently. 'That's my last word. I haven't got all day.'

'OK,' said Rachel.

He handed over the money, then reversed his

vehicles up to the barn door, let down the tailgate, and together they herded the pigs into the horsebox.

'I'll come back for the feed and the boar tomorrow, OK?'

'Yes, fine. If I'm not here, you know where to find them. Goodbye, Mr Jarvis. Thank you.'

Rachel watched the red rear lamps of the horsebox getting fainter and fainter as he drove away in the gloaming. She smiled a little ironically, knowing that she had been robbed, but also quite aware that she would have given the pigs away, if necessary, just to be shot of them. The feeling of deliverance from the responsibility for them was enormous. 'There's only you left, you daft old thing,' she said cheerfully to the boar, tipping his solitary meal into his trough. 'And that's only till tomorrow, isn't it?'

The boar looked up at her, his small red eye alert, his moist pink snout twitching, and grunted. She poured the remains of the bucket of water into his drinking trough, almost light-headed with relief at not having to hump seven or eight heavy buckets from the well. Then she unhooked the lantern and went back to the house.

It was not yet six o'clock; there was no radio or television to keep her company, and nothing in particular to be done. So she took the lantern upstairs to her father's room and resumed the sad but necessary examination of his possessions. She put the lamp on the night-table, and looked around the room. In the narrow, light oak wardrobe hung Ernest's clothes. His best suit had, of course, gone with him to the grave. The rest of his clothes were few: a khaki greatcoat, of the army-surplus variety, two pairs of brown corduroy trousers and a brown-and-cream striped flannel shirt. On a shelf were several string vests, and a pair of cream woollen long johns. On the floor of the wardrobe, thick knitted socks were stuffed inside heavy dubbined boots. Rachel closed the door, unwilling to decide how best to dispose of these things.

To one side of the wardrobe, and close to the wall, was a small trunk, little bigger than a suitcase. It was made of navy blue leather and had leather handles on either side. The initial letters ANC were painted in white on the domed lid. Rachel knew it was her mother's marriage chest, and that the letters stood for Amy Nora Cropthorne.

Her heart beating a little faster, Rachel knelt down, took the bunch of keys from her pocket and tried them in the lock of the chest until she found the one that opened it. She lifted the lid, and found a neatly laundered pile of Fifties-style cotton frocks, and a beautiful patchwork quilt, obviously very old, to judge by the faded colours of the patches, and the extremely tiny stitches that held them together. On top of the quilt was a Victorian box, of rosewood, inlaid with mother-of-pearl. Gently, Rachel raised the lid of the little box. Inside was a prayer-book, with a picture of Adam and Ned slipped between its pages. Then she discovered a faded framed photograph of her parents' wedding, their birth and marriage certificates, and Amy's death certificate. There was also an envelope, with 'Rachel' inscribed on it in her father's uneducated hand, each letter separately and laboriously written. Inside was a note:

These are for you Rachel, and your Mum's clothes and that.

I am sorry there is not much money.

Your loving Pa, Ernest Cropthorne.

In a separate package, fastened with a rubber band, she found one thousand seven hundred pounds, in ten-pound notes, all of them fairly recently printed. He must have exchanged them each time the notes were redesigned, she thought sadly. Poor man, he must have scrimped and saved for years to do this, and I never thought he cared for me at all. She picked up the photograph and studied it closely. She had never seen a picture of her mother, and had thought that none existed. Rachel had known that she resembled Amy, had the same fair hair and grey eyes, but now, holding the photograph close to the lantern, she saw that the likeness was uncanny; they could easily have been twins. For the first time, she understood why there had been such an unbreakable emotional barrier between herself and her father. Poor man, she thought, I could never have been any kind of comfort to him, looking so like her. It must have been agony for him. Suddenly, tears rushed to her eyes and fell unchecked down her face, as she hugged the precious photograph to her breast. She wept for the tragedy of her mother's death, the equal tragedy of her father's life, and a bit for herself for having been denied the happy childhood those two people would have given her.

Stanley, although he was not yet entirely prepared to admit the fact to himself, was in heaven, his domestic life transformed. Each evening, on his return home, he found the house warm and in perfect order, the children's homework done, and a delicious-smelling meal in the oven. Antonia Updike, sent by the agency in response to his urgent appeal for domestic assistance, had proved more than adequate to the challenges confronting her in Lovelace Road. Forty-two years old, and of striking appearance, she was tall and had black hair worn in a loose knot on the nape of her slender neck. Her eyes were large, very dark, and interestingly tilted at the outer corners. She had set about her new employment with enthusiasm and efficiency, and in the space of a week she had not only organized the restoration of the master bedroom to a degree of comfort that amazed Stanley, but had also bullied a plumber into repairing the damage to his much-loved bathroom. This room, in addition to its perfectly-working fittings, was now equipped with thick white bath towels and Floris's *Fougère* soap and bath essence, which left an agreeable, if faint, scent on his skin, very soothing to Stanley's spirits, as he prepared to sleep in his own bed once again.

At the end of the second week, the house was so unbelievably tidy, clean and comfortable that even the twins were impressed and became half in love with the charismatic Antonia and anxious to please her. Like most boys of their age, they were pretty heartless when it came to matters of their own convenience, and poor, long-suffering Madge was dumped with scarcely a twinge of guilt. Ciaran was the only one of the three to miss her mother at all, and in the end even she found herself quite able to transfer her affections to Antonia, particularly when she was singled out for special attention. She loved the private sessions in Antonia's room, having her fair hair cut into a beautiful Renaissance bob, or her nails carefully filed and painted with transparent polish. Amazed by the transformation in her appearance, which she could see reflected in Antonia's mirror, Ciaran had heaved a great sigh of happiness and gazed at her benefactor with adoring tawny eyes. 'You're going to be a beauty, Ciaran,' Antonia had said, and laughed.

By the end of January, Stanley and his children had begun to take for granted the newcomer's harmonious presence in their lives. Adam went so far as to speak to his father about his wish that she should become a permanent fixture. 'She's terrific, Dad. She can even do algebra, and Latin, too.'

'I'm not surprised to hear it. She certainly seems to be extremely competent, and in many directions.'

'She's fun, too. She's going to help me redecorate my room. She said she would, if you agree.' Adam looked at his father, his small intelligent dark eyes bright with hope. 'If we should get a CD-ROM, Dad, she knows her way round that, too.'

'Really?'

That night, after supper, a delicious tagine of lamb, with sun-dried apricots and couscous, Antonia brought coffee to the sitting-room, where Stanley was comfortably settled in front of the sweet-smelling log fire. 'Antonia,' he said, accepting his cup of coffee, 'Adam tells me that you are computer literate. Is this true?'

'I'm afraid it is, Dr Madoc.'

'If it isn't an impertinent question, my dear, why are you working as a domestic economist, when your education and qualifications so obviously lead one to assume that a career in a comparatively intellectual sphere would be more appropriate?'

Antonia smiled. 'Do you not think that domestic economy requires a certain organizational capacity and intelligence, as well as a fundamentally caring attitude towards one's fellow creatures, Dr Madoc?'

Stanley blinked, a little nervously. 'Er, yes, I suppose it does.' He hesitated. 'But compared with, say, a career in financial services, the pecuniary rewards are not particularly great, I would have thought.'

'Depends how you calculate it, doesn't it? Take this job, for example. I have no personal overheads in the way of board and lodging, and if I need to, I can use your car. As a matter of fact, after I've paid into my pension funds and life insurance, I seem to be able to save a good deal of my salary.' Antonia looked at Stanley seriously. 'But for me, it's really more a question of the quality of one's daily life. You see, I actually enjoy keeping house, cooking, shopping, gardening, whatever. I really love doing all these things. In a job like this, I get to do it full time, so it makes good sense to me as a career.'

My dear young woman, said Stanley to himself, with

feeling, you sound like the perfect wife. He cleared his throat. 'So, what's your view about the usefulness of the CD-ROM, as far as the children's education is concerned, Antonia?'

'No question, it would be a most valuable asset to them all. These days, it's a positive handicap not to have one at home.'

'Do you really think so?'

'Yes, I do.'

The next day, Stanley, with his usual caution and thoroughness, investigated the possible bargains to be negotiated. Two days later, the longed-for CD-ROM was installed, and Antonia's position as bringer of joy to the household was confirmed. It was more than confirmed, it was celebrated with a bottle of champagne brought home by Stanley to launch their collective career in cybernetics.

The children were already familiar with the workings of this modern miracle, so that Antonia was not often distracted from the preparation of supper to come and sort out a problem. Stanley, however, had a very limited knowledge of its mysteries, largely a matter of the two-fingered tapping-out of his scripts on a word processor, but curiosity drove him to ask Antonia to give him some lessons. These took place, at his request, after the children had gone to bed. This was to avoid their mocking laughter at his slowness in grasping the new knowledge, and his difficulty in retaining it thereafter.

'It's OK, don't worry about it,' said Antonia kindly. 'It'll come.'

'Do you really think so?' Stanley was excessively humble in the face of her cleverness, and her cool beauty.

'Yes, of course I do. You're just a victim of the generation gap, that's all.'

That night Stanley lay in his bed, racking his brains,

badly needing to think of a way of proving to Antonia that he was in fact no fool, that he was a man much respected for his sharp wit and keen intelligence, that he was accustomed to holding his own among the great and the good.

At last, after several sleepless hours, an idea came to him, and after breakfast, he spoke to her. 'My wife's obligations to her late father are taking so long, Antonia, and I owe so much hospitality since the Christmas festivities, that I was wondering whether you would be prepared to organize a small dinner party for me?'

Antonia's dark eyes lit up. 'But of course! What fun; I'd love to. How many guests had you in mind, Dr Madoc?'

'Oh, er, what about eight?'

'Eight guests, or eight altogether?'

'Eight guests, I think,' said Stanley.

'Eight guests and yourself, then.'

'No. Eight guests, me, and you too, of course.'

'Great. What evening will it be?'

'How about tomorrow week; eight o'clock? I'll speak to a few friends, and let you have the list by tomorrow evening, and confirm the day.'

'OK, fine. When we know the guest-list, I'll consult with you about the menu.'

'I shall leave all the decision-making in your capable hands, Antonia.'

Happily, Stanley drove off to his lecture, secure in the knowledge that for once he was in a position to entertain his peers in a style appropriate to his, and their, just deserts. Unworthily, at the back of his mind hovered the fervent wish that Rachel would not spoil his plans by coming home before the party had taken place.

His confidence in Antonia was not misplaced. The dinner was a huge success, from elegant start to convivial finish. The twins and Ciaran, though resentful at being fed early and banished to their own quarters, were permitted by Antonia to sit on the stairs and listen in, once the guests had entered the dining-room, its table ablaze with tall candles, sparkling glass and shining, newly polished silver. In front of each lace-covered place setting, Antonia had placed a small crystal bowl containing snowdrops, their nodding heads reflected in the deeply-waxed mahogany table, its colour almost blood-red in intensity.

With Stanley's permission, Antonia had hired a friend of hers, an out-of-work actor, to perform the function of waiter. Eric changed the plates, offered each course according to her instructions, and served each wine with impeccable courtesy, moving unobtrusively round the festive table in his white coat.

The meal began with a hot spinach soup, each bowl hidden beneath a lid of golden puff pastry. There followed a salmis of pheasant with redcurrant sauce, a mousseline of potatoes and celeriac, with a side salad of watercress. It was so extremely delicious that there was a brief lull in the conversation as the guests gave the food their astonished full attention. The pheasant dispatched, there was a burst of animated and very cheerful chat as Eric deftly removed the plates and placed two cheeseboards and a decanter of port on the table. Finally, the guests were offered a lime sorbet, with a glass of Beaumes de Venise.

Antonia, in her role as hostess, was elegant in a slim black wool trouser suit, worn with a low-necked white silk shirt that emphasized the length of her neck. Her abundant black hair, released from its usual constraints, framed her face, with its winged dark eyebrows and kohl-ringed slanted eyes. With studied grace, she listened courteously to the conversation of the guests, rather than taking a prominent part in the animated but self-consciously arcane exchanges that flowed from side to side, and sometimes the entire length of the table. Charming and attentive, she laughed at the erudite jokes, the loudly trumpeted and frequently slanderous remarks, quietly encouraging the performers to further indiscretions. The wine flowed, each bottle more seductive and potent than the one before, and the scholarly bitchiness grew ever more personal and intense, to the enormous pleasure of Stanley's chosen few.

'Wonderful evening, old man!' Professor Winthrop helped his wife, flushed and inclined to hiccup, into her pink mohair evening coat. He looked at Stanley, a hint of speculation in his malicious old eye. 'Rachel still away, I take it?'

Stanley looked grave. 'She is indeed, I'm afraid,' he replied, in a sepulchral tone. 'Her father passed away, after a long illness, poor man. She has to sort out the estate.' He managed to convey that the winding-up of a considerable property was the reason for Rachel's continued absence.

'Oh, how sad, how awful for her, poor thing!' exclaimed Mrs Winthrop. 'Do give her our love, Stanley, won't you?' She put a swift hand to her mouth, looking apologetic.

'Yes, I will. Thank you, Rosemary. Good night.'

Stanley, full of pleasantly urbane goodwill, a sensation not often experienced by himself, received the compliments of his guests and wished them good night, finally closing the door as the last of them drove away in their minicab, soon after midnight. He did not notice his children, as they silently made themselves scarce, and went at once to the kitchen. There he found Antonia, her jacket removed and wrapped in her blue-striped butcher's apron, stacking the dishwasher, while Eric washed up the saucepans. 'That was a perfect evening,' he said quietly, trying not to be too fulsome in his thanks. 'Thank you so much, both of you.' He took his wallet from his inside pocket. 'Eric, how much do I owe you?'

'Let's see. I got here at seven, didn't I? It's twelve-twenty now; it'll be nearly one before we're finished. Would thirty quid be OK?'

'Absolutely.' Stanley handed over the money, said good night and went to bed. He would have liked to express his appreciation of Antonia's efforts on his behalf with much greater warmth, but a curious shyness had seemed to stifle this impulse. He lay in his bed, his hands linked beneath his head, and relived the special enchantment of his dinner party, his eyes closed, his lips forming a small pleased smile from time to time.

After a while there was a light tap on his door, and Antonia came in, wearing a pink towelling bathrobe. 'Hello,' she said. 'I saw your light, and wondered if you'd like a cup of tea, or anything?' She crossed the room, her bare feet silent on the thick new carpet, and stood beside the bed, smiling.

Stanley, aware of his vulnerability, but incapable of dissembling any longer, held out his hand and gazed up at her with imploring eyes. 'Darling Antonia, there *is* something you could do for me, if you could bear it?'

She took his hand, and sat down on the edge of the bed. The bathrobe fell open, revealing her smooth slender legs. 'What can I do for you, Stanley?' she asked. Tentatively, he placed his hand on her naked thigh. She laughed softly, and bending over, kissed him on his eager mouth. 'I thought you'd never ask,' she said.

On the day following her exploration of Ernest's desk and Amy's marriage chest, Rachel decided to cycle into Ely and find a solicitor to deal with the settlement of her father's affairs.

She found a legal practice without difficulty, and after a twenty-minute delay, during which she sat in a cold waiting-room, she was shown into a small, book-lined office. A grey-haired, middle-aged woman sat behind a large, tidy desk. The solicitor introduced herself, and invited her client to be seated. Rachel explained her business as briefly and as concisely as she could.

'You have the death certificate, Mrs Madoc?'

'I have.' Rachel handed it over.

'And as far as you are aware, you are the only surviving relative of the deceased?'

'That's right.' Rachel took from her bag a large brown envelope into which she had put all her father's papers, the title deeds of the farm, the documents relating to his tax affairs, his vet's bills, and his Post Office book. In fact, the envelope contained the entire contents of Ernest's desk, and the story of his life. 'I think that's everything, really. My father may not have been a man of any substance, but he seems to have kept his affairs in good order.'

'That's excellent news. It will simplify matters enormously.' The solicitor looked at Rachel kindly. 'So there's nothing else, really, except the farm buildings and the land, to be valued and disposed of? What about stock? Are there animals to be sold?'

'Yes, there were pigs. Fifteen in-pig gilts and the boar. I sold them to the next-door farmer for seven hundred pounds. Plus eighty pounds for the left-over feed and straw.'

'Strictly speaking, my dear, you shouldn't have done that. Have you got the money with you?'

'Yes, I have. Should I give it to you?'

'That would probably be best, if you don't mind, Mrs Madoc. It will go into our clients' account and earn a little interest for you, while we wait for probate to be granted.'

Silently, Rachel handed over George Jarvis's grubby notes, and the lawyer wrote a receipt for them. The question of whether to mention the seventeen hundred pounds in her mother's marriage chest hovered in Rachel's mind, and the angry voice of her father seemed to speak in her ear: 'Don't bloody tell 'em, gel. It's nowt to do with they; it's between thee and me. Keep thy trap shut.'

'That's all then?' The solicitor handed over the receipt.

'Yes, that's all.'

'Presumably you intend to dispose of the property, Mrs Madoc?'

Rachel hesitated, finding herself curiously reluctant to make such a decision straight away. 'Very probably, that will be the sensible thing to do in the end, but I need time to think about it.'

'That's understandable. There's no need for you to decide anything in a hurry, is there?'

'I'll let you know, when I make up my mind, of course.' Rachel looked steadily at the other woman. 'Could you tell me what your fee will be, for the work, please?'

The lawyer told her, and Rachel was unable to conceal her dismay. 'Good heavens, that seems rather a lot to me,' she said quietly.

The woman smiled, her face bland. 'Don't worry, I'm sure the money you've entrusted to us will cover it,' she said.

'I should hope so.' Rachel stood up. 'I'll be returning to Oxford in a couple of days. I'll leave the keys to the farm with Father Lovell at the Rectory in Deeping St Cuthbert.'

After leaving the office, Rachel bought herself a sandwich and ate it as she cycled back to Deeping. Before taking the lane out to the farm, she propped her bike against the churchyard wall and went to visit her father's grave. She sat down on the damp mossy ground beside the fresh pile of earth that marked

Ernest's last resting-place. 'Thank you, Pa,' she said. 'You didn't have to do that, you know. Seventeen hundred pounds, that's a lot of money in my book.' It gave her a strange, proud sensation, the knowledge that she had so much money; the power that it gave her, and the responsibility. I suppose I should really have told the solicitor about it, she thought, but I'm bloody well not, so there. Pa's right; they'd have it off me, if they knew I had it.

It took her three more days to sluice down the pig-pens, burn the rubbish and leave the house and barn in a reasonable state. Buying her daily bread at the shop in Deeping, she ran into the district nurse, and offered her the chickens as a thank-you present for her efforts on Ernest's behalf. Greatly to her relief, Brenda accepted the gift at once, and said she would collect them at the end of the week, when Billy would be at home, and could help her catch them. Rachel thanked her, said goodbye, then telephoned the taxi rank at Ely and ordered a cab to take her to the station the next day.

That night, after supper, she cycled deep into the fen, and stood for a long time in the great dark sinister place, silent except for the constant, scarcely audible trickle of water. She remembered her childhood in that desolate near-wilderness, recalling the lonely and sometimes frightening bike-rides to and from school, and the humiliation frequently endured at the hands of the daughters of the city fathers, the mocking of her clothes, and her fenland accent. Rachel had had a good ear, and by the time she had gained her place at Cambridge had pretty well rid herself of this supposed handicap. But what I can't eradicate, she said to herself, is the fact that Pa was my father, and Amy my mother, and this place is where we all belong, together.

She could see her parents, young and strong, in love with each other and their patch of land, excited by the idea of their coming child. She imagined them working together, Amy driving the tractor, turning the rows of potatoes, while Pa followed, bent double as he picked up the moist white King Edwards, swiftly filling the willow baskets ranged along the rows. She saw the great arching sky over their heads, sometimes vibrantly blue, more often cloud-driven and grey, and she saw the fiery sunsets that seemed to have ended most of the working days, rain or shine.

A pale half-moon rose in the east, enmeshed in the bare black branches of a willow tree, and Rachel remounted her bike and rode slowly home. She turned up the lantern hanging over the table, lit a stump of candle, and drank a cup of elderberry wine in memory of that far-off time.

In the morning, she humped her mother's marriage chest down the stairs, to be ready when the taxi came. On the way to Ely, she dropped off the keys at the Rectory. Father Lovell promised to forward any mail to Oxford, and wished her Godspeed. In the phone box, she called Lovelace Road to let them know that she was on her way home, but there was no reply.

The journey was long and tedious, and she arrived late at night, cold and exhausted. The house was in darkness, and silent, when she let herself in, trying not to make a noise as she carried in Amy's trunk. She crossed the hall in the dark, turned on the light in the immaculate kitchen and poured herself a small whisky. When she had drunk it, she rinsed the glass carefully, dried it and put it away, awed by the unfamiliar sense of clinical order in her own kitchen. She took off her boots, and went quietly upstairs, leaving her mother's chest in the hall.

At the door to the spare room, Rachel paused for a moment, wondering whether to make her return known to her substitute, the excellent Antonia. Then she decided that it might not be very kind to wake her at such a late hour, and continued on to her own room. She switched on the lights at the door. Everything was pin-neat, the bed turned down, the pillows fat and inviting. It looks unreal, like a picture in a glossy magazine, she thought. Stanley must be out at a dinner, she said to herself. She undressed, leaving her clothes on the floor, and fell into bed.

Lying there, trying to relax beneath the comfort and warmth of the soft duvet, Rachel became disturbingly aware that she had very little wish to see Stanley, much less share her bed with him. She felt a sudden sense of dismay, even slight panic, at the prospect of resuming her position as doormat to her formidable family, together with her chronic inability to be equal to their collective expectations of her. I expect it's just tiredness, she told herself drowsily, I'll be all right in the morning. Of course I want to see them.

Nevertheless, at the back of her mind hovered the realization that her weeks of solitude in St Cuthbert's Fen had been both self-revelatory and strangely rewarding. In that lonely place, she had come to feel an unlooked-for closeness, even love, towards both her parents and her origins, but more than that, she had experienced, for the first time in her life, the freedom, the inner composure, of belonging only to herself.

Chapter Five

On the day following Hugo's discovery of the gold-
mine in the cellar, he invited Henry to walk to the pub
in the village for a drink before lunch. 'Come on,' he
said, 'I could do with a beer, and a rest from adolescent
girls, couldn't you?'

Henry had never been on particularly fraternal terms
with his sister's husband, having almost nothing in
common with him, but he was flattered by this mild
display of male solidarity and agreed that a trip to the
boozer would be quite pleasant. He threw down his
newspaper, heaved himself out of his easy chair and
accompanied Hugo to the hall, where they put on rain-
coats and selected walking-sticks.

Watching them from an upstairs window as they
strode purposefully down the drive, Nelly laughed
aloud at Hugo's convincing performance as a middle-
aged retired army officer. I'm surprised he didn't
manage to find a brown trilby from somewhere, she
thought. As soon as she heard the clang of the iron
gate, she ran downstairs to the hall, where the black
1940s telephone stood in its usual place on the marble-
topped console table beneath a large gilded rococo
mirror. The girls had all gone out for a drive in the four-
wheeler, pulled by the ageing pony Murphy, whose
round grass-filled belly could scarcely fit between the

shafts of the cart. Elsie was preparing lunch, with two closed doors between the kitchen and the hall, so that Nelly felt quite confident that she would not be overheard when she telephoned her bank manager in London.

Ten minutes later, she replaced the phone in its cradle. She looked at her reflection in the blue, spotted glass of the mirror with a satisfied smile, and ran her fingers through her straight glossy red hair. The bridging loan she required had been arranged in a matter of minutes, and she had undertaken to call at the bank later in the week to sign all the necessary documents. Good on you, Nelly, she said to herself, you're pretty good at plotting. She gave the black telephone a friendly pat, straightened its thick plaited beige-coloured cord, and went to the kitchen to give Elsie a hand with the lunch.

At five to one Henry and Hugo arrived at the gate to *Les Romarins*, hotly pursued by the four-wheeler, pulled by the sweating Murphy. 'Hold the gate, Papa!' cried Phyllida, and Hugo obligingly did so. They swept past him at a brisk trot, all three girls convulsed with lunatic laughter as they careered round the side of the house in the direction of the stables.

'Thank God I haven't got children,' remarked Henry sourly, watching the girls disappear and waiting while Hugo closed the gate. 'Don't know how you stand it, old boy. It must be pretty good hell in that woman-dominated set-up of yours.'

Hugo laughed. 'Well, it *is* rather bedlam sometimes, but I can't imagine life without them, as a matter of fact.'

'Never regretted not having boys?'

'No, not particularly. Never really thought about it, Henry.'

'What about Nelly?'

'Don't know. Never asked her.'

'Oh.'

Lunch, at Elsie's insistence, was served in the dining-room, just as it would have been in Lady Tanqueray's day. Not wishing to upset Elsie, whom she knew to be deeply affected by Una-Mary's death, Nelly went along with this, and the family sat in the chilly room, inadequately warmed by a smelly paraffin heater, consuming Elsie's excellent toad-in-the-hole made with island sausages, followed by rice pudding with local cream.

After lunch, the girls helped Elsie with the washing-up, Hugo vanished into the bookroom with his notebooks, and Nelly took the coffee-tray into the drawing-room, where she found Henry, full of beer and solid food, half-asleep in front of the coal fire. 'Coffee, Henry?' she murmured.

'What, what?' He opened his eyes reluctantly. 'Oh. Yes. Thanks.' He took the proffered cup and drank the scalding coffee, making a lot of noise in the process.

Flinching slightly, Nelly drank her own coffee. What an unattractive man he is, she thought, I'm surprised Jane hasn't divorced him long ago. Mind you, she's not much to write home about herself, is she? Perhaps they deserve each other.

'Henry?' she said, and smiled at him in what she hoped was a friendly manner.

'Yes? What?'

'I rang my financial people this morning, and there seems to be no difficulty at all in raising the extra money I need to buy you out. Just tell me what you want, or get your lawyers to write to mine, and the whole thing can go through as soon as probate's granted.'

'Well, good. I suppose that saves a lot of trouble, really.' He blinked at her, his face flushed, looking older than his fifty-six years.

There's something about Henry that makes one want to kick him, thought Nelly. Poor man, he hasn't had a very satisfactory life, at all. 'One good thing,' she said cheerfully. 'You won't have to pay an agent's fee, will you?'

'So I won't. Good thinking, old girl.'

Unwillingly, but driven by a tiny prick of conscience, Nelly asked her brother whether there was anything of their mother's that he would like to have, as a memento of her. 'There are loads of old photos of us, as children, in her bureau drawers. Wouldn't you like some of them, Henry?'

'No, I wouldn't, thanks.' He looked at her, hesitating, reluctant to talk about the past. In the event, he did. 'You may think this place paradise, Nelly, and very possibly it was, and still is, for you. As far as I am concerned, I always felt as if it were Borstal here, and doubtless I always will.'

'Oh, dear, did you really? How awful for you. Why do you think that was? Can you remember?'

'I remember very well indeed. *You* didn't have to remain here, all alone, when Ma and Pa were *en poste* in Shanghai, Istanbul or wherever. My nurse was a cow, and drank; the governess was shagging the gardener's boy when she should have been with me. All the servants thought me a bloody nuisance and a weed, to boot, so they bullied me all the time and made me cry. It wasn't until you were on the way that Ma decided to stay at home, and by then I was fourteen, and at school in England.'

'But what about the holidays? It must have been lovely for you, with Ma at home at last?'

'No, it was too late by then. I'd hated her for years, for dumping me with the servants; abandoning me, really.' He looked at Nelly, his eyes empty and sad. 'If it had been nowadays, and if the old man hadn't been a big cheese in the diplomatic corps, they'd have had the social workers after them, wouldn't they? And serve them bloody right.'

Nelly sighed, and her heart felt heavy and full of guilt, as if she too had a share in the neglect and maltreatment of her brother. 'I don't suppose you were all that thrilled when I came on the scene, were you?'

'No, I wasn't. I loathed the very sight of you, horrid little screaming redhead. And to make matters worse, Ma *adored* you; always adored you, Nelly. She only tolerated me, I could tell.'

'Life's a bitch, Henry. Ma knew that. She knew she'd let you down badly; she told me so, several times.'

'Bet she didn't lose much sleep over it,' muttered Henry, determined not to be comforted in any way.

'Probably not,' replied Nelly quietly. 'She was too pragmatic and sensible to worry about things she couldn't change.' She put the coffee-cups on the tray, and stood up, preparing to leave him to his nap. 'So there's nothing at all you'd like as a keepsake?'

'No, nothing.'

Nelly went to the door.

'Actually,' said Henry, 'a case of wine would be nice.'

Nelly's heart stopped. 'Yes, of course,' she said, her mouth dry. 'Why don't we go down and choose something?'

'Oh, no, can't be bothered. Get Hugo to bring up a case or two of Beaujolais, will you? Jane likes Beaujolais; prefer the hard stuff, myself.'

'Right,' said Nelly. 'I'll do that, Henry.'

Phyllida, bored with winding up her younger sisters, decided to take the dogs for a walk. She took the track down to the beach, just as Una-Mary had done practically every day of her life, until age and arthritis overcame both herself and her dogs. Wiggy and Pepys sniffed the salt air eagerly, as they stumbled over the roots and sharp stones that littered the uneven ground. The late summer growth had not been cut back, and Phyllida, armed with a hook, slashed at the long, thorny, cranberry-red brambles that were doing their best to obstruct her path, and the vicious nettles that seemed to leap from the banks of the lane to sting the unwary passer-by.

On the beach, the light was already beginning to fade, the sun obscured by a wide bank of low cloud, pearl-grey, with the sky above a clean-washed and delicate blue-green, reflecting the calm, unruffled water. The tide seemed to be at the point when it was neither coming in nor going out; it seemed suspended, the water oily and still, with specks of brown seaweed clearly visible, hovering beneath the surface. It was as if the sea held its breath.

Phyllida walked slowly along the tideline, letting her Reeboks get wet, while the little dogs huffed along beside her, their noses dribbling, their pink tongues flicking in and out of their mouths, their bug-eyes cast upwards at their old friend, adoring and apologetic, as if they realized how boring they must be to take for a walk, but grateful nevertheless. 'Silly old things,' said Phyllida. 'It's your beach, too, you know.'

When she reached her rock, she sat down to give the dogs a breather, and took out her roll-ups. Carefully, she assembled her joint, licking along the gummed strip of the paper, and sticking it down. She put it between her lips, feeling in her pocket for her lighter. It wasn't there, nor in the other pocket of her jacket, nor in the pockets of her jeans. 'Shit,' she muttered, under her breath, and put the cigarette back in the tin. Where the hell did I put it? she asked herself, and picking up a piece of driftwood, threw it a little way down the beach. The dogs wagged their tails. 'Go on, fetch it!' The dogs looked out to sea, ignoring the stick.

From behind the rock came a small dragging sound,

of something being scraped on wet sand. The dogs pricked up their ears, looking at Phyllida, but seemingly unwilling to investigate the matter further. 'Cowards,' said Phylly, and swiftly shinned up her rock to have a look. She peeped over the top, and saw below her, a few metres away, the tall blond young man she had observed the evening before, raising lobster-pots in the bay. He was turning the seaweed with a small rake, gathering clams and putting them into a bucket.

Phyllida watched him for a few minutes, then hauled herself to the top of the rock, and crouched on the summit. 'Hi,' she said.

At the sound of her voice, the stranger looked around, shading his eyes against the low sun that had dropped below the band of cloud and thrown a sparkling path across the sea. He could not see anyone, and shook his head, resuming his clam-gathering.

Phyllida laughed. 'Up here!' she called. 'Look up here!'

The man straightened his back again, then looked directly at her, squinting in the sun. 'Hello,' he said. 'Who are you?'

'My name's Phyllida Turnbull. What's yours?'

'András du Toit. Are you a tourist?'

'No, I'm not.' Phyllida pointed to the cliff-face. 'My grandmother's house is just up there. I've been coming here all my life.'

'Oh, I see.' András looked at her, and brushed the sand from his hands. 'Your grandmother is Lady Tanqueray from *Les Romarins*, then?'

'Was,' said Phyllida quietly. 'She died ten days ago. We brought her ashes from London and scattered them in the bay. It's what she wanted.'

'I'm very sorry. I didn't ever meet her, but I believe she was a very nice lady.'

'Yes,' said Phyllida. 'She was.'

'Now I understand about the flowers. I saw the daffodils floating on the sea. They were for your grandmother, no?'

'Yes, they were.' A wave of misery threatened to engulf her, and to avoid giving way to tears Phyllida slid down the rock, and ran across the sand to his side. 'Give me the rake,' she said. 'I'll turn the sea-wrack, and you gather the clams, OK?'

'OK.'

For a few minutes they worked together in silence. The two dogs came furtively round the rock and lay down on the sand, watching and waiting, until the bucket was full. András stood up, stretching his back. 'Thanks for your help,' he said. 'I've got enough now.'

Phyllida handed him his rake. 'What are you going to do with the clams? Sell them?'

'No. There's no market for them. My mother will make soup with them, with cabbage and leeks.'

'Sounds good,' said Phyllida, sounding unconvinced.

András laughed. 'It's better than it sounds, as a matter of fact. Garlic, and herbs, and quite a lot of cream goes in, too.'

'I'm sure it's terrific.' Phyllida gazed at him, her hazel eyes curious. 'Whereabouts on the island do you live, András? How come I've never bumped into you before?'

András returned her gaze, coolly. 'I imagine because my mother's family, the Langlois, live on a small farm on the other side of the island, the French side. They have a dairy herd, and grow some potatoes. They don't move far from home, except to take the milk to the harbour every morning, by tractor.'

'And your father's family? The du Toits?'

'We are neighbours of the Langlois. There's only Mum, Dad and me on the island now, though Dad has cousins on St Aude.'

'So, you and your dad fish for a living, right?'

'Right.'

'How long have you been catching lobsters in our bay, András?'

András picked up his bucket, and laughed again. 'Do you think we've been poaching your lobsters, Miss Turnbull?'

'Don't call me that. My name's Phyllida.'

'OK, then, Phyllida.' They began to walk towards András's boat, moored in the shallows.

'And *have* you been poaching?'

'No, we haven't. Dad noticed that this bay was practically deserted, so he found out who it belonged to, and went to ask your grandma if we could put down lobster-pots, and gather mussels and stuff.'

'Oh. Good. That's all right, then.'

'Yes, but I suppose now we'll have to check it out with the new owner. Is that your dad?'

'No, it's my Uncle Henry, Mum's brother. But Mum is trying to buy him out, so we can keep the house. Mum loves it here, and so do I.' She watched as András stowed the bucket of clams in the prow of the dinghy. 'Don't mention the lobster-pots to Uncle Henry, András. I'm sure he'd say no; it's how he is. I'll speak to Mum, and tell her about you. It'll be fine with her, I'm sure.'

'Thanks, that's kind of you.' András held out his hand, and Phyllida shook it, as if sealing a bargain. 'Would you care to come out in the boat sometime, perhaps?' he asked. 'Dad doesn't always fish with me; I'd be glad of your company, any time.'

'That'd be cool, András. Thank you, I'd love to.'

András unfastened the painter, pushed the dinghy into deeper water and leapt into the boat. He lowered the outboard engine and pulled the cord. The motor spluttered into life, he grabbed the tiller and pointed the boat seawards. 'Bye,' he called. 'See you around.'

'When?' shouted Phyllida.

'When what?'

'*When* shall I see you again, András?'

'Oh, any time!'

'What about Sunday? I could bring a picnic; we could go to one of the uninhabited islands, couldn't we?'

'OK, if you like. Twelve o'clock, here?'

'Brilliant!'

Phyllida stood on the water's edge, watching the dinghy heading across the bay. Just before it disappeared behind the northern point, András turned and raised his arm. Smiling, unaccountably happy, Phyllida waved back. Then, calling the dogs, she turned and ran across the darkening sand, heading for the cliff path, and *Les Romarins*.

Hugo and Nelly sat by the fire in the drawing-room after supper, watching the *Nine o'Clock News*. Rather to their surprise, Phyllida had chased them out of the kitchen after the meal was finished, and had ordered her sisters to help wash up and tidy the kitchen. Their eyes round with amazement, Sophie and Gertrude had obeyed her, dumbfounded at this volte-face from the normal disinclination of their older sister to co-operate in the matter of household tasks. Her usual tactics were never to do anything except under extreme duress, an attitude readily copied by her siblings.

Nelly, having adjusted the ancient TV set as best she could, curled herself up on the long Knole sofa beside her husband and tried to be interested in the international events of the day, which seemed, as usual, to be of the horrific variety, a distressing catalogue of disasters, both natural and man-made. 'She's still smoking pot, you know, Hugo,' she said quietly. 'I can smell it.'

Hugo sighed. 'Oh, dear. Can you really?'

'If you'd seen as many dope cases as I have, darling,

you'd recognize the symptoms and the smell immediately.'

'She seems rather better these last few days, doesn't she?' Hugo tried to sound calm, and unruffled about the problems of his difficult daughter. 'Look at tonight; she actually offered to clear up after supper. That's good, isn't it?'

Nelly smiled. 'Yes, of course it is, in the short term. In the longer term, what are we going to do about her?' Sighing, she leaned against Hugo. 'Poor Ma, her dying has got in the way of everything, hasn't it? We still haven't found a school that would be prepared to accept Phylly, so taking her A levels this summer must be seriously up the spout by now, to say the least. As for the question of drink and drugs, that has to be equally or even more important, doesn't it?'

'You're the expert, Nelly. What do you think we should do? Or rather, what do you think she'd *allow* us to do, to help her?'

'If an unknown adolescent presented with exactly the same problems, I'd know precisely what I'd prescribe to help her, and equally make an informed choice of appropriate psychiatric treatment. But it's so difficult when the patient is your own child, Hugo. I can't help blaming myself, and you too, and asking myself what it was we did wrong to make her behave in such an irresponsible and self-destructive way.'

'You don't think it's just normal adolescent behaviour, gone horribly wrong? Not such a big deal, really?'

'I wish I *could* think that, I really do.'

'But you can't?'

'No,' said Nelly, 'I can't.'

'OK, point taken. What are we going to do?'

'I haven't the least idea, except try and get her to see a psychologist, and attend a drug clinic.' She laughed, wryly. 'Trouble is, I'm pretty sure she'd tell me to get lost, if I suggested such a thing.'

'I've been thinking,' said Hugo, taking off his spectacles and polishing them with his handkerchief. 'I have a sort of idea, but you might not agree.'

'Try me.'

'I wondered whether, instead of returning to London next week, with you and the other girls, she and I might stay on here for a while.'

'What, just the two of you?'

'Yes, why not? One, it's a great place for me to get on with my book. Two, I could probably settle Phylly down to a sensible programme of study again, and work with her when she needs help. Three, and most importantly, I shouldn't think she'd find any drug-pushers here, so once she'd used up her present hoard, and finds she doesn't need it any more, that particular problem could be resolved without a fight.'

Pensively, Nelly considered Hugo's suggestion. She watched the television pictures of a long line of starving children queuing for a bowl of rice at a feeding station, but was unable to respond with her usual concern to their tragic situation, so sharply was her attention focused on the potentially disastrous circumstances of her own daughter. 'I suppose,' she said slowly, 'it could be just what she needs. She'd have your undivided attention, for one thing, and get away from me, for another.'

'Don't be silly, my love. She doesn't need to get away from you. Why should she?' Hugo laughed, and put his arm round Nelly's shoulders.

'It's par for the course, darling. Girls *do*, that's all. The others'll be the same, you'll see.'

'God, will they really? How very dire of them.'

'I suppose, said Nelly, thoughtfully, 'giving your plan a try could be quite a useful exercise for us all. We could see how we got on, with you working here most of the time, and me continuing to work in London, and coming home at weekends.'

Hugo looked worried. 'Wouldn't that cost an awful lot?'

'Yes, it would,' agreed Nelly, 'but we could always let part of the house to help pay for it, couldn't we? The rents in London are astronomic now, though I don't suppose you've noticed, my love?'

'Can't say I have, no.'

'Typical,' said Nelly, and kissed his ear.

At that moment, Phyllida came into the room, bringing a tray of coffee. She smiled benevolently at her parents' display of affection, and put the tray down on the low table. She poured the coffee, handing their cups to Nelly and Hugo. She poked the fire into a brighter blaze, then sat cross-legged in front of it, her hands held out to the flames, hogging all the heat in the process. 'Mum,' she said. 'Have you ever heard of some people called du Toit, on Florizel?'

'Doesn't ring a bell,' said Nelly. 'Why?'

'Oh, nothing. I just met a guy on the beach, gathering clams, that's all. He's called András du Toit, and he says Granny gave his father permission to put down lobster-pots in the bay, and collect mussels and stuff.'

'Well,' said Hugo, 'I suppose in that case, *she* must have known him, mustn't she?'

'András?' Nelly sipped her coffee. 'Doesn't sound like an island name, does it? Though, of course, du Toit would be quite common.'

'His mother's maiden name was Langlois,' said Phyllida, glancing briefly at her mother. 'Perhaps it's something to do with that family? They're farmers, over on the French side.'

'Really?' Nelly studied her daughter's slender seated figure, the leaping firelight burnishing her smooth young face and her spikes of bright hair. Diplomatically, she resisted the temptation to probe, and exchanged a small complicit smile with Hugo.

'It's not just his *name*,' Phyllida went on. 'He

doesn't *look* like an islander, either.' She turned towards them, and grinned teasingly. 'He is very, *very* tall, with terrifically fair hair, and very, *very* blue eyes. What do you make of that?'

Hugo smiled. 'You got me there, sweetheart.'

'Me, too,' said Nelly. 'He sounds quite a dish. Is he?'

'Lush,' said Phyllida, and they all laughed

The following morning, when Elsie came to give a hand with the washing, Nelly sounded her out on the question of whether she would be prepared to take on the care of Hugo and Phyllida during her own working week in London.

'No problem,' Elsie reassured her, cheerfully. 'I don't suppose the job would be much different to looking after Lady T., really, would it?'

'Thanks, Elsie,' said Nelly. 'That's a huge weight off my mind.'

They hauled the sheets out of the old twin-tub and carried the basket of wet linen to the little orchard behind the house, and pegged it out on the line, in the moist, sweet-smelling air.

'Elsie?' said Nelly, with pegs between her teeth, 'do you know anyone called du Toit?'

Elsie looked thoughtful. 'There's not many of them on Florizel, Miss Nelly. Quite a few on St Aude, I think.'

'It seems my mother gave permission to a Mr du Toit and his son András to fish in the bay. I just thought you might know them.'

'Ah,' said Elsie. '*That* du Toit. You mean the one with the fair-haired lad?'

'That's him.'

Suddenly, Elsie looked wary, and hung up another sheet in silence, avoiding Nelly's eye.

'What's up, Elsie? Was it something I said?'

'It's not something we like to talk about, Miss Nelly.

It's to do with the war. Those were bad times, so my mother says.'

'You mean the German occupation?'

'That's right.' Elsie looked at Nelly, her cheeks flushed. 'It's a shame,' she said. 'That poor lad's grandmother, Michèle Langlois, was carrying on with a German soldier, and he was sent away to the Russian front, and got killed at Stalingrad, so the story goes. After he'd gone, she found out that she was in the family way, and she had this little girl, Rosie.'

'Well,' said Nelly, gently. 'Was that so very terrible?'

'Yes, it was. After the Liberation, there was a lot of blaming went on, and name-calling, specially of girls who had been too friendly with the Germans.'

'How awful.'

'Yes, it was worse than awful, my mum says. They cut off all their hair, shaved their heads really, then they stripped them naked and ran them through the streets like cattle, whipping them and chucking rotten eggs and tomatoes and stuff at them.'

'Is that what happened to András's granny?'

'Yes, and when she'd been run through the streets they threw her into the harbour, all covered in filth, poor little thing.'

'God, how frightful. Was she OK?'

'Yes. Her dad got her out and rowed her home right round the island. After that, the whole Langlois family was branded *collaborateurs*, and poor little Rosie grew up as a *collaborateur*'s bastard. Everyone turned against them.'

'And what about Rosie's son, András? Surely that's all water under the bridge, nowadays?'

Elsie sighed. 'I don't know, Miss Nelly. People have long memories here, you know. And there's the Langlois themselves. They're proud folk of good island stock. They're not great forgivers, either. They keep themselves to themselves; they don't mix much.'

'So,' said Nelly, picking up the empty basket, 'it's a question of the sins of the father, is it? Or rather, the grandmother? How very depressing.'

'Depressing's the word,' said Elsie. 'Let's have a cupper, shall we?'

'Yes, let's.'

Chapter Six

Rachel was woken by Ciaran, putting a mug of tea on her night-table. Opening her eyes, she saw her three children, wearing their outdoor clothes, and ready to go to school.

'Hello, Mum,' said Adam, grinning at her. 'Why didn't you let us know you were coming home?'

'I tried to ring from the phone box in Deeping, but you were all out,' she replied sleepily. 'Goodness, what's the time?'

'Ten past eight,' said Ned. 'We're off now, Mum. We just came to say hello and goodbye.'

'Dad said you were dead tired,' said Ciaran, 'so Antonia's bringing you some breakfast.'

'Oh. How kind.'

'Come on, you lot!' Adam exclaimed impatiently. 'We'll be late!'

Ciaran gave her mother a clumsy kiss, and the children left, slamming the door behind them.

'See you, darlings.' Rachel drank the tea, which tasted faintly, though not unpleasantly, of roses, then lay back on her pillows. She listened to the sounds of departure: the slamming of the front door, followed by the twins' raucous farewells, then the bang of a car door, and the crunch of gravel under tyres as Stanley drove down the drive.

Rachel turned her head and looked at Stanley's half of the bed. The pillow was dented, the sheet slightly rumpled; his pyjamas lay on top of the duvet at the foot of the bed. How odd of him not to wake me, she thought; not even to say hello. She lifted her eyes to the ceiling and stared at it intently, trying to locate the scars of the disastrous episode of the burst pipe, but could see nothing. The entire ceiling was immaculately plastered, and newly painted a soft broken white. The sheets on the bed were new, white and hemstitched, and felt as if they were made of Egyptian cotton, soft and silky to the touch. The carpet, too, was new. Rachel had noticed how thick and warm it had felt under her bare feet, as she prepared for bed the previous night. Thank heaven for the insurance, she thought; it seems to have taken care of everything, in spite of me forgetting to get the pipes lagged. She would have liked to get out of bed and go to the loo, but felt unwilling to be caught in the act by the mother's help, or whatever she called herself. Antonia, she said to herself, that's rather a fancy name for a mother's help, I would've thought.

There was a tap on the door, and it opened to reveal a tall, dark, elegant woman carrying a tray. 'Good morning, Mrs Madoc,' said Antonia. 'I do hope you slept well. You must be exhausted after such a long journey.' She put the tray carefully down on the nighttable, removing the empty mug at the same time. She smiled at Rachel, showing perfect white teeth. 'I've brought you some breakfast; then you can have a nice leisurely bath. Everything's under control downstairs, so you can just relax, and unwind.'

'Thank you.' Rachel ran her tongue over her dry, cracked lips. 'It's very kind of you; you shouldn't have gone to the trouble.'

'No trouble at all, Mrs Madoc. It's what I'm here for, isn't it?' Antonia went to the window and pulled back the curtains. The rain fell steadily on the black branches of the chestnut tree outside the window, and spotted the glass. 'Horrid day, I'm afraid. Bed's the nicest place when it's raining, isn't it?' She picked up Stanley's pyjamas from the foot of the bed. 'Time these were washed,' she said briskly. 'I'll put clean ones out for him when I make the bed.'

Rachel opened her mouth to protest, but Antonia had already gone, the door closing softly behind her.

For a few moments Rachel lay where she was, feeling extremely agitated. She was astonished at how expertly the woman had manipulated her, simultaneously putting her in her place and leaving her no room in which to assert herself. By the simple device of bringing her breakfast in bed, Antonia had confined her to her room, out of harm's way, no doubt. Humiliation and anger made her cheeks burn and her nose run; she got swiftly out of bed in search of a tissue. She found a box in the bathroom, next to a large bottle of *Fougère* bath essence. Blowing her nose, Rachel observed with dismay the tatty lace edging of her own nightdress, itself none too clean, and in need of laundering. It was not difficult to imagine the fastidious Antonia snatching it away with disdain, to join Stanley's pyjamas in the washing-machine. Angrily, she cleaned her teeth, using her husband's toothpaste, not his usual brand, she noted. Then she dressed quickly in the clothes she had worn the day before, in spite of the fact that her sweater smelt of trains. Sod it, she said to herself, I don't want her bloody breakfast. She picked up the tray, glancing with derision at the pretty china, the perfect toast, the chilled orange juice and the coffee, together with a sprig of sweet-smelling yellow mahonia in a glass, the whole charmingly arranged on a snowy tray-cloth with a matching napkin.

Quite aware that she was behaving childishly, but

spurred on by a slow-burning anger, Rachel took the offending tray downstairs and put it ostentatiously on the kitchen table.

Antonia turned from the sink, where she had been polishing silver. 'Oh!' she said, sounding surprised, and raising her arched eyebrows. 'Is anything wrong, Mrs Madoc?'

'I don't eat breakfast,' said Rachel brusquely. 'And *never* in bed, unless I'm ill.'

'I'm very sorry. I was only trying to help. Dr Madoc said . . .'

Rachel interrupted her. 'I don't give a damn what he said. How the hell would he know how I feel? He didn't even wake me up to find out.'

'I'm sorry. I expect he thought you could do with a rest, after the difficult time you've been having with your father.'

'Yes, well. That's as maybe.' At the mention of her father, Rachel felt her anger and frustration draining away, to be replaced by the shameful realization that she had been acting entirely unreasonably. She looked across the table at the self-possessed Antonia, still tenderly polishing the silver teapot, and managed a small contrite smile. 'I expect you both meant well,' she said quietly. 'Sorry.'

Antonia inclined her head graciously, but said nothing, and Rachel left the room. She went into the sitting-room, closed the door, and picking up the telephone, dialled Madge's number. The bell rang and rang, but there was no reply. She replaced the phone, and stood staring at it, frowning uneasily. She looked around the room, taking in its unbelievable tidiness and cleanliness. The carpet was impeccably hoovered, the covers of the sofa and chairs were taut and straight, the cushions plumped up and arranged in straight lines. Books and magazines were in neat piles on the occasional tables, which also bore sparkling crystal vases of daffodils. The room smelt of polish and flowers, and bore little relation to the relaxed, untidy family room Rachel had left behind her, a few short weeks ago. It feels like a posh consultant's waiting-room, she thought spitefully; probably a fashionable gynaecologist's.

Suddenly, she was gripped with an intense desire to trash the place, to eradicate all traces of the usurper's presence in her house. She longed to reclaim her own territory, and her own lifestyle, along with her husband, her children, and especially, Madge. I must speak to Stanley at once, she told herself, and sort this out.

She went out to the hall, put on her coat and changed into her boots. Wrapping her red scarf round her neck, she saw that her mother's marriage chest was no longer where she had left it the night before. She went to the kitchen door. 'Where is my little blue trunk?' she enquired politely. 'Did my husband move it?'

Antonia was now engaged in making pasta dough. A small shiny apparatus for turning the dough into tagliatelle stood ready on the table beside her. She gave Rachel a tranquil smile. 'No, it was me. I put it in the cloakroom, to be tidy, Mrs Madoc.'

'Put it back where you found it, please. I'm going out.'

Rachel would have liked to sweep out of the house at once, but first she had to run upstairs to fetch her bag and her keys, and then get her bike out of the cloakroom. There, she was obliged to drag out the trunk herself, in order to reach the bicycle. She put her bag in the basket, wheeled the bike across the polished floor of the hall, manoeuvred herself and her machine through the door, and let it bang behind her. She cycled down Lovelace Road and into the Woodstock Road, then pedalled hard in the direction of St Giles and the city centre, with the unreal sensation that she was trying to escape from something, actually running away.

She turned into the Broad, then dismounted, pushing the bike across the road, and went into the Turl, walking along the narrow pavement until she reached the gatehouse of Stanley's college. She locked her bike, propping it against a wall, and approached the porter's lodge. The porter was a pompous and suet-faced individual with egg on his tie. In response to Rachel's enquiry as to whether or not Dr Madoc was in his room, he replied that he thought he very probably was, and suggested that he ring and make quite sure.

'No, it's OK. I'll just go up and see.'

'Very well, Miss. You know where to go, I take it?'

'Yes, I do. And it's Mrs, actually. I'm Mrs Madoc.'

Rachel walked round the quad until she reached the entrance to the third staircase. She glanced at the list of the occupants' names elegantly hand-painted on the board at the foot of the stairs, then went up the wide steps of venerable, unpolished oak to Stanley's room on the first floor. After pausing for a moment to collect herself, she knocked on his door.

'Come.'

She turned the handle of the handsomely panelled door, and entered the room.

'Rachel! What on earth are you doing here?'

'What do you think, Stanley? I've come to see you, of course.'

'That's not possible, I'm afraid.' He consulted his watch, shooting back the impeccably ironed cuff of his brilliantly white shirt. 'I'm expecting someone for a tutorial, any moment now.'

Stubbornly, Rachel sat down on the window-seat. 'I'm sure you could easily postpone the tutorial, if you wanted to, Stanley.'

A distant clock struck the quarter, followed by a knock on the door. Stanley looked at Rachel with a triumphant smile, but she remained obstinately where she was. His face dark with vexation, he got up and went to the door. Listening to the brief, barely audible exchange on the landing, Rachel asked herself what the hell she thought she was doing here, what was the purpose of her visit, and what did she really hope to achieve? She experienced a moment of pure panic, then told herself coldly to get a grip. Her reason for coming was to explain to Stanley that she very much resented being patronized by the domestic help; that she felt Antonia's presence deeply humiliating on a personal level, and that she, Rachel, wanted her out of the house with the least possible delay.

Stanley came back into his room and seated himself at his desk, looking extremely displeased. He drummed his fingers on the desk-top, and waited for Rachel to tell him what was on her mind.

'Stanley?'

'Yes?'

'Why didn't you wake me this morning?'

'No particular reason. I thought you needed the sleep.'

Rachel raised her anxious grey eyes to his shrewd dark critical gaze. 'What gave you that idea?'

'Well, for one thing, you left your clothes scattered about on the floor last night, Rachel. I had to pick them up for you when I came in; the room was a shambles.'

'What was so surprising about that? I quite often leave my things on the floor, don't I?'

Stanley pursed his lips. 'Yes, you do, more's the pity.'

'What do you mean by that?'

'I mean, Rachel, that for the last few weeks, since Antonia took over the management of the house, the place has been a pleasure to come home to.'

'Are you implying that before she came, it wasn't a pleasure to come home to?'

'In a word, Rachel, yes.'

'I see.' Rachel stared out of the window. She felt slightly wrong-footed at this attack on her capacity as a home-maker, but, curiously, not at all hurt by it. For a moment, she almost laughed out loud at his cool sweeping away of her sixteen years of child care and boring housework. She turned back to face him. 'I suppose, if we could afford it, you would like to employ that supercilious creature on a permanent basis?'

'Yes, I most certainly would, and so would the children, I'm sure.'

'Really? So who's been putting such an idea into their heads, I wonder?' She got to her feet, and approached the desk. 'Well, we *can't* afford it, can we, Stanley? So it's a non-starter anyway.'

Stanley took off his spectacles and polished them carefully. He blinked at his wife short-sightedly, and smiled. 'We could afford it, Rachel, if you had a job.'

There was a long silence, broken at last by Rachel. 'Are you seriously suggesting that I go out to work, in order to pay someone to look after my house and care for my children?'

'Yes, that's exactly what I mean.' He put his spectacles back on his nose. 'Sit down, my dear,' he said, in the manner of one addressing a recalcitrant child. 'I don't think you quite realize how totally inadequate you are in the area of domesticity. You have a good brain, Rachel, and a good history degree. Don't you think that it's time for you to resume life in the real world, outside the confines of the family? Ciaran is twelve now; she doesn't need you at home all the time. Surely you can see that it would be advantageous to us all if you were able to pick up the threads of your own career?'

'What career? I never had one, did I, Stanley? I

111

married you practically as soon as I graduated, remember? I've never even had a *job*, much less a career.'

'It's never too late to start, is it?'

Rachel stared at the implacable, closed faced of her husband, and asked herself what had happened to the man she had married, the humorous and engaging young Welshman of sixteen years ago. He has become a pompous bore, she told herself, and as social-climbing and bitchy as the rest of the pack. He's boxed me into a corner, she thought, and put me in the wrong, when the whole purpose of my coming here was to tell him that I refuse to have this Antonia woman under my roof a moment longer than necessary. She took a deep breath and folded her arms. 'She'll have to go, Stanley.'

'Who'll have to go?'

'Antonia, of course. I can't stand her.'

'You've barely set eyes on her, Rachel. Do try not to be infantile.'

'I don't care what you say, Stanley. I've seen and heard quite enough of her to convince me, thank you. I don't like her; she must go as soon as possible.'

'I disagree.' Stanley looked at his watch again. 'I have a luncheon engagement, Rachel. I'm afraid this interview must end. I'll speak to you this evening.' He stood up and, taking her by the elbow, propelled her to the door. 'Think about it, Rachel, please. Take your time, by all means. I think that you may well find some merit in the idea I've proposed to you.'

Finding herself thrust unceremoniously out of Stanley's room and standing alone on the landing, Rachel's first reaction was one of childish fury. She aimed a powerful kick at the beautiful old door, almost breaking a toe in the process. A yelp of pure agony escaped her; tears sprang to her eyes and filled her nose as she hobbled down the stairs, clinging to the wooden balusters for support. At the foot of the staircase she leaned against the whitewashed wall for a moment, and blew her nose, trying to regain some composure. With bleary eyes, she peered at her watch: twelve-twenty. I'm not bloody going home to be patronized by that cow, she said to herself; I'll go and see if Madge is in now, and take her to the pub for lunch.

She retraced her steps to the gatehouse, walked past the porter's lodge without acknowledging his presence, unlocked her bicycle and made her way back to St Giles. At Little Clarendon Street she turned left and headed for Jericho.

Madge lived in the basement flat of a red-brick artisan's house, in one of a maze of narrow streets to the west of Walton Street. After taking two wrong turnings, Rachel eventually found the right street and dismounted outside number 167. She peered down the concrete steps into the dank well, which contained little except a battered door and a single grubby window, screened by a yellowing scrap of coarse lace. There were no lights on inside the flat, as far as she could see, and an empty milk bottle stood on the doorstep. She must still be out at work, Rachel thought. Disappointed, she leaned against the railing, wondering whether to write Madge a note to let her know that she was back in Oxford.

An extremely young woman, little more than a girl, with an untidy mass of badly bleached hair, black eyebrows and brilliant orange lips advanced towards her, pushing a buggy designed to accommodate twins. In fact, a single very large baby, of about eighteen months, occupied the pram, and was half-smothered by a mountain of bulging supermarket bags. The young woman stopped at the next-door house, apparently intending to propel the entire load down the steps without first removing either child or shopping.

'Can I help?' offered Rachel.

113

'Ta,' said the girl. 'Cop 'old of these, then.'

Rachel took the six supermarket bags from her, and waited until the buggy had been bumped down to the door. The woman unlocked the door, and pushed the baby inside. Rachel followed her down, and handed over the shopping. 'Um,' she said, 'I was wondering. Could I possibly leave a message with you, for Madge? She's the one who lives next door; I expect you know her?'

'I know 'er all right, but she's gone.'

'Gone?'

'Gone. Not there any more, geddit?'

'Why not?'

'Landlord booted 'er out; couldn't pay the rent, I daresay.'

'God, how awful,' said Rachel, feeling physically sick at the very idea of Madge and her little boys on the street with no home.

'Was it you she worked for, then?' The blonde young woman studied Rachel sharply, and frowned.

'I'm afraid it was, yes,' admitted Rachel sadly.

'What she do then? Nicked somethink, was it?'

'No, of course not. She was my best friend, as a matter of fact.'

'Really? Doesn't sound much like it, if you ask me.'

'It would never have happened if I hadn't had to go away. My father was sick, well, dying, really. It was my husband's decision to get a live-in housekeeper.'

The girl uttered a coarse laugh, full of derision. 'Well, fancy that! And I bet she's young, and a class act, with no kids, eh?'

Rachel stared at her, slowly taking in the implications of this assessment of Stanley's choice. 'You're quite right,' she said quietly, and felt her ears burning with embarrassment. 'That's exactly what she is.'

'Poor cow.' The girl removed the snot-nosed child

114

from her safety harness, and sketched a sympathetic smile at Rachel.

'Do you mean Madge, or me?'

'Whatever. If the cap fits, darlin'. No smoke an' all that crap.' The baby began to scream.

'I must go,' said Rachel quickly, and made for the door. 'If you do happen to see Madge, please ask her to come and see me, will you?'

'What name shall I say?'

'Rachel. She'll know.'

In the public bar of the pub, Rachel ordered half a pint of bitter and a ham sandwich. She found an empty seat in a corner, next to a line of fruit machines, and sat down. Ignoring the dull mechanical clunks and whirrs from the gambling area, she ate her sandwich, and drank her beer slowly, while trying to make sense of the feelings of dismay, rather than anger, that informed her heart and mind. Her primary concern had to be for Madge and her children. What had happened to them? Were they OK? She thought it very unlikely that Madge had gone to social services for help, or signed on. Rachel knew that she'd already had a couple of spells in prison, for petty larceny. She also knew that Madge's constant nightmare was the thought of her kids being taken into care. Her instinct was to keep her head down, not to tangle with the authorities in any way – hence the fact that she chose not to apply for a council flat, preferring to pay an exorbitant rent to an un-scrupulous landlord. Poor Madge, she thought, she's never had a chance, has she? Pregnant at seventeen, dumped at eighteen. Loitering with intent, whoring for a meal; pregnant again at twenty-three, the father a handsome black lorry-driver who had dossed in the flat for a while to help with the rent. But he, too, had shown no interest in being a father to the delightful Mike, and the inevitable happened. He vanished without a trace, leaving behind him a saxophone in a leather case, which Madge immediately flogged to pay the four weeks' rent owing. There's nothing I can do for her, unless she shows up, Rachel told herself sadly, and turned her mind to her own immediate problems.

Taking extremely small sips of her beer in order to make it last, Rachel was able to give herself time to think about Stanley, and the evident failure of their marriage. She tried to come to terms with his insulting claim that she was an inadequate wife and mother, or, at any rate, an inefficient provider of a comfortable home for himself and their children. She considered the merits of the few dons' wives of her acquaintance, and was forced to admit that in terms of their smart clothes, flawlessly managed houses, and impressive entertaining, there was no contest. She had never even tried to compete with them in any way, and had no wish to start doing so now. I suppose he thinks I'm holding him back socially, she said to herself numbly. So what if I am? He knew *exactly* what he was in for when he married me, didn't he?

Rachel had been twenty-one when she met Stanley, and in her last year at Cambridge. She had just sat the final examination of her history degree. Freed at last from her desperate, last-minute revision, and feeling pretty sure of a good second-class degree, or even the remote possibility of a first, she had cycled out to the Orchard at Grantchester and treated herself to tea under the apple trees. Even after three years in their company, Rachel had not integrated particularly well into the normal run of well-heeled undergraduates. Many of them had been at public schools, and exhibited all the confident, and in some cases over-confident attitudes of their background and education. To the shy and rather inhibited daughter of a fenland farmer, they had seemed like creatures from another planet, glamorous but extremely intimidating. As for

Rachel's impact on *them*, it had been negligible; she was practically invisible, hovering on the fringes of their glittering world. She had never been invited to go out in a punt during the long, hot summer afternoons and evenings, and had never even been asked to the cinema, much less a May Ball.

Arriving at the Orchard, hot after her cycle ride, Rachel had joined a short queue at the serving-hatch. Then she carried her tray of tea and a deck-chair to the farthest end of the orchard, away from the laughter and chat of the other parties, mostly young men in white trousers and boaters, and girls in antique frilly blouses and beribboned straw hats, who had punted up from Cambridge, meandering slowly through the water-meadows bordering the Granta. It must be lovely to do that, she had thought, but entirely without envy. For Rachel, just being there at all, living and working in such a centre of excellence had been a completely satisfying experience, albeit a solitary one in most respects. Depending on her results, she now expected either to apply to do research for a PhD, or, if she failed to get a first, take a teacher-training course. There are worse careers than teaching, she told herself; plenty of free time for travelling, maybe even working abroad, in America perhaps?

She unfolded her deck-chair, placing it carefully under a gnarled old apple tree, the last pink-and-white petals of blossom still clinging to its branches, and speckling the grass beneath like confetti. She sat down in her deck-chair, drank her Earl Grey tea with a slice of lemon, and ate a small buttery scone with runny strawberry jam. It was delicious. The combination of the slightly sharp tea and the intense sweetness of the jam seemed to Rachel a perfect paradigm of a cool, English summer's afternoon. She poured herself a second cup of tea, took her book from her bag and opened it at the marked page.

'Excuse me. Am I intruding?'

Rachel looked up from her book. A short dark-haired man with small intense black eyes stood before her, carrying a tea-tray. Vaguely, she recognized him, a don from the philosophy school, though she had never spoken to him, and could not remember his name.

'The Orchard is rather packed this afternoon. Might I perhaps share your table? Would you mind?'

'No, of course not. Please do.'

'Thank you; how kind.' He put his tray on the table. 'Stanley Madoc,' he said. 'How do you do?'

'How do you do,' said Rachel. 'My name's Rachel Cropthorne.'

'Yes, I know.' He sat down on his swiftly erected deck-chair and smiled at her. 'You're a historian, aren't you?'

'I hope to be, with a bit of luck.' She lowered her eyes to her book, wondering how it was that Stanley Madoc knew her name.

'Calvino,' he remarked, picking up his teapot. 'Which story are you reading?'

'*The Cloven Viscount.*'

'Is it good?'

'Very.'

'I haven't read it; what's it about?'

'It's about a nobleman, cut in half by a Turkish cannon-ball, on the Bohemian plain.'

'Sounds ghastly.'

'No, it's not. It's good.'

'Turkey,' said Stanley Madoc, cutting a slice of cake into bite-size pieces, 'what a wonderful country. Have you been there?'

'No, I haven't.' Since the intruder seemed disposed to talk to her, Rachel replaced her bookmark and closed the book. She took another sip of her cooling tea. 'As a matter of fact, I haven't been anywhere.

London's the furthest I've ever been, and I didn't think much of it, actually.'

Stanley Madoc laughed, and ate two pieces of his lemon sponge. Intrigued, he studied Rachel with mocking boot-button eyes. 'Are you asking me to believe that you've never been abroad? Never even crossed the Channel?'

'Not even on a day-trip.'

'Why not?'

'Can't afford it. As it is, I have quite a struggle to manage on my grant, in order to stay here.'

He flicked a crumb from his shirt-front. 'I thought you were an exhibitioner, Rachel?'

'Yes, I am.' She smiled timidly, pleased at this small evidence of recognition. 'That doesn't really cover all one's needs. I expect you know that?'

'It's true, of course. It was the same in my day. I used to work on a building site, during the vacations, to earn the difference. Can't you do something like that?'

'I do work.'

'So, what's the problem?'

'I work for my keep, on my father's farm.'

Stanley Madoc frowned. 'Is that wise?'

'It may not be wise, but it's necessary, especially in the summer.' Rachel raised her grey eyes to his, and in the verdant shade of the ancient tree he thought that she looked like a drowned child, with her straight lank greenish-pale hair, and her greenish-grey eyes in a narrow colourless face.

A curious sensation of elation rose within Stanley Madoc, and a sort of amused tenderness towards this little odd-girl-out, Rachel Cropthorne. 'Why especially in summer?'

Is he thick, or what? Rachel asked herself impatiently, but answered him politely. 'Because that's the busiest time of the year for us: harvest, though that's probably too romantic a word for it at our place.

Our crops are quite boring: potatoes and sugar beet.' She looked steadily at Stanley. 'It's a crap farm, I'm afraid, and my dad's a crap farmer.'

Shocked at Rachel's brutal assessment of her father, Stanley changed the subject. 'So, what are your plans for the future?'

'If I manage to get a double first, I'd like to stay on for a doctorate. It's probably more likely that I'll get a second, in which case I'll do teacher training.'

Until that moment, Stanley had never exhibited the slightest sign of impulsive behaviour. 'Either way,' he said lightly, 'why don't you spend the long vacation with me in Turkey?'

Rachel had stared at him incredulously. 'You're not serious, are you?'

'I am. Never more so.'

They had taken their trays back to the serving-hatch, then cycled back to Cambridge together. A week later, the exam results were posted and Rachel discovered that she had in fact achieved a good second. Not particularly disappointed at this news, she went round to Stanley's lodging. He had answered the door.

'Did you mean it about going to Turkey?'

'Of course.'

'I'd like to join you, if I may. I'll have to get a passport, though.'

'That shouldn't be difficult, Rachel.' He had held open his door. 'Come in, my dear.'

The trip to Turkey had been more than a revelation to Rachel, it was a time of real, unalloyed happiness. Stanley was the very first man to show the slightest interest in her, and she was putty in his hands. Together, they inspected the ancient sites, swam in the warm shallow sea, and sunbathed naked in tiny secret coves. At night, they ate in cheap local café's, then slept together in the lumpy bed provided by their shared hotel room.

After six weeks of this idyllic existence, Rachel discovered to her consternation that she was pregnant. Stanley, on being informed of the situation, was at first taken aback and inclined to blame Rachel for her carelessness, then, surprisingly, changed his mind and expressed himself delighted. They would marry immediately; it was not a problem. No-one need know.

They returned to England, and went straight to St Cuthbert's Fen, intending to get married by special licence in St Cuthbert's church.

'What's the hurry?' Ernest had asked, sourly. He was not at all impressed by Stanley.

'I'm afraid there's a good reason, Pa,' Rachel had told him quietly. 'I'm expecting.'

She had entirely failed to anticipate the likely reaction of Ernest Cropthorne in the face of what he thought of as his daughter's shotgun wedding. 'For that's what it bloody well is, my gel!' he roared, beside himself with humiliation, rage and disappointment. 'We Cropthornes may be rubbish according to some folk, but we've never had a bloody whore in the family, and that's the God's truth!'

'We've heard quite enough, Rachel,' said Stanley, white with anger. 'We'll leave at once. Goodbye, Mr Cropthorne.'

'Fuck off, and take the baggage with yer. I'll not have 'er 'ere.'

They got married in Wales, with Stanley's parents as the only witnesses, then travelled to Oxford for the start of the university year, and Stanley's new appointment.

The rupture with her father had been absolute. When the twins had been born, Rachel had written to him, and sent a photograph of the baby boys, but had received no response. She had not tried to contact him again, and when the children showed a natural curiosity about her family home, or her parents, she

121

learned to be evasive, sidestepping the subject, aware that this was Stanley's wish. Each year, at Christmas, she sent a card from them all, but that was all.

Sixteen years is a long time, thought Rachel, gazing into her empty beer glass. The pub was quiet now, the lunch-time drinkers gone, the fruit machines silent. Sixteen years and three children, and now, suddenly, everything is changed. I'm no longer good enough for Stanley. He wants someone posher and smarter than me, is that it? Is he having an affair with this woman, or am I leaping to conclusions, being paranoid? She looked at the clock above the bar: two forty-three. I'll cycle to the school and meet Ciaran, she thought, getting up to leave.

At the school gate, she waited for the children to come out. Just before three-thirty, she felt a touch on her elbow, and turned to see who it was.

'Hello,' said Antonia. 'I wasn't sure if you were going to meet Ciaran, so I came, just in case.'

'Yes, of course. I'm sorry, I should've made myself clear, this morning.'

'Well, since you're here, I'll go home and put the kettle on, OK?'

'Fine,' said Rachel. 'See you later.'

The children swarmed out of the building and she peered anxiously around, trying to locate her daughter. A little tug on her sleeve announced Ciaran's arrival, and they walked slowly home together, Rachel pushing her bike.

'Did my grandpa die?'

'Yes, he did, darling.'

'Did you bury him in the cold ground?'

''Fraid so; it's what one does.'

'He wasn't burnt, then?'

'No.'

After a while, Rachel asked how they had all been

getting on in her absence. 'OK,' said Ciaran, and gave a little hop. 'Antonia's ace, Mum. She can do the CD-ROM brilliantly. Adam is in heaven now; his homework is a doddle he says. She gave a knock-out dinner party for Dad, too. You should have been there, Mum, it was terrific. She let us sit on the stairs and watch. It was just like on the telly, really, *really* cool.'

'How lovely.'

Ciaran looked up at her mother. 'Have you noticed my hair, Mum? Antonia did it for me; it's brill, isn't it?' She turned slowly round, for Rachel to admire the cut.

'Very nice, darling. Is there anything she isn't good at?'

'I shouldn't think so, no.'

That night, in bed, Rachel turned to her husband. 'Are you having an affair, Stanley?'

'What on earth do you mean?' He looked startled.

'I mean, are you sleeping with Antonia?'

'Certainly not! Whatever gave you such an idea, Rachel?'

'So, why do you want to keep her on?'

'I've already explained why,' said Stanley, patiently. 'She is a very good housekeeper. You are not, and your considerable other abilities should be put to better use out in the real world, working.'

'And if I refuse?'

'Please don't refuse. I'm sure that in due time you will thank me for this, my dear. At least, give it a try.'

'You've made up your mind, haven't you? You're making me redundant here, aren't you?'

Stanley laughed, took her in his arms and made swift and energetic love to her. When it was over, he kissed her. 'You'll never be redundant in *that* department, darling Rachel,' he said, and tweaked her nose. 'I'm so glad you're home.'

Chapter Seven

Nelly returned to London with Sophie and Gertrude. She was worried that the girls had missed more than a week of school, and concerned that she herself had cancelled many appointments, some of them rather urgent ones. Never particularly good at dividing her life into compartments of equal importance, she felt miserable to be leaving her beloved island, as well as Hugo and Phyllida, but nonetheless anxious to resume her own work, and the conscientious overseeing of her daughters' education. As the plane took off from Guernsey and banked steeply, heading towards the mainland, she stared at the sullen grey waves below, glimpsed through shredded low cloud, and thought of her mother, whose ashes were now mingled for ever with the rocks and sand below *Les Romarins*. Darling Ma, she thought sadly, I've been too busy to give you a thought for days.

''Snot fair,' said Sophie, resentfully.

Nelly sighed. 'What isn't fair?'

'Bloody Phylly. Why should *she* have a holiday with Papa, and us have to go back to school?'

'You know quite well what the reason is, Sophie. Be your age.'

'But it *isn't* fair, Mum,' insisted Gertrude, a whining note creeping into her voice. 'She behaves like a stupid cow, and has a holiday. We do absolutely nothing, and get punished, don't we? It's very hacking-off.'

'Don't you think being expelled from school is a punishment?'

'You know what we mean, Mum. We think she ought to be *seen* to be being punished, and really in disgrace. It doesn't seem to Gertie and me that Papa is all that angry with her, now. In fact, you both seem to have forgotten that she actually spent a night in the slammer. It's not a lot of fun for Gertie and me, now, with gross old Miss Gurnhill watching us like a hawk all the time, in case we give the school a bad name, like Phylly did.'

'Lower your voice, please, Sophie. Do you have to broadcast our private affairs to the entire world?' Nelly spoke quietly, but she sounded upset and angry. 'Would you really have liked these things to happen to you?'

Sophie and Gertrude looked at each other, smirking with embarrassment, aware that they had gone too far. 'No, I suppose not,' said Gertrude. 'Sorry, Mum.'

'Sorry.'

'OK,' said Nelly. 'You're not quite as unkind, or as silly, as you sometimes sound, then.'

On Sunday morning Phyllida went into the book-room where Hugo was working and explained to him that she was going on a picnic, so wouldn't be cooking lunch. She offered to leave him a sandwich, and promised to make a proper meal in the evening. Hugo looked vaguely up from his work and said, 'Fine, fine. Whatever you say, darling.' He smiled and went on writing.

Phyllida went to the door. 'Papa?'

Hugo looked up again, blinking. 'Mm?'

'Did you hear what I said? Is that OK?'

'Is what OK?'

'Is it OK if I go out to lunch, and cook supper instead, this evening?'

'Of course, why not?'

'I'll leave you a sandwich, OK?'

'Thanks.'

Phyllida shook her head, closed the door quietly behind her and went to the kitchen. There, she made thick sandwiches of Elsie's wholemeal bread, filling them with salami, olives, salad and hard-boiled eggs. She wrapped them in plastic film, setting two aside in the fridge, for Hugo. She put the rest into her grandmother's old lidded picnic-basket, with apples, cheese, a bottle of white wine, two glasses and a corkscrew. As an afterthought, she added paper napkins, a bottle of water and two tin plates. Then she wrote a note for her father: *Papa, Your sandwich is in the fridge. See you later, Love P. XX.*

Outside, although the sky was a soft duck-egg blue and the sun shone, there was a cool breeze and Phyllida was glad of her fisherman's sweater. She carried her basket in one hand and her gumboots in the other, as she descended the cliff path to the beach. As she stepped out onto the sand, she saw that András was sitting in his boat in the shallow water, at the other end of the cove. Great, she thought, he hasn't forgotten, and she ran swiftly along the tideline towards him. He saw her coming and raised his hand in greeting, then, with a single oar, manoeuvred the dinghy close to the water's edge. Phyllida changed into her gumboots, chucked her Reeboks into the boat, handed the basket to András, and climbed aboard. 'You didn't forget, then?' she said, sitting down on the central thwart, facing him.

'No, I didn't forget.' He sculled away from the shore, lowered the outboard into the water and pulled the cord. He sat in the stern, his hand on the tiller, and they headed out to sea. 'Put on that life-jacket,' he said.

Obediently, Phyllida put it on. 'Where are we going, András?'

'Ecqurihou.'

'I've never been; is it far?'

'It takes about ten minutes to get there. It's time I went anyway; I've got some pots out there. With a bit of luck, we might get a lobster for our lunch.'

'Cool,' said Phyllida, impressed. 'How will we cook it?'

'Make a fire; boil it in sea water. Look behind you, I brought a bucket.'

Phyllida turned, and saw not only the necessary bucket, but kindling and a pile of cut-up driftwood. 'Matches?' she enquired cheekily, and laughed, the wind whipping her few remaining long locks of hair into her eyes.

András tapped the breast-pocket of his life-jacket, and smiled at Phyllida, amused by her bossy manner, and by the stiffly gelled, coppery spikes on top of her head. The boat surged through the green waves, and after a few minutes András raised an arm and pointed. 'There it is.'

Phyllida looked, and saw the island, still far away, a craggy little black rock, quite alone, surrounded by the marbled green-and-white waters of the wintry ocean. 'Does anyone live there?' she asked.

'Only sea birds. It's never been inhabited, as far as I know.'

As they drew near, Phyllida could see the orange marker buoys that revealed the presence of the lobster-pots. András cut the engine and drifted alongside the buoys, pulling up and inspecting each of his traps in turn. It was a good haul: four lobsters in the big pots and a quantity of spider crabs in a smaller pot, which had been reinforced with chicken-wire, to make escape impossible. He extracted the crabs with care, transferring them to a large nylon net, originally used for

127

packaging onions. He secured the top tightly, and hung the net over the side of the boat, to keep the catch alive in the water. Three of the lobsters were thrust into another net and hung beside the crabs, and the fourth he put into the bucket beside Phyllida.

András stood up in the boat, and sculled slowly towards the shallow waters of a minute rock-encircled cove surrounding a tiny beach of pristine white sand, a soft green froth on the tide's edge the only mark of impurity of any kind. When the prow of the boat hit the sloping sandy shore, it stopped with a gentle crunch, and Andnás shipped his oar, hopped nimbly over the side and held onto the gunwale. 'Bring the lobster and the rest of the stuff,' he said. 'Then I'll pull her out of the water.'

Phyllida grabbed the bucket and the picnic-basket, lowered herself carefully into the few inches of water, then carried her provisions a little way up the beach, above the tideline. She sat down on the dry sand and watched as András, waiting for the pulsing movement of small waves to assist him, propelled the heavy boat into a safe position, then heaved the anchor over the side to prevent it drifting away. He extracted his kindling and driftwood from their niche under the prow, carried them up the beach, set them down in front of Phyllida and sat down beside her. He took off his life-jacket and folded it into a thick cushion. 'Better to sit on these,' he said. 'Underneath, the sand's quite wet.' She followed his example, then watched as he dug a hole in the sand, lined it with smooth round stones and set about making a fire.

'You've done this before,' she said, smiling.

'Certainly have.' Skilfully, András fed kindling into the small blaze. 'You have to make your own entertainment in a place like Florizel, otherwise you'd die of boredom. There's no cinema, no clubs, and only a couple of rather dozy pubs, full of old men waiting to die, and a few tourists in the summer.' He glanced at her, his blue eyes challenging. 'It's a crap place, Phyllida. Hadn't you noticed?'

'No,' she replied, stoutly, 'I hadn't. I love it here; I always have, and I expect I always will.'

'That's because you don't live here. You can get away whenever you want to; trot off back to London.'

'But this is such a beautiful place, András. Can't you see how stunning it is? You want to *try* living in London; you'd soon change your mind. That's a crap place if you like, polluted, noisy, and full of ill, worried, rude people crammed into overheated, over-crowded tubes and buses. It's sheer hell living there, I can tell you.'

'I'd love it.'

'You wouldn't.'

'I *would*!' András snapped a branch in two and laid it precisely on his twigs, supported by the stones on either side. 'OK,' he said. 'Let's cook.' He took the lobster in its bucket down to the sea, half-filled it with water, carried it back and set it carefully on the fire. Phyllida, slightly surprised at his vehement rejection of her beloved island, unpacked her picnic-basket thoughtfully, and uncorked the bottle of wine. 'Is that the kindest way to cook a lobster?' she asked meekly. 'Bringing it to the boil from cold?'

'No-one really knows. Crabs have a nervous system, so you can kill them quickly by shoving a sharp knife between the eyes, but lobsters don't have brains, so you can't deal with them like that.'

'Perhaps they don't feel anything at all, then?'

'Perhaps they don't. One hopes not.'

Phyllida poured two glasses of wine and handed one to András. He took it, and smiled at her apologetically. 'Sorry. It was rude of me to put down your island, Phylly.'

She laughed, and took a sip of her wine. 'As a

129

matter of fact, I can understand perfectly how you could feel the way you do. It's a question of having choices, isn't it?'

'Exactly.'

Since it occurred to her that the salami would not go very well with the lobster, Phyllida unfolded her sandwiches and removed the rose-pink, fat-flecked discs of sausage, and they ate them with their fingers as a starter, tasting delicious with the cold, dry wine. As the lobster slowly came to the boil, turning a vibrant coral colour in the process, she arranged the salad, olives, eggs and brown bread on the two tin plates. When the fish was cooked, András drained the bucket, then split the lobster lengthways through its tail with his sharp folding fisherman's knife. He placed a half-tail on each plate, then cracked the big claws with a heavy stone, ready for extracting the delicious, tender meat.

'Brilliant!' said Phyllida. 'What a treat! My sisters would be livid, if they knew.' She laughed, and picking up her fork, began to eat.

Silently, their appetites sharpened by the fresh sea air, they ate every crumb of food, except the apples. With a little sigh of satisfaction, Phyllida wiped her face and fingers on her napkin and refilled their glasses. 'Thank you, András,' she said. 'That was absolutely delicious; you're a terrific cook.'

He smiled. 'It's a question of good raw materials, isn't it?'

Phyllida opened her mouth to say that he wouldn't be able to buy a live lobster in London without having to take out a mortgage on it, then closed it again, and bit into her apple.

'Phyllida?'

'Mm?'

'Why didn't you go back to London with your sisters? Aren't you still at school?'

'No, I'm not, since you ask. I got the chuck.'

'Got the *chuck*? Whatever for?'

'Oh, I screwed up. Drink, drugs, you name it, I did it.'

'Why?'

'Why not? It just seemed like a good idea at the time. Everyone does drugs and stuff in London. I got found out, that's all.' She turned her large hazel eyes on András, smiling, trying to appear world-weary and experienced, but without succeeding. Instead, she sounded childish and resentful. 'Other people do *far* worse things than grass, and don't get busted.'

'What sort of things?'

'Oh, snort coke; even shoot up, some of them.'

'Really? How pathetic.'

'Why is it pathetic? You sound like my parents, András.'

'Isn't it pathetic to make a balls of everything right at the beginning of your life, when every door is open for you, and when there's nothing to stop you from doing anything at all that you want?'

'Perhaps that's the trouble,' said Phyllida quietly. 'Perhaps I'm bored with the endless work and exams, and my mum's ambitions for me. Perhaps I don't want to be a clone of her, go to university, have a great career and all that.' She looked at him as he sat beside her, stirring the fire with a stick. 'Don't you understand that, András?'

'Yes, of course I do, but from where I'm at, it seems like a terrible waste. Criminal really.' He turned his head and looked at her thoughtfully. 'So, what is it you really want to do?'

'Nothing. Just chill out, here, with Hugo.'

'Hugo?'

'Papa, then. He's my dad. He's a writer; he's really cool. Money's not such a big deal for him. I'd much rather be like him; perhaps be a writer, too, who knows?'

131

András gave her a small ironic smile and raised his eyebrows. 'It's very convenient for your dad that he's got a wife like your mum, don't you think?'

Phyllida flushed, her cheeks burning at this implied criticism of her father. 'It's not like that at all, András – not at all! They're a great partnership; they adore each other. I don't know any other parents I'd rather have.'

'So why do you make your mother sound like a pushy, over-ambitious woman, Phylly?'

'I don't mean to; she's not really. She just decides what she thinks is the right thing for us.' Then, inexplicably, Phyllida dissolved into tears; tears of shame, regret and bitterness.

When the sobs had subsided into a watery snuffling, András touched her hand. 'Tell me about it, if you like.'

So she stared out to sea, and told him everything. She told him about the summer holiday in Scotland, and her initiation into drugs and sex by the glamorous Kit, as well as the driving lessons. 'He was a shit, actually,' she said. 'I never saw him again, horrid little creep, and good riddance. He was utterly gross, in every respect.' András laughed, and so did she. 'I never told Mum or Hugo about him, they'd have agonized about it, thought it was all their fault, or something stupid. You know – letting me go there in the first place. But I did tell Granny. She wasn't specially surprised. She said much the same thing had happened to *her*, in the Thirties, before the war, would you believe?'

'*Really?*'

'Yes, really. She told me that it was when her mother took her to London to do the season – you know, all that sad deb stuff. Apparently the debs, and the blokes wheeled in to dance with them were a pretty wild bunch. They did everything – booze, drugs, sex, the lot!'

'I suppose every generation has to reinvent these things for themselves, wouldn't you say?'

Phyllida frowned. 'I suppose. But I don't think Hugo and Mum got up to stuff, much, before they were married.'

'I wouldn't bet on it.' András smiled at her and his intensely blue eyes seemed to Phyllida to offer her not only friendship but understanding, and an unusually tolerant mindset for someone of her own generation, or nearly. 'My grandmother sowed her wild oats, too,' he confided. 'Except that in her case, things didn't work out according to the conventional pattern, which is one of the reasons why I'm here, as a matter of fact.'

Thoroughly confused, Phyllida stared at him. 'What's your *grandmother* got to do with your existence, András?'

'It's a long story, Phyllida. Do you really want to hear it?'

'Yes, of course I do.'

András piled more wood on the fire and the bright flames leapt up again, making a rosy circle of light around them. 'My granny is called Michèle Langlois. Her family are farmers on the other side of the island, the French side, we call it. In 1940 the German army invaded the islands, as you probably know. Florizel was one of the last to be occupied. The islanders offered no resistance, and on the whole the Germans behaved quite well in their turn.'

'I know a bit about it,' said Phyllida. 'My granny wasn't here during the war, because Grandpa was working in Intelligence in London, and she was with him, but of course, Granny's *parents* were here at *Les Romarins*, all through the Occupation, I think.'

'Yes,' said András, 'and by all accounts they got on quite well with the German officers.'

'Oh? Who told you that?'

'Common knowledge; everyone knows your business here, Phylly. How could they not?'

'I suppose.'

'Anyway, they weren't the only ones. The Langlois family had a couple of Germans billeted on them at the farm, and one of them was a guy called Werner Balthus. He was a very nice man and the whole family liked him. He and my granny fell in love. He was about twenty when he came to Florizel, and Michèle was two years younger. No-one in the family minded about him being a German, and they planned to marry after the war.'

'And did they?'

'No, they didn't. At the end of '42 Werner was posted back to Germany, everyone assumed he would be sent to the Eastern front. My granny wrote to him at the address he gave her but never got a reply. She thinks he must have been killed almost at once, at Stalingrad. Thousands of young Germans were.'

'How dreadfully sad.'

'Worse than sad, I'm afraid. You see, after he'd gone, she found she was pregnant, and my mum was born in October 1943. She looked just like him: fair hair, blue eyes.'

'Just like you?'

'Yes, just like me.'

'You don't look much like an islander, I must say,' said Phyllida quietly.

'More like a German?'

'Yes, much more like a German. Is that so bad?'

'Yes, it is, here.' András turned towards her, his face taut, dark with anger. 'Do you know what happened to girls who slept with the enemy, after the Liberation?'

'No, I don't,' said Phylly, her heart full of foreboding.

'Shall I tell you?'

'OK, tell me.'

'The local people rounded up the girls and shaved their heads, and then ran them naked through the streets, chucking rotten fruit and eggs and shit at them, and beating them with sticks, like driving cattle. Some of them even got tarred and feathered, and worse.'

'God, how awful. Is that what happened to your granny?'

'No, not the tar, thank God. But she was chucked into the harbour, half-conscious, and left to drown.'

'What happened?'

'Her dad took out a boat and saved her. He rowed her home, right round the island. It took him four hours, in a heavy sea.'

'Poor things, how horrible.' Phyllida turned to András, her eyes bright with pity and distress. 'And what about the baby? What happened to her?'

'She grew up on the farm with Michèle and the old people. She was a lovely little girl, very pretty, but of course she had this label German bastard pinned on her from the very beginning, so she had a rotten time at school, and even worse when she grew up and found she had no friends.'

'What, none at all?'

'Just this one guy, Pierre du Toit.'

'Is that your dad, András?'

'Yes, it is, worse luck.'

'Why worse luck?'

'I don't really mean that. Poor chap, he does his best, I know. But he's only a peasant, Phylly, with little or no education, and no interests outside his boat, his bottle and his bed.'

'In that order, András?' asked Phyllida, smiling.

He laughed ruefully. 'Yes, more or less.' He looked at the sky. 'It's time we got back. The light's beginning to fade already.'

They packed up the basket, smothering the remains of the fire with sand, returned to the boat and made a fast passage back to Florizel on the incoming tide. It was five o'clock when they reached the cove below *Les Romarins*.

'András,' said Phylly, 'would you like to come up to the house, meet Hugo and have some tea?'

'Yes, I would,' said András. 'Thank you.'

The friendship between the two young people was to prove a fruitful experience for them both. Hugo took to András immediately, recognizing from the beginning his quality and natural intelligence, and admiring his evident serious quest for knowledge.

Having taken the decision to work on the island, Hugo had lost no time in having a computer installed at *Les Romarins* and getting himself on line. He was happy to show the delighted András how to find his way round the Internet, but was quick to point out its limitations. 'There's still nothing to touch visiting the actual places and reading all the available literature, as far as real research goes,' he said. 'To rely on the Internet entirely would be rather like getting your information from a popular digest instead of using the British Library, in my view.'

Phyllida, too, began to settle down to her own work once more, during the day. At four o'clock, when she guessed that András would be in the bay checking his pots, she would take the dogs and run down to meet him. Sometimes he was with his father, and she would just wave and walk on with the dogs, but more often he was alone, and would come up to the house for tea, to return books and borrow others. Every so often, he brought a gift of fish – langoustines, crabs, oysters or mussels. On these occasions he would stay for supper, going home in the darkness, his port and starboard lights visible from Phylly's lookout on the cliff-top, as his boat chugged quietly across the bay.

*   *   *

Towards the end of February, Nelly and the younger girls came for the weekend, bringing with them the wine expert from a famous auction house. He was to inspect and value the contents of the cellar, prior to its shipment to London, and eventual sale.

Hugo and Peregrine, for this was the elegant young man's name, walked together along the aisles of the cellar. As they progressed, Hugo held up his hunter lantern and Peregrine, his hand trembling with excitement, wrote down the details of each bin. 'My God,' he said, 'I haven't seen anything like this for years. I can't believe it wasn't all drunk decades ago.'

'I think my father-in-law was a compulsive buyer of wine,' said Hugo. 'He loved the idea of the cellar beneath the house, full of secret treasures. Of course, he's been dead for a long time now, and my mother-in-law nearly always drank gin.'

Peregrine pursed his lips. 'Gin,' he remarked dryly. 'That's a very *Thirties* drink, don't you think?'

Hugo laughed. 'Una-Mary was a very Thirties person, and none the worse for it.'

After four hours of this intensive inspection and cataloguing, Peregrine turned to Hugo. 'Unless I am seriously losing my touch, I estimate that the contents of this cellar should fetch half a million, give or take twenty per cent.'

'Well, that's brilliant news. It's my wife's business, of course; it all belongs to her. Make sure it's in her name, won't you?'

'Yes, certainly.'

'We might decide to keep a few cases,' said Hugo, looking longingly at the Pomerols.

'Yes, of course. Just let me know the details.'

That evening, András walked up from the beach with a sack of mussels. He was introduced to Nelly, Sophie and Gertie, and invited to stay to supper. The younger sisters fluttered around, setting the table and giggling self-consciously, while András, aided by Phylly, prepared a huge dish of *moules marinière*. The entire family, with Peregrine and András, sat round the long table in the warm kitchen and ate this delectable seafood, with hunks of crisp baguette and a chilled Pouilly-Fumé.

'This wine is a bit posh for this sort of food,' said András, laconically.

Hugo laughed, amused by this assertion. 'What would you have chosen, András?'

'A dry cider, or a Muscadet, perhaps.'

'Do you like wine, András?' asked Nelly. 'Does it interest you?'

'Very much, but I don't often get the chance to drink anything as good as this, Dr Turnbull. It's delicious.'

Nelly smiled at him. 'Call me Nelly,' she said. 'Everyone does, here.'

The following morning Hugo and his daughters took Peregrine to catch the Guernsey launch for the first part of his return trip to the mainland. They drove to the little harbour in the four-wheeler, leaving Nelly alone at *Les Romarins*. She washed up the breakfast things, pleasantly aware of the silence around her, broken only by the click of china on the draining-board, the soft drip of the slowly running tap. Bliss, she thought. It's heaven to be here, away from the noise and the dirt, and tensions. One feels so safe and secure on an island; un-get-at-able, I suppose you'd call it. No-one can get me on a bleeper here, thank God.

There was a knock on the back door and Nelly looked round, surprised. No-one she knew, like Elsie, would knock; they would walk straight in. She dried her hands on the tea towel, and went to the door. On the step stood a tall, handsome, well-built woman in her fifties. Like most islanders, her skin was tanned and leathery, but her hair, although greying, was fair, and her eyes a clear blue. Nelly noticed at once her resemblance to András, and had little difficulty in guessing the identity of the stranger. 'Good morning,' she said politely.

'Mrs Turnbull?'

'Yes,' said Nelly, not bothering to correct her.

'Rose du Toit.'

'How do you do?' said Nelly. 'How can I help you?'

'It's personal.' Rose du Toit looked over Nelly's shoulder into the kitchen. 'Can we be private?'

'Yes, of course,' said Nelly. 'Do come in. I'm on my own, there's no-one here.' She led the way to the kitchen table and they sat down.

'It's András,' said Rose du Toit brusquely. I thought it might be, said Nelly to herself, and waited. 'He's my only son, and I won't have him messed around, that's all.'

'How do you mean, messed around?' Nelly spoke calmly, in her usual unruffled professional manner.

'I want him left alone. I want your husband to stop lending him books, putting ideas into his head, making him dissatisfied with his lot. I want your flighty daughter to stop playing games with him, leading him on.' She paused for breath, her face flushed, her eyes angry and resentful. 'Haven't I had enough trouble in my life, Mrs Turnbull, without having the only decent thing I've ever had stolen from me? I'm not a fool; I can see which way the wind's blowing, make no mistake. Does your girl know that András is already engaged to be wed? He's going to marry Madeleine du Toit, and it's a good match for him. András will carry on with the fishing after my man packs it in, and then his sons after him. It will all stay in the family. It's our way. It's how it should be, and how it's going to be.'

After a short pause, during which Rose du Toit

stared at her unblinkingly, challengingly, her chin thrust forward belligerently, Nelly spoke. 'Is that all?'

'Isn't it enough? Haven't I made myself clear?'

'Indeed you have, perfectly clear.' Nelly cleared her throat. 'I must tell you, Mrs du Toit, that I, personally, have no intention of interfering with anyone's life in any way. I can't, of course, speak for my husband or daughter.'

'You can tell them what I said, can't you?'

'Yes, I can do that, if you wish.'

Rose du Toit stood up. 'Be good enough to do so, then,' she said, and took her leave.

Nelly said nothing about Rose's visit until that afternoon, when she and Hugo took a rare walk together, without their daughters. The girls had all gone down to the beach in search of András, and Hugo and Nelly walked right round the *dépendances* of *Les Romarins*, inspecting the walls and roofs of the byres and barns, the high granite orchard walls, and the fencing that enclosed the small, scrubby fields of sheep that surrounded the property. 'There's a fair old bit needs doing,' said Hugo. 'Henry was quite right when he said the place was crumbling.'

'Doesn't matter,' said Nelly comfortably. 'We'll do it a bit at a time. After all, it's stood up for more than two hundred years. It's not going to collapse now.' She sat down on a damp wooden bench. 'Sit down, darling. There's something I must tell you.'

Hugo sat beside her, and she told him about Rose du Toit's visit and her angry accusations. He listened carefully, but remained unmoved. 'Poor thing,' he said. 'She is a bitter and rather difficult woman, by all accounts. It's hardly surprising, is it?'

'Shall I say anything to Phylly?'

'No, I wouldn't. If it's true about the engagement,

140

she'll find out soon enough. András will tell her.'

'And will you stop lending him books, Hugo?'

'Most certainly not. He is an exceptionally bright young man; it would be a crime not to help him expand his horizons, and I shall continue to do so, until *he* tells me not to.'

Nelly smiled. 'I thought you'd say that,' she said.

Chapter Eight

The beginning of March brought a change in the weather. An endless succession of soft rainy days was replaced by a blue sky, a keen sharp wind, and the opening buds of daffodils, tossing their heads in the gardens of Lovelace Road.

Rachel, at first deeply resentful of Stanley's manipulation of her in the matter of obtaining paid employment for herself, applied in a half-hearted manner for several local jobs, rather hoping that her applications would fail. In fact, this was exactly what happened, the rejections arriving with insulting speed. If a reason for her failure was given, which was rarely, it was usually a vague excuse that she was over-qualified for the vacancy in question. Otherwise, the problem seemed to be her lack of experience and references, in view of her age.

After two frustrating weeks, and seven interviews, she became angrily determined to get a job, *any* job, just to prove that she could, so that it was with some relief that she finally obtained a very badly-paid one as personal assistant to the fund-raiser of a local charity. The offices of this organization were up a flight of concrete stairs in an ugly modern building, part of a new development off the Iffley Road. Once inside the office suite, however, the atmosphere was one of heated opulence. In spite of the fact that the double-glazed windows were firmly locked, the radiators were turned to maximum so that the staff were driven to shedding their garments layer by layer throughout the day, though even this did not prevent them from sweating profusely, which did nothing to improve the already stale atmosphere. Three pale young girls sat at a communal table in the outer office, opening envelopes and extracting cheques, postal orders and occasionally banknotes.

Mrs Montgomery, Rachel's boss, the motivating force behind this charitable mail, sat behind a splendidly impressive mahogany desk in the back room, more often than not talking into one of several brightly coloured telephones. The walls of her room were papered with green-and-gold embossed vinyl, on which hung enlarged photographs of pathetically emaciated but nonetheless appealing African children. The floor was covered in an expensive-looking and very thick carpet, and the comfortable leather chairs seemed to Rachel to be inappropriately luxurious for the offices of a charity. Surely, she told herself, the bulk of the money donated should go to feed the mouths of the children so tellingly displayed upon the walls, rather than the elaborate decoration and heating of the office?

Mrs Montgomery was a small, very thin woman, probably in her fifties, with carefully waved grey hair, immaculately made-up face, and long red fingernails. She wore chic Chanel-type suits and a great deal of costume jewellery. Her room smelt strongly of Chanel No 5, and at the end of each roasting day Rachel returned home with a splitting headache and in a very bad temper. Only pride prevented her from giving notice after the first week. Her work consisted solely in chasing up the recipients of Mrs Montgomery's mailshots, and endeavouring to pin them down as regular contributors to the charity, preferably by direct debit. She sat in Mrs Montgomery's room while she carried out this distasteful task, passing the calls to her boss if she detected any sign of backtracking on the part of the unfortunate victim on the line. The sound of the honeyed tones of Mrs Montgomery's voice, drooling down the instrument, would remain with Rachel for a long time.

She stuck it out for three weeks, and then came down with a heavy cold. Arriving home on Friday evening with a high temperature, and coughing and sneezing in a very antisocial manner, she was easily persuaded by Stanley to go to bed, and allow herself to be looked after. By Sunday morning, after two nights and a day of rest, hot lemon and paracetamol, she felt quite a lot better, and when Stanley, with unusual thoughtfulness, brought her the *Sunday Times*, she spent the morning reading its many sections, including the sport, and felt fairly happy to accept the fact that the multi-talented Antonia was downstairs, cooking Sunday lunch for the family. For the first time, it occurred to Rachel that it might actually be rather good to have a job – a decent job, of course – and be able to relax like this when she felt like it. She turned the pages until she found the section marked 'Appointments', and was surprised to see how many were being advertised. Among the impressively large ads in search of senior executives, at what seemed to Rachel astronomical salaries, a very small and insignificant one caught her eye. It was tiny in comparison with the rest: six lines of a single column. *PHOTOGRAPHER'S ASSISTANT, W1*, she read. *Must have drive and ability to cope under pressure. Excellent opportunity for enthusiastic non-clock-watcher. Experience not necessary. Attractive remunerative package*. There followed a London telephone number.

Intrigued, Rachel read the ad again, then she got out of bed, took her pocketbook from her bag and made a careful note of the telephone number, under P for Photographer. When Stanley came up to see whether she was well enough to come down to lunch, she said she didn't really feel quite up to it yet, and he promised to send a tray up for her. The tray duly appeared, carried by Adam, and she thanked him gravely, doing her best to look suitably feeble as she lay against the comfy pillows.

Adam put the tray on the bed, and stared at her, frowning. 'You all right, Mum?'

'Just tired, darling. I'll be OK tomorrow.'

'Oh. Good.' He took himself off, embarrassed, unable to think of anything more to say to his mother. Typical male reaction to indisposition in their womenfolk, Rachel said to herself, without malice, and smiled. It's not on Adam's agenda at all; he just can't take it seriously, can he?

After lunch, Ciaran came up to tell her that the boys had gone out, and that she was going ten-pin bowling with Stanley. 'Dad says, will you be OK on your own?'

'Is Antonia going with you?'

'Oh, she's gone already. She's gone out with Eric.'

'Who's Eric?'

'He's an actor, Mum. He's really cool.'

'How exciting,' said Rachel.

'Will you be OK, then?'

'Yes, of course I will. Have a good time.'

When she heard the front door slam, and the car being driven away, Rachel picked up the *Sunday Times* and reread the advertisement. I wonder if he or she works from home, she thought. They might be there right now; it's worth a try. She went round to Stanley's side of the bed, where the extension phone stood on his night-table. She opened her pocketbook at P and dialled the number. The phone rang for quite a time and she was about to hang up, when it was answered, by a man. 'Yes?'

'Are you the photographer advertising for an assistant in the *Sunday Times*?'

'Yes.'

'I wondered if the post had been filled?'

'No.'

'I would like to be considered for it, please.'

'OK. Can you come round now? I'm in all afternoon.'

Rachel swallowed nervously. 'I'm afraid I can't come today,' she said. 'I'm in Oxford, actually. But I could come tomorrow, if that's convenient?'

'OK. What about twelve-thirty?'

'Yes, I could do that. Thank you. What's the address?'

He gave the address, and Rachel wrote it down. 'And the name, please?'

'Simon Ruskin.'

'My name's Rachel Madoc. I look forward to meeting you, Mr Ruskin.'

'OK, fine. See you tomorrow.'

Rachel replaced the telephone, amazed at the ease with which she had organized her interview. She decided that she would not mention it to anyone, in case the whole thing came to nothing. She would pretend to go to Mrs Montgomery's, as usual, and catch the first train to London instead. Feeling quite excited, and a great deal better, she went to her cupboard to select what she hoped would be the correct gear for a photographer's assistant. After careful thought, she decided on her Gap jeans, a clean white shirt and the Doc Marten boots she wore practically all the time. She would wear her navy-blue Oxfam pea-jacket, just as she usually did. She didn't think that a London photographer's non-clock-watching assistant would wear a camel-hair Jaeger job, which had been Stanley's Christmas present to her two years ago. Better to be a bit too relaxed than too middle-class and posh, she thought. I should look as if I actually need the bloody job, after all.

The question of her clothes dealt with, Rachel got dressed, made the bed and went downstairs, taking the *Sunday Times* with her. She found the house warm, quiet, and astonishingly, unnaturally tidy. She went into the sitting-room and deliberately dropped the disordered pages of the newspaper onto the sofa. She blew her nose, and threw the crumpled tissue on top of the pile of neatly laid, unlit logs in the fireplace. Then she went to the kitchen, and decided to create a bit of friendly chaos by doing some cooking. She got eggs and milk from the fridge and took down the heavy earthenware crock of flour from its shelf above the worktop. She retrieved her old griddle-pan from the back of a cupboard, gave it a smear of oil and put it on the gas to get hot. Scotch pancakes were one of the few things that Rachel enjoyed cooking, and was in fact rather good at. She made her batter with her balloon whisk as she had always done, ignoring the brand-new electric hand-mixer prominently displayed on the worktop. She lit the oven, turned it to low and put in a large platter to get warm, ready to receive the pancakes. The griddle began to give off a faint smoke and Rachel dropped spoonfuls of batter onto it, and watched, fish-slice at the ready, as the little bubbles formed, and then burst, on the uncooked top of each small pancake. She flipped them over, one by one, admiring each beautiful cooked surface, brown and freckled, like the best kind of egg.

After twenty minutes, she had made about eighteen pancakes. She covered the dish with a folded tea towel to prevent the sweet-smelling golden discs drying out, then put her cooking things in the sink. She looked at her watch: four-thirty. As if on cue, she heard the arrival of the car, the opening of the front door and the cheerful entry of Stanley and Ciaran. Smiling, pleased at her afternoon's work and good timing, Rachel put on the kettle, and taking mugs and plates from the dresser, set them on the table. In a couple of minutes, having hung up their coats in the cloakroom, Stanley and Ciaran came into the kitchen.

'Hello,' said Rachel. 'Had a good time?'

'Excellent,' said Ciaran. 'I won!'

'Well done, you,' said Rachel, grinning.

Stanley sniffed the air. 'Been cooking, Rachel?'

'Certainly have; look in the oven.' She measured tea into the pot, and filled it with boiling water.

Ciaran opened the oven door. 'What is it?'

'Scotch pancakes. You can put them on the table, and get the butter from the fridge, please, darling. We should have some honey somewhere, too.'

Stanley hovered in the doorway, looking unaccountably nervous.

'What's the matter, Stanley?' said Rachel. 'Come and sit down and have some tea.'

'The thing is, my dear, I believe you have inadvertently piled Ossa upon Pelion.'

'I've *what*?'

'What Dad means, Mum,' said Ciaran clearly, 'is that Antonia got tea ready for us before she went out.'

'Oh, really? How very kind of her,' said Rachel, doing her best not to overreact to this news. 'Well, I daresay her contribution will keep, won't it? It'll do for tomorrow, I'm sure. Let's have the pancakes now.'

Ciaran looked mutinous. 'I don't *want* pancakes, Mum. They're boring. Antonia's done chocolate brownies, my favourites.'

'OK, we can have the pancakes *and* the chocolate brownies, can't we?'

'No, we can't,' said Ciaran, turning the screw with considerable relish. 'Because she's made Barra Brith

148

for Dad. He loves it; his mother used to make it when he was a little boy.'

Rachel stared at Ciaran, appalled at the insensitivity displayed by her daughter, but did not reply.

'It's a Welsh delicacy,' Ciaran continued briskly, in case her mother was unaware of this interesting fact. 'It's a kind of fruity bread.'

Rachel turned to Stanley, expecting him to applaud her efforts on their behalf, and sweep aside Ciaran's objections, but he did not. He said nothing, and remained where he was, in the doorway. Ciaran stared her mother out, with unyielding obstinacy. Finding herself isolated, and more hurt than she would have believed possible, Rachel tried to laugh it off. 'OK, where is this wonderful tea, then?'

'In the dining-room,' said Ciaran, visibly brightening. 'We *always* have Sunday tea there now. Had you forgotten?'

The pancakes, now getting cold and leathery, were left on the table, and Ciaran picked up the teapot and led the way triumphantly to the dining-room. At the door, Rachel hung back. As Stanley edged his way past her, she laid a hand on his arm. 'I suddenly don't feel so good, Stanley. I think I'll go back to bed.'

'Whatever you like, dear.'

'Stanley?'

'Yes?'

'Oh, nothing.'

Back in bed, she lay miserably staring at the ceiling, depressed and sad, but curiously unable to relieve her feelings by weeping. She heard the boys returning home, their loud voices downstairs, and the occasional burst of laughter. She found it hard to understand the sense of alienation from them that filled her whole being. Have they stopped loving me, she asked herself, or worse, is it *me*? Have *I* stopped loving *them*? Reluctantly, she came to the conclusion that it seemed

149

quite likely that she had. It's something to do with Pa dying, she thought. They didn't really care at all, did they? They all shied off the subject as if his death was totally unimportant and irrelevant to the Madoc family. Perhaps it's because I feel guilty about neglecting Pa myself, being ashamed of him, letting Stanley persuade me into his bogus middle-class values. Nobody forced you down that road, Rachel, she reminded herself; you went willingly enough at the time, didn't you? Trouble is, you weren't much good at social climbing, were you? Which is why he prefers bloody Antonia, and he's not the only one, it seems.

At eight o'clock, Ciaran appeared at the door with a tray. 'Why are you in the dark, Mum? Still got a headache?'

Rachel turned on the bedside lamp. 'Yes,' she said. 'I have, rather.'

'I've brought your supper. Dad thought you'd probably only want the soup, and some bread.'

'Thank you,' said Rachel quietly, feeling quite unreal, as if she were in hospital and Ciaran was a nurse, attending impersonally to her needs. 'What are you all having?' she asked, more for something to say than any real desire to know.

'Cold duck, and a *gratin dauphinois*, and an orange salad with balsamic vinaigrette.'

'Sounds delicious,' said Rachel faintly.

'Oh,' agreed her daughter, heading for the door, 'it will be, absolutely. Antonia's food always is.'

The next morning Rachel got out of bed at half-past six, while Stanley was still asleep, and took a bath. She got dressed in the clothes she had chosen the day before, brushed her hair and applied a light, natural-looking make-up. Then she put lip-gloss, some tissues and a comb into her bag, and went quietly down to the kitchen. There, she poured herself a glass of milk, and put an apple in her pocket. She sat at the table and scribbled a note to Stanley: *Have gone early to work – will probably be late this evening. R.*

She cycled to the station, rather enjoying the comparative lack of heavy traffic at that early hour. She parked her bike, locking it carefully, then went to the ticket office and bought a day return to Paddington. On the platform she looked at her watch: she was in plenty of time. Thinking that it would be a bore if Mrs Montgomery were to ring her home number to ask why she hadn't come to work, she decided to phone her, on the off chance that she was already in the office. The phone was answered immediately, though not by Mrs Montgomery herself. It was one of the outer-office girls, aptly named Charity.

'Hi. It's me, Rachel,' she said. 'I'm afraid I've got an awful cold, so I won't be coming in today. Could you tell Mrs Montgomery, please?'

'Will do. Get well soon, Rachel. Bye.'

'Bye.' Relieved, she hung up and joined the rest of the commuters on the platform just as the London train pulled in.

She arrived at Paddington station at nine forty-five. She was not at all sure where to find Blomfield Road, so she looked for a bookstall in order to buy the London A-Z. Having done that, she bought herself a coffee, and sat down at an empty table to drink it, at the same time consulting the A-Z. To her surprise, she discovered that Blomfield Road appeared to be quite close to the station, though separated from it by the menacing-looking Westway. The best option seemed to be taking the Underground to Warwick Avenue, and then walking to Blomfield Road. She looked at her watch again: almost a quarter past ten. She was miles too early for her interview, but she thought that she might as well locate the place, and then walk around until it was time to ring the bell.

Rachel negotiated the underground system without difficulty and emerged into the watery sunshine at Warwick Avenue. From there it was a short walk to Blomfield Road, and as she turned into the street she was surprised, and pleased, to find that it ran alongside a canal. The houses, some very grand and smartly painted, and one or two quite shabby and badly in need of redecoration, seemed a bit like rather more impressive versions of those in Lovelace Road, except that they weren't red brick, but painted stucco. Finding the number that Simon Ruskin had given her, she was quite relieved to see that the house was one of the shabby ones, in fact probably the shabbiest of all, with several bald patches where the stucco had fallen off the brickwork. She went past the house and walked slowly along the canal, enjoying the pale sunshine, and watching the ducks on the water. A large number of drakes were milling about in quarrelsome, aggressive groups, pestering the few nervous females, then suddenly taking off in swift flight, for reasons best known to themselves. A narrow boat chugged by and she watched it out of sight, wondering where it was going and whence it came.

At twelve-twenty, Rachel turned and walked back to the dilapidated house. There were six names on the entryphone panel at the side of the door, including two marked 'Ruskin'. Simon Ruskin's was the top one, and she pressed it. There was a crackle, and a disembodied male voice said, 'Yes?'

'It's Rachel Madoc. I have an appointment with Mr Ruskin at twelve-thirty.'

'OK. Come up. It's the top floor.'

The front door clicked open and Rachel went in, letting it swing to behind her. The long narrow hall, decorated in a faded hand-blocked art nouveau wallpaper, led to a staircase that must once have been elegant, its first long flight culminating in a lofty

Venetian window that overlooked a long, narrow, rather run-down garden. She continued up three more flights to the second-floor landing, where a scarlet-painted door stood open. She tapped on the door, waited for a response, and when none was forthcoming, went in. She found herself in what she took to be a loft. It was a large bare space, with all the former stud partitions ripped out, to judge by the marks left on the walls. Three square windows looked into the tops of the trees on the street side, and a similar number gave onto the garden at the rear of the house. As well as the partitions, the ceilings had also been removed, exposing the original wooden joists and purlins of the roofspace. Against the wall on the garden side, between two of the windows, stood a large wood-burning stove, with a hefty black flue soaring up through the roof. A supply of logs lay in a neat stack close by.

In the centre of the loft, and resembling an intelligent child's construction toy, stood what looked like the superstructure of a giant and enormously high four-poster bed, made of pine and stainless steel. Access to the top of this astonishing platform was by means of a set of steel steps, and Rachel could see that there was some kind of small cubicle or room on top, making a connection between the platform and the roof. It was painted matt black and was difficult to see clearly against the dark timbers of the roof. On the floor, underneath the platform, stood a long leather chesterfield, of the kind one might expect to find in a common-room or a men's club; it was a shiny brown, the colour of a conker. This comfortable piece of furniture rested on a square of sisal matting, cut to fit inside the supporting legs of the platform, and on either side were two oversized photographic lamps, large white umbrellas with fat silver-coated electric-light bulbs. Behind the chesterfield, against the bare brick wall at the far end of the loft, were a sink, a cooker, and a small fridge arranged under some industrial shelving, all in stainless steel. This intimidatingly functional scheme was slightly relieved by a few colourful cans of tomatoes, bottles of oil and wine, and a large packet of Jordan's Porridge Oats. Between the windows on the street side was more industrial shelving, carrying books and videotapes. Surplus books and some mounted photographic blow-ups were propped against the walls, and piles of magazines were stacked underneath the low table in front of the chesterfield.

Rachel stood in the doorway for a few minutes taking everything in, then tapped on the door again. 'Mr Ruskin?' she called. 'Are you there?'

A muffled voice, apparently coming from the roof, called back. 'Hang on a tick, I'm in the darkroom. I'll just be a moment.'

Rachel closed the door, and waited. After a short pause, there was the sound of a door sliding open, then sliding shut again, and Simon Ruskin came swiftly down the ladder. 'Come in, sit down, how do you do?'

'How do you do?' Rachel was surprised and immensely reassured to see that her prospective employer appeared to be very young, possibly in his twenties. Tall, and slenderly built, he had close-cropped brown hair, three days' growth of beard, a long narrow nose, and amazing, almost colourless blue eyes. He wore a single fine gold earring and the kind of crumpled black jacket and trousers that come either from Oxfam or from an Italian designer. His grey silk shirt was collarless, and he had a long mulberry-coloured silk scarf wound round his neck. When he smiled, his thin face took on the guileless look of a child, and any nervousness Rachel might have felt disappeared from that moment.

'Coffee? Glass of wine?' he offered.

'No thanks,' said Rachel, sitting down on the sofa, 'I'm fine, I had a coffee at the station.'

'Good. Right. OK.' He sat down beside her. 'Um, what can I tell you about the job? Basically, it's dogsbody and troubleshooter. Booking the shoots, and making sure I caption the Polaroids correctly for the feature-writer if the job's for a magazine, that's very important. Then there's checking on the supplies – film, chemicals, paper, stuff like that. Usually, after a mag-shoot, the film goes to a lab for processing, then we deliver to the client. We hold onto the black-and-white Polaroids that I do to check the composition before I take the colour transparencies, so there's no possibility of a cock-up when everything's ready for the scanner.'

'Doesn't sound terribly difficult,' said Rachel. 'What about correspondence, filing, that kind of thing?'

'A bit of that, yes. Can you type?'

'Well, I can, but not frightfully fast.'

'I've got an oldish AppleMac. It's useful for letters, filing, accounts and stuff. Could you handle that, do you think?'

'As long as I could ask you if I got stuck, I expect I could. I'm a graduate, I'd learn pretty fast, I'm sure. Have you still got the instruction book?'

Simon laughed. 'I expect so; I'll look it out.'

Rachel looked at him and thought how nice he was, and how very badly she wanted the job. 'Have you got other applicants to see?' she asked.

'Yes, I have, two. One this afternoon, and one this evening.'

'Oh. Yes, of course. I understand.'

'You haven't asked about the pay.'

'Oh. So I haven't.'

'You'll probably think it far too little, as a matter of fact, especially as you're a graduate.'

'Try me.'

He told her the sum he had in mind. She looked at him and smiled. 'I don't think that's too little. That would be fine.'

'Good,' said Simon. 'The job's yours, if you really want it.'

'Thank you very much; I really want it.'

He held out his hand and she shook it. 'Please call me Simon,' he said. 'May I call you Rachel?'

'Of course, what else?'

'When can you start?'

'Would next week be OK? I have to give notice to my present employer, and I think I must try and find a room near here. I don't think it would work very well, commuting from Oxford every day.'

'Just a room?' asked Simon. 'Not a flat?'

'Couldn't afford a flat; it'll have to be a room.'

'This house belongs to my grandmother. She's widowed, and quite broke, but she can't bear the idea of selling up and moving, so she lets rooms to make ends meet. I don't think she charges exorbitant rents. Would you like me to ask her if she has a vacancy? It would certainly be very convenient if she had, wouldn't it?'

'*Convenient?*' exclaimed Rachel, amazed at the speed with which her life was arranging itself. 'It would be a miracle!'

'Hardly,' said Simon. 'Wait till you see the rooms, Rachel. They're pretty cheesy, I should warn you.'

As the train sped towards Oxford, Rachel sat in her window seat watching the countryside flash past, and reflected on her good fortune in finding both a job and a lodging that she knew would suit her very well. Simon's grandmother had turned out to be a delightfully vague old lady in her late seventies, who lived in the drawing-room on the first floor of the house, overlooking the canal. It was a charming, though extremely disorganized and dusty room, crowded with beautiful old furniture and occupied by several Burmese cats. She had offered Rachel a small room on the ground floor, with a window looking over the rear garden, and Rachel had accepted at once. Now, sitting in the train, she felt tired but extremely happy, and full of an unaccustomed self-confidence. She looked forward with considerable relish to giving notice to Mrs Montgomery, and with some complacency to informing Stanley of her success in the world of gainful employment. Cycling slowly home from the station, she thought about Simon, how laid-back he was, kind, sympathetic, but manifestly entirely uninterested in questions of personal detail. He had not asked her about herself, whether she was married or had children, or what her previous jobs had been. Neither had he asked for references of any kind. Come to that, she thought, I didn't ask *him* for a reference, either. I chose to take him on trust; I guess it's the same for him.

As she turned into the gateway, the thought struck her that Simon had offered her the job before he had interviewed the other two applicants. Oh well, she said to herself, I expect he thought of something kind to say to them.

When Rachel informed him that she had taken a job in London, from Monday to Friday, Stanley had been extremely annoyed at not being consulted in the matter. 'What you mean,' said Rachel, 'is that I should have asked your permission first, don't you?'

'Certainly not. That's not what I meant, at all. I just think you should have *discussed* it with me, that's all.'

'So that you could try to stop me, Stanley?'

'Don't twist my words, Rachel.' She smiled faintly, but said nothing. 'Well, anyway,' he went on, 'the money will be useful, as we agreed.'

'What money is that, Stanley?'

'The money to pay Antonia's salary, of course.'

'You're not serious?'

'Of course I am,' said Stanley. 'It was the reason for your taking a job in the first place.'

'Forget it. The money you will save for my food, laundry, bathwater and so on will more than cover that.'

'I disagree.'

'Get real, Stanley. I've done *exactly* what you pressured me into doing. I've got a job, and I shall need all my salary to cover my expenses in London during the week, as well as my train fares. You'll just have to get used to it, won't you? I'm sure Antonia will cope splendidly. She might even be able to cook some nice economical dishes, instead of her fancy cordon bleu stuff every day. She could save quite a bit of money that way. What do you think?'

Predictably, Antonia coped very well indeed. She lost no time in taking advantage of the situation, and on the night following Rachel's departure to London she appeared in Stanley's room when the other occupants of the house were fast asleep, and slid silently into bed beside him.

Chapter Nine

Easter came early, at the end of March, and Nelly, Sophie and Gertrude arrived in Florizel on the afternoon of Good Friday. Hugo drove the four-wheeler down to the harbour to meet them, and carry the luggage home.

'Where's Phylly?' asked Sophie, when they were all safely on board, and Murphy was plodding slowly up the hill again.

Hugo smiled. 'It may surprise you to know that she is at this moment finishing an essay, in order to get it out of the way before you two disruptive creatures arrive.'

'Oh.' Gertrude pulled a face at her sister.

'That's very good news, darling,' said Nelly, installing herself beside her husband on the driver's bench. 'You really think she's settled down to work again?'

'Looks like it. I don't know about the *quality* of the work, but it strikes me as excellent.'

'She asks you to read it, then?'

'She does.'

'Good.'

At the top of the hill, Murphy had a rest, and was then persuaded to break into a gentle trot. In twenty minutes they drove through the gates of *Les Romarins* and came to a halt beside the front door. It was a still late afternoon, the air fresh and salt-laden, and the house and garden seemed to swim in the blue, crepuscular, fading light. The lights were on, and the windows shone, warm and glowing against the stark granite walls of the house.

For a fleeting second, Nelly expected to see the door open and Una-Mary to appear, white-haired, smiling, wearing her ancient Guernsey sweater and baggy tweed skirt, flanked by her two little dogs. A sharp pain smote Nelly's heart as she reminded herself that they would not be spending any more holidays with her mother; not Easter, not Christmas, and not the long summer vacation.

The door opened and Phyllida came down the steps to welcome them, followed by the two dogs, wagging their tails and yapping in a fussy manner, from force of habit. 'Guess what?' said Phyllida. 'Baz just rang up from France. He wants to come and stay.'

'Hello, darling,' said Nelly, jumping down from her seat. 'Don't I get a kiss?'

Phyllida laughed, and hugged her mother. 'Of course you do, what else?' She turned to her sisters. 'Don't just sit there! Chuck the bags down!' The bags were duly passed down and stacked on the step.

'OK,' said Hugo. 'You take over, Sophie, and you can help her, Gertie. Make sure you give Murph a proper brushing, while he has his oats. And hang the tack up properly, please. Don't just leave it in a tangle on the floor, right?'

'OK, Papa; don't fuss.'

Hugo watched the girls out of sight, as they drove round the corner of the house to the stable, then picked up the two remaining bags and followed his wife and eldest daughter into the house.

'The kettle's boiling,' said Phyllida. 'Elsie made a ginger cake, specially for Gertie, she said.'

'What a star she is.' Nelly smiled. 'She never forgets things like that, does she?' She took off her coat and muffler and ran her fingers through her hair, peering at her reflection in the looking-glass above the hall table. 'What did Baz say, Phylly? Did he leave a message or anything?'

'He left a number, for Papa to ring back. There it is, by the phone.'

Hugo picked up the notepad and studied it. 'It's not his number in the Touraine. That's the code for Paris – he must be at his office.'

'Well,' said Nelly, 'if he wants to come and stay, it's for you to decide, isn't it? I'll only be here for ten days or so this time. How do you feel about coping with him on your own, darling? And what about Olivia? Is she coming too?'

'He didn't mention her,' said Phylly.

If Hugo detected a certain reluctance in Nelly's re-action to the possibility of a visitor, he chose to attribute it to simple tiredness. 'I'll see if I can reach him now,' he said. 'Go and have your tea, darling. You must be knackered.'

In the kitchen, Nelly was pleased to see the familiar black kettle simmering on the hotplate. The table was properly laid with a cloth, cups, saucers and plates, as well as a blue jug of jonquils, whose sharp intense smell made a little scented cloud that hovered in the warm air. The teapot, one of the few remaining pieces of a complete Quimper set of china that had formed a cherished part of Nelly's childhood, stood on the stove with the tea-leaves already spooned into it, waiting for the boiling water. The stiff, upright figures of Breton men and women, wearing their traditional dress, dec-orated its fat, comfortable sides. It was a pity, but did not really matter, that a large chip on the lip of the spout made it impossible to pour the tea without drip-ping. On the table was a fresh, uncut wholemeal loaf on a proper breadboard, butter in a cow-shaped dish and a jar of honey. The ginger cake, moist and sticky, its top decorated with pieces of preserved ginger, sat rather regally on a paper-lace doily in a silver entrée dish. Nelly leaned against the stove, warming her hands, while Phyllida made the tea, then put the pot on the table. They sat down together.

'How are you, darling?' Nelly took a sip of scalding tea, and smiled at her daughter.

'I'm OK.'

'Really OK?'

'Yes, really.' Phyllida cut thick slices of bread and offered one to her mother. 'I like it here, you know, Mum. I wish we could live here always, all of us.' She looked at Nelly, her eyes serious. 'Papa misses you, you know.'

'I miss *him*, Phylly. I miss you, too.'

'So why can't we all be here, together?'

Nelly sighed. 'You know why not, darling. My job; the girls' school; your school too, I expect, when we sort things out.'

'I don't want to go back to school in London, Mum. I'm much better here, working with Papa. He's light-years ahead of those dozy cows who taught me at school. I really like working with him, one to one. It's a much more mature system, and much more rewarding.'

'But if he took on three of you, all at different stages, how would he have time to do his own work?'

'Well, yes, I suppose that's true.' Phyllida buttered a slice of bread. 'He seems to find time to talk about books and things to András.'

Nelly said nothing, spread honey on her bread, and waited.

'He's coming to lunch on Sunday, and bringing oysters or langoustines, depending on the catch.' She glanced at Nelly. 'Is that OK with you?'

'OK? Of course it is, what a terrific treat. Have you planned anything for the rest of the meal?'

'Hugo and I thought that lamb would be the traditional thing, so he had one of ours killed. Alain did it a few days ago, and we cut it into joints, and I put most of them in the freezer. The leg for Easter Sunday is hanging in the still-room.'

Alain was Elsie's husband, and had managed Una-Mary's small flock of sheep for her, cut the hay crop and harvested the little field of potatoes, early and main crop. Without any particular consultation between Nelly and himself, he seemed happy to continue in this supportive role on her behalf. She was quite surprised at the speed with which Hugo and Phylly had taken to island life, and very surprised indeed at her daughter's lack of concern at the grisly fate of one of their own lambs, its leg now hanging in the still-room, stiff and cold, waiting to be roasted. After so many years of living and working in the city, Nelly was inclined to think of legs of lamb and chickens coming to her kitchen sanitized and plastic-wrapped, with no thoughts concerning the method of their slaughter. This was pretty strange, she pondered, when so much of her professional life had necessitated a close involvement with death and dismemberment of the human variety. 'Well done, both of you,' she said. 'You seem to have organized everything splendidly.'

'Oh, it was mostly Hugo. He's really into food these days; he's got a stack of Granny's old cookbooks by the bed.'

That's the second time she's called him Hugo, thought Nelly. I suppose this is growing up?

Sophie and Gertrude came noisily through the garden door, and washed their hands at the sink.

'You smell of horse, foul things,' remarked Phyllida.

'*And?*' Sophie glared at her older sister.

163

'You could've had the sense to take your coats off, dick-heads.'

'Look who's talking,' said Gertrude belligerently. 'Since when did *you* have much sense, Phylly?'

'That's quite enough, do you mind?' Nelly spoke automatically, quietly, regretful that an all too rare private conversation with Phylly had been blown away. She poured tea for the younger girls, and they sat down and helped themselves to bread.

Hugo came into the kitchen, looking preoccupied, polishing his spectacles. They were the same steel-wire-framed ones he had worn as an undergraduate, and at forty-two he still had the slightly vulnerable air that had been so appealing to Nelly all those years ago. His sandy hair was cut short in exactly the same way, and his blue eyes were as kind, and as perspicacious, as they had always been. He smiled benevolently at his family as they sat round the table in the lamplight, their coppery hair shining, their identical hazel eyes bright with affection and competitiveness. He sat down next to Nelly, and put on his spectacles. 'Basil,' he said, 'is a pain in the arse.'

'Oh? Why?'

'He's doing research for a French documentary about the Occupation of the islands. He wants to come here and talk to some of the people who lived through it, find out how they survived, what it was like, all that.'

'Is that such a good idea, Hugo? Raking up the past, after so long? Won't it cause trouble?'

'That's exactly what I said to Baz, but he said that the spin they're putting on it is the heroism of the islanders, their courage and endurance, that sort of thing. Nothing else, he said.'

'Are you really sure?' Nelly looked worried.

'That's what he said.'

'Did you say he could come, darling?'

Hugo sighed. 'Yes, of course. How could I refuse?'

'When's he coming?'

'Sunday evening.'

'Shit!' said Nelly crossly. 'It's too bad. I was really looking forward to it being just us, on our own. I don't *need* this, Hugo.'

'I'm sorry, darling. I'd have got out of it if I could, but you know what Baz is like, don't you?'

'Yes, I do. He goes looking for trouble. It's what he does, all the time. He's like all reporters, he's got a nose for a story, and if there isn't one, he'll invent one.'

'God,' said Hugo. 'I hope he won't do that here.'

Easter Day dawned bright and clear, with a brisk easterly wind, and they walked across the fields to attend the Family Eucharist. The hedgerows were starred with primroses, and sheets of blue periwinkle had appeared in the grass overnight. The little church was packed with worshippers, and greenery and flowers decorated every window-sill, as well as the lectern, the pulpit and the altar, filling the air with the fresh, verdant smell of living things, newly resurrected from the dead of winter. It's strange, said Phyllida to herself, going to church here is quite different from London, or Assembly at school. Somehow, there, it all seems boring and pretty pointless. Here, it always feels as though everyone is actually listening to the words of the service, and is quite sure that Jesus really *did* rise from the dead. Halfway through the proceedings there was a slight commotion as the small pupils of the Sunday School came in through a side door, and mounted the steps to the wooden gallery at the back of the church, where they settled themselves in whispering rows, hymn-sheets rustling, ready to augment the choir when required. The small regular choir was composed of elderly females, whose grey heads were covered with rather saucy-looking black diamond-shaped caps with golden tassels. Since the sound

produced by these ladies was not particularly mel-
lifluous, the addition of the cheerful trebles of the
children was a fortunate circumstance, Hugo thought,
as he stared blandly at the Easter lilies adorning the
pulpit, his face giving nothing away.

He had risen early to prepare his leg of lamb for the
oven, spiking it with slivers of garlic close to the bone,
in accordance with Mrs David's instructions, and fes-
tooning it with branches of rosemary, secured with
string. After a liberal sprinkling of virgin olive oil, and
a good grinding of black pepper, the leg had been
loosely wrapped in foil and placed on a grid in a large
roasting-pan, ready to go into the oven just before they
left for church. Calculating that the appetites of the
young people would be huge, he peeled two dozen
potatoes and left them in a saucepan of cold water. He
was halfway through a similar number of carrots when
Phyllida appeared, yawning, and set about preparing
breakfast. She made coffee and toast, and put a pan of
water on the stove for boiled eggs. When the table was
ready, and the rest of the family began to appear, she
performed her grandmother's Easter ritual. She poured
a bottle of red food-colouring into the boiling egg
water, then carefully lowered five pure white eggs into
the pan. When the timer rang after four minutes she
removed them from the heat, and transferred each
gaudy orange-pink egg into a white china eggcup.

'How lovely, Granny's Easter eggs!' Nelly exclaimed,
coming into the room. 'Thank you, darling.'

Phyllida did not see András or his family in church,
but they met him on their way home as he emerged
from the cliff-path below the sheep-field, carrying a
sack over his shoulder.

'What've you got?' called Phylly.

'Oysters!'

'Cool!' exclaimed Sophie and Gertrude together and

ran to inspect the booty. Good-naturedly, András opened the sack, and allowed the girls to take a look at the catch. Phyllida came up and joined them. 'Goodness,' she said, peering into the sack. 'What a lot, András. I hope you left some for your parents?'

'They don't eat them.'

'You're kidding?'

'No, I'm not.' He laughed. 'It's like owning a sweet-shop, Phylly. You never eat sweets.'

'But you do.'

'Yes, of course.' He picked up the sack. 'Come on, you girls, there's a lot of opening to be done.'

While András, assisted rather ham-fistedly by Sophie and Gertrude, opened the oysters on the slate shelf in the still-room, Phyllida arranged the prepared half-shells on plates lined with the seaweed he had brought with him from the beach. She cut lemons into quarters, four for each crowded plate. 'A dozen oysters each; what luxury,' she said. 'Do you think we'll have room for Hugo's lamb?'

'Try me,' said András, smiling.

'Me, too,' agreed Sophie. 'I'm starving.'

'So'm I.'

'Well,' said Phyllida. 'That's all right, then.'

After eighteen years of raising children and keeping her career going at the same time, organizing the household, shopping and cooking with the aid of various au pairs and daily helps, Nelly felt a curious sense of disbelief at the display of domestic competence exhibited by her husband and children. Everything was under control; there was no crisis for her to deal with. Hugo had removed the foil from the lamb and it was browning nicely. The parboiled potatoes had been transferred to a baking-dish with a little oil, and were roasting under the joint. The carrots, fragrant with mint, simmered on the hob, and a jar of mint jelly had been fetched from the store-cupboard.

'Where shall we eat?' asked Nelly. 'Dining-room, or here?'

'It's still a bit cold for the dining-room, isn't it? Let's eat here.'

'Yes, OK.' Nelly picked up a tea towel and wiped down the kitchen table. 'If we're going to eat in here more often than not, perhaps we should get a bigger table? There's plenty of room for one, isn't there?'

'Good idea.' Hugo looked at Nelly thoughtfully. 'I've been having vague thoughts about central heating, myself. Would you think that a terribly naff idea, darling?'

Nelly smiled. 'I think it's a great idea, as long as it doesn't involve having poncy modern radiators, or anything like that.'

'Good, we'll investigate the possibilities.' Hugo opened the door of the oven, and saw that the potatoes were a delicate golden colour and smelling delicious. 'We're nearly ready; I must make the gravy. Come on, woman, don't just stand there chatting. Set the table; open the wine; make yourself useful!'

Nelly laughed, and putting her arms round him, kissed the back of his neck. He turned, basting spoon in hand, and kissed her properly. 'I'm glad you're here, my darling,' he said quietly. 'I don't like it on my own.'

'You've got Phylly.'

'You know what I mean.'

'Yes, I know what you mean. I don't like it on my own, either. Happy Easter, my love.'

At a quarter to four Basil Rodzianko disembarked from the steamer from France and stood on the quayside, looking around him. The granite harbour of Florizel was extremely small, and consisted of half a dozen little shops, all closed, a post office, a bank, and an incongruous-looking modern telephone kiosk. There was no sign of a taxi or public transport of any kind, and since he had chosen to come on an earlier boat, there was no-one there to meet him. Four other passengers had disembarked at the same time as himself, and he made haste to enquire of one of them the whereabouts of *Les Romarins*. '*Les Romarins?*' repeated the man, then pointed to the road that climbed straight up the hill, and away from the harbour. 'Go straight on up, then past the pub and the church. It's a big house, about fifteen minutes' walk from the church. You can't miss it.'

'Thanks very much,' said Basil. He lingered, hoping to be offered a lift in the man's pony and trap, but an invitation was not forthcoming. The trap was driven away up the hill, and Basil picked up his grip and followed it. It took him ten minutes of muscle-cramping toil to reach the top of the hill, and the pub. Regrettably, this turned out to be closed, like everything else, it seemed. He took off his long black leather coat, bought on one of his assignments in Istanbul, and spread it on the ground. Thankfully, he sat down on it, stretching out his traumatized legs on the soft green grass of the roadside. He looked around him, soothed by the simple charm of the few low stone buildings, and the leafy hedgerows, studded with primroses, that lined the narrow road. There was no sound, except the occasional shrill burst of song from a robin that haunted the thick hedge. What a peaceful place, he thought, even though it's agony getting here.

His period of rest and relaxation was, however, to be short-lived. The wind had dropped, the afternoon was mild, and suddenly clouds of midges, attracted by the smell of his sweating body, began to attack him, getting into his thick, dark, bushy hair and beard, down his red plaid flannel shirt, and even inside his trousers. Basil sprang to his feet, cursing, and swatting himself violently in an attempt to rid himself of his tormentors. He ripped off his shirt and swung it vigorously round his head to disperse the voracious hordes of insects, then picked up his coat and grip and ran as fast as he could to escape from them. He presented a very strange spectacle as he sped down the lane, his chest naked except for a string vest, and a steel identity disc on a black leather bootlace round his neck. His flight from the midges had not been fast enough to avoid being bitten, however, and as he ran Basil could feel the itchy swellings rising on his back and forehead, in his ears and on his scalp. He did not dare stop to examine the damage, for fear of a fresh onslaught. Then, his lungs bursting, he raced round a bend in the lane and saw what he took to be his goal, *Les Romarins*, its mellow granite buildings enclosed by a high wall and surrounded by fields of sheep. He turned into the short gravelled drive that led to a gated archway in the wall. Before opening the gate he paused to put on his shirt, at the same time examining the painful eruptions on his body, forcing himself not to scratch them.

It was quite a few years since Basil had spent any time with Hugo and Nelly, his oldest and once closest friends. Their friendship went back to school and university days, and Phyllida was his god-daughter. Not that I'm much of a godfather to her, he said to himself wryly, I can't even remember her birthday. He pushed open the gate, walked up to the house, and rang the bell. No-one came to the door, and he frowned, irritated with himself for being early, for arriving before the agreed time. They've all gone out, he thought; damn. Half-heartedly, he rang again, and miraculously, he heard the sound of footsteps, and the door was flung open. Apart from the jagged spikes of hair and the gold stud in her nose, the slender girl who stood in the doorway might have been the eighteen-year-old Nelly, and Basil's heart lurched within his breast.

'Hi, Baz,' said Phyllida. 'You're early. Everyone's gone down to the beach. Come in, I'll make you some tea.'

Basil rearranged his thoughts, and smiled at his godchild. 'Hello, Phylly. Great to see you again. It must be three or four years now?'

'Yes, it must be. Since you got married, I suppose.' She took his coat, and hung it on the row of pegs in the hall. 'Come through to the kitchen. It's warm in there. We haven't lit the fire in the drawing-room yet.'

'As a matter of fact, I'm boiling hot,' said Basil, following Phyllida to the kitchen. 'I ran practically all the way, because of the midges, but I still got bitten.'

'Oh, dear; poor you.' Phyllida laughed, and glanced at him. 'You do look a bit blotchy. Never mind, I'll find the stuff for you; that'll take the swelling down.' She opened the kitchen door, and at once Basil saw a very tall fair-haired young man standing at the sink, washing dishes. 'András,' said Phyllida, 'this is my godfather, Basil Rodzianko. Baz, this is András du Toit.'

'Hi,' said Basil.

'Hi.' András held up his wet hands apologetically. 'Can't shake hands, I'm afraid, Mr Rodzianko.'

'Call him Baz,' said Phyllida. 'We all do, don't we?'

'Yes, of course. Please do.'

Nothing changes, Basil said to himself, as he sat at the table watching them drying the dishes and putting them away in their proper places, under Phyllida's strict eye. She's exactly like her mother, bossy but mercifully beautiful. What a difference that makes.

The work finished, Phyllida made tea and brought it to the table. Pushing a mug in Basil's direction, she noticed his blotched and swollen face. 'Oh, God!' she exclaimed. 'I forgot the spray for your bites. I'll get it now.' She got up from the table and left the room.

Basil took a sip of his tea, and looked covertly at

171

András, curious as to his origins. 'Do you live on the island, András?' he asked.

'Yes, I do.' Coolly, András returned Basil's gaze. 'And you, where is your home?'

'I live in France, but I'm hardly ever there. My work takes me all over the world.'

'Is that interesting?'

'Yes, it is, very. But there are times when I'd like to spend more time at home, with my wife, in the Touraine.'

'Do you have children?' András sipped his tea.

'Sadly, no. Olivia's commitments are almost as frustrating in that respect as mine. She's in Japan at the moment; she has an exhibition in Tokyo next week. She'll be supervising the hanging, right now.'

The door opened and Phyllida came in, carrying a can of sting-relief. 'There you are, Baz. That should do the trick.'

'Perhaps I'd better adjourn to the bathroom and deal with them properly. The little sods have got in everywhere.'

'Good idea,' said Phyllida. 'I'll show you your room.'

'Interesting man,' said András, when she came back.

'Yes, he is.'

Basil lost no time in embarking on his research programme, and the following morning he was out and about before midday, having borrowed a bicycle, making enquiries as to where the oldest inhabitants, those with wartime memories of Florizel, were to be found. His approach was direct, straightforward and friendly. He decided that the pub might prove a useful starting-point, and this turned out to be a fruitful line of investigation. The landlord, a cheerful man in his fifties, was happy to oblige him with several names of island pensioners. 'There's one of them, right there,' he said, pointing to an elderly white-haired man sitting alone beside the open fire, an empty beer glass on the table in front of him. 'That's Charlie Smith. He was here right through the war.' The landlord looked at Basil, grinning. 'A glass or two might oil his tongue, I daresay.'

'Right. A pint of whatever he's drinking, please, and a small vodka for me.' He sauntered over to the fireplace, and put the drinks on the old man's table. 'Lovely fire,' he said. 'Do you mind if I share your table?'

The old man looked at Basil, his rheumy eyes suspicious. 'It's a free country,' he said. 'There's other tables.'

Basil ignored this, and sat down. 'I bought you a drink,' he said. 'I hope you don't mind?'

Charlie Smith looked at the full pint of golden ale. He blinked, and pursed his lips. 'I suppose I doesn't mind, if you wants to throw your money about.'

Basil put his cigarettes and lighter, and the extremely small and inconspicuous tape recorder down on the table in front of him, and raised his glass. 'Cheers,' he said. Charlie Smith responded with a grunt, and took a powerful swig of his beer. As he did so, Basil, with a slight and deft movement of his hand, switched on his recorder. 'This is my first visit to Florizel,' he said. 'It's a beautiful island, isn't it? Have you lived here all your life?'

'Man and boy. You lives where the good Lord puts you, doesn't you? Nobody asks you do you want to, do they?'

'That's true,' said Basil. 'I was born in Paris myself. I didn't have any choice in the matter, either.' He smiled, and took a sip of his drink.

'You're French, then?'

'No. Half-Russian, half-English. My father was a Russian Jew. He spent the war moving from place to place in Paris, dodging the Gestapo. Thousands of

Jewish people like him were caught, and deported to the Nazi concentration camps.'

'Well, there's war for you. Not a lot you can do about it, is there?'

'That's very true,' agreed Basil. 'The ordinary man in the street doesn't have much say in the matter in wartime, poor chap. He just keeps his head down, and waits for better times, doesn't he?' He paused for a moment or two, then continued. 'I imagine life went on pretty much as normal on a tiny island like this? The war must have passed you by, more or less?'

'Like hell it did!' said the old man vigorously, and blew his nose loudly with a khaki handkerchief. 'It was bloody 'orrible. They tried to send everyone to England before the Jerries got 'ere, and it was a right ole shambles. Some people got the shits up an' rushed down to the boats, leaving everything just as it was, doors open, dinner still on the table, an' that. Just a handful of families stayed behind; it was terrible. The next day there was cows roaring all over the island, mad with pain. Their udders was bursting with milk, poor ole critters. They 'ad to be shot, you understand?'

'How distressing,' said Basil, quietly.

'It weren't just the beasts,' the old man went on, leaning forward confidentially. 'There was a good few villains got up to no good, looting 'n' that. Some of the 'vacuees got off the boat at Guernsey an' came back, an' when they got 'ome they found everything nicked, windows smashed, all the animals gone. Them bastards even took the bloomin' lino off the floor!' Charlie Smith took another long pull at his drink, then thumped the glass on the table emphatically. 'And that was *before* the Jerries got 'ere. I never did hear of anything stolen by *they*, not all during the five years they occupied us, an' that's the God's truth. They might've took a few houses for the soldiers, but the Jerries

174

didn't go in for *looting*, not that I ever 'eard tell, anyway.'

Basil smiled sympathetically, realizing that he had struck gold during the very first hour of his investigation. 'So, the Germans were OK, were they?'

'Some were; some weren't.'

'How do you mean?'

Charlie Smith gave Basil a wintry smile. 'It's not a thing we like to think about. There's no good looking down that road, is there?' Basil said nothing, and waited. 'It was the camps, really, an' what they called the forced labour. Not *us*, you understand. The ordinary German soldiers left us alone, pretty much. But there was this German thing called the OT, *Organisation Todt*. It was supposed to be secret, like, but we all knowed what it was. They were building these underground tunnels and that, an' they'd got the slave labour working down there, French, Russkies like you, all sorts. They were half-starved, weak as women, poor sods, an' if they slacked off or fell down, the OT men beat them up, even kicked their 'eads in, if they couldn't get up again, an' every night the dead bodies got chucked into the sea, an' were bashed to bits on the rocks. We all knew about it, but there wasn't nothing we could do to 'elp them poor devils. We dursn't.'

'Very understandable,' said Basil.

'An' yet, you know, them German soldiers could be ever so kind. There was bugger-all to eat sometimes, you understand. Nearly everything we growed 'ad to go to feed the German army, so we often went without. We couldn't even grow enough to feed them soldiers, an' sometimes they would come to our farm to see if we 'ad spare milk, or eggs to sell, an' they would give us bread, or cheese, and they'd give chocolate to the kids. They did like kids, you could tell.' Charlie Smith looked at Basil, a strange expression on his wrinkled old face. 'So you can understand why we looked the other way, and kept our traps shut, can't you? What could we do to help them poor buggers of slaves, anyways, when all's said and done?'

By the end of the week Basil had travelled the length and breadth of the island, talking to all the elderly people he could find. Some were quite willing to relive their wartime memories, and one or two seemed positively eager to denounce local collaborators, those islanders who had been only too willing to do business with the occupying army. Many, on the other hand, gave Basil short shrift, one old farmer going so far as to set the dogs on him.

Nelly, stitching the ripped leg of his trousers, was not at all sympathetic. 'Poor old man, I don't blame him, Baz. I know it's just another assignment as far as you're concerned, but I don't feel at all happy about it.'

'Why not? I'm not here to do a hatchet job on the islanders; far from it. It will be a testament to their endurance and courage during the Occupation.'

'Pull the other one, Baz.' Nelly looked at him with a flash of scepticism. 'I know you. I wish you'd try to remember that this is my island, too.'

'But you weren't even born, my love.'

'That's not the point. My family was here.'

András, too, was deeply angry and distressed that a friend of the Turnbulls should be going round making trouble, stirring up memories best forgotten. Meeting Phyllida on the beach on Friday evening, he came straight to the point. 'What the hell is going on, Phylly? Why has this man Rodzianko come here, poking his nose into other people's business, asking questions, raking up the past?'

'Is that really what he's doing, András? Are you sure?'

'Of course I'm bloody sure. He was over at Roc aux Chiens yesterday, talking to our neighbour. My mother saw him go in; he was there for over an hour. Naturally, she's convinced they will have been gossiping about my grandmother and the German soldier.'

'And what about you, András? Do *you* think that's what they were doing?'

'What else *can* I think?'

Phyllida sighed. 'God, I hope you're wrong. In any case, I shall speak to Baz about it, and find out.'

'As a matter of fact, Phylly, I'd prefer to speak to him myself, if you don't mind. I don't want to hide behind you, or Hugo.'

Phyllida looked slightly surprised, then smiled and touched his hand. 'Right,' she said. 'Come on, let's go now. No time like the present.'

They found Basil in the drawing-room, listening to his tapes, and making transcripts.

'Baz,' said Phyllida, closing the door. 'András would like a word with you.'

'Oh?' Basil switched off his tape recorder, and closed his notebook. 'How can I help you, András?'

András sat down on the sofa, and Phyllida sat beside him. 'I don't want to make a fuss, or be rude to you, since you're a friend of the Turnbulls, but I think you should know that you're making life very difficult for my parents, and my grandmother.'

'Really? In what way?'

'Well, for one thing, you were at Roc aux Chiens yesterday, weren't you?'

Basil consulted his notes. 'Yes, I was.'

'And you visited the Boudins?'

'Yes, I did.'

'And I expect they told you all about the wartime scandal in my family?'

Basil looked András straight in the eye. 'No,' he said, 'they did not.' He rewound his tape, then played it

177

back, and Phyllida and András listened to the quavering voice of old Mrs Boudin describing how they used to scavenge in the German rubbish heaps after dark, searching for scraps of food, and how she and her little brother had once watched as a lorry had driven up and parked quite close to them, on the edge of the cliff. Two OT men, with swastika armbands, had got out of the cab and let down the tailgate of the lorry, then heaved three naked bodies onto the rocks below the cliff. 'It haunts me still,' said the old lady. 'I put a bunch of flowers on those cliffs every year.'

András stared at the tape recorder. 'Is that all?'

'That's all. Isn't it enough?'

András flushed angrily. 'Of course it is; don't treat me like a child.' Then, in a low, halting voice, he related the story of Michèle, his grandmother, and her lover, Werner Balthus, and their baby daughter Rose, András's mother. He hesitated briefly, then told Basil about the terrible humiliation Michèle had suffered at the hands of her fellow-countrymen, after the Liberation.

'How very sad,' said Basil, gently. 'For him, the German father, as well.'

'Do you really think so?'

'Yes, of course I do.'

'They think he was probably killed at the battle of Stalingrad, in January 1943. That would have been very soon after he was posted from Florizel, at the end of '42. I believe thousands of young German soldiers were slaughtered in Russia.' András lifted his eyes, and met Basil's serious grey ones. 'So you haven't been rootling round, looking for *collaborateurs*?'

'No, not specifically. Of course, I can't stop people telling me things, András. But if anyone should happen to mention your family, I won't use the material, I promise.'

'No,' said András. 'Don't promise anything. History

is history, and I'm not ashamed of my part in it. I don't think my grandmother is, either. It's my mother who minds so much.'

'You know,' said Basil, thoughtfully. 'There is a remote possibility that I might be able to trace your grandfather. I have many friends in the information business, and at the very least we could probably find out what happened to him. How would you feel about that, András? Would you like me to try?'

'Could you really do that?'

'If you really want me to.'

For the first time, András smiled. 'Thank you,' he said. 'That would be very kind of you. I would like to know what happened to him.'

'Right,' said Basil. 'You must give me all the information you have. Names, dates, regimental number and so on, everything you can. OK?'

'OK.'

Chapter Ten

Rachel settled quickly and happily into her job in London. She found the work fascinating and of absorbing interest. No longer having the daily hassles of housework, cooking and childcare to contend with, she experienced little difficulty in sorting out Simon's files, accounts and correspondence, and soon brought these under control. A good deal of her time was spent working with him, on location. Most of his commissions were photo-shoots of the interiors of the houses of celebrities, usually for publication in glossy magazines. Sometimes this entailed driving out into the countryside, the back of his estate car jammed with all his equipment, camera bags, tripods, and lighting gear. Rachel's job was to organize these elements correctly, so that Simon had everything exactly where he needed it, at the right time, and in the right order. Her other responsibility on these occasions, though less well defined, was to act as a buffer between the owner of the house, if present, and the 'stylist' almost always sent by the magazine to rearrange the furniture, pictures, books and flowers in order to achieve more photogenic compositions. Predictably, the owner of the house, particularly if a woman, was liable to become rather nervous at this cavalier treatment of her cherished home, and would become increasingly tense as curtains were draped in a different way, and Paisley throws and modish tasselled antique cushions were produced from the stylist's van, and substituted for her own things. Though owners rarely gave vent to their outraged feelings, it was fairly obvious that they were not at all happy about it, and at such times it was Rachel's task to pacify them, preferably by taking them for a walk in the garden, or some equivalent ploy to remove them from the action, thus leaving the stylist free to reinvent the place in her own image.

'Isn't it odd, Simon?' Rachel remarked, as they drove home from one such assignment. 'Presumably the magazine people must see some merit in the place, or they wouldn't want to do a piece about it, would they? It seems a bit perverse to go to so much trouble to fog the issue with the whims of the stylist, I'd have thought.'

'Well,' said Simon. 'It's what they do, and of course sometimes it makes sense, in the interests of a good feature. But you're right; there's far too much fiddling and twitching goes on.'

'I can't think why the owner doesn't tell them to go to hell, if he or she can't bear it.'

Simon laughed. 'I'm afraid we've got them over a barrel in that respect. They want the publicity, for one reason or another. So they put a brave face on it, and let it go. No-one without an axe to grind would put up with the intrusion.'

Rachel became very fond of her little bedsit, and equally attached to her landlady. Because Rachel's room had only a small camping-gas burner on which to prepare a hot meal, Mrs Ruskin told her to keep her food in the fridge in the kitchen, and to use the cooker, the sink and the washing-machine, all of which Rachel did. She could not help noticing that the old lady did not appear to make supper for herself, since the kitchen was always empty when she went into it for any reason. One evening, when she was reheating a Chinese takeaway, Mrs Ruskin came to prepare her cats' supper. She smiled vaguely at Rachel, took a large can of cat food from the fridge and scooped the contents onto three saucers. She put them on the floor, then came over to the stove. 'Mm,' she remarked. 'Delicious smell you're making. It reminds me of Hong Kong.'

'Really? Do you know it well?'

'Lived there for twenty years or so. Best days of my life, my dear.' She gazed longingly at Rachel's supper. 'Dim Sum,' she said. 'My husband's favourite food.'

Rachel smiled. 'Have you eaten yet?' she asked. 'There's loads here, I always seem to get far too much for one. Would you care to join me?'

'Thank you, dear, I would.'

Life in Lovelace Road went on perfectly smoothly without Rachel. Stanley's routine was impeccably maintained by Antonia, and nothing was allowed to ruffle the smooth passage of his days and evenings. The quarrelsome, noisy behaviour of the young people on their return from school, together with their reluctance to settle down to their homework, was a thing of the past, and by means of an insidious blend of bribery and flattery Antonia soon had all three firmly under her thumb. The only one who was not entirely happy with the new regime, and who consciously looked forward to the homecomings of Rachel at the weekend, was Ciaran, though she never mentioned this fact to anyone. In the unlikely event of being forced to make a choice between her mother and Antonia as the manager of domestic affairs, she knew that she would have unhesitatingly opted for Antonia. After all, she reasoned, she was able to see her mother at weekends, wasn't she? Antonia was not only a much better cook, but could, and did, help with her schoolwork. Since the advent of the CD-ROM all three children were getting excellent grades at school, due to the superior presentation of their work as well as its content. Stanley, impressed and delighted at their progress, began to have serious aspirations for their futures, particularly those of the twin boys, in which Oxbridge places figured prominently.

On a less rarefied intellectual level, but of equal importance to Stanley, his sexual appetites were more than gratified once or twice a week by the delectable Antonia. From time to time, in rare moments of honesty, Stanley asked himself what it was that Antonia saw in him, a short, dark, hairy little Welshman of no great physical beauty. Whatever it was, he wasn't going to rock the boat by asking her to define her feelings towards him. Staring out of his window in college, he watched a group of undergraduates chatting in the quad below. Suddenly, a vision of Rachel rose in his mind: not the middle-aged Rachel of today, but the young undergraduate sitting in the green shade of an apple tree in the Orchard at Grantchester, so many years ago. She was lovely then, he thought, just as Antonia is so perfect now. He sighed, and turned away from the window. Trouble is, he said to himself, childbirth ages women so quickly, poor creatures. They lose that special bloom; that's their tragedy.

In the middle of May Rachel informed Stanley that she would be going abroad for about ten days, on a shoot. Far from raising difficulties, Stanley smiled at her quite amiably and wished her a pleasant trip. He had for some time been toying with the idea of giving another little dinner, and he saw immediately that Rachel's absence on business would provide a perfect opportunity for Antonia to exercise her particular talents once again.

Simon and Rachel arrived at Pisa airport in pouring rain and a violent thunderstorm, and were met by their hostess's chauffeur, holding up a placard saying RUSKIN. The camera equipment having been safely checked out and installed in the boot of the long black Mercedes along with their personal baggage, the chauffeur drove skilfully but rather hair-raisingly through the evening traffic and out onto the Florence *autostrada*. Rachel knew very little about their destination except that it was the home of a Danish writer of romantic fiction, married to a minor Italian aristocrat. Since she was an old friend of Simon's family, Ulrica Ericsson had expressed a preference that he should do the publicity shoot, and had invited him to stay at the *palazzo* rather than book into a hotel.

After half an hour's driving through the dark, rain-lashed countryside, they left the motorway and headed south, following the signs to San Gimignano. Disappointingly, the night was so dark and the torrential rain so persistent that it was impossible to get even a glimpse of the landscape through which they travelled. After what seemed like hours, but was in fact only about fifty minutes, they turned on to a minor road, which, in spite of the lashing rain, Rachel could see was bordered on either side by Corsican pines, their rough brown trunks illuminated by the powerful beams of the car's headlights. In another fifteen minutes the car slowed to a crawl and drove through an imposing stone gateway, then plunged steeply downhill through a wooded valley, finally coming to rest at the foot of the steps to the wide arcaded entrance to a Renaissance *palazzo*.

At first glance, the place seemed shut up, as if it were empty or abandoned, then the wide carved doors of the entrance were flung open, a stream of golden light poured into the darkness, and a servant in a white coat ran down the steps carrying an enormous black umbrella over his head. He opened the car door, Rachel got out and ran up the steps at his side, protected by the umbrella. She waited in the doorway, watching, shivering in the chill, as first Simon, and then all his gear were delivered safely into the shelter of the porch, out of the rain.

'Simon! You are here! What a terrible storm to arrive in, my darling!'

They turned, as a tall and powerfully built woman of sixty-something, silvery blonde and golden-skinned, wearing a long electric-blue djellaba and a lot of heavy silver jewellery, came smoothly down the honey-coloured marble staircase and into the vaulted entrance hall.

'Ulrica! How lovely to see you again.' Simon went swiftly to meet her, they exchanged air-kisses at the foot of the stairs, then he turned to introduce Rachel. 'May I present my assistant, Rachel Madoc. Rachel, this is our illustrious hostess, la Contessa di Volpini, aka Ulrica Ericsson.'

Ulrica laughed. 'Not *illustrious*, my dear Simon, merely *successful*. That's an entirely different thing.' She came over to Rachel, her big hands outstretched. 'Hello, Rachel, how nice to meet you. I'm sorry you had such a hard time getting here.'

They shook hands, and Rachel smiled, thinking of her grim nocturnal bicycle rides through the fenland backwaters of Deeping St Cuthbert. 'It seemed to me the essence of pampered luxury, as a matter of fact, Contessa,' she said quietly.

'Call me Ulrica, my dear. The other is my little aber-ration.' She slid a hand under Rachel's elbow, and held out the other to Simon. 'Come. Supper is waiting upstairs; *andiamo*.'

As they mounted the wide shallow steps of the curved marble staircase, Rachel gazed about her, enthralled, almost awestruck at the majestic beauty of the soaring limewashed walls of the hall, which rose through two floors to a high vaulted ceiling far above. From this lofty apex hung a massive carved and gilded chandelier whose multitudinous lights cast a fairy-tale glimmer that underlined the exquisite construction of the vaulting. Below them, in the hall, several enormous baroque mirrors, with candle sconces incorporated into their ornate gilded frames, faced each other and were reflected in endless tunnels of flickering light. On either side of the dark, intricately carved Renaissance double doorway stood solid heavy chairs of the same period, but the hall was otherwise completely bare, and almost monastic in its austerity.

At the top of the first flight of stairs, Ulrica paused beside a door. 'This is a little cloakroom, Rachel. I'm sure you'd like to freshen up.' She pointed to a second, impressive-looking double door. 'There's the *salone*; join me there when you're ready.'

Obediently, Rachel went into the cloakroom. It was very small, absolutely functional, and everything in it was pink. Even the water in the loo, unbelievably, looked like pink champagne. She washed her hands and brushed her fair hair, looking at herself objectively in the pink mirrored panel over the basin. In fact, the colour of the glass was remarkably flattering, and the face that looked back at her seemed to Rachel quite pleasing, at least healthy-looking, with flushed cheeks and soft, lustrous grey eyes. Nonetheless, she applied some gloss to her lips, and tucked her new linen shirt into the waistband of her denim skirt a little more elegantly.

In the *salone* the contessa waited, drink in hand, seated on a small white upholstered and gold-fringed chair before an immense stucco fireplace which soared up to the ceiling and was adorned with the coat of arms of the Volpini family. A log fire burned in the fire-basket, and Rachel made her way towards it, across a vast expanse of pink and grey carpet, as her hostess rose to greet her. 'These places are all very well in the really hot weather,' she said, with a sweep of her arm, 'but I still like a fire in the evening.'

'I quite agree. Even in May, an open fire is nice.' Rachel sat down, accepting the aperitif offered. 'You must forgive me if I seem to be staring rather rudely,' she said, 'but this house is so extraordinary, it's impossible not to.'

'Come,' said Ulrica. 'Let us take a little walk, and I'll show you my favourite bits and pieces.'

Together they examined the faded frescoed walls, with their garlands of fruit and flowers, and their toga-draped Roman emperors, and gazed up at the breathtaking high timber ceiling, its massive beams and joists all intricately painted in a design of birds, insects, flower motifs and fruit, in shades of brown, chrome yellow, vermilion and off-white. To Rachel, who had never seen such decoration before, it gave the impression of having an enormous patterned carpet stuck on the ceiling; she thought it strange, but utterly beautiful. The spacious formal room was furnished with conventional, expensive, overstuffed off-white armchairs and sofa, but the real interest lay in the exquisite antique pieces scattered around, in the shape of brilliantly waxed satinwood writing-desks and tables, carrying silver-framed family photographs and tall glass vases full of white peonies. On a library table stood a pair of gilded lamps, with gold-lined, glossy black shades. A heavy-looking silver tray held bottles, ice and glasses, with new books and magazines stacked nearby. Behind this table, in semi-obscurity, stood a curious ebony pole on a stand, supporting a Venetian carnival mask, its pale green face grotesquely distorted by an unnaturally long nose. From the back hung a pure white horse's tail, crimped and brushed into a snowy mass, and bound with a glittering golden cord.

'Horrible, isn't it?' said Ulrica, and laughed, just as Simon entered the room. 'There you are, my dear boy, at last.'

'Sorry,' said Simon. 'Just checking the cameras and stuff. I'm always paranoid about them getting damaged.'

'Would you like a drink, or shall we eat at once?'

'Eat, please. I'm starving.'

In the *sala da pranzo* it was immediately apparent that Ulrica had not allowed her Scandinavian origins to be completely overwhelmed by the traditions of her country of adoption. Like the *salone*, the walls of the small octagonal room were adorned with their original frescos, but these were quite informal, almost childlike, depicting a soft, crepuscular landscape with gentle hills and trees in shades of grey and misty green. In the centre of the room, standing on a circular carpet of natural sea grass, was a round table covered in a white floor-length damask cloth, and laid for three people, with antique blue and white Danish porcelain and heavy silver cutlery. The beautiful Gustavian high-backed chairs waiting at each place still had their original pale blue paint, and their newly upholstered padded seats and backs were covered with a pale blue and white broadly-striped cotton fabric. Identical chairs, the rest of the complete set, stood against the walls. From the leafy painted ceiling hung a large milk-glass chandelier, converted to electricity but nonetheless exquisitely delicate, its many tear-shaped crystal drops trembling on silver wires, and shedding rainbow streaks of light on the tablecloth beneath.

They sat down at the table, and Ulrica rang a small silver handbell. A secret door in the painted wall opened silently, and the white-coated manservant who had greeted their arrival appeared, carrying a tray. He placed hot porcelain bowls before them, and offered a tureen of a delicious-smelling soup with clams floating in it. Equally silently, he put a basket of bread rolls on the table, poured chilled white wine, and departed.

Simon took a mouthful of his soup. 'Mm,' he said, 'wonderful.' He looked at Ulrica and smiled. 'Where is Gianni? Not at home, just now?'

'No, the brute, he isn't.'

Rachel looked up, startled, but Ulrica laughed her big booming laugh. 'Don't worry, it's not a big deal. He'll be back when he's spent everything in his current account, and can't get any more credit. I'm used to it now. I don't care any more.'

'Still,' said Simon, frowning, regretting that he had brought up the subject of the errant husband, 'it must be pretty lonely for you, stuck out here on your own?'

'Funnily enough, no; it isn't really. Apart from the writing, there's a great deal to see to. The *contadini* are only too thankful that I'm here, to keep things going, pay the wages. I like them, and I think they quite like me, though that's probably only because they need me.'

'I shouldn't think that's the only reason, Ulrica,' said Simon gently.

'Well, one hopes not, of course.'

The door opened, admitting the ubiquitous Cesare, who removed the soup bowls, then served a dish of calf's liver with butter and sage, accompanied by baby broad beans with *pancetta*.

Ulrica looked enquiringly at Rachel. 'You haven't got a thing about liver?'

'No,' said Rachel, though she did in fact detest any form of offal. Politely, she took a mouthful, and to her intense surprise it tasted sweet and tender, the sage providing a perfect marriage of flavours, the entire dish a million miles from the grisly overcooked lumps of grey culinary horror she had previously encountered at home, unfortunately cooked by herself. She smiled at

Ulrica, and cut another delicate pink morsel. 'It's absolutely delicious,' she said, with perfect truth.

Cesare poured a young Chianti Classico, beautiful in the glass and intensely fruity in the mouth.

'Is this your own wine, Ulrica?' Simon asked.

'It is. What do you think?'

'Excellent.' He laughed. 'I could get quite used to this kind of thing, couldn't you, Rachel?'

'I most certainly could,' she replied. 'I'm making the most of every moment.'

'Basically,' said Ulrica, 'it's what keeps me here. I couldn't think of leaving now. Where else would I be so spoiled?'

The calf's liver was followed by a green salad and some *stracchino* cheese, after which they returned to the *salone*, where coffee and grappa was waiting in front of the fire.

Rachel was feeling delightfully relaxed, even drowsy, after the long day's travelling, and the good food and wine. She leaned against the soft cushions of a deep sofa, drank her coffee, and listened to the conversation of Simon and Ulrica. This seemed mostly to concern his parents, particularly his mother, who, it transpired, was a noted interior decorator. It had been Alice Ruskin, egged on by Ulrica, who had banished to the *soffitta*, or worse, to the saleroom, the heavy nineteenth-century furniture that had clogged the beautiful rooms of the *palazzo* when Gianni and Ulrica had married and moved in. 'Mind you,' said Ulrica, smiling, amused by the memory, 'Gianni wasn't exactly a pushover when we started chucking the stuff out. He fought tooth and nail for every grotty little knick-knack, bleating about *la famiglia*, wringing his hands, crossing himself and whispering *Mama mia* under his breath, just like a bad movie.'

Simon laughed. 'Poor old Gianni. He was no match for Ma and you, was he?'

'Poor Gianni nothing! He has the soul of a servant, and the cupidity of one, too!'

Why did you marry him, if he was so awful? was the question that rose in Rachel's mind, though not to her lips. The answer came at once. 'Twenty-one years ago, when we met, he was really very amusing, very attractive in a boyish way, and seriously good in bed.' Ulrica looked at Simon and laughed coarsely. 'As a matter of fact, he thought me a great tart to go to bed with him before we married.'

'Good heavens! Why?'

'In Italy, darling, nice girls don't.'

'It didn't stop him marrying you, did it?'

'No chance. He needed money. I had it. That's life, Simon.'

'I suppose.' Simon put down his cup and rose to his feet. 'We must start work at crack of dawn, to catch the early light. Thank you for a lovely dinner, Ulrica.'

'Yes, indeed,' said Rachel, getting up.

'It's wonderful to have you here, both of you. You're in your old room, Simon, and Rachel is two doors further on. Can you find your way?'

'Surely.' Simon took Ulrica's hand and kissed it. 'You're not going to bed yet?'

'No. I never go to bed before two or three in the morning. This is my time for work, when I have total quiet, and no interruptions.'

They said good night and Simon led the way up another flight of the marble stairway, and showed Rachel her room. 'Six o'clock start?' he said. 'Is that OK for you? You won't be too tired?'

'No, I'll be fine. Good night, Simon. See you at six.'

Rachel went into her room, closing the door behind her, and found herself in the most desirable bedroom imaginable. It was not very big, the walls were simply decorated in natural lime plaster, and the original dark timbers supported the ceiling. The door through which

191

she had just come, however, and a second one leading to a small white bathroom, were painted in the romantic eighteenth-century pastoral style, probably executed by the same artist employed in the dining-room, for the colours were identical, soft greens and blues, warm ochres and broken whites. Around each door was a frame, painted directly onto the wall, a broad band of raw umber. The double bed was turned down, the bedside lamps switched on. The sheets and pillowslips, hemstitched and brilliantly white, had obviously been ironed by hand with loving care. The coverlet, made of an antique crimson and gold textile, had been folded, and lay across a bench at the foot of the bed, beside her suitcase.

On the other side of the room, facing the door, tall, elaborately-pelmeted curtains of a warm apricot silk were closed against the night air. Rachel crossed the room, pulled them back, then opened the French windows, and stepped out onto a balcony. This narrow space was guarded by a low wall, about a metre in height, that ran along the length of the building, connecting the upper rooms. She placed her hands on the stone coping and took deep breaths of the cool night air. The rain had ceased, but the night was very dark, and starless; she could not distinguish between earth and sky. In the pale beam of light from her window she could see the fat, bursting buds of a wisteria whose gnarled leafy branches crawled snakelike through a metal pergola covering the shaded terrace of the first floor, immediately below, where they had spent the evening. Beyond that, in the garden, she could dimly make out the shapes of some green clipped shrubs and the tall black spires of cypresses. She looked to her right, and to her left, but all was dark and quiet. No light, or sound, came from Simon's room. He's probably asleep already, she thought, and went back into her room, and to bed.

*　*　*

Rachel woke at half-past five, got out of bed at once and went out onto the balcony. In the early sunlight she could now see the garden of the *palazzo*, a parterre of clipped box hedges, filled with roses and embellished with life-size Renaissance statues of nymphs and satyrs, some half-obscured by ivy, and all heavily encrusted with lichen. Behind the formal, intricate patterns of the parterre rose a screen of dark trees, massed cedars and cypresses competing for space, and beyond that was the magical landscape of Tuscany. Swathed in early mist, she saw a gentle, smiling pastoral landscape of olive groves and vineyards, punctuated by tall black lines of cypresses, and culminating in soft round blue hills melting into an opalescent sky.

'Unbelievable, isn't it?'

Rachel turned, and saw Simon sitting on the wall, clad only in a towel. Suddenly conscious of her own semi-nakedness in her thin cotton nightdress, she folded her arms protectively across her breasts, and smiled. 'Yes, it is. It doesn't seem possible that the weather was so awful last night, does it?'

'This is our reward: the perfect Tuscan light, clean and new. We'll start straight away, in the garden.'

'Right,' said Rachel. 'I'll be down in ten minutes.'

While she was dressing, there was a tap on the door and a pretty, dark-haired young girl, wearing a grey cotton dress and a white apron, came in with a tray of tea and cake. '*Buongiorno, Signora*,' she said, putting the tray down on the night-table.

'*Buongiorno*,' Rachel responded shyly; '*grazie*.'

'*Prego!*' The girl smiled, and left the room as swiftly as she had entered it.

My God, thought Rachel, what a time to be at work. Are the servants here all absolute saints, or what?

She brushed her hair, put on her jeans and a T-shirt,

slipped her feet into her old brown leather loafers, then quickly drank some tea. She picked up her clipboard and went down to the hall, where she found Simon already loading film into several different cameras. Ulrica was nowhere to be seen, and they went out into the garden and wandered around, choosing the best angles, making notes, deciding on the order of the work. They stood together on the gravelled path bordering the parterre, looking back at the *palazzo*, calm, elegant, its apricot-tinted walls warm in the early sunlight. A deep loggia, pierced by a series of rounded arches, ran along the entire length of the ground floor, like a cloister. Its stone pillars were repeated on the shaded terrace of the first floor, its pergola supporting the huge grey limbs of the wisteria, already revealing drooping racemes of scented blue blossoms. Above the double row of pillars they could see, set back a few feet, the low wall fronting the balcony to the bedroom floor, and the open French windows of their own rooms.

'What a perfect building.' Rachel shook her head in wonder and admiration. 'It's so splendid, and yet so utterly simple, really.'

'Don't you think that's what perfection is?'

'Yes,' said Rachel, 'I suppose I do.'

Throughout the early morning they worked, as the sun climbed up the sky, and the temperature rose. In the garden the only sound was the drone of bees. From the house came the faint whine of a vacuum cleaner, then silence. At ten o'clock Simon decided that the angle of the sunlight was too high and therefore too harsh for outdoor photography, and they moved into the *palazzo* to begin work on the entrance hall, with its sweeping marble staircase, vaulted ceiling and details of Renaissance carving. When all the photographic possibilities had been explored, they moved upstairs to the *salone* and set up the cameras once again. Ulrica was still nowhere to be seen, but the rooms were in impeccable order, the flowers fresh, no sign at all of the previous evening's entertaining, and no sign of the servants.

'That chap Cesare must be what used to be called a treasure,' Rachel remarked, as she looked around in vain for a cushion to plump up, or a magazine to straighten.

'Actually,' said Simon, 'he's a bit too much of a treasure. Lie down on the sofa, Rachel. Make a few dents in the cushions – it all looks a bit *dead*, unnaturally tidy, don't you think?'

Quite glad to have a moment of rest, Rachel lay down on the sofa as instructed, and closed her eyes. She heard the whirr and click of the camera and sat up, startled.

'Nice picture,' said Simon, smiling. The polaroid slid out of the camera, and he put it under his arm for a moment. 'Stay there,' he said. He peeled off the print and studied it, bending the sides to crop the image to the composition he wanted. 'Great.' He picked up his hand-held camera and came close to the sofa. 'Lie down again,' he said. 'Now, look at me. Look at the lens.'

'Why?' said Rachel feebly, protesting, but obeying the instruction nevertheless.

'Because.' He leaned over her, the camera to his eye. 'Rachel?'

'What?'

'You have a lovely face.'

Before she could say anything, she heard the click of the shutter, followed by several more. 'Gotcher!' said Simon, and laughed.

'Have you quite finished?' She sat up, trying to look displeased, but failed. 'I suppose you say that to all the women you photograph?'

'Say what?'

'Oh, the bullshit about having a lovely face.'

'That wasn't bullshit, Rachel.'

'Oh? What was it then?'

'The truth.' He went back to the big camera, checked the light again, and prepared to take the picture. 'OK, you can get up now. Chuck a book or something on the floor beside the sofa, will you?'

Slowly, Rachel got to her feet, fetched a book from the library table and placed it on the floor beside the sofa. Then she got out of the frame, and sat down to wait as Simon shot his pictures. Watching him as he worked, she was suddenly aware that she had never really looked at him properly before. If she had been asked to describe him, other than as her rather eccentric young employer, she might have said that he was tall and skinny, with cropped mousy hair and very pale blue eyes, which made him look slightly manic, and that he had a preference for oversized second-hand clothes. Now, wearing only a pair of baggy Madras cotton shorts and espadrilles, she saw that his body, though extremely slender, was in fact well-proportioned and quite muscular. If he grew his hair a bit, and had a shave, she thought, he might be quite attractive. She smiled at herself mockingly. Do I just think that, all of a sudden, because he said I have a lovely face?

They were carefully packing away the exposed plates when Cesare came into the *salone* and announced that lunch was ready to be served on the terrace. 'Good timing,' said Simon. 'I'm starving, aren't you, Rachel?'

'Yes, I am.' She looked at her watch and saw that it was one-fifteen. 'Is that really the time?' she said, surprised that the hours had passed so quickly.

On the terrace they found Ulrica, looking bronzed and cool in a white cotton burnous, relaxing in a long cane chair under the shade of the wisteria, a glass of chilled Punt è Mes in her hand. She waved towards the trolley of drinks. 'Help yourselves, darlings. I'm too lazy to get up.'

'I think we've earned a drink,' said Simon. 'What would you like, Rachel?'

'Oh, anything, thanks. Water would be nice.'

'Really?'

'Yes, really.'

He poured mineral water into a tall glass, added lemon and ice and handed it to her. 'There you are.'

'Thanks.'

He fixed himself a Campari, and they sat down in the chairs on either side of Ulrica. Simon, his eyes squinted against the noonday glare, let his gaze travel over the formal garden and through the dark trees to the wooded hills beyond, and the olive groves and vineyards that were the only evidence of the presence of a human hand at work. 'Is that a chapel or something, Ulrica, over there in the olives?' he asked, pointing to a pale, slender tower on the flank of a hill in the middle distance.

'Yes, it is. Or rather, was,' said Ulrica. 'It was a ruin, as a matter of fact. It was empty, abandoned, for years. But, a while ago, it was bought by an elderly couple. She's a dealer in antique gardening books, and rather well-known in that world, I understand. They keep themselves pretty much to themselves, and that suits me. I'm the same, most of the time. They seem quite content up there, alone in their funny little chapel.'

'How romantic,' said Rachel. 'Are they Italians?'

'Chiara is, but he's a *Tedesco*, I believe.'

Cesare appeared with a dish of gnocchi in a tomato sauce, which he placed on the table.

'What's this one called, Cesare?' Ulrica got up and approached the lunch table.

'*Strangolaprieviti, Signora.*'

197

'Sounds rather sinister,' said Simon. 'What does it mean?'

'Priest-choker,' said Ulrica, and laughed.

'*Why*, for heaven's sake?'

'Search me, darling. Italian ambivalence on the subject of their clerics, perhaps? Who knows?'

Chapter Eleven

Nelly sat at her desk in her consulting-room, completing the notes on the last of her afternoon's patients, a brave, frail little girl of six, suffering from Hodgkin's disease. In spite of her upbeat prognosis for the child's eventual recovery, and her many years' experience, Nelly was still not entirely capable of distancing herself from the tragedies that visit the very young, and often asked herself why she had opted for a consultancy in paediatrics in the first place. The sight of the child's bald head, and her small face bloated as a result of the steroid therapy had the curious, though fleeting effect of making Nelly feel guilty, as though by prescribing the chemotherapy and the drugs she herself was responsible for the discomfort and the distressing side-effects experienced by the young patient. She finished the notes, filed them, and closed down the computer. She looked at her watch: ten to six. Time to go home; check out the girls' homework, and prepare supper. She lifted the phone, and buzzed the partnership secretary. 'I'm going home now, Rosemary. No messages or anything for me, I hope?'

'Yes, there's one. Will you ring a Mr Peregrine, when you have a minute?'

'Yes, OK. Thanks.' Nelly replaced the phone, looked

up the auctioneer's number in her Filofax, then dialled it. 'Peregrine? It's Nelly Turnbull.'

'Hello, Nelly. How are you?'

'Busy.'

'Same here. Good news, I think. We got just over four hundred K for your little lot.'

'Is that good?'

'Pretty good, I'd say. Aren't you pleased?'

'Sorry! Yes, of course I am. Thank you; you've done an excellent job.'

'Well, good. I'm glad you're not disappointed. Cheque should be with you shortly.'

'Thanks again, Peregrine. Goodbye.' Replacing the phone in its cradle, Nelly went to the window, and watched the taxis drifting past in the rainwashed, lamplit street below. I don't feel especially pleased, she thought moodily; I feel unreal, and unsure. What do these huge sums of money really mean, in the final analysis? Will it actually make us any happier as a family, having two houses instead of one, with me and the girls dividing our lives between the two places? I hate not being with Hugo. I miss him badly, in our daily life and every night, in bed. I miss Phylly, too, and I worry about her, all the time. Just when we seem to be understanding each other, I've created an unnecessary distance between us. I'm beginning to realize that it was a pretty ill-conceived idea, thinking we could live in two places at the same time. It's not working; not for me, at any rate.

At the back of Nelly's mind hovered another and more fundamental consideration. Slowly, she was beginning to realize that by taking on *Les Romarins* at all, she ought also to be preparing to devote at least part of her time to the island's affairs and well-being, as her mother and grandparents had before her. Aware that Basil's research into the occupation of Florizel had aroused old animosities, and drawn unwelcome attention to the Langlois and the du Toits, and others like them, she had the guilty feeling that she should be there, on the spot, to accept responsibility for his actions, if necessary. Feeling depressed and confused, she put on her coat, picked up her bag and her keys, went down to street level, got into her car and drove home.

Sophie and Gertrude smiled at her benignly when she poked her head round the door of Hugo's room. For once, they were doing their prep without the noisy altercation that was their more usual mode of study. 'Hi,' she said. 'OK?'

'Hi,' said Sophie. 'What time's supper, Mum?'

'About an hour.'

'Cool.'

Nelly went down to her basement kitchen. She opened the drawer of the long wooden table and took out the drawings and estimates she had commissioned for the proposed division of the house into two flats. She looked at them for a moment, and then it dawned on her that it would not now be necessary to do the work at all, nor to have a tenant. She had more than enough money to pay off the bridging loan; both places were now hers, absolutely. She could do exactly as she pleased. Frowning, she shoved the plans back in the drawer, poured herself a drink, and began to prepare supper. When the chicken was in the Aga, and the potatoes simmering on the hotplate, she phoned Hugo in Florizel and told him the good news. 'The weird thing is, darling, I don't feel all that excited,' she said. 'I begin to have the feeling that money wasn't the real problem.'

'So, my love,' said Hugo quietly, 'what *is* the real problem?'

'It's us. I don't like being split up like this. I really think we should be all together, at *Les Romarins*. I know Ma expected that we'd live on the island, if we bought out Henry.'

'Trouble is,' said Hugo, 'the girls' education. That would be an even bigger problem, wouldn't it? Especially at this stage?'

'I know.' Nelly sighed. 'That's what's pissing me off.'

At the end of five days' intensive work, Simon had pretty well satisfied himself that he had made an excellent photographic record of the *palazzo*. In addition, he had taken many shots of Ulrica herself, in the garden, on the terrace, working in her study, a small, dark room overlooking a vine-shaded courtyard at the back of the house. He had even persuaded Cesare to permit himself to be photographed without his white jacket, shirtsleeves rolled up, preparing a *minestra* in the gloomy subterranean kitchen.

The leisurely, warm days of unbroken sunshine began to take on a pattern of their own. The bulk of the commissioned work was done during the long, quiet mornings, followed by lunch with Ulrica. In the afternoons, Simon and Rachel explored the area around the *palazzo*, taking pictures in the olive groves and vineyards, and in the *fattoria*, the buildings and cellars where the wine was made, and the olives pressed. One afternoon they borrowed Ulrica's elderly Jeep and went to visit San Gimignano. Here they wandered around the narrow streets and squares, admiring the traditional tower houses, the status symbols of power of the city's medieval families. They bought a guidebook and learned that out of the seventy-six original towers, only thirteen now remain. They found the *Cappella di Santa Fina* in order to see Ghirlandaio's murals, their backgrounds depicting a landscape showing the city bristling with the famous towers. They drank iced tea in a café already crowded with tourists, although it was only mid-May, then drove back to the *palazzo* through the tree-lined lanes that criss-crossed the vineyards of the superb Tuscan landscape. Just before they reached the drive to *La Felicità*, Simon slowed down and turned into a lane on the right-hand side of the road. 'I have a feeling that this probably goes to the little chapel. Shall we take a look?' The narrow, stony track plunged downwards, and then, surprisingly, began to climb uphill.

'Are you sure, Simon? This looks like a farm road to me. It's a single track.'

'Just a bit further. At least until we can find a place to turn, and go back.'

In a couple of minutes they arrived at a farm gate, and Simon stopped the Jeep, intending to turn in the gateway. He got out to open the gate, and as he did so he saw the chapel, about two hundred metres distant, surrounded by tall black cypresses and ancient olive trees, on the far side of the steep, narrow valley. 'There you are, Rachel. I knew I was right. It's here, come and look.'

She came to the gate and stood beside him, and silently they gazed at the small stone building, half-hidden by its encircling trees. All around them was a deep silence, as if the land slept in the heat of the late afternoon. Even the ubiquitous summer sound of the cicadas had ceased.

'How beautiful,' said Rachel, 'and how withdrawn, private, and inaccessible.' She looked up at Simon, and smiled. 'It reminds me of my own home, in a way.'

'Your home in Oxford?'

'No, no. My family home, in the Fens, near Ely. It doesn't *look* like this, not at all. It has the same air of detachment and isolation, but it's not a lovely old building like that chapel; it's more a hideous ruckle of sheds, plonked down in a wasteland of mud and water.' She laughed.

'You sound as if you love it, all the same?'

'I do.' She folded her arms on the top rail of the gate and gazed across the valley at the chapel. 'I'm only just beginning to realize it, but I *do* love it. It's quite possible that I'll end up living there, one day.'

'So you're not planning to live in Oxford all your life?'

'No,' she said, 'I don't believe I am.'

Curious, but careful not to intrude on Rachel's private life, Simon did not enquire whether Stanley would be part of her long-term planning. Instead, he opened the gate, and turned the car round. 'Somehow, the chapel doesn't look like the kind of set-up where you could just breeze in, and ask to take a picture, does it?'

'Absolutely not,' said Rachel.

'Better ask Ulrica to telephone first?'

'I think so.'

When they got back to *La Felicità*, Ulrica had not yet come down from her siesta, so they decided to have a swim in the pool. This was concealed within a carefully planted grove of cypresses, so closely packed together that they formed, to all intents and purposes, an outdoor room. Rachel went upstairs to change into her bathing-suit, and feeling slightly self-conscious about her body, which was flat-chested, with heavy hips and thighs, the legacy of her child-bearing years, she wrapped her towel around her waist to conceal these defects. She walked down a winding path to the green, shady pool, where she found Simon already floating lazily on his back, his eyes half-shut against the fierce glare of the blue sky above.

The swimming-pool was not the usual kind of cheerful turquoise-tiled affair, but had been hewn from the living rock. It was fed from a spring, its water untainted by chemicals and very cold indeed. Rachel let her towel fall, and sat down on the edge of the pool, trailing her legs in the water, to acclimatize her body to the drop in temperature. Never particularly athletic, she was not much of a swimmer, and it had never occurred to her that this handicap did not necessarily rule out the enjoyment of bathing.

'Aren't you coming in? It's heaven, after the first few agonizing seconds.'

'In a minute.'

He turned and swam towards her, and, thinking that he planned to pull her into the water, she forestalled this humiliating possibility by plunging in. This bold action on Rachel's part proved to be a near-catastrophe, for she sank like a stone, swallowing a good deal of water in the process. Finding herself on the dark rocky bottom, she pushed off as hard as she could with her feet, and, with bursting lungs, shot out of the water, coughing and spluttering, her hair plastered over her face.

'Rachel! What the *hell* are you doing?'

'Go away! I hate you!' Desperately, she struggled to the stone rim of the pool, but her fingers could not get a firm enough grip, they kept slipping off, and she began to swallow water again. Then she felt a firm strong arm round her body, and quiet, soothing words in her ear. 'It's OK. Stop fighting. Keep still.'

Exhausted, Rachel stopped thrashing about and let herself go completely limp. She took several deep shuddering breaths. 'I'm OK now, Simon, thank you,' she said. 'I can manage.'

'No, you can't. I'll take you to the steps, Rachel. Just do exactly as I say, OK?'

'OK.'

'Turn towards me, and link your hands behind my neck, right?'

'Right.'

'Now, try to relax and I'll swim backwards to the steps. You do nothing, just let your legs float behind you, OK?'

'OK.'

'Trust me?'

'Yes, I trust you.'

Slowly, Simon swam across the pool, dragging Rachel with him, and carefully manoeuvred her to safety on the steps. He sat beside her, his arm round her shoulders, while she recovered both her breath and her composure. 'Poor thing,' he said gently. 'You gave yourself a fright.'

'It's just that there's no rail to hang onto.' She spoke forlornly, pushing the wet hair back from her face.

'Are you totally put off, or shall we have another try?'

'What, go in again?' She sounded horrified.

'Why not? I'm with you. I won't let you drown.'

'Well, perhaps. If you really think I should?'

'It would be a pity not to, wouldn't it? Come on, I'm right beside you.'

Feeling foolish, but unwilling to appear cowardly as well, Rachel lowered herself into the water, and putting her feeble breast-stroke to the test, swam to the opposite side of the pool, where she was able to grab hold of a metal ring, let into the rock face. Simon swam beside her, and she turned towards him, triumphantly.

'You're quite right, it's a really lovely feeling. I could quite easily get to like it, in about twenty years' time.' She smiled, shyly. 'I've only ever swum off a pebbly beach in Turkey, years ago. It's just about the total extent of my experience, unless you count the Pembrokeshire coast.'

'No swimming in Oxford?'

'Not as far as I'm concerned. The children swim at school.'

They swam back to the steps without incident, and then walked back to the house, where they found Ulrica on the terrace, with the drinks trolley beside her. They sat beside her, cool and comfortably relaxed after their swim, drinking chilled lemon juice, and told her about their afternoon in San Gimignano, and finding the way to the chapel. 'I'd love to take some pictures there,' said Simon. 'Do you think your friend would mind very much, if we paid her a visit?'

'I could always ask her. I'll phone her this evening. I'm sure she won't mind.'

At half-past ten, tired after the long hot day, Rachel thanked Ulrica for another perfect meal and happy evening, and went up to bed. She took a shower, and put on her nightdress, newly washed and ironed in her absence by the indefatigable and kind Angelica. She lay down on her bed and thought about the day, about herself, and about Simon. This place has done something to me, she said to herself. Is it the sun, or the food and wine, or even the landscape? I'm beginning to feel somehow *cured* of something; not exactly insecurity, more a sense of inferiority and my failure to satisfy Stanley's and the children's expectations. Look at Ulrica: she's a happy woman, totally in control, and she doesn't allow the ghastly Gianni to wreck *her* life. Is she unconsciously teaching me something, perhaps? And look at Simon: he's the same, in control, living his life exactly the way he wants, or needs to. In her mind's eye she saw herself thrashing ineffectually around in the pool, and felt once more Simon's arm around her panicking body, strong and reassuring. He's like Ulrica, and the whole atmosphere of this place, she thought: kind, calm and non-judgemental. How stupid I was to feel embarrassed about my lumpy legs, she said to herself, and smiled ruefully. I don't suppose he even noticed, and if he did, he wouldn't care. He'd just think it was an inevitable part of the ageing process, like wrinkles and stretch marks.

She got up from the bed, and pulling back the heavy silk curtains, went out onto the balcony. The night was brilliantly starlit, the air cool, and as her eyes became accustomed to the light, she saw that each clipped piece of topiary was outlined with silver, and each pale rose glimmered on its thorny stem. From the black dense thicket beyond came the long haunting lament of a nightingale, and from a great distance came the faint but unmistakable response of another. A lump rose in Rachel's throat. Tears filled her eyes and fell unchecked down her face; tears of joy for the beauty of the world; tears of sorrow for the cruelty inflicted on each other by its inhabitants.

'Rachel?'

She turned and saw Simon, sitting on the wall of the balcony, in front of his room. 'Oh,' she said. 'Hello.'

'Are you OK?'

'Yes, I'm OK.'

'You're crying?'

'Yes, I'm crying.'

'Why? Was it the business in the pool? Did it upset you?'

'No, not in the least. It's not that, Simon.'

He got off the wall, and came to her side. 'What is it then? Tell me.'

She glanced at him fleetingly, and asked herself whether she was about to make a complete fool of herself, and if she was, whether she particularly cared. She looked up into Simon's serious, pale, concerned eyes, and decided that she did not. 'It's this place,' she said in a low voice. 'It's so beautiful, it makes me weep, and it fills me with sadness that Gianni can corrupt it for Ulrica.'

'As Stanley does for you, Rachel?'

She dropped her eyes. 'Yes,' she whispered, her heart pounding; 'as Stanley does for me.' She crossed her arms across her heart, suddenly chilled to the bone.

'Rachel?'

'Yes?' she replied, her teeth chattering.

'May I kiss you?'

'Why? Because you're sorry for me, Simon?'

'No; because I love you.'

She looked at him, her eyes bright. 'You know very well that I'm married and have three children. Quite apart from that, I must be at least ten years older than you.'

'What the hell has that got to do with it?'

'Don't you think it matters?'

'No, I don't.'

They stared at each other for a long moment, then he put his hand on her bare shoulder. 'So, may I kiss you, darling Rachel?'

'Yes, of course you may.'

He took her in his arms and kissed her, and a wave of pure joy and intense physical pleasure, of a kind she had never before experienced, surged through her entire body, leaving her both breathless and defenceless. She leaned against him, her arms round his waist, inhaling the scent of his sunburnt skin. He kissed the top of her head. 'Rachel?'

'Mm?'

'Is it too soon to go to bed together?'

She smiled, and raised her face to his. 'No, it's not too soon,' she said.

In the morning, when Angelica brought Rachel's tea, she found her fast asleep in Simon's arms, but did not find the circumstance at all surprising. Very quietly, she put the tray down on the night-table, and, smiling to herself, tiptoed from the room.

Basil Rodzianko came out of the Métro at St Michel, walked across the bridge to La Cité, turned right and made his way past Notre Dame in the direction of the Ile St-Louis and his mother's apartment, where he planned to spend the night. He did not often do this, preferring, when working in Paris, to catch the fast train to Orléans, and go home to the barn in the deep, silent wooded countryside where he lived with his wife, Olivia. Tonight, however, he was tired and pre-occupied, and beginning to regret his promise to András to try to trace his grandfather, Werner Balthus. At first things had gone fairly well, and he had fol-lowed the trail of the missing man from Florizel to Dresden, the city of his birth, presumably on leave before his departure to the Eastern front. There was evidence that his regiment had gone to Stalingrad, but he could find no mention at all of Werner's presence at the battle, hardly surprising in view of the thousands of troops pressed rapidly into service during that terrible conflict. The casualties had been so enormous that there were no proper lists of the dead and wounded, and no way of identifying survivors.

Discouraged, pretty sure that Balthus had indeed met his end at Stalingrad, Basil had nevertheless per-suaded a colleague in Berlin to trawl through the records in search of a Werner Balthus, born in Dresden in 1920. Two days later he had received a fax with the news that a Werner Balthus had been working as a technical translator in Munich from 1947 to 1985, when he had reached retirement age, and received his pension. The money was regularly mailed to the *fermo posta* service in Trieste. It appeared that he had given up his flat, paid all his bills and taxes, and gone to Italy. But exactly where he had gone no-one knew, or, frankly, cared.

Frustrated, and irritated with himself for getting involved in such an improbable wild-goose chase merely to turn away Nelly's harsh judgement of his methods of research, Basil crossed the Pont St-Louis and walked along rue St-Louis-en-l'Ile towards the side-street where his mother lived. He turned the corner and followed the high stone wall to the gated carriage-entrance to a seventeenth-century mansion. Hester's narrow door was on the left-hand side of the *porte-cochère*, and concealed the steep flight of stone steps leading to her apartment in the *entresol* above. He walked through the *porte-cochère* into the court-yard, and, not wishing to make his mother come down to let him in, stood under the window of her studio and whistled. Almost immediately Hester appeared at the open window and tried to see through the leafy branches of the tree that grew beneath it. 'Baz? Is it you, darling?'

'Yes, it's me. Chuck the key down, will you?'

After supper, and a couple of Armagnacs, he decided to use his mobile phone to call Hugo and give him a progress report.

'So that's it?' said Hugo, when Basil had told him the results of his enquiries so far. 'The trail's gone cold?'

'It looks like it, Hugo. I'll keep going; try to think of something, but it doesn't look very brilliant, I'm afraid.'

'Poor András. Do you want me to tell him, Baz?'

'No, don't do that. I wouldn't want him to give up hope at this stage. I'll write to him, care of you, OK?'

'OK.'

After a pause, Basil asked after the family. 'And Nelly? How is she?'

'Pissed off,' said Hugo.

'Oh, dear. What's up? Not still angry with yours truly, I hope?'

'No, I don't think so. It's more what you might call a general malaise. She can't decide whether she wants to live here, or in London.'

'Poor old thing. It'll work out, I'm sure.'

'I hope,' said Hugo. 'Good night, Baz. Thanks for ringing.'

'Good night. Talk to you soon.' Basil switched off his phone, and drained his glass. Unbelievable, he said to himself. There they are, lucky sods. Loaded, with three great kids, two good careers, and the stupid woman

211

still makes heavy weather of everything. He was gripped with a familiar, latent sadness, and felt a stab of real grief, even agony, for the loss of his first love, Nelly. Swiftly, he picked up his phone again, and called Olivia. 'Hello, darling. Have you gone to bed?'

'No, not yet. Still working.'

'I miss you.'

Olivia laughed, softly. 'I miss you, too, of course.' After a pause, she spoke again, slightly impatiently. 'Any special reason for phoning, Baz?'

'No. Just felt like a chat.'

'Oh. Trouble is, the paper's drying out. I must hang up, I'm afraid.'

'OK. Good night, darling,' said Basil, miserably, and switched off his phone.

Simon and Rachel left the Jeep at the farm gate, and walked together through the olives to the old chapel. Chiara Balthus had invited them to lunch, and had raised no objection to Simon bringing his camera with him. The last two days had been a time of great happiness for them both. They had sunbathed, swum in the pool and made love whenever the opportunity arose. Both wished that their present idyll would never end, but equally looked forward to the return to London, where they would have greater privacy. For Rachel, the only shadow that clouded her happiness was the knowledge that she would, naturally, have to return to Oxford at the weekends.

'Must you really?'

'Yes, of course. What else? The children will expect me to be there.' She sighed, and slid her hand through Simon's arm. 'As a matter of fact, I don't think Adam and Ned would miss me at all, they're fifteen now, and pretty wrapped up in themselves, quite independent. But Ciaran might; she's only twelve.'

'Would you miss *her*, Rachel?'

'Yes, I would.'

'Let's not talk about it.'

'No, let's not.'

The chapel, when they reached it, looked much as it must have done for centuries: plain, its grey stone walls innocent of decoration or windows, its squat bell-tower surmounted with a metal cross, green with verdigris and tipping slightly to one side. At the west end the original wooden doors were closed, and the whole place appeared shut up, impenetrable. They stood for a moment, uncertainly, and then a stout white pug with a black face and ears walked on stiff little legs round the corner of the building, caught sight of them and began to bark hysterically. It was followed immediately by its twin, which joined in the fuss, and then by a formidable-looking woman of indeterminate age, wearing baggy white silk pyjamas, with a scarlet Indian turban wound round her head. She was carrying a watering-can and a pair of secateurs. 'Hello!' she shouted, over the din. 'You must be Rachel and Simon?' She yelled at the dogs in what sounded like abusive Italian, and they subsided submissively, snorting and shaking their heads, so that flecks of snot flew in all directions, mostly onto their mistress's trousers.

'Basta! Diavoli!' She advanced towards the visitors, holding out a green-stained hand. 'Chiara,' she said. 'Come into the garden.'

They followed her round the side of the chapel and onto a brick terrace, furnished with a blue-stained rattan sofa and chairs, overlooking an apparently neglected garden, a cool green oasis of olives, figs and evergreen oaks, growing in rough grass, and without flowers of any kind. The terrace stretched the length of the building, and both terrace and garden were reflected in the sliding glass doors that had replaced most of the original stone wall, to stunning effect. The trees that grew on the edge of the terrace were so tall and luxuriant that it had not been necessary to erect the usual pergola for the sake of shade, and a beautiful shadow of fig-leaves spread itself over the pink, powdery bricks of the floor, like a dark stain.

Silently, speechless with surprise and admiration, Simon and Rachel followed Chiara and her dogs through the open glass doors and into a large general-purpose room. A tray of drinks waited on a low octagonal table, its wood stained a translucent Prussian blue, so that the grain showed clearly through the colour. The floor was a continuation of the terrace, herringbone-patterned pink brick, and on it stood antique rattan furniture, of a more elaborate design than the chairs on the terrace, but stained the same subtle blue. The long sofa and several deep chairs were made comfortable with thick cushions, covered in a pink and blue Indian Paisley fabric. The frames of the glass doors had been manufactured from silvery weathered oak, and facing these doors were built-in bookcases of the same matured wood. On their shelves were a great many beautiful, leather-bound antique botanical books, which formed the basis of Chiara's profession as a dealer in such things.

Interspersed between the books was a huge collection of biological memorabilia, in the shape of antique drawings and paintings, cases of dried and mounted flowers, and individual fossils of prehistoric ferns, shells and invertebrates collected over the years. Glass test-tubes, in wooden racks, held single specimens of wild flowers, freshly picked every day.

Watching Simon gazing around him, taking in all the details of her unorthodox but beautiful home, Chiara smiled. 'Go ahead,' she said. 'Take your pictures.' She turned to Rachel. 'Come with me, my dear, and we will make a salad, no?' Leaving Simon on his own, she took Rachel into the kitchen, where a big rush basket stood on the tiled worktop, filled with a brilliant still life of tomatoes, bell peppers, aubergines and zucchini. Chiara took hard-boiled eggs from a pan of warm water, and ordered Rachel to halve them, while she swiftly sliced tomatoes, peppers and rose-pink salami and arranged them on a large olive-green platter.

Left to himself, Simon lost no time in exposing the major part of a roll of film, first in the house and then in the garden. He was quietly wandering back to the house through the trees when he saw an elderly man, tall but stooped, white-haired, his skinny arms tanned by the sun, suspending a cardboard contraption from the lower branches of an apple tree. The man turned as Simon approached, and greeted him in perfect English. 'Mr Ruskin? How do you do?'

'Simon, please. How do you do?'

The two men shook hands and Werner Balthus introduced himself. Curiosity getting the better of him, Simon asked about the strange object in the tree. 'What is it for?'

'It's my usually unsuccessful attempt to trap the codling moths before they lay their eggs, and their grubs eat our apples.'

'Does it work?'

'No, it doesn't!'

The women appeared, bringing the lunch out to the terrace, and Werner and Simon joined them. Having plied their guests with enormous plates of the salad, together with thick slices of rustic bread and glasses of rough red wine, Chiara and Werner sat back and encouraged the visitors to talk about themselves. This they did, with as much discretion as possible, but it was pretty obvious to their hosts that they were deeply in love. For their part, Simon and Rachel observed with pleasure the manifest attachment between the elderly couple, always a matter of some surprise to the young. Simon, having politely asked their permission, took a number of informal pictures of them, separately

215

and together, and one of Werner with Rachel.

At four o'clock, they rose to leave. 'Thank you so much,' said Rachel, giving Chiara a shy kiss on the cheek. 'It was very kind of you to allow us to invade you in this rude way.'

'My dear child, it was a pleasure.'

They said goodbye to Werner, and Chiara and the dogs accompanied them as far as the boundary, on the edge of the valley.

'I wonder?' said Simon. 'I think I may have some really good pictures here, Chiara. Would you mind very much if I tried to place a feature about you, in a magazine?'

'Not at all, why not? It might sell a few books, who knows? The only thing I ask, Simon, is please don't identify the location of this place. We'd hate that. But you can give the address of my shop, in San Gimignano, if you like.'

'Fine; understood.'

They said goodbye again, walked back to the Jeep, and drove slowly through the lanes to *La Felicità*.

'Home tomorrow,' said Simon.

'Yes.'

'Will it make a difference, do you think?'

'No,' said Rachel, 'I'm sure it won't.'

'I love you, Rachel.'

'And I love you.'

Chapter Twelve

Rose du Toit dressed herself in her black Sunday-best suit, although the weather was very warm for late May. For the umpteenth time she counted the ten twenty-pound notes she had withdrawn from her Post Office savings account, then carefully replaced them in the stiff brown envelope provided by the cashier, and put it in her handbag, next to her purse. She looked at herself in the mirror that hung beside the kitchen door, and hooked a long strand of fair hair behind her ear. She wondered whether it might be sensible to wear a headscarf, in case the wind got up while she was on the boat, then decided not to bother. She was, after all, only going to see Charlie du Toit, and the only thing he'd be interested in was the money she brought with her.

She walked down to the harbour, and then watched as the steamer arrived at the quayside and three passengers disembarked. Rose was the only person making the short trip to St Aude, and she sat on deck, watching the rapacious seagulls that flew alongside, waiting for any waste scraps that might be hurled overboard. Promptly at three-fifteen the boat arrived at St Aude harbour, and Rose hurried down the gangplank. She made her way to the centre of town, where her brother-in-law had his butcher's shop. She found him attending to a customer, and waited until the woman had departed with her parcel of pork chops, and bones for the dog. Charlie pulled down the blind in the shop window, and turned the sign hanging on the glass door to CLOSED. Then he ushered Rose through to the back, to the kitchen-parlour.

'Cupper tea?' he offered.

'No thanks,' said Rose. 'Best get on, I'll be catching the five-fifteen back.'

'Right. You got the money, then?'

'I have.'

'OK, let's have it.'

'All in good time,' said Rose, sitting down at the table, her blue eyes cold in her handsome face. 'First things first. What date have we settled on for the wedding?'

'She says she'll not wed till she's twenty, and that's not till November's end.'

'Before Christmas, then? What about the Saturday before?'

'I'll ask 'er.'

'Not *ask*, Charlie. *Tell*, all right?'

'OK, Rose, whatever you say. I'll tell 'er.'

'That's settled, then.' Rose looked sternly at her brother-in-law. 'She's in good health, is she? No problems down below, or anything?'

Charlie flushed, a deep embarrassed beetroot red. 'Madeleine's a fine healthy girl, Rose. She'll give young Andy lots of strong lads to dig the spuds, and help in the boat in due time.' He looked at Rose, his lips pursed, finding the interview rather distasteful. 'God willing,' he added, sanctimoniously.

Rose snorted derisively. 'You can leave God out of it!' she said. 'Get your pad out, Charlie, and we'll draw up the contract.'

Back in Florizel, Rose waited a week, biding her time,

choosing her moment to inform András that he would be marrying his cousin Madeleine on the Saturday before Christmas, in St Aude's church.

Unable to believe his ears, András put down his knife and fork. 'You didn't consult me about this, Mother, did you?'

'It wasn't necessary. It's a good match for you, and anyway, I've signed the contract.'

András stared at her. 'You've done *what*?'

'Signed the contract, *and* paid your Uncle Charlie two hundred pounds.'

Horrified, András pushed back his chair and got to his feet. 'Forget it, Mother. I won't marry her.'

'And why not, young man?' Rose, her eyes blazing, stood up and confronted her son across the table.

'Why the hell should I? I don't love her; I hardly know the bloody girl. I've no intention of marrying her, or anyone, and you can't make me.'

'I certainly can. I've signed the contract, and given Charlie two hundred pounds to seal the bargain. As far as I'm concerned, it's legal.'

'In the circumstances,' said András quietly, pushing his chair into the table, and preparing to leave the house, 'that was a very rash and stupid thing to do, Mother. I doubt Charlie'll give the money back, when you tell him there isn't going to be a wedding.' He went to the door, taking his lamp from the hook beside it. 'I'm going out now. I don't know when I'll be back.'

'Stay where you are, and listen to me!'

András paused, waiting silently.

'This is all because of your bloody friends, isn't it? Madeleine's not good enough for you now, is that it? You thought you could belong to the snooty world of the Tanquerays and the Turnbulls, didn't you? Well, I've got news for you, young man. They'll never let that girl of theirs marry an islander, believe you me, specially one with a dodgy background, like yours, however much you run round after them, and lick their arses. They're all friendly and smarmy on the surface, and very charming I dare say, but when the chips are down, it's another story, you can bet your bottom dollar on *that*. They're a lot of patronizing, stuck-up gits, and I despise them. Who do they think they are, anyway?'

'They're kind and civilized people, not a bunch of ignorant peasants, like us,' replied András, and made his escape through the door, but not before Rose, in her fury, had swept the plates off the table with a tremendous crash.

He ran swiftly along the lane behind the cottage, and down the cliff-path to the boat, where Pierre was preparing for a night's fishing. 'I'll come out with you, Dad.'

Pierre looked at his son, sharply. 'You OK, boy?'

'I'm OK, Dad. Mum's just smashed all the pots again, that's all.'

'Oh, merde!' Pierre grinned, nervously. 'It's like that, is it?'

András jumped into the boat, Pierre cast off, and soon they were heading out towards the fishing grounds. 'You bin upsetting the old woman then, Andy? Why did she trash the crocks, boy?'

'She wants me to marry Madeleine du Toit, Dad. I told her I wouldn't, that's all.'

'Oh, well, it's early days. P'raps you'll think better of it; Charlie's girl's a fine strong lass, and no mistake.' Pierre looked at his son, his eyes avaricious. 'She's an only child, Andy. There'll be a good bit coming her way, later on.'

'Forget it, Dad. I don't love her.'

'What's love got to do with it, son?'

Phyllida sat on the driver's bench of the four-wheeler, waiting for the launch from Guernsey which would bring her mother and sisters to Florizel for the half-term holiday. The weather was perfect, with long days of unbroken sunshine, clear blue skies, and a sea warm enough to make swimming almost a pleasure. In spite of the beauty and warmth of the island, and the prospect of seeing Nelly and the girls again, she was feeling far from happy. She had the impression that for some reason András was avoiding her, and now rarely saw him on her nightly visits to the cove. Since it was the closed season he had removed his lobster-pots from the bay, and had stopped bringing gifts of fish to *Les Romarins*, or even borrowing books from Hugo. Once or twice Hugo had remarked on this, and Phyllida had responded non-committally. 'Busy, I expect. It's the tourist season, after all.' Hugo was not fooled by this explanation, and thought it much more likely that András had been in some way upset by the letter from Basil that he had passed on to him, and would have given much to know what it had contained. Knowing Baz as he did, Hugo thought it quite possible that he had been at best insensitive in the writing of the letter, and, at worst, inadvertently wounding. That's the trouble with these multilingual guys, he said to himself, they're inclined to drop clangers in all their languages. Nonetheless, while concerned to see his daughter looking sad and withdrawn, he did not think it wise to interfere in any way. He would wait, and discuss the matter with Nelly when she came home.

Scanning the horizon, Phyllida saw at last the distant speck of the launch as it sped over the sea towards Florizel, making an impressive bow-wave and leaving a long creamy wake behind it. When the boat slowed down and came alongside, she got down from her seat and held Murphy's head, waiting for the family to come ashore.

The first to reach the four-wheeler was Sophie, red-faced, hauling a heavy suitcase. At sixteen, she had suddenly grown a lot taller and thinner. She grinned at her sister, displaying perfect white teeth.

'You've dumped the beastly braces!' exclaimed Phyllida, taken by surprise.

'Gross, weren't they?'

'They were, rather, yes.'

'Can I drive home?' demanded Gertrude without preamble, coming up and chucking her bag into the back of the cart.

'I doubt if you could be trusted, my dear child,' replied Phyllida in a lofty tone. 'You need quite a bit of practice, one would imagine.'

'Bollocks,' said Gertie amiably, and climbed into the back.

'Hello, darling. Where's Papa?' Nelly put down her grip, and gave Phylly a hard hug.

'Working,' said Phylly, returning the hug. 'He's finishing a chapter.'

'How far has he got?'

'Sixteen, I think.'

'Oh, good. We'll see something of him, then.'

'It's only the first draft.' Phyllida climbed back onto her seat.

'That's the hardest part.'

'I know,' said Phyllida. A bit like life, she said to herself.

Nelly sat beside her on the driver's bench. 'How's everyone? Elsie? Alain?'

'Fine. Elsie's doing the lunch today, specially. I should warn you, it's her Lancashire hotpot.'

'How frightfully uncool of her!' remarked Gertrude loudly, from the back.

'Literally and figuratively, my dear!' added Sophie facetiously, and both girls dissolved into idiotic giggles.

Phyllida and Nelly exchanged an unamused glance, and ignored them.

'How's András?'

'He's OK, busy with the tourists, I think. He takes fish to the hotel and the pubs every day, just now.'

'Yes, of course,' agreed Nelly. 'I don't suppose he has much spare time?'

'No.'

Something in Phyllida's subdued tone advised Nelly not to pursue the subject. She had been on the point of asking whether Basil had made any progress in his search for András's grandfather, but now she held back, with the intention of raising the matter with Hugo when they were alone.

From the book-room, which was now his permanent place of work, Hugo heard the crunch of wheels on the gravel drive, and the loud confident voices of his younger daughters. He put the cap on his pen, and went out to welcome them. At the same moment Elsie appeared from the kitchen, a delighted smile on her kind face, and wiping her hands on a tea towel. In the ensuing commotion, Hugo did not think it appropriate to embrace his wife in the manner he would have wished, but waited until the girls and Elsie had taken themselves to the kitchen to see to the lunch. 'Drink, my darling?' he offered.

They went to the drawing-room, cool, tidy and deliciously scented by the sweet peas and roses that had been picked by Phylly early that morning, and placed in bowls on every available surface. Hugo closed the door and took his wife in his arms. Sometimes he felt that it was almost worth enduring the long separations from Nelly, for the sake of the energizing sexual rush that her homecomings always generated in him. Their embrace was passionate and lengthy, and both fervently wished that they could ignore their obligations to their children, and go at once to bed. Duty and common sense prevailed, however, as it almost always had

223

to, and reluctantly they unwound themselves from each other, laughing.

Hugo went to the library table, where gin, bottles of tonic, ice and lemon stood waiting on Una-Mary's heavy silver tray, in time-honoured fashion.

'Who did the lovely flowers?' Nelly buried her face in a bowl of sweet peas.

'Phylly, I expect. I didn't notice.'

'They smell divine. The whole place smells like I remember it; like home.'

Hugo handed her a glass, clinking with ice, and touched her cheek with a cold hand. 'And you, my dear love,' he said softly. 'You smell like home to me.'

'Do I?'

'Yes, you do.'

It was not until later on the first evening of her holiday that Nelly spoke to Hugo about Phyllida, as they walked together in the garden after supper. 'She seems rather quiet, and a bit depressed. Is it András?'

'Mm, I think so, but I don't quite know the score. Baz wrote to him, care of me, but that's all I know about it. I'm not going to pry, if he doesn't want to talk about it.'

'No, of course not.' Nelly broke off a sprig of rose-mary and rubbed it between her hands, releasing its beneficent aroma. 'Baz hasn't got very far with his search for Balthus, I take it?'

'No, I'm afraid not. At least, he *did* find out that he wasn't killed, and worked as some sort of translator after the war, in Dresden I think he said. They know that he retired in '85, but after that the scent went completely cold, it seems.' Hugo shook his head. 'I can't help feeling that it was probably a bad mistake to try looking for him in the first place. Chances are, András will be terribly disappointed now, overreact, and feel even more angry about what he thinks of as Basil's witch-hunting. That's probably why he's gone to ground, as far as we're concerned.'

'Poor boy,' said Nelly, thoughtfully, frowning at her mangled sprig of rosemary. 'It must be awfully hard, not knowing who he is.'

'He's the du Toits' son, darling.'

'You know what I mean.'

'Yes,' said Hugo, and sighed. 'Of course I do.'

Life in the du Toit household grew more difficult with each passing day. Rose kept up an unrelenting campaign to pressurize András into agreeing to the marriage with his cousin. Her methods of attack swung between her usual noisy and domineering insistence on the inevitability of the proposed match, and a slightly more subtle, albeit whining approach.

She would wait until she had managed to get András on his own, and then conjure up a pathetic word-picture of herself as an injured woman, the victim of her mother's sins of the flesh. 'Can't you understand what this means to me, András? When you and Madeleine have kids, they will be third generation du Toits, and when your gran dies, everyone will forget about the Langlois, the war, and all that. She's seventy-seven now, she'll not last much longer, anyway. Your sons will probably never have a clue about her.'

'They would if I told them about her.'

Rose flushed angrily. 'Why would you want to? Is that the way for a son to treat his mother?'

'I thought we were talking about Gran?'

'Are you mad, or just stupid? It's me that's got the "bastard" label round her neck, or had you forgotten that?'

'It's not a thing I think a lot about, Mother, except when you bang on about it. Is it *really* so important?'

Her reply was brusque. 'Yes, it bloody is, to me. And always will be.'

'I can't understand why, when Dad doesn't give a toss, one way or the other.'

'He's not a man whose opinions matter much to anyone, András.' She spoke with withering contempt. 'Or hadn't you noticed that, either?'

Since receiving the note from Basil Rodzianko, with its inconclusive news of his grandfather, András had been half-tempted to show it to Rose, and even more inclined to pay a visit to his grandmother, at the Langlois place. Now, after almost ten days of his mother's alternate rages and pleadings, he saw clearly that such an action would probably bring down even more opprobrium on his head, as well as accusations of treachery and betrayal, if she knew that he had told not only Phyllida Turnbull, but also the feared and unwelcome interloper Rodzianko the closely guarded and shameful family secrets.

A couple of times he thought about going to see his grandmother, for he felt pretty sure that she would be glad to hear that the man she had once loved had not been killed after all. But then, he said to himself, what if it turned out that he *is* actually dead, *now*? Or is never found? Wouldn't that be harder to bear? Better leave it alone, and wait and see if anything happens.

Every night he went out in the boat with Pierre, and every morning delivered the catch to the regular customers. One afternoon, instead of taking his usual few hours' sleep, he rode his old bike to the other side of the island, and spied on the Turnbull girls from the cliff-top. Hidden among the gorse bushes, he watched the two younger sisters playing with the dogs in the surf, while Phylly lay on a flat rock, reading a book, a little way up the beach. He remembered with an emotion approaching grief the day they had spent together on the uninhabited island; how naturally and easily she had told him about her adolescent problems; her sudden tears, followed by a giggly account of old Lady

Tanqueray's own youthful misdemeanours. That's how it is with them, he thought. They laugh; they cry, but nothing's particularly serious, because problems get solved for them, everything comes easily. Mum's probably right, I'll never be one of them, never.

Suddenly, he remembered seeing the daffodils floating on the sea, and how peaceful and beautiful it had seemed to him, as he had drifted slowly past in his boat. That's exactly the difference between them and us, he said to himself; I'd never have thought of doing that, in a million years.

For half an hour he lay concealed in the bushes, watching, and increasingly conscious of a sour taste in his mouth, the bitterness of having raised his sights too high, in a selfish attempt to escape from the dead-end existence that was his island birthright, and now, it seemed blindingly obvious, even his duty. When he saw Sophie and Gertrude come out of the water, and run up the beach to join their sister, he got up, mounted his bike and rode slowly back to Roc aux Chiens. By the time he got home, he had already half-convinced himself that agreeing to marry his cousin would be the best thing for everyone. If it would make such a difference to his mother, what right had he to refuse? With a leaden heart, he recalled the words of his father: 'what has love got to do with it, son?'

For two days, although he could not yet bring himself to say the words that would relieve his mother's distress, he felt as though he were under some kind of grim spell, and was engaged in reconstructing himself, though whether this was as an unwilling bridegroom, or as the proverbial sacrificial lamb, he was not entirely sure.

On the third evening he did not go out in his father's boat, but sailed his own dinghy round the coast to the cove below *Les Romarins*. There, he spent some time pretending to check his marker buoys, at the same time keeping half an eye on the shore, in case Phylly should appear at her usual time. It was his firm intention to speak to her; to ask her to tell Basil Rodzianko not to continue his search; to explain to her that his mother was understandably hurt and angry about Basil's intrusion into their lives, and that he blamed himself for having connived at his interference.

He waited for over an hour, then, seeing Phylly emerging from the hidden cliff-path onto the beach, turned the boat round and headed for the shore. By the time the boat's prow scrunched onto the sand, she was waiting for him.

'Hi,' she said, but she was not smiling.

'Hi.' He shipped his oars, and jumped out of the boat and into the shallow water.

'How are you, András? You haven't been to see us?'

'No.'

'Is anything wrong? I've missed you. We all have.'

'Well, I've been quite busy. This and that; you know how it is, don't you?'

'Yes, I know how it is,' said Phylly, swallowing nervously.

András, still standing in the water, crossed his arms and attempted to look her candidly in the face, but he could not. His eyelids drooped, and he stared at his feet. He cleared his throat. 'I have something to say to you, Phylly. That's why I'm here.'

'Oh?'

'You people have no idea how it is for ordinary folk like us, who live from hand to mouth, relying on good weather to make a living, and a very modest living at that, like my father does, and I do.' His voice was unsteady, and he sounded remarkably unconvincing.

'András, what the hell are you on about?'

'I've come to tell you that I can't go on seeing you, or being friends with Hugo. My mum is shattered by the gossip and rumours your friend Basil has stirred up by coming here, and it's beginning to seem to me that you're punishing her all over again, for a crime she didn't commit.'

'But no-one has suggested for a second that we're talking about any kind of *crime* here. You know that perfectly well, András.'

'That's how *you* see it, Phylly. But it's not how it looks from our side of the fence. *You* have nothing to lose, *we* have everything; especially my gran and my mother.' He raised his eyes briefly. 'Can't you understand that?'

'If it comes to the crunch, András, we all have something to lose, or would rather forget, probably. My great-grandparents were here all through the war, and I'm sure they did their best in the circumstances, though *you* might not agree. They used to have the German officers to tea every so often, did you know that? I imagine they thought that it would help to keep things ticking over smoothly, but after the war they were publicly accused of being collaborators.' She looked hard at András, frowning, her eyes dangerously bright. 'I expect your mum thinks that too, doesn't she?'

András did not confirm or deny this, but his burning cheeks answered for him. Many times he had heard Rose's angry accusations, denouncing the Tanquerays for entertaining the occupying forces at *Les Romarins*. He felt confused and wrong-footed, as though Phylly had somehow turned the tables on him. 'Be that as it may,' he said lamely. 'What I've really come to say is that I'm probably getting married, Phylly, so I can't go on seeing you any more.'

Phyllida stared at him, stunned by this news. 'Who to?' she said at last, unwillingly, but desperate to know.

'Madeleine du Toit.'

'What, a *cousin*?'

'Yes, a cousin.' He glanced at her again. 'It's for the

best, if it makes my mother feel less of an outcast, more secure.'

'You can't be serious, András.'

'I am.'

'I don't believe you.'

He looked down at her then, his face drawn, his blue eyes clouded, hopeless. 'You'll have to believe it, and so will I.'

She put out a tentative hand and touched his sunburnt arm. 'How could you even *think* of doing such a thing, Andás?'

Carefully, he removed her hand from his arm. 'You don't understand anything at all, do you, Phylly?' he said sadly, and turning, pushed his boat off, and, jumping in, rowed swiftly away from her on the falling tide.

She stood at the edge of the water, her hand to her mouth, and watched him go. Then she turned and went home, her mind in total confusion and full of a numb despair.

At the end of the half-term holiday, Nelly and the younger girls prepared for the return to London, and as the day of departure drew near, she became more and more depressed. Her week on the island had been for her a time of total happiness, and her relationship with Hugo seemed to have grown into a new dimension of fulfilment and mutual understanding. She no longer felt the necessity to be the prime catalyst in their marriage, and now seemed to have rid herself of the intolerance concerning her husband's perceived lack of drive and competitiveness that had frequently driven her mad in the early days of their partnership. Now that their children were growing up, she was beginning to see him in a different, and very attractive light. In a curious way, it was almost as if they were finding again the man and woman they had once been, before children and their respective careers had blurred the picture, once or twice near-fatally.

At supper, on the last night, Nelly did a very uncharacteristic thing. She burst into tears.

'Mum!' cried Sophie, alarmed. 'Whatever's the matter?'

'What is it, my darling?' Hugo got up from his seat, and put his arms round her. 'Tell me; what's the matter?'

'I can't bear it,' she sobbed. 'I really can't. I hate us being separated like this, I want it to *stop*.'

'But, darling, it was your idea.'

'No, it wasn't, Hugo. It was *yours*. You said if I didn't have my job, I'd go barmy, and you'd have to divorce me!' She blew her nose. 'Please, please, can't we all go home tomorrow, and be together?'

'*No!*' Phylly stood up, her face ashen. 'I can't leave,' she said, and rushed from the room, banging the door.

'Oh, dear,' said Hugo, sorrowfully. 'I can't go without her, darling. It's a mess.'

Chapter Thirteen

Rachel and Simon had returned to London at the end of May, in a state of euphoria, with little heed as to what difficulties might lie ahead to threaten their happiness. It was, of course, a great convenience to them to be living under the same roof, and Rachel continued to rent her room from Mrs Ruskin. She did not sleep in her own bed very frequently, but enjoyed the feeling of independence the room gave her, and the luxury of a quiet place in which to be absolutely alone when she felt like it. The photographs of *La Felicità* proved to be sensational, and were greeted with enthusiasm by the magazine editor. The cheque for the work appeared with unusual promptness, and, to celebrate, Simon took Rachel out to dinner at *Le Gavroche*.

At first slightly overawed by the plush atmosphere and the attentive service, she soon succumbed to the excellence of the food and wine, and enjoyed herself. 'It was lovely, Simon,' she said, as they drove home in a cab. 'But I wouldn't want you to spend money like that every day. I'm quite happy with a take-away, you know.'

'Right,' he said, and laughed. 'Next time, I'll buy you a wok.'

'You know what I mean.'

'I know what you mean, but I disagree. Sometimes it's nice to spend money, if you have a really compelling reason.'

'Like the Italian shoot?'

'That, of course, but mostly, us.'

'Oh.'

Simon took her in his arms and kissed her, a considerable achievement in the dark confines of the taxi. 'What a strange creature you are, my darling,' he said gently. 'You're not at all used to being looked after, or given treats, are you?'

She shook her head, as it rested in the crook of his shoulder, her cheek against the rough linen of his jacket.

'Could you get used to it, do you think?'

'Yes, I think I could.'

The pictures that Simon had taken of Chiara and Werner Balthus at *Cappella della Vigna* were, in their turn, all that he had hoped for, reflecting exactly the romantic nature of the location, as well as the slightly eccentric appearance of its elderly inhabitants. A little reluctantly, for he would have preferred to keep the pictures as a private memento of his love for Rachel, Simon allowed his agent to hawk them round the Sunday newspapers and within a week had sold them for a gratifying fee.

'Chiara will be pleased,' said Rachel. 'If it helps to sell books for her, as she said, why not?'

'Let's hope it does,' agreed Simon. 'Remind me to send them a copy when it's published, won't you?'

The midsummer weeks passed in a haze of happiness and a series of interesting and enjoyable commissions. On Friday nights, Rachel returned to Oxford and her family. Adam and Ned were fully committed with extracurricular activities on Saturdays and Sundays, so that she saw comparatively little of them. Ciaran, on the other hand, was always delighted to see her, and Rachel guessed that she deliberately kept some of her weekend free to be with her. If Stanley felt able to dispense with it, they took his car, and drove out of Oxford to visit places that had a special interest for Ciaran. Rather to Rachel's surprise, her daughter, though not yet thirteen, nurtured an ambition to become an architect. One afternoon, after they had inspected Blenheim Palace together, they sat on the grass beside the lake, away from the crowds, and Ciaran told her mother of her secret hopes. 'Don't tell anyone, Mum; they'll only put me down. The thing is, you need three A's to train anywhere that's any good, so my chances must be pretty slim, mustn't they?'

'Why should you think that, darling? I went to quite an ordinary school, and managed to get into Cambridge. You're at an excellent school, so your chances should be as good as anyone else's, shouldn't they?'

'I don't think my teachers would agree with you. They think my work is crap.'

Rachel laughed. 'You'll just have to show them that they're wrong, won't you?'

Ciaran gave her mother a conspiratorial smile. 'Like you showed Dad?'

'How do you mean?'

'Well, his gob was seriously smacked when you got that job in London. I could tell.'

'Really?' said Rachel, sounding surprised. 'And what about you, darling? Was your gob smacked, too?'

'Yes, it was. Well, actually, I was more like really hacked off with you for dumping me. Then, after a bit, I could see how it made you happy, and you stopped crawling to Dad, which was really cool.' Ciaran looked at her mother, her foxy gold-flecked eyes strangely perceptive, serious beneath the fringe of wispy fair hair. 'I miss you a lot, Mum, but it's terrific that you've got a proper paid job, and aren't just a slave to us all any more. It's made you a real person.'

'It's not all that wonderful a job, darling, by some people's standards.'

'But you like it?'

'Yes, I do. I love it.'

'Well, then,' said Ciaran, 'that's all that matters, isn't it?'

'What about Antonia? Is she a slave to you all?'

'No way! She's got us all sussed, and no mistake! Except you, that is.' Ciaran shot a malicious glance at Rachel, and grinned. 'It's Dad who's *her* slave, in my opinion.'

'How do you mean?'

'Oh, nothing. It's just that he toadies to her all the time, and she despises him for it, I can tell.'

'Really, Ciaran! You're making it up!' said Rachel, suppressing a desire to laugh.

'I'm bloody not!'

'You bloody are!'

'There's something else you ought to know, Mum.' Ciaran examined her fingernails, in an elaborate display of nonchalance.

'Oh? What's that?'

'I don't know if I ought to tell you.'

'Tell me.'

'It's Dad and Antonia.'

'What about them?'

Ciaran giggled. 'They creep about the house at night sometimes, Mum. I can hear the floorboards.'

'Perhaps they're going to the loo,' said Rachel lightly, curiously unmoved by these revelations.

'No,' said Ciaran seriously, suddenly quite anxious to dispel any illusions her mother might have on the subject. 'They're not going to the loo, Mum. One would hear them pull the chain, don't you think?'

On a misty evening in late June, Olivia Rodzianko
herded her geese into their shed and carefully locked
the door, to protect them from the fox that lurked in the
woods bordering their few hectares of land. She stood
for a few minutes, watching the western sky changing
from pink to a deep purply blue, and listening to the
muted complaints of the geese as they settled themselves for the night. The wooded, watery landscape of
the Sologne, where she lived with her husband Basil,
had become a place of vital significance to Olivia, and
the leitmotif that underpinned her work as a print-
maker. At twenty-eight years old, success had come
early for her, and she exhibited regularly in Paris and
London, and occasionally in Tokyo and New York.
Since Basil's work as a correspondent took him abroad
for much of the time, living and working alone had
become a way of life for her, and one which suited her
very well.

When the geese had ceased their nocturnal mutter-
ings, she turned and walked back to the barn that was
both her home and her workshop. It was an un-
compromisingly tough-looking building, constructed
from huge blocks of limestone, with a disproportion-
ately deep stone-tiled roof, punctuated along its length
by the catslide roofs of dormer windows. Neither she
nor Basil had much spare time and even less inclination for gardening, and the rough, patchy grass that
surrounded the barn remained in its natural state,
except for an annual mowing in late August. The
meadow-grass did, however, produce sequential
summer flowerings of daisies, dandelions, buttercups,
cornflowers and brilliant scarlet poppies. Mulberry
trees and ivy grew against the walls of the barn, and a
load of firewood was stacked against the gable-end.
Olivia's scooter was propped against the kitchen door,

with the goose-food bucket beside it. The keeping of geese had been an unlooked-for enterprise, initiated by the gift of six goslings from her nearest neighbour, a farmer from whom she bought milk, eggs, butter and cheese on a daily basis, as well as fruit and vegetables in season. The Crouziers had become good friends, and from time to time Olivia and Basil accompanied them to the local weekly market. There they would inspect the wonderful produce, do some shopping, and then repair to the town's best restaurant to indulge in a serious gastronomic lunch. It was at this same local market, at Christmas time, that Olivia planned to dispose of her fierce, quarrelsome and noisy tenants.

The house, when she entered the kitchen, was empty and peaceful, for Baz had driven their English weekend guests to the station at Orléans, and had not yet returned. She went into the long room in which she spent the major part of her time, whether working, eating or relaxing in front of the wide, open fireplace that dominated the end wall. She debated whether or not to light the fire, decided against it, and sat down on the long, low sofa, gathering together the scattered pages of the English newspaper left behind by the visitors. She set aside the colour supplement, and settled herself comfortably against the cushions to read it. She turned the pages slowly, one by one, reading about new English books she would probably never buy, plays she was unlikely to see, and bizarre fashion of the tarty, transparent tendency that was of minimal interest to her. Impatiently, she flicked through the remaining pages until a colour spread caught her eye. It showed a handsome, elderly man, blue-eyed and white-haired, sitting on a rattan sofa, evidently in conversation with a much younger, fair-haired woman, sunburned and smiling. They held glasses of wine in their hands, and sat in the shade of a superb fig tree, the essence of cool, summer idleness. Other spreads showed an attractive middle-aged woman wearing white pyjamas and a red turban, inside a beautiful house full of books, lunching on the fig-shaded terrace, and walking in a wild and romantic garden.

Reading the captions, Olivia was not surprised to learn that the location of this summer idyll was Tuscany. *Chiara Balthus and her husband Werner*, she read, *live in a delightful converted chapel in Tuscany, not far from San Gimignano, where Chiara deals in antique books from her little shop in one of the medieval streets.* What a lovely place, said Olivia to herself. I must go to Tuscany again and look at the frescos in Arezzo. She looked thoughtfully at the pictures once more, puzzled, frowning. *Balthus*? she asked herself, where on earth have I heard that name recently? 'Werner Balthus,' she repeated, aloud, and read the piece again, trying to recall where she had heard the name.

The slam of the car door announced Basil's return, and a moment later he came into the room. 'The Brits are all the same,' he said, and laughed. 'They never expect trains to depart punctually; they keep wanting to stop and look at things. We only just got to the station in time.'

'Baz?' Olivia looked up at him. 'What was the name of that German guy you were looking for?'

'Balthus. Werner Balthus. Why?'

'Take a look at this, darling. I think I've found him for you.'

Three days later Hugo received a package from France, containing the colour supplement and a letter from Basil.

Dear Hugo, he read, *Olivia found this quite by chance, and I feel pretty certain that this is our man. Shall I hand over to you now, or would you like me to shoot down to San Gimignano on my next free week-*

*end, suss out the wife's bookshop and sound her out?
Either way, I'm sure we're on the right track. If we are,
I hope it won't turn out to be a disappointment to
young András.*

Love to N and P, Baz.

Phyllida was at her desk, working, when Hugo came
into her room and showed her the letter and the
article. Silently, she read the letter, then studied
the spreads and their captions. Hugo sat down and
waited for her reaction. Presently she looked up
and smiled faintly, but her eyes were clouded and
anxious. 'He looks a nice old man, doesn't he?'

'Yes, he does.'

'He and his wife look very fond of each other,
wouldn't you say, Papa?'

'Yes, darling, I would.'

She blinked nervously. 'So what has Baz actually
achieved, other than stirring up a potential hornet's
nest?'

'Good question, Phylly.'

'Perhaps it would be best to say nothing about this to
András, just drop the whole thing?'

'Do you really think that, my love? Personally, if
András really wishes to know the truth about his
grandfather, I think he has a right to see this.'

'Even if it causes more humiliation to him and his
family than they've already suffered through Baz's
troublemaking?'

'Baz was only doing his job, Phylly. He didn't deliberately set out to inflict pain on anyone, I'm sure.'

'Are you?' Phyllida's voice was scornful. 'I think
that's exactly what makes people like him tick; they
don't give a toss about destroying people's lives.
Specially Baz, when he thinks he's onto something.'

Hugo sighed. 'OK. You're probably right. Let's forget
it. Sorry I brought it up, Phylly.' He got up and left the
room, leaving the supplement on her desk.

At lunch, Phyllida did not raise the subject, but seemed preoccupied and subdued. Hugo, anxious not to put any kind of pressure on his daughter, read the *Florizel Gazette* as he ate, and returned to his room. Back at her desk, Phyllida continued writing her essay, glancing from time to time at the spread of Werner and the young woman under the fig tree. I suppose she could be his daughter, she thought, then dismissed the idea. Obviously, it would have said so in the caption, if that were the case. The more she allowed herself to study the pictures, the more convinced she became that this sympathetic-looking old man was indeed András's grandfather. The eyes, nose and cheekbones seemed to her to be identical. It was easy to imagine him as a young man, blond, blue-eyed, handsome – just like András, in fact.

That evening, having folded the supplement carefully and put it into the inside pocket of her jacket, she called the two dogs and went down to the beach. She walked slowly along the tideline, her eyes scanning the quiet waters of the cove, half-dreading, half-hoping that András would put in an appearance, but he did not. On the following two evenings she came down again, and wandered up and down for over an hour, but there was still no sign of him.

On the fourth night he came into view, as Phyllida sat on her rock, patiently waiting. If he saw her sitting there, he gave no sign, and steered the boat across the bay.

'András!' Climbing down from her rock, Phyllida ran to the water's edge and waved, trying to attract his attention, but without success.

'András!' she called again, louder this time. 'I've got something to show you! Please come!'

He turned and looked at her, shading his eyes. 'What do you want?' he shouted back, rather rudely, as though she were a stranger.

'Just come!'

'What for?'

'*András!*' she yelled, losing patience. 'For Christ's sake stop pissing me around, will you?'

He did not reply, but turned the boat and steered towards the shore. 'What do you want with me, Phylly? Or are you just playing games?' He shipped the outboard motor, jumped out of the boat, and came towards her, his face grim.

'This.' She took the folded supplement from her pocket and offered it to him. 'Basil's wife found it quite by chance, in France. He sent it to Hugo, to give to you.'

András wiped his hands on the seat of his jeans, and took the paper from her. He opened it carefully, stared incredulously at the pictures, and read the text. Phyllida watched him anxiously, her arms folded, saying nothing. Suddenly, it occurred to her that this was not a moment András would wish to share with anyone, least of all with her, and she turned and walked away to the other end of the beach. There, she stood gazing out to sea, remembering the daffodils floating on the water for Una-Mary, and wishing passionately that her grandmother had not chosen that moment to die, when she, Phylly, still needed her so badly. Why is life so bloody difficult, she asked herself sadly. She turned her head and saw András walking towards her, and when he drew close she noticed that his face was dirty and streaked, as if he had been weeping, and immediately she began to cry herself.

'Don't cry, Phylly. It's OK.' He produced a grubby, oil-stained rag from his pocket and gave it to her.

'I'm sorry,' she sobbed, 'but I've been so worried about all this. You must understand, András, I never meant to hurt you; none of us did.' She blew her nose, and looked at him, red-eyed. 'You've been crying yourself, haven't you?'

'Yes, I have. It's not every day you find a grandfather, is it?'

'So you're not angry?'

'No, of course not. It's the best possible news. That is,' he added cautiously, 'if it really *is* him.'

'András.' Phyllida looked up at him, and spoke gently. 'You're the spitting image of him, can't you see that?'

'Am I really?'

'Yes, of course you are.' She took a step towards him, and took his hand in hers. 'I know that you're supposed to be engaged to someone else, András, but I would like you to kiss me. Just once, for friendship's sake, if you wouldn't mind.' Without speaking, he took her face in his hands and kissed her. It was not a passionate kiss, but very gentle and undemanding. Nevertheless, it told Phylly all she needed to know. 'Thank you,' she said. They smiled at each other, then walked slowly back to the boat together.

'If Hugo could fix it for you, would you like to go to Tuscany and meet your grandfather?'

'I'd love to go, of course, but first things first, Phylly. I must show the paper to my grandmother, and see how she feels about it. May I take it?'

'Yes, of course, it's yours.' She hesitated for a moment, then continued. 'What about your mum, András? Will you tell her?'

'I'm not sure. I don't think so. Not just yet, anyway.' He pushed the dinghy into deeper water, then jumped on board and lowered the outboard motor. 'I'm sorry I was so rude about your friend Rodzianko, Phylly. It was good of him to go to so much trouble. Please ask Hugo to thank him, will you?' András pulled the cord of the engine, and it throbbed into life. He looked at her, and smiled ruefully. 'I'm sorry I was rotten to you, too, Phylly. It was stupid of me, I know.'

'Forget it; it's not important.'

'See you.'

'See you.' She turned and looked around for the dogs, but they had got bored and gone home. She ran across the hard wet sand and up through the over-grown cliff-path to *Les Romarins*. When she reached the top, she stood at the cliff edge and looked down into the cove to catch a last glimpse of András, but the boat had already disappeared round the point, leaving behind a faint wake of lacy white foam on the glassy waters of the bay.

In the kitchen Hugo was preparing supper, frying bits of bacon and garlic on the range, making a delicious smell. For the first time in days, Phyllida realized that she actually felt quite hungry. 'I gave András the paper, Papa. He said to tell Baz thank you, when you speak to him.'

'Oh, good. I'll do that.' Hugo glanced at his daughter, trying not to seem too inquisitive, and added cubes of lamb to his pan, and a handful of chopped dried apricots.

'Smells good,' said Phylly. 'Anything I can do?'

'No, there's just rice to cook, in a minute. Set the table, if you like. Better still, pour us a glass of wine.'

Phyllida looked at the back of her father's neck with respect and deep affection. She was entirely aware that he was intensely interested in the unfolding saga of András and Werner Balthus, and equally that his apparently laid-back attitude to her recent problems with drink and drugs was a cover for his profound concern for her safety and happiness. She fetched the glasses and a bottle of Beaujolais, and pulled the cork with precision. Then she poured the wine, handed a glass to Hugo and took a sip herself. 'He's going to show the paper to his grandmother, and then decide what to do after that,' she said.

'Seems like a good idea; no point in rushing things.' Hugo put down his glass, filled a pan with water for the rice, and put it on the stove to boil. 'What about the mother, Phylly? Rose du Toit?'

'What about her?'

'Won't she have to be told?'

'I don't know, Papa, and I don't think András does, himself.' Carefully and neatly, she set out the knives and forks on the table. 'Mrs du Toit is a very difficult woman, you know. She's deeply, deeply sad. She hates everybody, and everyone rather hates her.'

'Even her own son, darling?'

'Especially him.'

On a warm Friday evening in June, to celebrate the last of Sophie's GCSE exams, she and Gertie went to a party at a friend's house, a few streets away. Pretty sure that she had done reasonably well, Sophie was in a mood to enjoy herself, and would have done so, had the party not turned out to be surprisingly dull. For a start, there was nothing except fruit-cup to drink, and by the taste of it, fruit was the only thing except water in its composition. There was a great deal of food, mainly bowls of potato crisps and rolls full of egg and salad, which was OK, but did rather remind one of the church fête. The music was utterly banal, in Sophie's opinion, though she did not, of course, say so, merely widened her eyes at her sister in an expressive gesture that made Gertrude do the nose-trick into her fruit-cup.

David Truman, a boy fairly well-known to the girls, sidled up to Sophie and was given a more enthusiastic welcome than might have been the case had there been any real talent in evidence. 'This is strictly for teeny-boppers, don't you think?' he asked quietly. 'Shall we split?'

Sophie quite liked David Truman. She rated him for his occasional wit, and for the convenient fact that he was eighteen and had a car of his own. 'OK, why not?'

she replied, tipping the remains of her fruit-cup into a pot plant. 'You coming, Gert?'

'Yes, if that's all right?' Gertrude looked enquiringly at David. If he was taken aback at being lumbered with both sisters, he did not show it. 'Fine, let's go,' he said. They squeezed through the crowded hallway and out onto the pavement. David's clapped-out *deux chevaux* was parked at the end of the street, and they piled into it, Gertrude in the back. 'Where are we going?' she asked, as they pulled away from the kerb.

'World's End,' said David. 'It's a club. It's just opened; it's quite a gas.'

Gertrude almost blurted out that they weren't supposed to go to clubs in term-time, then thought better of it, and waited for her sister to say something, but she did not. Delighted to be speeding towards the King's Road in an open car, Sophie chattered away to David, and when he lit two cigarettes and handed one to her, she took it. He did not offer one to Gertrude. In fact, they seemed to have forgotten that she was there at all.

The club was in a cellar, a series of small interconnected rooms, with no windows and poor air-conditioning. The walls and ceilings were lined with aluminium foil, which reflected both the intense body-heat of the several hundred members present, and the strobe lights that flashed in time to the beat of the heavy-metal music piped throughout the premises. Admission to the place appeared to be a simple question of the handing over of several twenty-pound notes, to Gertrude's surprise, and she followed David and Sophie down some badly-lit stairs, sticking close to her sister.

They fought their way to the crowded bar, and David bought three cans of lager. 'Is this OK?' he said to Sophie. 'It seemed a bit of a hassle, asking for different drinks.'

'Yes, of course. This is fine.' Sophie drank half her

can at one go. 'It's fearfully hot in here. Beer's what one needs.'

'Want to dance?'

'Yeah, why not?'

David swallowed the rest of his drink, Sophie dumped her can, and they were soon lost in the scrum of the dancers, leaving Gertrude on her own, clutching her ice-cold lager. She took a sip, decided that it tasted like sick, and squeezed her way to the bar. 'Do you have any wine?' she asked the barman, when she finally managed to grab his attention.

'Red or white?'

'White, please. Dry, if you have it.'

The barman filled a glass from a wine box, and handed it to her. 'That'll be five quid, Miss.'

Five pounds! thought Gertrude. It's robbery! Reluctantly, not daring to make an issue of it, she handed over some of the taxi-money Nelly insisted they always had with them. Since there was nowhere to sit down, she leaned against the bar, jostled by people eager to quench their thirst, and drank the small glass of wine. Even with her limited experience of wine, she thought it tasted pretty revolting. The place grew hotter and hotter, the music louder and louder. There was no sign of David and Sophie. Annoyed with them for abandoning her, Gertrude permitted herself to be chatted up by the barman. 'Go clubbing often, then?' he asked.

'No, I don't,' she replied. 'This is my first time, as a matter of fact, and I can't say I think much of it, to tell you the truth.'

The barman grinned. 'Been stood up, have you, darling?' he said, and took himself off to the other end of the bar.

Nelly had spent a miserable evening, alone in the empty house. After her solitary supper she had gone out into the small back garden, to water the pots and deadhead the few rose bushes that flourished there. She wondered what Hugo was doing at that moment, whether he had watered the tomatoes, and remembered to put the bamboo shades over the summer bedding she had planted during the half-term break. A wave of homesickness engulfed her, and for the hundredth time she asked herself what the hell she thought she was doing there, separated from Hugo, lonely, unhappy and with the increasingly alarming knowledge that her vacillating state of mind was adversely affecting her work. Ten years ago, she thought, I wouldn't have had the slightest doubts about my life. I would have been absolutely sure that I wanted to be right here, where my job is, and going to Florizel for the holidays, just as we always used to.

The watering-can was empty, and she went to fill it from the rainwater butt. Frowning, she watched the thin trickle of water as it slowly filled the can. The trouble is, she said to herself, things are different now. Mum's gone, and I'm not young any more. I suppose that as long as you've got a parent alive, and a family home to go to, there's still a bit of the child left in you; in a sense, you're still keeping your options open. So now it's me that's got the family house, and soon it'll be the girls' turn to have careers, and husbands and things, perhaps coming home to Florizel at Christmas, as I always did. But that's all at least three years away, and in the meantime I'm stuck here without Hugo, and will be, at least until Gertie finishes school. Oh, God, she said to herself, lugging the heavy can across the paving-stones, slopping water over her shoes, I do miss him dreadfully. I need to have him with me, I really do. This whole situation is a huge mistake. The fact is, I want to go home, to him, and to Florizel. Either that, or we shut up *Les Romarins* and all live together here. I can't go on like this, that's for sure.

Nelly finished her watering and went indoors. She thought of phoning Hugo right away, but not wishing to worry him by getting upset herself, and weeping over the phone, decided to wait until the morning. Instead, she watched *News at Ten* and then the movie that followed, finally falling asleep in front of the television. She was abruptly woken by the ringing of the telephone, staggered to her feet and went to answer it. It was twenty past one, so unlikely to be Hugo, and as she put the receiver to her ear she heard the sound of coins working their way through a pay phone.

'Mum? It's me!' Gertrude's voice sounded shrill, panicky.

'Is anything the matter, darling?' asked Nelly as calmly as she could.

'Yes, plenty. We're at St Stephen's Hospital, Mum.'

'Has something happened to Sophie?'

'No, it's not Sophie, Mum. It's David.'

'David?'

'A chap we know. We all went to a club, Mum. He must have taken something. He passed out while they were dancing, and Sophie made them send for an ambulance and they brought us all here.' Gertrude's voice shook. 'He's still unconscious, Mum.'

'Gertie, darling, stay where you are, and I'll come at once, as quickly as I can.'

'We're not allowed to *go* anywhere, Mum. The police are here. They want to talk to us. They're with the doctors now.'

'I see. Well, try not to get upset. Just tell them the truth. Is Sophie there?'

'No, she's hanging about outside the place where they've taken David, in case he wakes up. She's worried sick.'

'Right, darling. I'll be with you as soon as I can.'

'OK, Mum. Thanks. Bye.'

* * *

Nelly replaced the receiver, then picked it up again and dialled the number at *Les Romarins*. The phone rang for a long time, and was eventually answered by Hugo, sounding wide wake and slightly alarmed. Nelly told him what had happened as concisely as she could, and Hugo said that he would take the first plane out and be with her as soon as possible. 'I'll phone from Heathrow, and if there's no answer I'll go straight to the hospital,' he said. 'See you soon, darling. Try not to worry.'

Nelly reached St Stephen's just before half-past two and went straight to A and E. She introduced herself to the young doctor on duty, who told her that they had been unable to resuscitate the boy, that he had died soon after admission, as the result of a presumed lethal combination of drugs and alcohol. The police were at this moment interviewing Sophie and Gertrude.

Nelly's heart sank. 'How dreadful,' she said quietly. 'Has the family been contacted?'

'Yes, of course. The parents are with him now.'

'Good. Or rather, awful,' said Nelly. 'Poor things, I feel terribly guilty at being so thankful that my girls are all right.'

'They're very upset, especially the older sister.' The doctor shook his head, and sighed. 'One never gets over the feeling of inadequacy in the face of this kind of disaster. The appalling waste of a young life.'

'I know. I've seen quite a lot of this sort of thing in my time, believe me. You never do get used to it, I have to tell you.' Nelly smiled at the young man. 'Do you think the police would object if I sat with my daughters?'

'I don't suppose they would. They've been in there at least an hour; they must be almost finished.' He took Nelly to a side room, knocked, and poked his head round the door. 'Excuse me,' he said. 'Dr Turnbull is here, the girls' mother.'

'Come in.' The officer in charge was a grey-haired and rather grim-looking man. 'Take a seat please, doctor.'

Sophie and Gertie sat side by side on two hard chairs, in front of the desk. As Nelly entered the room their heads turned in her direction, their faces pale, anxious, and, in Sophie's case, blotched with tears. Restraining a strong impulse to gather her children to her breast and comfort them, Nelly smiled at them and sat down on the chair indicated.

'This is an extremely serious matter, Dr Turnbull,' said the police officer reproachfully, as though by smiling at her daughters, Nelly had failed to grasp the gravity of the situation.

'Yes, of course it is,' she agreed quickly, trying not to antagonize him. 'It's a terrible tragedy,' she added, thinking how inadequate her comment sounded in the circumstances.

The man turned back to the girls. 'Well, I think that's about all for the present time,' he said. 'The tape recordings of both your statements will be typed up at the station. You should both come tomorrow afternoon, with your parents if you wish, to read the statements and sign them. Is that quite clear?'

'Yes,' said the girls in unison, their voices sounding thin and frightened.

The policeman looked at Nelly. 'Is the father not available?'

'Yes, he is,' replied Nelly, evenly. 'He is on his way from the Channel Islands at this moment.'

'On business, is he?'

'No, our home is there.'

'So you're not resident in London, then?'

Oh, God! thought Nelly, why did I mention the island? 'Yes, we are,' she said. 'We live in Holland Park.'

'So you have two homes?'

'Yes.'

'I see.' He stared at Nelly coldly, with ill-concealed disapproval. 'There will be an inquest, as I've no doubt you are aware. Your daughters will have to give evidence, and they must remain in London until everything is finalized.'

'I understand,' said Nelly, standing up, and doing her very best to remain calm, polite and unruffled. 'Is that all for the moment? May I take my daughters home now, please?'

'You may,' the policeman agreed, grudgingly. 'You should bring them to the station tomorrow at four o'clock.' He wrote something on a piece of paper and handed it to her. 'Here's the address. Please be punctual.'

Silently, the girls followed their mother from the room. In an equal silence, Nelly drove through the quiet London streets, and they reached home just as dawn was breaking. In the kitchen, Nelly made tea, and they sat at the table to drink it.

'Are you angry, Mum?' Sophie raised her swollen eyes to her mother's.

'No, not angry. Just thankful that you're both all right.'

'What about David?' asked Gertrude, sadly.

'Indeed.' Nelly looked at Sophie, frowning. 'Did you *know* he took drugs, darling?'

'No, I didn't. I don't know him particularly well. I wasn't surprised, though. Nearly everyone does drugs, Mum, you know that. It's not such a big deal, really.'

'Do you not think that being dead is a big deal, Sophie?'

'Yes, of course I do. I'm, sorry, Mum.' Tears filled Sophie's eyes again, and fell down her face. 'Of course, I'm sorry.'

'Well, don't cry. It was hardly your fault, was it?'

'I don't know. Maybe I could have stopped him, if I'd thought, but it all happened so quickly. This guy came up and said, "Here you are, Dave, I owe you one." And Dave said, "Thanks man," and popped something in his mouth. He was dancing the whole time; he never stopped.'

Nelly shook her head. 'Why don't you both go to bed now, and try and get some sleep. We'll talk about it later, when your father gets here.'

'You're not going to work today?'

'No, it's my Saturday off. I'll be here to go with you to the police station, and so will Papa.'

Hugo phoned from the airport as he had promised, then got a cab to the house. Hearing his taxi in the street, Nelly opened the front door and ran down the steps to meet him. He paid the driver, then turned and put his arms round her. 'Are they all right?'

'The girls are, thank God, but the boy died, Hugo.'

'God, how dreadful.' Hugo released Nelly, and passed his hand over his face. 'What kind of a world do we live in, for Christ's sake?' he asked wearily. 'We've been through all this with Phylly. I can't believe it's happening again.'

'Come in, let's not talk on the step.' They went into the house together. 'You decided not to bring Phylly with you?'

'Yes. She wants to be there for András at the moment, while he makes up his mind whether to write to his grandfather in Italy. We must let her know the girls are OK; she'll be worrying.'

'Yes,' said Nelly, 'we must.' She led the way down to the basement kitchen. 'So it looks as though the old man in the Sunday supplement really is the guy Baz was trying to find?'

'Yes, I'm sure it's him. Even at his age, his resemblance to András is extraordinary.'

Coffee was waiting on the stove, and Nelly poured two mugs. 'The girls are asleep, poor things,' she said. 'We have to take them to sign their statements this afternoon, and there'll be an inquest later, of course.'

After the visit to the police station, the two girls, sad and subdued, helped Nelly prepare supper, and they decided to eat in the garden.

'Papa?' Sophie's voice was muted.

'Yes?'

'I suppose all this is going to get into the papers, isn't it? Like it did when Phylly crashed Mum's car?'

'Yes, I suppose it's rather likely.'

'We were talking about it, Gertie and me, Papa, and we know what will happen at school. It'll be the end for both of us, as far as the Head's concerned. She's never taken her crap little eyes off either of us, since Phylly was expelled.'

Gertrude blinked myopically at her mother, her cheeks pink with indignation. 'She's utterly odious, dismal old cow. When I think of the money you and Papa shell out in school fees, I find her attitude pretty offensive.'

'I expect she feels she has to protect the school's reputation,' said Nelly mildly. 'It's understandable, isn't it?'

'Mum!' said Sophie earnestly. 'Please try to listen to what I'm saying! We don't want to go back to school, not to *that* school, anyway. Please don't try to make us jump through the same hoops as Phylly did, and then get the sack, which is what'll happen. In any case, I've finished my GCSEs; it's not a problem. I hate it there; we *both* do, don't we, Gertie?'

'Absolutely!'

Suddenly Hugo spoke, with uncharacteristic firmness. 'If that's how you both really feel, leave it to me. I'll deal with Miss Gurnhill on Monday, and as soon as the inquest is over you can come home to Florizel.'

'But you'll have to go to school somewhere,' said Nelly, feeling that the situation was getting out of hand. 'You can't just walk away from your education, and I'm quite sure there's no need to. After all, you've done nothing wrong.'

'We have, Mum. We went clubbing in term-time. It's against the rules.'

'Whatever,' said Nelly impatiently. 'In any case, I'm sure we can find a sympathetic school that you'll both enjoy.'

Gertrude looked at her mother with bright, hopeful eyes. 'We've been thinking, Mum. What about your old school?'

'*My* old school? You mean the convent?'

'Yes, the convent. You liked it there, didn't you?'

'Well, it was all right, I suppose. Yes, I did like it.' Nelly frowned. 'But a *boarding*-school, with *nuns,* in the *country*? Wouldn't you find it terribly boring, after London?'

'No, we don't think so, Mum.' Gertrude looked seriously from Nelly to Hugo and back again. 'London's a really septic place these days, Mum, you don't seem to realize. You can't go anywhere without coming face to face with drug-pushers. They're everywhere; on the streets; outside the school gates. There are even kids selling them *inside* the school, which might pull the rug from under ghastly old Gurnhill, if she knew. At least with the nuns we wouldn't have all that hassle to deal with, would we?'

Nelly smiled. 'Nuns aren't all sweetness and light, as I remember,' she said. 'Some of them can be great disciplinarians. You might find it all quite hard to take; it's a bit like being in prison.'

Sophie laughed, to the enormous relief of both her parents. 'Even the horriblest nun couldn't be as poisonous as Miss Gurnhill, hairy old lesbian!'

Nelly shook her head in disbelief. 'I find it hard to believe you're really serious,' she said. 'But if you like, we could all drive down and visit the convent, and then see what we think?'

'Brill.'

Chapter Fourteen

On Sunday morning András got up early and cycled to the Langlois farm to visit his grandmother, taking with him the colour supplement Phyllida had given him. It was a crisp clear day, and a stiff breeze blew off the sea. The narrow road to the farm was deeply rutted, damaged by the tractors that constantly made their way along it in all weathers, towing trailer-loads of straw bales for the cows, or milk churns from the farm to the creamery, or paper sacks of new potatoes to the harbour, for export to the mainland. The Langlois farm, surrounded by its fertile green fields, was quite close to the cliffs and overlooked the narrow channel that separated Florizel from France. On clear days, like today, you could plainly see the little houses along the French coast, and at night the flash of the lighthouse at Cap de Carteret.

András stopped for a moment, looked out across the sea, and thought about his German grandfather coming from France on a troopship, all those years ago. Had the weather been fine, like today, or had the sea been wild and turbulent, as it so often was in that strip of water? He wondered whereabouts in Germany the Balthus family had lived, and whether any of them were still there nowadays. Why had Werner himself settled in Italy? Presumably because he had married an

Italian, or maybe it was a simple question of taking his retirement in a Mediterranean climate?

Pushing his bike, András approached the farmhouse of his second cousin, Denis Langlois. He propped his machine against the wall and knocked at the back door. It was answered by Denis's wife, Monique.

'Hello, Monique. How are you?'

'Hello, Andy, haven't seen you for weeks. Come to see Gran, have you? She's been looking out for you, man. You should come a bit oftener.'

'I know,' said András, following her to the kitchen. 'It's not very easy. Work gets in the way, doesn't it?'

Monique smiled knowingly. 'Work and the girls more like, Andy, eh? I hear you're engaged already?'

'No, I am *not*,' said András loudly. 'Who told you that?'

'Guess!'

András flushed angrily. 'I know who it was, and it's a load of shit. I wish she'd get off my back.'

Monique laughed. 'Fat chance of that, man. The old girl's looking after her interests, isn't she? Making sure you stick around and look after her in her old age.' She gave him an inquisitive look. 'Got other ideas, have you, then?'

András, irritated, shook his head noncommittally. 'How's Gran?' he asked. 'Is she about?'

'Yes, of course. She's out the back, doing the hens. You know the way?'

'Thanks. I'll go and find her.'

Michèle Langlois was not cleaning the hen-house. She had already finished that self-imposed task, and was now engaged in picking up the little green apples that lay in the grass after the June drop, in the orchard beyond the poultry paddock.

At seventy-seven years of age, Michèle was still a fine-looking woman. Although her once golden hair was now white, and worn in the traditional old lady's bun, her cheeks were pink in her sunburned face, and her calm blue eyes were clear and bright. Long years of activity in the capacity of unpaid general dogsbody to the Langlois family had kept her fit and slender, and her only concession to her age was a reluctant admission to having a bit of arthritis in her wrists. She had been born on the farm and had lived there all her life, thanks to the generosity, love and support of her parents, and subsequently that of her brother, who had inherited the place when their father died. It was to his son, Denis, and his wife Monique that Michèle now looked for the roof over her head, and for her board and lodging.

Bringing up her daughter Rosie in her parents' house had not always been easy, particularly as Rose had been such a difficult child, quick to see animosity where none existed, always ready to be aggressive and unpleasant to her elders, and to fight with her young cousins. Nonetheless, with a lot of goodwill on both sides, and a great deal of hard work on Michèle's part, things had gone on fairly well until the day of Rose's marriage to the fisherman Pierre du Toit. Although glad to see the back of her, no-one in the Langlois family was particularly delighted at this union, for they had always assumed that Rose, a typical Langlois, fair and blue-eyed like her mother, would find a more acceptable mate, in spite of the misfortunes surrounding her birth.

It was, therefore, a circumstance of very great joy to Michèle when the baby András, born six months after the marriage, grew to have an astonishing resemblance to his grandfather, Werner, the only man Michèle had ever loved. Now, living out her active but tranquil existence on the family farm, her grandson was the focus of her life. Each day, as she toiled in the garden, she would look from time to time across the fields in the direction of Roc aux Chiens, hoping that András would find time to come and see her, just as she had gazed longingly at the German barracks, so long ago, waiting for Werner.

Having tracked his grandmother to the orchard, András stood for a moment, watching her as she filled her big basket with the fallen apples, acutely aware that in all probability he was about to shatter the peace of her uneventful, sequestered days. Slowly, he walked towards her, his boots dragging in the unmown grass, and she turned towards him, her face lighting up with happiness at the sight of him.

'Hello, Gran.'

'Hello, my dear boy.'

He kissed her on both cheeks, then picked up the heavy basket. 'Let's sit down, Gran. I've got something to show you.'

'Really? Whatever can that be?'

A Victorian garden seat, its paint shabby and peeling, beyond repair, had been relegated to a sunny corner of the orchard and it was to this place that András led Michèle. They sat down, and carefully, he extracted the folded supplement from his pocket. 'Sorry it's a bit crumpled, Gran, but I think you should see this.'

'What is it?' Michèle took her spectacles from her apron pocket and put them on, then unfolded the paper. Silently, she looked at the pictures, and attentively, read the text. When she looked up, her face was pale, but composed, with two bright spots of colour on her cheeks.

András cleared his throat uneasily. 'Do you recognize that old man, Gran?'

She smiled. 'Of course I do. It's Werner, Rosie's father, and your grandfather. I thought he'd died, long ago. I can't believe he's alive, after all these years. It's wonderful.'

'He's married, Gran.'

'That doesn't matter, András. Dead or alive, married or single, I'll always love him.'

'Would you like to see him again, if that were possible?'

In the long silence that followed, András began to regret asking such a loaded question, and was about to suggest that such a meeting would be impossible to arrange anyway, when she made this tactic unnecessary. 'I don't think so, no. I wouldn't want to make trouble for him with his wife.' Michèle looked again at the paper. 'She looks quite a remarkable lady, doesn't she?' Then she raised her eyes to his. 'But I *would* like him to know about you, András. And Rose, too, of course.'

'Would you really?'

'Yes, I would. I've always felt sad about him not knowing. Perhaps you should write to him, András, explain how it was, send some photos?' She studied the paper. 'There isn't an address, though, is there?'

'Well, it does mention Mrs Balthus's shop in San Gimignano. That would find him, I expect.'

'Yes, I see.'

'In any case, Hugo would know how to suss that out, I'm sure.'

'Hugo?'

'Hugo Turnbull at *Les Romarins*, Gran.'

'Don't the Tanquerays live there any more?'

'Old Lady Tanqueray died. It's Nelly's house now.'

'Really? Nobody tells me anything, these days.'

'I do.'

'Yes, dear, you do.'

András stood up, preparing to leave. 'So, I'll write a letter to Werner Balthus, shall I? And send a few photographs, maybe? Why don't you write him a note yourself, and it can go with mine?'

'Is that a good idea, do you think? Wouldn't Mrs Balthus mind if I did that?'

'It's no-one's fault what happens in wars, Gran. Of course she won't mind; she doesn't look that kind of person.'

'All right, I'll think about it.' She got up and they walked slowly back to the kitchen door together, András carrying the basket of apples. Suddenly, Michèle gave her grandson a reproving tap on the arm. 'And incidentally, András, I don't like you referring to Werner as "that old man"! He doesn't look old to *me*, not at all. So don't say it again, please.'

András laughed. 'OK, Gran. I won't, I promise.' At the kitchen door he embraced her and mounted his bike. 'Do you want to keep the paper?' he asked.

'Yes, I'd like to, if I may?'

'Of course, I was sure you'd want to. I'd better just take the details of Mrs Balthus's shop, though, hadn't I?' He took his folding knife from his pocket, and skilfully cut out the vital information at the end of the piece, then handed the precious supplement back. 'I'll go over to *Les Romarins* tonight and see Hugo, then I'll call back in a couple of days for your letter, OK?'

'Yes,' said Michèle, 'OK.'

On a Saturday morning in the middle of July, Rachel received a letter from the solicitor in Ely, informing her that probate had been granted, the farm at St Cuthbert's Fen was now officially hers, and that she was free to sell the property should she so wish.

Stanley, with his habitual bland assumption of his right to interfere in Rachel's affairs, demanded to see the letter. Rachel handed it to him, across the breakfast table. He read the letter, then handed it back. 'Good,' he said, 'and about time. We must sell it at once, we need the money.'

'Why?'

'Why?' Stanley looked furtively towards the kitchen, where Antonia was engaged in paying the milkman. He lowered his voice. 'Because it costs a lot having a resident housekeeper now that you're working, Rachel, and more especially as you don't make the contribution we agreed.'

'I don't remember making any such agreement, Stanley.'

'Don't quibble, Rachel. Either you chip in, or we dispense with Antonia's services, and you quit your job and come home.'

'Get lost, Stanley.'

'I beg your pardon?'

'I said, get lost, Stanley. Or if you wish me to be more explicit, get stuffed.'

Stanley rose to his feet, throwing down his snowy linen napkin, and left the dining-room, the embodiment of affronted dignity.

Rachel watched him go, heard the front door close behind him, and calmly put her letter back in its envelope. She poured herself another cup of coffee, and lifted the pot invitingly, looking round the table. 'Coffee, anyone?'

Adam and Ned both sat staring at her with disbelief, as if she had suddenly grown horns. Their jaws, munching toast and marmalade, moved in unison. They shook their heads.

'Yes, please,' said Ciaran, pushing her cup towards her mother, and grinning all over her face.

Stanley returned home at teatime, after spending most of Saturday angrily pacing about his room in college, trying to figure out how to clip Rachel's wings and bend her to his will. He was aware that his customary bullying tactics no longer had the desired effect on her, and asked himself how it was that she had become so assertive, not to mention astonishingly vulgar in her attitude towards him. Never in his life had he been told to get stuffed by a woman. Surely the mere taking of a job had not wrought this remarkable change in her mindset? After sixteen years or so of marriage, during which time she had feebly relied on him for direction and support of every kind, often causing him much exasperation in the process, he found it incredible that a few short months on her own could have brought about such a difference.

The house was quiet when he entered. The sitting-room was empty and so was the study, though the twins' school books were open on the table; evidently they still had work to be completed. Feeling neglected, but also slightly mortified at his own capacity to sulk in the face of Rachel's obduracy, he took a volume of Isaiah Berlin's essays from the bookcase, and made his way to the back garden. There, he found Antonia, wearing shorts and gardening gloves, engaged in what seemed to him to be a major project. Spread about the scruffy lawn were several dozen large black plastic pots containing flowering plants of every description, though on account of his ignorance of horticultural matters, he was unable to identify very many of them. Antonia had already dug over the entire border, and had enriched the soil with fertilizer of an organic nature, to judge by the smell. 'Good heavens,' said Stanley, seating himself in a deck-chair beneath the chestnut tree. 'You look very busy, my dear.'

'And not before time,' she replied briskly, energetically excavating a large hole with a shiny new stainless-steel spade. 'It's such a shame that no-one looks after the garden; it's been horribly neglected.' Expertly, she tipped a bushy plant with mauve flowers out of its pot and placed it carefully in the hole. Then she replaced the earth around it, gently firming it in with her foot. 'It'll look magnificent in a week or two; you'll see, Stanley.'

'You certainly seem to have taken matters in hand, Antonia.' He cleared his throat nervously. 'All this stuff must have cost quite a bit, I imagine?'

'Not really. About two hundred quid for the plants, plus another ninety or thereabouts for the compost and fertilizer, and some proper tools.'

'Isn't that rather a lot, just to smarten up the garden? How did you pay for everything?'

'Oh, I paid by plastic. I'll give you the receipts; it's not a problem.'

Stanley, dismayed, angry and nauseated by the smell of chicken manure, got up from his seat. 'Where are the boys?' he asked, preparing to retreat indoors.

'Tennis, I think. Or maybe rowing. I can't remember.'

'And Rachel?'

'She's gone out with Ciaran; she didn't say where. They took a packed lunch.'

'I see.'

Rachel and Ciaran did not get home until half-past seven, having spent an enjoyable afternoon on the river. Since Antonia was out for the evening, and Rachel felt no special inclination to cook supper, she bought fish and chips for five hungry people on the way home. Ciaran carried the large warm fragrant parcels into the kitchen and turned on the oven to keep them warm.

The twins were in the study, working, and Stanley was in the sitting-room, reading. Antonia had already gone out, and Rachel decided to have supper in the kitchen, considering it to be an appropriate setting for a simple meal of fish and chips.

'Dad won't like it,' said Ciaran, nervously.

'He can always take his and eat in the dining-room, if he feels like it,' responded her mother, imperturbably. 'That is, if he could be so pathetic.'

Ciaran's eyes widened. She was quite aware of the tension existing between her parents, but this was beginning to sound like open warfare. She was about to be proved entirely accurate in this conjecture.

They put knives and forks, bread and cheese, a bottle of tomato ketchup and a jug of tap water on the kitchen table, and at eight o'clock Ciaran was dispatched to call the family to supper. In an embarrassed silence, Rachel divided the fish and chips equally between the warmed plates and Ciaran handed them round.

'Really, Rachel, isn't this rather sordid? Couldn't you manage to cook something for us?'

'My dear Stanley, I fail to see why I should. If you want something fancy every night of the week, you should either cook it yourself or ask Antonia to leave something ready-prepared.'

'She's very busy with the garden, just now. She can't be expected to do everything.'

'I get the impression that's *exactly* what she does, Stanley.'

Stanley shot a sharp look in Rachel's direction, and she returned the look coolly, without blinking. Slowly, a deep magenta blush crept up his neck, and into his face. He longed to ask her precisely what she was implying, but did not dare, fearing she would tell him, and humiliate him in front of the children. *Pas devant les enfants* came unbidden into his head, but where such an idiotic phrase originated he had no idea, and managed to restrain himself from actually saying it out loud. They finished the meal in silence.

At half-past ten they went to bed. Rachel washed, cleaned her teeth, slipped into her pyjamas, got quickly into bed and opened a book.

Stanley, after a lengthy spell in the bathroom, got

into bed beside her. 'Have you thought any more about the farm, Rachel?'

'No, I haven't.'

'I think you should.'

'Why?'

'You know perfectly well why.'

Rachel put down her book. 'I take it that you have in mind that I sell my own farm, and hand the proceeds over to you, is that it?'

'Well, I certainly think it would be logical, and fair, to use the money to pay for the domestic and child care we currently employ.'

'We had domestic help in the shape of Madge, Stanley, and I had to find her wages out of the miserable housekeeping allowance you saw fit to dole out when it was convenient to you.'

'Madge was a complete disaster, as well you know, Rachel. Antonia is in an entirely different class.'

'A very expensive one, I imagine,' said Rachel. 'Or do some of her duties come free, Stanley?'

'I don't know what you mean.'

'Of course you do. Do you think me a complete moron; that I don't know what you get up to when I'm away, you stupid little man?' She looked at her husband with quiet derision, her eyes mocking his pompous, hypocritical self-righteousness. 'Even the kids know you're screwing Antonia,' she added scornfully.

'I'm sure they *don't*!' he exclaimed angrily, before he could stop himself.

Rachel smiled. 'Don't worry about it; I really don't care what you do. It makes us quits in that department anyway. I have a lover myself.'

Stanley stared at her. 'You're not serious?'

'I am, absolutely. And I've got news for you, Stanley. Until quite recently, I had no idea what real love, or even good sex, was about. What I had with you was

266

just a sort of blundering initiation, and thereafter a matter of routine copulation, if and when you felt like it. The fact is, you're lousy in bed. On a scale of one to ten, I wouldn't even give you one.'

There followed a very long silence. At last Stanley spoke, very quietly and rather meekly, a new departure for him. 'Rachel,' he said. 'Why don't we go back to how we were, before your father died?'

'You mean me give up my job?'

'Yes.'

'Forget it, Stanley.'

'It's that photographer chap, isn't it?'

'Yes, since you ask.'

'I thought he was quite a young man, in his twenties?'

'He's twenty-seven, ten years younger than me.' She looked at him coldly. 'Antonia, I understand, is also a few years your junior, is that right? Or are we talking double standards here?'

'I could divorce you, Rachel.'

'Go ahead, if that's what you want, Stanley.'

Stanley got out of bed and put on his slippers. 'I think it would be better if I slept in the spare room,' he said.

'Good idea,' said Rachel. 'Though maybe you'd be more comfortable in Antonia's bed, or is she still out with her boyfriend?'

When he had departed, closing the door with elaborate dignity behind him, Rachel lay down, put a pillow over her head and laughed until she almost cried. She was astonished, and even a little ashamed, at the degree of bitchiness of which she now seemed only too capable in her dealings with Stanley. At the same time, she felt profound relief that the charade of their marriage was at last at an end.

On Sunday night Rachel returned to London, taking

the solicitor's letter with her. She found Simon in his studio, watching a video. She lay down on the sofa beside him, he put his arm around her and they watched the last quarter of an hour of *Trainspotting* together.

'Have you ever done drugs, Simon?' she asked, as the credits rolled.

'Had a few smokes, nothing much, when I was a student. What about you?'

'Never. I'm too scared of losing control, I think.'

'You don't mind drinking a glass of wine, though? That's a drug, too, isn't it?'

'True.' She turned in his arms and kissed his ear. 'I daresay that had quite a bit to do with my eagerness to share my bed with you.' She smiled. 'In fact, I'd love some wine, right now. Or better still, a little brandy.'

Simon got up, went to the shelf over the sink where he kept the drink, and poured two brandies. He sat down beside her, handing her a glass. 'You don't regret it?'

'Regret what?'

'Getting into bed with me.'

'Never.'

'Don't ever change, please.'

The next day, as they were driving down to Kent on a shoot, Rachel told Simon about the letter she had received from the lawyer in Ely. 'Stanley wants me to sell the farm, of course. He has no interest in the place; he just thinks it's the rather embarrassing evidence of my squalid background.'

'And you, Rachel; is that how you see it?'

'Absolutely not.'

'So, what's the problem? Don't sell it, of course.'

'Wouldn't it be terribly impractical to keep it? It's pretty much of a wreck, really; it badly needs things repairing. Like the roof, for instance. And there's quite a bit of land, too. You can't just leave fields to do their own thing; you have to clean the ditches, things like that.'

'Is that what your father did?'

'Yes, poor man, he did.' Rachel sighed, and stared out of the car window at the passing landscape, suddenly depressed, remembering her father's last weeks of life. 'I feel bad about it, Simon. I never tried to help, or even went to see him, for years and years. I walked away, really.'

'I don't suppose you'd have done that on your own, Rachel. I guess Stanley had a hand in it, didn't he?'

'Well, a bit. But I should have stood up to him. I know that now, when it's too late.'

They arrived at their destination, a village set among hopfields, and asked the way to the converted oasthouse that was to be the subject of the shoot.

'Lovely place,' remarked Simon, as they drove through a pair of white-painted gateposts, 'but a bit gentrified, don't you think?'

Rachel laughed. They parked the car beside the stylist's van, and prepared for a long day's work.

Driving back to London in the cool of the evening, Rachel began to tell Simon about her childhood with her father, and about her last visit to him, his illness, death and funeral. Simon listened attentively, saying nothing, until they were driving through Richmond Park, and she fell silent.

'Is that all?'

'Yes. Not much of a life, was it, poor man?' Her voice broke, and Simon could tell she was crying. He drove into the next parking area, stopped the car and turned off the engine. He turned towards her, and wiped the tears from her cheeks with his thumb. 'Why didn't you tell me all this before now?' he asked gently.

'I don't know why.' She smiled wanly. 'I suppose I wasn't thinking about it. I was too happy; I forgot.'

'Then you got the letter, and remembered?'

'Yes, I suppose so.'

'Do you know what I think?'

'What?' said Rachel, blowing her nose.

'I think you need to go there, don't you? Take a good hard look; try to remember everything that ever happened there; *everything*. And then make up your mind what you want to do.'

'But that would be quite difficult, Simon. Work, and Oxford on Fridays.'

'It's not at all difficult. Tell Stanley you're not coming this weekend, and we'll go together to Deeping.'

'Would you really? Come with me, I mean?'

'What else? I can't think of anything I'd rather do.'

'Really?'

'Really.'

They arrived in St Cuthbert's Fen at noon, having shopped in the Deeping mini-market, collected the keys of the farm from Father Lovell, and paid a brief visit to Ernest Cropthorne's unmarked grave. 'I must get him a stone,' said Rachel, as they walked back to the car, then took the single-track road out to the farm. 'Do you know,' she said, sounding surprised, 'I haven't the least idea where my mother is buried. How strange that I never asked Pa.'

Simon drove slowly along the narrow road, exulting in the vast blue vault of the sky and the towering white cumulus clouds driven like galleons before the salt-laden east wind. Tall reeds bordered the lane, swaying and rustling in the breeze, alive with nesting buntings. As they approached, the male birds, a drab brown colour, but with elegant white ruffs under their black heads, shot hysterically out of their hiding-places and bounced along in front of the car in a series of short agitated flights. Beyond the reeds, fields of potatoes were in full leaf, a glorious vibrant green, and cattle grazed in water-meadows, knee-deep in the lush grass. Along the banks of an invisible stream grew pollarded willows, the pink stems of their new season's growth bending gracefully towards the water below, their delicate pointed leaves stirred by the warm flow of air.

'My God,' said Simon. 'It's beautiful, Rachel.'

'It is, but it doesn't look like this in winter, you know.'

'I bet you get some wonderful sunsets?'

'Well, yes, I suppose we do.'

In a few minutes, they arrived at the cattle-grid that served as a gateway to the farm, drove into the yard, and stopped the car. They got out and stood for a moment, deafened by the sudden silence, dazzled by the interminable distances all around them. To the east a faint gleam on the horizon suggested the sea, though as the coast was at least sixty miles away, this seemed improbable. The high-pitched twittering of skylarks made pinpricks of sound in the upper air, and house-martins swooped low around the house and barn, bringing food to their young, their shrill cries as they approached their nests provoking a clamorous response from their offspring. Around the door to the house an overgrown rose flaunted dark drooping crimson blooms on long arching thorny branches. An ancient wisteria, growing along the eaves, hung extravagant panicles of white blossom from its contorted grey limbs, like so many scented wedding bouquets.

'*White* wisteria; isn't that rather unusual?'

'It's always been there,' said Rachel. 'I think my mother must have planted it. It must be getting on for forty years old, near enough.'

The tall trees that grew in the little copse behind the house were in full leaf, and giving sanctuary to robins and blackbirds, long-tailed tits and wrens. The hot sun had dried up the malodorous midden in the yard, and the scents of flowers and cool green leaves flowed around the little house, attracting flights of foraging bees.

Rachel unlocked the door and they went into the kitchen, taking the shopping with them. The house felt cool, though not particularly damp, and the smell of corruption she remembered seemed to have disappeared, leaving in its place a faint odour of disinfectant. They opened the windows all over the house and immediately the scent of roses and wisteria filled the rooms. Rachel's spirits rose, and she turned to Simon. 'What shall we do? Have a picnic, or would you like to explore first?'

'Let's have a picnic.'

They had brought with them rugs, pillows and sleeping-bags, in case the household linen was damp, and they took the rugs out to the back of the house and spread them on the rough grass under the lime trees. Rachel unpacked the shopping, and selecting some ham, a loaf of crusty bread, cheese and tomatoes, put everything onto her father's old mahogany tray and carried it outside, followed by Simon with glasses and a bottle of white wine, cooling in a bucket half-filled with ice-cold well water.

They ate the food and drank the chilled dry wine, then lay side by side, dozing under the shady trees, or gazing up into the green canopy of translucent leaves, while a robin sang over their heads, and the house-martins skimmed over the grass nearby, quite unperturbed by their presence.

The distant church bell struck three, and reluctantly, Rachel sat up. She stretched out a hand and touched Simon's face. 'Wake up, we have things to do.'

He opened his eyes slowly, and smiled at her. 'What things?'

'Oh, you know. Check out the buildings; get the stove going if we want a proper supper; make the beds.'

'*Beds?* Won't one be enough?'

She laughed, and bending down, kissed him. 'Yes, I expect it will.'

'Kiss me again.'

'No!' She scrambled hastily to her feet. 'Come on, first things first.'

'Must we really? What a slave-driver you've become, all of a sudden.'

They carried the remains of the picnic back to the kitchen, and Simon washed the plates and glasses, while Rachel lit the stove. Fortunately, she had had the good sense, all those months ago, to leave kindling, coal, and a box of matches beside the Dover stove, and it now obliged her by allowing itself to be ignited without difficulty.

'Now we must get logs in,' she said. 'Let's hope no-one's been around doing themselves a favour.'

They took the large round willow log-basket, and made their way to the woodshed at the back of the barn. All the firewood was there, neatly stacked, and they filled the basket.

'What happened in there?' Simon pointed to the barn door.

'Pigs.'

'Really?'

Rachel pushed open the big double doors, and they went in. The place smelt fresh and clean, and two pairs of swallows flew in and out of the ventilation holes, attending to their nests high in the peak of the iron roof. Apart from the empty pens, there was no evidence at all that at one time successive groups of fifty or more pigs had been reared and fattened there.

'When did the pigs go?'

'Oh, after Pa died. I sold them to the chap down the road, and all the feed and straw and stuff.'

'Wasn't there an awful lot of mucking-out to do, when they'd gone?'

'Tell me about it!'

'Who did it?'

'Who do you think?' She laughed. 'Me, of course. Who else?'

'All by yourself, Rachel? In the middle of winter?' He sounded incredulous.

She smiled. 'Does it matter?'

'Yes, it does.'

They returned to the house, stoked up the fire, and went upstairs. In Ernest's bedroom, they turned the mattress before making up the bed with sheets and blankets Rachel took from the painted chest. She examined the grey, lumpy pillows and shook her head. 'These are really disgusting,' she said; 'they'll have to go. Poor old Pa, I expect he was past caring. It's a good job we brought yours with us.'

When the bed-making was finished, and their bags had been brought up to the bedroom and unpacked, they took a walk round the four small fields that now belonged to Rachel. The one closest to the yard appeared to have a patchy crop of potatoes, evidently the product of last year's imperfect harvesting, resulting in a sporadic new growth. 'I wonder if there's anything worth eating?' said Rachel. She fetched a fork from the barn and lifted a clump, loosening the earth under the green tops. 'Look!' she exclaimed, kneeling down and plunging her hands into the dark soil. 'New potatoes!'

Simon took them from her, making a pouch with his shirt to receive the moist white tubers. 'Aren't they stunning?' he said. 'They don't look or smell at all like this in the supermarket, do they?'

'No,' said Rachel, getting up and adding two more to the precious hoard. 'We'll have them for supper, with the chicken. I must see if I can find the mint patch, after all this time.'

They found the mint where it had always been, by the back kitchen door, and half smothered by nettles.

274

They put the potatoes and a bunch of mint into a blue china bowl on the dresser, then continued their walk round the little farm. The three remaining fields had now reverted to meadow, and were waist-high in timothy, vetches, rye grass and a dazzling array of ox-eye daisies, corn-cockles and scarlet poppies, sheltered by the thick overgrown hedgerows of black-thorn and hawthorn.

'Thank heaven I brought the cameras,' said Simon. 'Let's get up at sunrise tomorrow, and take some pictures.' He turned to Rachel. 'That is, if I have your permission, my darling?' Without waiting for an answer, he put his arms round her and kissed her, then held her tightly against his body as they stood together in that exquisite lonely place. A wave of absolute happiness flowed between them, and for both it seemed a long moment of silent but total commitment. 'I love you, darling Rachel,' he said quietly, 'and I love this place.'

'So do I, Simon. I'll never sell it.'

'Amen to that.'

Chapter Fifteen

Werner Balthus's response to his grandson's letter arrived in the middle of July. Since writing to his grandfather András had taken extremely good care to be in the vicinity of the letter-box at the normal time of delivery every morning, in order to prevent the reply falling into his mother's hands, with predictable consequences. He took the letter with the unfamiliar Italian stamp from the postman, slipped it into his back pocket, and went out to deliver the orders for fish, as usual. In the evening he sailed his own dinghy to the cove below *Les Romarins* and found Phyllida waiting for him.

Silently, he handed her the unopened letter, and she took it. 'What's the matter, András? Why haven't you opened it?'

'I'm scared shitless.'

'Why?'

'In case he doesn't want to know.'

'Do you want me to open it for you?'

'Please. If you wouldn't mind.'

Phyllida opened the letter and took out two sheets of paper, folded round another sealed letter, which was addressed to Michèle Langlois. This she handed to András, and he put it carefully into his pocket.

'Shall I read it to you, András?'

He nodded, and they sat down together on Phylly's rock.

My dear András, she read in a low voice, *it was with a strange combination of shock and joy that I received your amazing letter a few days ago, and I must tell you at once how very delighted, as well as surprised, I am to learn of your existence, and also of course that of your mother, after so long a time has passed since I was in Florizel.*

You will find also a letter to your grandmother Michèle, in which I have much to tell her, but I also wish to explain to you, András, that I wrote many times to my dear Michèle after I left the island, but never received any answers, not even one. When the fighting was in the end over, and the terrible truths about Auschwitz, Treblinka and the other dreadful death camps were made known to us all, I did not feel it would be acceptable for me, as a German, to come again to Florizel, but I did not forget the happiness I had known there, and never will.

My wife, Chiara, knows that I was for a time in Florizel, and understands very well the circumstances that war often precipitates. She was a child herself during the war, here in Tuscany, and when I showed her your letter, she was almost as excited as I. Chiara and I married only ten years ago, and, naturally, have no children. She asks that, if it is convenient, you come as soon as is possible to visit us, here at Cappella della Vigna.

I remain, my dear András,
Your grandfather,
Werner Balthus.

Smiling, Phyllida handed the letter to András, and he read it again, to himself.

'Will you go?' she asked, when he had finished.

'Yes, if you'll come with me.'

* * *

277

On his return to Roc aux Chiens, András got on his bike and rode over to the Langlois farm to see his grandmother. He found her in the scullery, scraping potatoes for the evening meal. András kissed her cheek and produced the letter he had brought for her. At the sight of it, Michèle turned pink, and, holding up her wet hands, told András to put it in her apron pocket, and this he did. Then she picked up her knife and continued with her job. 'Did he write to you, too, András?'

'He did.'

'Was he pleased to hear from us?'

'Yes, he was, very pleased. He asked me to go and stay with him and his wife at *Cappella della Vigna*. That's the name of the place where they live.'

Michèle turned to him, her eyes shining. 'That's exactly what I hoped he'd say.' A shadow crossed her face, and she frowned. 'What about money, dear? Can you afford the fare?'

'No, I can't.' He shifted his feet uneasily. 'I think it's possible Phyllida will come too, and Hugo – Mr Turnbull – will help pay for the trip.'

'Why should he want to do that, András?'

'I think he felt embarrassed about his friend coming to Florizel and stirring up gossip and stuff. Hugo was very glad that by a fluke Rodzianko did manage to find my grandfather, and he'll be anxious to help in any way he can, I know. He's like that.'

'Well, that would be very kind of him.' She smiled. 'But you must tell me if you need any more. I've got a little bit put by; it's yours if you need it. Or your Uncle Denis would help, I'm sure.'

'Thanks, Gran, but I hope it won't be necessary. I'll ask if it is, OK?'

'Yes, dear. OK.'

'I'll be off, then. I expect you'll want to read your letter?'

'Later on, I will. After supper.'

278

At Roc aux Chiens, his parents were halfway through their supper when András got home. 'You're late!' Rose spoke sharply, as he went to the sink to wash his hands. She got up, and, taking his supper from the oven, put it on the table. 'It's all dried up, I dare say,' she said, sitting down again, 'but it's your own bloody fault, if it is.'

'Sorry, Mum.' András sat down, and picked up his fork.

'Where've you been, anyway?'

'To Gran's.'

'To *Gran's*? What for?'

'I had a letter for her.'

'A *letter*? What sort of a letter? Who would write to *her*, may I ask?'

András put down his fork, and cleared his throat. 'My grandfather wrote to her, Mum, and to me.'

'Don't be bloody stupid. Your grandad's dead these nine years or more.'

'Not my grandfather Langlois, Mum. My other grandfather, Werner Balthus.' András looked at his mother boldly, full of a new-found confidence. 'That journalist bloke, Rodzianko, found him. He lives in Tuscany.'

'Where's Tuscany, when it's at home?' asked Pierre.

'In Italy,' said András, 'and I'm going out there to stay with him.'

'Over my dead body you are, young man!' Rose, white as a sheet, her blue eyes glacial with hatred, banged on the table with her fist, making the plates jump. 'First that bloody Russian comes here, causing trouble for me; the so-called *friend* of your precious Turnbulls, and now *you* want to run off and suck up to that fly-by-night Hun that got Mum in the fucking pudding club. If that scabby Kraut wasn't killed at Stalingrad, or wherever, why didn't he come back after the war and make an honest woman of her? And of *me*?' Angry tears spurted from her eyes, and she pushed back her chair and went to the window, turning her back on them.

András sighed. 'If he'd actually *known* about you, Mum, he would have come back, I'm sure.'

'Like hell he would! It seems to me he didn't give a toss about us. I expect he left a trail of little German bastards behind him wherever he went, the womanizing shit!' She turned from the window, her arms folded belligerently, the tears gone. 'Is he married, then?'

'Yes, he is, to an Italian woman.'

'There you are, then! Loads of kids, I dare say?'

'No,' said András. 'They have no children.'

'Aha!' Rose uttered a coarse, mocking laugh. 'So *that's* the way the wind's blowing, is it? No flies on *you*, young Andy, eh?'

Pierre, who had remained virtually silent throughout, now raised his voice in protest. 'Now then, Rosie, there's no call for that sort of talk, is there?'

'And *you* can shut your fucking face, you stupid old bugger! It's no bloody concern of yours.' She flounced out of the house, banging the door behind her. In a moment they heard the squawking of hens, and a volley of foul language as Rose shut them up for the night.

'Let's go for a pint, Andy? Give 'er time to cool off?'

'Better do the washing-up first, eh, Dad?'

A week later, Phyllida and András took the launch to Guernsey, flew to Paris and got a connecting flight to Pisa. Hugo, although still worried about his younger daughters, had been almost as thrilled as the young people at the turn of events, and was intensely relieved that Basil's meddling with the island history had at least had the merit of locating Werner Balthus. He persuaded András to speak to his grandfather on the phone, ask his permission to bring a friend with him, and confirm the dates of the visit, and all this András did, slightly nervously, for his way of life so far had had little need for long-distance telephone calls.

Hugo, having seen them off on the launch, made his way back to the empty house, feeling curiously deflated after the small excitement of obtaining a passport for András and arranging the journey to Tuscany. Slowly, Murphy plodded up the hill, then ambled along the lanes to *Les Romarins*. Hugo felt no great desire to get home in a hurry. It's always the same, he thought, it's the one left behind who feels somehow abandoned, and lonely. What the hell's the matter with me, he asked himself impatiently. It's what I've always wanted, isn't it? A place to work in solitude, no distractions, no noisy teenagers, and no traffic. I've been banging on about it for years, and now I've got it, I don't much like it. Still, he reflected, they'll soon be home for the summer, won't they?

Nearing the gate, Murphy, anticipating his snack and a good roll in the paddock, broke into a geriatric trot, staggered up the drive and came to a disconcertingly sudden halt at the door of his stable. 'Bloody old fool,' said Hugo tolerantly, and got down from his seat.

Brushing Murphy's moulting piebald flanks as he crunched his way through his nuts, Hugo's thoughts returned to his present solitary state, and persistent mood of self-pity. It's not so much the girls, he said to himself, it's Nelly. I miss her dreadfully. Why are we wasting our lives, being apart for so much of the time, like this?

Murphy finished his food and blew into his manger, in the hope of finding a few last bits. Hugo put down the brush, undid the halter and took the pony back to his paddock. He stood by the gate and watched as the elderly animal lay down and rolled ecstatically in the grass.

Hugo checked the gate, and walked back to the

house. Perhaps I'm being stupid, just because Phylly's gone, he said to himself. I can see how seriously she's involved with András, and I suppose every father feels a pang of bereavement when his daughter transfers her affections, but of course that has to happen sooner or later. In any case, he's a very nice young man. I trust him absolutely, and I like him a lot. In the kitchen he poured himself a beer and looked in the fridge to see what he could find for lunch, which turned out to be not much, except a small piece of Parmesan cheese. 'Sod it,' he said. 'It'll have to be pasta.'

He worked all afternoon, well enough, but aware of the empty house around him, the cool flower-filled drawing-room, the children's abandoned rooms up-stairs, and Una-Mary's big beautiful bedroom, now his and Nelly's, but with only himself to sleep in it.

At four o'clock Elsie arrived with the shopping, and brought him a cup of tea.

'I've left some ham in the fridge for you, Mr Hugo. Will that be all right? I've got my B and B visitors arriv-ing this evening, so I'm a bit pushed.'

'Yes, of course. Thanks, Elsie, I'll be fine.'

At seven o'clock he closed down his computer, fixed himself a whisky, and read the *Florizel Gazette*, left for him by Elsie, from cover to cover.

Walking in the garden after supper, deadheading a few faded roses as he passed, it suddenly occurred to him that he had not told Nelly about Phylly's trip to Tuscany with András, much less consulted her on the matter, taking the view that she had enough to cope with already. He went straight indoors and called her. She answered at once, and he launched into a long account of the events of the last couple of weeks, the invitation to visit *Cappella della Vigna*, the hastily organized arrangements. 'They left this morning,' he finished, lamely, 'on the launch.'

'Darling Hugo, you sound exhausted, and sad.'

'I am.'

'You're missing Phylly, I expect.'

'It's not Phylly I'm missing. It's you.'

'Well, my darling,' said Nelly cheerfully, 'you won't be missing me much longer. I've got news for you.'

'What's that?'

'I am about to hand in my resignation at the hospital, Hugo, and with any luck I should be on Florizel with you, permanently, by the end of October at the latest.'

'Good heavens! You're not serious?'

'I am. As a matter of fact, I was on the point of calling you, to tell you that I got the written confirmation from Reverend Mother today. It was here when I got home this evening. The girls can start in September.'

'Are they pleased?'

'I haven't told them yet. I wanted to tell you first.'

'But what about your consultancy, Nelly? What about the little girl you told me about? The one with Hodgkin's?'

'She died, Hugo.'

'*What*? You didn't tell me, Nelly. What happened, for God's sake?'

'Her mother couldn't handle the suffering the therapy caused the patient. She decided to suspend the treatment. After a couple of months the child had a severe relapse, and she died. It made me angry, as well as very depressed. I know that I don't distance myself from the patients as much as I should. It's bad for them, and it's not good for me, Hugo.'

'Oh, darling, I am sorry.'

'It doesn't matter. Now will probably be a good time for me to start something completely new. It might be possible to arrange a consultancy on Guernsey, say three days a week. Then later on, I'd really like to open a general clinic on Florizel. We certainly need one, don't we?'

'My darling, are you really sure? Wouldn't you find it incredibly parochial, after London?'

Nelly sighed. 'People are people, Hugo, wherever they live. They get sick; then they either get better, or they die. They're all the same. The most valuable contribution I could possibly bring to the island would be to take on a job that most people with my qualifications and experience would consider a waste of their skills.'

'Your mother would be proud of you, Nelly.'

She laughed. 'Don't be fooled by the high-minded talk, my love. If you want the real truth, it's because I can't bear being parted from you any longer.'

'You'll be parted from the girls when they go away to school, won't you?'

'Well, that's our next big leap in the dark, isn't it? But at least you and I will be doing it together. I'll tell you one thing: I can't possibly miss them as much as I've missed you.'

'That makes two of us, sweetheart.'

At the end of July, Nelly and the girls came home to Florizel for the long summer holidays, to Hugo's great relief and happiness. Even the constant bickering and argumentative attitude of Sophie and Gertrude failed to spoil his pleasure in their noisy presence, filling the house with life once again. Even a slammed door had become for him a reassuring sound, though he was quite aware that this euphoric mood would probably wear fairly thin in a week or two.

Nelly, for her part, although overjoyed to be at home and once more sharing a bed with the man she loved, nevertheless lost little time in finding something new to worry about. She had never entirely shared Hugo's relaxed attitude towards Phyllida's close friendship with András, and was finding it difficult to approve of his decision to send them abroad together to stay with strangers. Nelly liked András, thought him intelligent and extremely handsome, but considered eighteen years old to be a very young age for Phylly to be seriously involved with a man, any man. But then, she reflected, I don't actually *know* that she *is* sexually involved with him, do I? And, at eighteen, I was having a very active double sex life myself, with Baz as well as Hugo, so what does that say about me, I wonder? It says I've had two lovers, and one of them became my husband, what's so amazing about that? Nelly sighed, aware that she was not only confusing herself, but getting seriously off the point. I wonder what Ma would have thought if she'd known what I got up to at Cambridge? she asked herself wryly. Probably not much, she never was one for the moral high ground. So what am I working myself up for now, for heaven's sake?

There was a lot of cooking and cleaning to be done at *Les Romarins*, with the family at home and Elsie preoccupied with her summer visitors. For this Nelly was rather thankful, for it meant that she was busy from morning till night with the daily domestic routines of the lovely old house. Deliberately she chose not to ask for much help from the girls or from Hugo, since by working alone she was able in a strangely comforting way to communicate with her mother once more, by plugging into the ancestral rhythms of her old home.

One afternoon, she was in the kitchen, kneading dough, when a shadow fell across the table and, startled, she looked up to see that Rose du Toit had entered the house without knocking, and now stood confronting her, looking grim. 'Hello, Mrs du Toit,' said Nelly, 'this is an unexpected pleasure.'

'Pleasure is not uppermost in my mind, Mrs Turnbull.'

'Oh, dear, I'm sorry to hear that.'

'Since you are not often here,' Rose continued, her

tone heavy with implied criticism, 'you may not have heard that my boy András is now formally engaged to Madeleine du Toit. The date is set.'

'No,' said Nelly. 'I hadn't heard.'

'The wedding will be the Saturday before Christmas.'

'Really?' Realizing that Rose's visit was unlikely to be brief, Nelly divided her dough, put it into the prepared tins, and put them on the back of the range to rise. 'I was just going to make some tea,' she said. 'Perhaps you'll stay and have a cup with me?'

'No, thank you.'

'Well, do sit down, anyway.' Nelly half-filled the big black kettle and put it on to boil. She spooned tea into the pot and got two mugs from the dresser.

'I said I didn't want any.'

'The second mug is for my husband, Mrs du Toit.'

'Oh.'

Nelly got milk from the fridge and poured it carefully into a jug, aware that she was stalling in her desire to avoid an unpleasant confrontation. She made the tea, and poured out two mugs. 'I won't be a moment,' she said, and left the kitchen, carrying Hugo's tea. She went to the book-room and put the mug on the desk beside him.

'Thanks, love,' he said, without taking his eyes from the screen in front of him.

'Rose du Toit is here, Hugo. I think she intends to give me a roasting about Phylly and András.'

Hugo looked up, surprised. 'Oh, shit, what a pain. Do you want me to come and cope with her?'

'I would like that, very much, but I don't think it would be a good idea. It would look as if I were afraid of her, and also as if I had good reason to be, wouldn't it?'

'Well, yes, I suppose that's true. But if the going gets rough, call me, won't you? After all, it's me that's been interfering in András's life, not you. You've been in London, for weeks.'

'Yes, she managed to get in a dig about me being an absentee wife, practically before she'd got through the door.' She sighed. 'I'd better go; try and sort things out, if I can.'

Back in the kitchen, Nelly sat down at the table and picked up her mug. There was a long silence, during which she drank her tea rather self-consciously and tried to think of something uncontentious to talk about. Rose sat clutching her capacious handbag, her knuckles white with tension, her eyes lowered, her expression sullen. Poor thing, thought Nelly, she really does have problems. With a history like hers, it's hardly surprising. She was just about to say something, when Rose spoke. 'I suppose you think I should be grateful to that journalist friend of yours, for finding my father, after all these years?'

'Well, it is rather exciting, isn't it?'

'Not to me it isn't, and I'll not pretend I'm pleased, because I'm not. Not after fifty-six years of being called a German bastard, I'm not.'

'That's very understandable,' said Nelly quietly. 'It must have been terribly hard for you, growing up in such a situation.' She hesitated, feeling her way. 'But it's all so long ago, does anyone really remember the war, or even think about it any more?'

'Plenty do, by all accounts, else why would they have blabbed to your Russian friend?'

Nelly swallowed nervously. After a moment, she looked at Rose, with a timid smile. 'I expect your mother was glad to hear that Mr Balthus is still alive, though, wasn't she?'

'I don't know if she was, and I don't care. It's down to her if she wants to believe all the lies he's very likely written to her; lies and excuses for letting her down the way he did. He didn't write to *me*,' Rose added resentfully. 'Didn't have the bloody nerve, I dare say.'

'Maybe he was waiting to hear from you first?'

Rose stared at Nelly incredulously. 'Why the hell should *I* want to get in touch with *him*, I should like to know? I'm not one of your crawlers, like András and my mother. I wouldn't demean myself, Mrs Turnbull, sucking up to him and his Italian wife, not for one second I wouldn't.'

'Oh, dear,' said Nelly. 'I'm sorry, I didn't mean . . .'

'In any case,' interrupted Rose. 'That's not what I've come here to discuss.'

Nelly said nothing. It was her turn to stare at her own hands, folded round her mug. She waited uneasily, fearful of what she was about to hear.

'By what right or authority did your bloody interfering husband send my son away to Italy in the company of your daughter, may I ask?'

'Mrs du Toit,' Nelly stammered, then stopped, indecisively. She looked at Rose's implacable face, and quailed inwardly. The last thing she wished to do was add to Rose's evident pain and anger, but equally she felt that she must make some mild defence of Hugo's actions. 'I'm sure my husband meant well,' she said appeasingly. 'After all, András is twenty-three years old; he's not a child any longer, is he? Surely, he's of an age to make his own decisions?'

'And what put that idea into your head?'

'Isn't that what every young person has a right to do?'

'That may be so with your sort,' replied Rose, unimpressed. 'You've got the means for it, haven't you? Your girls will be just like you, won't they? Go away to college, and all that? Do exactly as they please in life?'

'Probably,' said Nelly wearily, 'but what has that to do with András making his own decisions? Is there any reason why he shouldn't, like everyone else?'

'Are you stupid, Mrs Turnbull, or just trying to put me down? That girl of yours has turned his head, as well you know, and now he's trying to wriggle out of his engagement to Madeleine.'

'Mrs du Toit,' said Nelly. 'Phyllida is only eighteen. She's far too young to be seriously involved with anyone, I promise you.'

'That's not the point!' exclaimed Rose. 'I don't give a toss whether they fuck or not, that's what lads do. It's breaking his marriage contract that I'm on about.'

Nelly, thoroughly rattled and rather astonished that Rose should use such offensive language to her in her own kitchen, got to her feet, hoping to bring the interview to an end without further harsh words, but Rose forestalled her. She, too, leapt to her feet, and thumped the table furiously. 'Don't think you can just show me the door, and there's an end of it!' she shouted. 'You're all the same, you people; always have been and always will be. You think that because you've got money, that entitles you to call the shots, tell people what to do, don't you?'

'I certainly don't think that,' said Nelly quietly. 'I never have, and I never will, and neither does my husband.'

'Yes, you bloody do, the both of you.' Rose drew herself up to her considerable height, and looked down at Nelly, her scornful anger filling the kitchen. 'What makes you think your family money gives you the right to rubbish other people, even enticing their kids away, encouraging them to ditch their own kith and kin and try to better themselves, like your precious Hugo has egged on my András, and even sent him off on a posh holiday, too. He'll not be content with the life of a fisherman after that, will he?'

Nelly sighed, tiredly. 'I can understand that it could seem like that to you, Mrs du Toit, and I'm very sorry indeed if it does, I really am. The last thing I would wish to inflict on you is any more pain, or any more trouble, believe me.'

Rose gave a harsh, derisive laugh. 'What a load of bullshit. You're all exactly the same, mealy-mouthed and polite to a fault. You can't even tell the bloody truth as you see it, can you? Your old grandmother was just the same, and your daft old grandad, too. There they were, as comfy as hell, right through the war by all accounts; plenty of food and fuel. They were pretty friendly with the German officers, so the story goes; even invited them to *tea* in this very house.'

'Perhaps they were doing their best not to antagonize the Germans, for everyone's sake?'

'Pull the other one! They were doing what a lot of people did, looking out for number one. Cosying up to the enemy, just like my mum did. Your grandpa and grandma were just as bad as she was; bloody traitors, in fact, the lot of them.'

'How can we know what it was really like, living through the Occupation? I expect everyone had to make some compromises, don't you?'

'It's called *collaboration*,' said Rose, brusquely, 'and that's what the Tanquerays were up to, in my book.'

Nelly, suddenly exhausted, sat down abruptly and put her head in her hands. 'Please, can we stop this?' she asked, wearily. 'It's pointless, and we're getting nowhere.' She looked up, her face drawn, and near to tears. 'I do understand how bitter you must feel; it's perfectly natural. What I don't quite understand is why you seem to think you have a monopoly on suffering, Rose. It's all around us, all the time, isn't it?'

Rose stared down at her arrogantly, her blue eyes icy, her arms crossed, the embodiment of self-righteousness. 'Don't you *dare* call me Rose, you patronizing cow,' she said, her voice cold with disdain. 'You, Nelly Turnbull, are a rich, spoiled tax-dodger. Why, you don't even live here properly. You just flit back when it suits you, don't you? At least old Lady T. was a bit better than that. She was a real islander, for all her posh ways, and that's something you'll never be, not in a million years.' She picked up her bag, turned on her heel, and walked out without another word.

Nelly watched her go. Then she blew her nose, got to her feet, and put her now well-risen loaves into the oven. She set the timer, and turning, saw Hugo standing in the doorway. She smiled wanly. 'Did you hear all that?'

'Quite a bit of it. I kept popping out to listen, just in case she actually attacked you, you poor old thing.'

'Is it too early for a drink, Hugo? I really could do with one.'

'Certainly not,' he replied. 'It has to be six o'clock somewhere.' He got whisky and glasses from the cupboard, and poured a couple of stiff drinks. 'Phylly was right, you know,' he said thoughtfully. 'Sad is the word for her, isn't it?'

'Sad, in the real sense, poor woman, and a bit pathetic.'

'That too,' said Hugo.

Chapter Sixteen

Antonia stood beside a magnificent clump of dahlias, the pretty sunburst kind in shades of yellow and cream, giving the ground a good soaking with the garden hose. This exercise took the best part of an hour each evening, and in view of the fact that their water was metered, was a source of acute though unexpressed financial anxiety to her employer.

Stanley, sitting in a deck-chair under the chestnut tree, raised his eyes from *Paradise Lost* and gazed at Antonia's beautiful bare back. He had an uneasy feeling that all was not well. In this he was not wrong, as he was soon to discover. He cleared his throat. 'Is everything all right, Antonia?'

She stuck the end of the hose into the base of the dahlias, and sat down close to his chair, disposing her sun-tanned slender legs gracefully upon the grass. She looked up at him, lifting the hair from her neck, and smiled. 'I was thinking,' she said, 'how nice it would be to have a holiday, Stanley. What do you think?'

'I suppose we could go to Pembrokeshire. The children still like it there, I think.'

'I wasn't really thinking of Wales, Stanley. Or the children, actually.'

'Oh. What were you thinking of, my dear?'

'I thought, perhaps, Crete? Just you and me, Stanley.'

'It sounds lovely, but what about the children? Wouldn't you like to go on holiday with them? I thought you were fond of them, my dear? They seem to like *you* very much, don't they?'

'Well, yes, I think they do. And I like them, too; of course I do.' Antonia stroked Stanley's bare arm with a slender finger. 'I just thought it would be rather heaven to have some time on our own. Wouldn't you like that, darling?'

'Yes, I would, very much.' Stanley took her hand in his, and kissed it. 'There's nothing I'd like more.' He frowned. 'The children might be a problem, though. We couldn't just leave them here on their own, could we?'

'Aren't there summer camps for teenagers, that sort of thing? Or what about Rachel, couldn't she look after them for a bit? It's her turn, after all, isn't it?'

'Well, she'll be here in a day or two. She's got several weeks' holiday, I understand. I'll ask her.'

'Either that, Stanley,' said Antonia lightly, withdrawing her hand, stretching herself out on the grass and closing her eyes, 'or I'm off.'

Stanley stared at her. 'What do you mean, you're off?'

'I mean, Stanley, that I shall leave; quit; go away; got it?'

'Antonia, are you by any chance threatening me?'

'Yes, Stanley, I am. Unless we have some time on our own, I am leaving. In principle, I have no objection to the kids, in fact I quite like them, but I have absolutely no intention of allowing them to dominate our lives, and turn my house into a teenage hell during the holidays.' She turned her dark, slanted eyes on Stanley, and smiled at him. 'If I were their stepmother, Stanley, it's quite possible that I might feel differently. As things are, I don't.'

At the very idea of having such a wife beside him, as

he advanced in his academic and social career, Stanley's bowels dissolved within him. He cleared his throat. 'Antonia, my love, are you suggesting that I divorce Rachel, and marry you?'

'You got it, Stanley.'

Upstairs, through the open window of Adam's room, the twins and Ciaran had been listening to this conversation. At its conclusion, they stared at each other uncertainly.

'They're planning to get rid of Mum, aren't they?' said Ned.

'It's a gross idea, "stepmother", isn't it?' said Ciaran, sounding alarmed at the thought.

Adam frowned. 'It boils down to a question of which of them we'd rather have, doesn't it?' He paused, his mind working fast as he considered his options. 'As far as Dad's concerned, Antonia wins hands down, it's obvious. She's got him over a barrel,' he said quietly. 'Us too, really.'

'Has she?' asked Ciaran timidly. 'Why do you think that, Adam?'

'Because she's clever, and efficient, and runs this place like clockwork. In five words, Dad couldn't do without her, and neither could we. It's a question of the improved quality of our lives, since she came.'

'But why couldn't *Mum* learn to be like Antonia?' said Ned. 'I bet if she really tried, she could be just as good at cooking, and gardening, and giving parties, all that stuff.' He looked at his siblings, hopefully. 'It's her duty, as a wife and mother, isn't it? It's what mothers are for.'

'But the thing is, Ned,' said Ciaran, 'perhaps Mum doesn't like doing these things any more? And frankly, I don't blame her. There's more to life than housework. You won't catch me doing it.'

'In that case, don't get married,' said Adam

censoriously. 'In Mum's case, she should have thought of that before. The fact is, she is married, and she's got us to consider. It's time she realized that a married woman's place is in the home.'

'You sound just like Dad,' said Ciaran, and giggled nervously.

'Oh, do shut up,' said Adam. 'We must work out a plan, and speak to Mum, as soon as she gets home.'

Three days later, Rachel returned to Lovelace Road for her three weeks' holiday. Simon had gone alone to Sicily, regretting that she felt unable to go with him, but understanding the reason. 'It's only three weeks,' she had said, hugging him.

'Three weeks can be a very long time, Rachel.'

'I know. I'm missing you already, my darling.'

'It's not too late to change your mind.'

'I can't. I must spend time with my children. You know that.'

'Yes, of course you must.'

She took a cab from Oxford station, and arrived home just as the family had finished dinner, and the children were helping Antonia clear the table and tidy up.

'Hello, dear,' said Stanley, setting aside his evening paper, and getting up from his armchair. 'Have you eaten?'

'No, I haven't.' Rachel looked at her watch, surprised that they had already finished supper. 'It's only just gone eight, Stanley. What's going on? Surely we eat at eight, don't we?'

Stanley looked sheepish. 'I'm sorry, dear, but Antonia's going to the cinema with a friend, so she served the meal at seven-fifteen tonight.'

'How very thoughtful of her, and of you, Stanley. Was it absolutely out of the question to keep the food on hold until I got home?'

'I'm sorry, dear. It was out of my hands, I'm afraid.'

'OK, never mind. I'll make myself an omelette, or would I be messing up the kitchen?'

'Better wait till she's gone, dear.'

'For heaven's *sake*, Stanley! Who's the boss here, or is that a rhetorical question? Where are the car keys? I'll go and buy myself a take-away.'

Silently, Stanley took the keys from his pocket and handed them over. With a grim expression on her face, Rachel took them. In the hall, she called 'Ciaran! Come here, please, darling.'

Ciaran appeared in the kitchen doorway, clutching a tea towel. 'Mum! We didn't hear you arrive!'

'Put down that cloth, and come with me, darling.'

'I can't. I haven't finished drying up the saucepans yet.'

'Do as I say, please.'

Ciaran hesitated briefly, then threw the cloth into the kitchen and followed her mother out to the car. Rachel drove out of the drive and turned towards the town centre. Mother and daughter grinned at each other. 'The hell with a take-away,' said Rachel, 'let's have supper in a restaurant, shall we? Could you manage another dinner, darling?'

'Easily,' said Ciaran, and laughed.

It was Adam who masterminded the conference between Rachel and her children, during which he intended to negotiate her return to the bosom of the family, under certain strictly laid-down conditions. 'The thing is, Mum,' he said solemnly, opening the proceedings, as the four of them crowded together in his bedroom. 'The thing is, one has to recognize the fact that Antonia is very well organized, very good at cooking and cleaning, all that stuff.'

'Better than me?'

'In a word, yes.'

'She's really ace at other things, too,' said Ned. 'Specially the CD-ROM. There's not a lot she doesn't know in that department.'

'Poor soul,' murmured Rachel, with an ironic little smile, 'how very dull for her.'

'Oh, *Mum*!' cried Ciaran, provoked by her mother's lack of gravitas; 'it's not at all dull; it's *vital*! No-one can succeed without technology nowadays. You must try and get your head round it.'

'Why should I, if I don't find it particularly rewarding? In any case, with such a technological wizard on permanent call, what's the problem? You don't need *me*, that's for sure.'

Ned looked at her, his black hair sticking up on the crown of his head, his dark Welsh eyes intense, the image of the young Stanley. 'But that's the point, Mum, we *do* need you.'

'Nonsense! Of course you don't,' said Rachel.

'You don't even try to understand, do you?' Ned wagged a reproving finger at her. 'Or are you being deliberately obtuse?'

'What about?'

'About Dad and Antonia, of course.'

'What about them?'

'They *sleep together*!' said Ciaran. 'I thought you knew that?'

'Yes,' said Rachel. 'I've known for some time, as a matter of fact.'

Silence. Then Adam spoke. 'Aren't you humiliated, or even angry?'

'No, not really. Your father has made such a thorough job of breaking my spirit that any love I originally had for him must have withered and died long ago.' Rachel looked at her three children with affection and sympathy as she watched them digest this unpalatable fact.

'Is that what always happens, when you've been

married a long time?' asked Ciaran, wiping her nose with the back of her hand.

'Quite often, I expect, but not always. I think lots of couples have very long and happy relationships.'

'Oh.'

'Be that as it may, Mum,' said Adam in his most priggish tones, 'it is a most unsatisfactory situation for us three, not to say an immoral one.' He glanced at his siblings for support. 'We all think you should resign from your job, and resume your rightful place in this house, as wife and mother. Especially the latter; it's your duty, you owe it to us.'

'Really?' Rachel laughed. 'And what do you propose to do about Antonia?'

'Tell her to leave,' said Ned.

'I see. And then what happens?'

'You come home, of course, Mum. This is where you belong, after all.'

'Let me see,' said Rachel slowly. 'You are all demanding that I give up my most interesting, rewarding and quite well-paid job, in order to resume my former boring and frustrating occupation as an unpaid domestic in this house, in spite of the fact that Antonia does the job a great deal better than I do. Is that right?'

'Yes.' Ned and Ciaran spoke as one.

'You needn't worry about not being as good as Antonia, Mum,' Adam assured her. 'I'm sure there are courses you could take in domestic economy, and proper real gourmet cooking, too, I dare say.'

'You could learn computer literacy, too, Mum, in your spare time,' added Ned enthusiastically. 'There are plenty of technical magazines in the shops; you'd soon catch up, if you tried hard enough.'

Resolutely, Rachel folded her arms. 'No,' she said firmly.

'But *Mum*! It's not *fair*!' A whining note crept into Adam's voice. In view of his failure to bounce Rachel into compliance, he quickly perceived that blackmail might prove a more effective persuader. 'If you really, really loved us, you wouldn't refuse to come home and take care of us, would you?'

'It depends what you mean by "taking care", Adam. I've learnt quite a few things since I've been working, and one of them is that caring for people should be a two-way thing; not only giving, but a bit of receiving as well. Otherwise, it finally boils down to a question of bullying, doesn't it?'

'Bullying?' exclaimed Adam, impatiently. 'What the hell are you talking about?'

'I mean, that if one person in a family, usually the mother, is expected to cook and clean, as well as doing the washing and ironing for everyone, with no time to call her own, and no money of her own either, then she is allowing herself to be bullied.'

'But that's your *duty*. It's what you're for.'

'Do you really think so, Adam?'

'Yes, Mum, I do.'

Appalled at the breathtaking selfishness and sheer brass neck of her children, even the gentle Ciaran, Rachel got to her feet. 'Clearly,' she said, 'this is a situation that needs sorting out, and I can see that there are no easy solutions. The rather crass and simplistic one you seem to have in mind is, to put it mildly, a complete non-starter, so don't hold your breath — you'll be wasting your time as well as mine.'

At the door she paused, her hand on the knob. 'I *had* hoped that you would all be pleased that I had three weeks' holiday, just so that we could spend a bit of time together. It appears that I was mistaken; all you're interested in is a rather crude attempt to turn me into a skivvy again.'

'Don't say that, Mum,' said Ciaran. 'It wasn't meant like that, honestly.'

'Think about it,' said Rachel, and left the room.

* * *

Depressed beyond belief by her children's low estimation of her competence, their dismissive lack of interest in her job, and their ability to rubbish its value and significance to her as a human being, Rachel left the house and went into town. She walked down St Giles', turned into Beaumont Street and entered the Ashmolean Museum. Feeling hot from her brisk walk, upset and missing Simon badly, she made her way to the little gallery that housed the works of Samuel Palmer.

It was cool in the dimly lit room, and she paused before each small exquisite painting, lifting the protective covers that shielded the fragile images from exposure to daylight. How I love these peaceful landscapes, she said to herself, with their gentle hills, and sheep under the sheltering clumps of trees; but mostly it's the light that's so enchanting. Moonlight or sunlight, breaking through great banks of cloud, shimmering like frost on the backs of the sheep or the rounded shapes of the hills, that's the genius bit, that's what makes them glow, and come alive.

She sat down on a bench and closed her eyes, soothed by the calm empty space and the eternal truths so clearly demonstrated in Palmer's paintings. They're not at all like St Cuthbert's Fen, she thought, but the *feeling* is the same; the big skies, the quality of remoteness and simplicity, a lost world, by today's standards. How strange, she said to herself, I grew up in a world like that, and then I lost it when I married Stanley. Now I've found it again, partly on my own, but mostly because of Simon. It was he who opened my eyes, and my heart, to what is real, beautiful, worth keeping and worth fighting for. Remembering the night on the balcony at *La Felicità,* the scented starlit garden, the nightingale's lament, and the man she loved holding her in his arms for the first time, Rachel experienced a sharp pang of loneliness, a desolation of her spirit, but also a recognition that she had at last broken free from the fetters of a loveless and philistine existence, and had willingly committed herself to the emotional tightrope of a real and powerful attachment.

She opened her eyes, disturbed by the entrance of an elderly man, accompanied by a small girl. Evidently, he knew the pictures well, for he answered the child's questions about them with patience and authority. Why didn't I try harder to do this kind of thing with my own children when they were little, she asked herself; especially with Ciaran? Perhaps it's not only Stanley who's to blame for their lack of sensitivity; their dogged determination to win; to be top in exams and get scholarships and stuff like that. Perhaps I could have tried harder myself to show them that there's a beautiful, secret world outside the bloody CD-ROM and the boring old Internet; a world of good simple things like ploughed fields, olive groves and vineyards, and work done as much for the love of it as for money. Of course, that's what I should have done, but how could I when I was so bogged down, allowing myself to be victimized, with scarcely a moment to think rationally, much less act on it?

Rachel remained on her bench all afternoon, then got up and went quietly back to the house. She found Stanley in the garden, playing bridge with the children. They had not missed her; they did not even look up from their cards as she sat down on the parched grass beside them. She waited until the rubber was finished, then spoke. 'Stanley, I've decided to take the children to St Cuthbert's Fen. It's time they saw my home, and understood my background. We'll go tomorrow, so I'll need the car.'

The children stared at her, astonished and speechless. 'You'd better go and pack what you need,' she said briskly. 'We'll start at six o'clock, OK? Don't forget your sleeping-bags.'

Stanley, perceiving instantly that Rachel's plan would serve to kill several annoying birds with one glorious stone, and visualizing himself on holiday with Antonia, readily agreed to let her have the car. With his family out of the way, he would lose no time in consulting his lawyers about the question of a divorce, and booking a flight to Crete.

Rachel and her children arrived at the farm a little before five o'clock, after a long and tiring journey. They had stopped for lunch and a break in Cambridge, and had looked in at the gatehouses of several colleges. Neither of the boys seemed inclined to show any interest in them, Adam remarking glumly that Cambridge seemed to him rather a provincial little place, compared with Oxford. He and Ned had then opted to remain in the car, while their mother and sister did a swift shop in a supermarket.

Rachel drove out of Cambridge and took the Ely road. 'Would you like to see the cathedral?' she offered, as they approached the city.

'Not particularly,' said Adam. 'What about you, Ned?'

'No, thanks.'

'I'd like to see it, please.' Ciaran sounded rather faint-hearted.

Rachel glanced at her. 'You're tired, darling, aren't you? We'll come another day; make a special journey, just us two, shall we?'

'Thanks, Mum, that'd be good.'

In five minutes they had left Ely behind and were on a minor road, heading for Deeping St Cuthbert. As they drove across the flatlands all three children fell silent, as if the unbroken endless fields and fens around them, and the distant shimmering horizons were alien to

302

them, and made them uneasy. At Deeping St Cuthbert, Rachel stopped beside the village petrol pump. It was an old-fashioned apparatus operated by an elderly woman, wearing a flower-sprigged apron and a cloth cap. 'Is this it?' asked Ned. 'Are we there?'

'Nearly,' said Rachel, and got out of the car to pay for the petrol in the post office. While she was there, she bought a packet of firelighters and a copy of the *Sun*, not to read, but in case she had forgotten to leave paper ready beside the Dover stove. She also bought some Mars bars, in order to raise the spirits of her passengers. These she distributed when she got back into the car, and they thanked her politely. She did a U-turn in the quiet High Street, and after a few yards turned into the single-track road that led to St Cuthbert's Fen. In ten minutes the car rattled over the cattle-grid, then came to a stop beside the midden. 'Here we are,' Rachel said, and turned off the engine. 'By the way, if anyone needs the loo, it's a long-drop. It's round the back, in a clapboard shed; you can't miss it.'

This announcement was greeted with an embarrassed silence. The children got out of the car and looked around them, inspecting the shambolic little house, the barn, and the quiet flat fields.

'I thought you said your father had a farm, Mum?'

'He did, Adam. This is it.'

Adam frowned. 'But farms are big agro-industrial estates, aren't they?'

'Not all of them. Some are very small.'

'I suppose it should properly be considered a smallholding, actually?'

'Adam,' said Rachel, with a touch of asperity. 'You can call it anything you like, a shit-hole even, if it satisfies your passion for concise definitions. But I shall continue to think of it as my father's farm, and call it what it's always been called, St Cuthbert's Fen.'

So there, you silly little prat, she felt like adding, but did not.

'Aren't there any animals?' asked Ned, trying to gloss over his brother's indiscretion.

'Not now, Ned. There used to be. Pigs and poultry, and in my grandparents' time they had a pair of heavy horses to pull the plough and the harrow.'

'Where were the pigs?'

'In that barn, but I sold them after my father died.'

'Oh.'

'Did you sell the chickens, too?' asked Ciaran.

'No, I gave them away.'

Adam, looking sulky, took the bags from the boot of the car. 'Where do you want these, Mum?' he mumbled.

'In the house, upstairs, please. Hang on, while I open the door.' She unlocked the door, and they all trooped into the kitchen. 'Put my bag in the front bedroom, Adam, please. You and Ned will have to share one of the two back rooms, so put Ciaran's things in the other one, OK?'

Ned opened the small boarded door to the narrow staircase, and the boys carried the luggage and sleeping-bags upstairs.

'*Boys*!' remarked Ciaran, grinning. 'They're deeply sad, aren't they? Specially Adam?'

'Adolescence is a difficult time, darling. Their hormones are all up the creek. I expect they'll grow out of it, eventually.'

'Not all of them do,' said Ciaran darkly. 'Some men are still pretty adolescent at forty, aren't they?'

'You've noticed?' Rachel laughed. She opened the kitchen windows, and the cool sweet air flowed into the room.

'Is this where my grandfather died?' asked Ciaran. 'In this very room?'

'Yes, darling, it is.' Rachel lifted the bags of groceries onto the table and began to unpack them. She pointed to the far end of the room, where her father's sickbed had been. 'The nurses brought one of the old iron beds down and erected it over there, so that he could be kept warm. It made it easier for them to nurse him, too.'

'Was it awful, Mum?'

'No, Ciaran, it wasn't awful, but it was pretty heart-breaking. I was very glad that I could stay with him, and look after him at such an important time.'

'Yes, I see.' Ciaran leaned against the table. 'I'm quite sorry I didn't know Grandpa, it would have been nice,' she said. 'Have you got any pictures of him, Mum?'

'Yes, I have a few, when he was young and married my mother.'

'Was she beautiful, your mum?'

'Yes, she was, but I don't remember her at all, darling. She died when I was born.'

'*Died*? When you were *born*?'

'Yes.'

'How terrible. Poor you.'

'I think it must have been terrible for my poor father, but I was hardly in a position to notice.'

'No, you wouldn't have been.'

Adam and Ned clumped down the wooden stairs and came into the kitchen. 'The bed in your room is already made up,' said Adam, 'but there's just iron beds and some rather revolting old mattresses in ours.'

'I know,' agreed Rachel. 'They are a bit ghastly. We'd better make a bonfire tomorrow, and burn them. Then we can drive into Ely and try and buy some new ones.'

'Wouldn't that cost an awful lot?' Ned looked worried, as if his mother was about to do something extremely rash.

'Yes, I expect it will,' said Rachel cheerfully. 'But if I'm going to live here eventually, I'll have to start replacing pathetic old objects like those mattresses, won't I?'

305

'*Live* here, Mum?' Adam looked horrified. 'You can't be serious?'

'I am, perfectly.'

'But it's a *slum*, to all intents and purposes, there isn't even a proper loo.' Adam's voice cracked, as his anxiety levels rose. 'Dad would be shattered if he saw it; you must know that. If the authorities saw this place, I'm sure they'd say it was unfit for human habitation, and put a demolition order on it.'

The three young people stared at their mother, Ned and Ciaran a little apprehensively, but Adam with a black determined hostility. Rachel looked from one to the other, apparently quite unruffled by this condemnation of her family home. Ignoring Adam, she turned to Ned. 'Take that basket, Ned, and get me some logs, will you? They're in a shed, behind the barn.'

Looking relieved, Ned did as he was asked, and vanished quickly through the door.

'Ciaran, could you riddle out the ashes in the stove? Then you can put in a firelighter and some kindling, and light it. The oven should be hot by seven, and we can cook supper.'

'Cool!' said Ciaran. 'Does that old-fashioned thing still work?'

'Certainly does. How else do you think we kept from freezing to death in the winter?'

Ciaran opened the iron doors to the grate and began to rake out the ashes and clinker into the tray beneath.

'Sit down, Adam,' said Rachel quietly, seating herself at the table. He sat, his face sullen and miserable, refusing to meet her eye. 'This visit is just an experiment, you know,' she said. 'We'll only be here for a couple of weeks, but if you really hate it so much, and aren't prepared to pitch in and give it a chance, then I'll give you the train fare, and you can go back to Oxford whenever you like. It's entirely down to you.'

'Dad wouldn't like it,' he muttered, red-faced, scarcely audible.

'Why not?'

'Because.'

'Adam,' said Rachel, sighing. 'Why wouldn't he like it?'

'Because of Antonia, of course. Don't you understand that, Mum?' He looked at her then, his dark eyes suddenly filled with tears of jealousy and self-pity. 'He doesn't want *us* there, does he? If you were in his shoes, you wouldn't either, would you?'

'Yes, I do see that.'

'*He* doesn't want us,' he said, trying in vain to choke back his tears, 'and now *you* want to chuck me out!'

'Adam,' said Rachel, resisting the urge to put her arms round him and hug him, 'that is arrant nonsense. I *do* want you here, very much, but you'll have to stop picking on everything if we're going to enjoy ourselves.' She put her hand gently on his tear-splashed one. 'I have feelings too, you know, darling.'

Adam stumbled to his feet. 'I'll go and help Ned with the logs.'

'Better still, take that bucket and get water from the well, if you wouldn't mind?'

Rachel waited for Adam to express astonishment that the farm was not connected to the mains water supply, but he did not. He picked up the bucket and went to the door. On the threshold he paused and turned towards her, frowning.

'How many pigs did Grandfather have, Mum?'

'About fifty, at any one time.'

'Did he have to carry all their water from the well?'

'Certainly.'

'And did *you* do that, last winter, before you sold them?'

'Yes, of course. There was no other way.'

'I see.' Without another word he went out to the

well, and presently Rachel heard the creak of the chain as Adam turned the wheel that hauled up the bucket.

'He'll be all right now, Mum, you'll see,' said Ciaran, cracking kindling over her knee.

'I hope,' said Rachel, and uncorked a bottle of wine.

Things could only get better, and they did. The next day they drove into Ely, and Rachel bought three new mattresses and some pillows, as well as sheets and pillowcases.

'Mum,' said Adam suddenly, 'would it be a good idea if I painted the kitchen? Or would you hate that?'

'I don't know,' said Rachel truthfully. 'I wouldn't want its character changed or anything.' She looked at Adam, realizing that he was doing his best to please her. 'You're right, the walls are pretty dingy, a couple of coats of limewash would be an improvement. Let's look for a builder's merchant, a proper old-fashioned one that still stocks that kind of thing.'

They found the builder's merchant, and bought a sack of lime, with brushes, scrapers, masks and several pairs of heavy-duty gloves. 'This stuff is lethal if you get it on your skin, I seem to remember, Adam. So for heaven's sake please be careful.'

'Can I help?' asked Ned, impressed by all the technical equipment.

'Yes, but Adam is in charge, OK?'

It took two days to prepare the kitchen walls, and another two days to apply the limewash. Rachel and Ciaran set up the kitchen table under the trees behind the house, and all the meals were prepared and eaten there, away from the chaos indoors.

Each evening, they walked through the flowering meadows to bathe in the shallow waters of the small brook that bordered the Cropthorne land. 'We used to have a little pond here, when my dad had a few cows,' said Rachel. 'It must have got filled in. The dam broke down, I suppose. I can't remember.'

Ned's eyes shone. 'Would it be OK to make another one, Mum? Big enough to swim in?'

Rachel laughed. 'Why not? It'd be jolly hard work though, wouldn't it?'

A week of swelteringly hot days passed. The kitchen painting was finished, the floor scrubbed and waxed and the furniture moved back indoors. The excavation of the pond began. Adam and Ned dug out the hole, and Rachel and Ciaran carried the spoil away in the wheelbarrow, and dumped it around the edge of the pond to form a sloping bank.

The two boys redirected the brook to flow into the hole and then, once the pond was full, out again on the opposite side, over a dam made from timber and clay. The pond took two full days to fill, and on the evening of the second day they had their first swim. The water was still pretty cloudy, but deliciously soothing on their sunburnt bodies. 'It's great here, Mum,' said Adam. 'I'm glad we came.'

'So'm I,' agreed Ned. 'It's much more fun than Oxford.'

'Good,' said Rachel. She got out of the pool, unpeeled the top of her swimsuit, and pulled on her T-shirt. 'Why don't we have our supper down here? I'll start getting it together, if some of you could come and carry things in twenty minutes or so?'

She walked slowly back to the house, through the long grass, happy and pleased that the holiday had not, after all, been a disaster. She went in at the back door and immediately, through the kitchen window, she saw Simon's car, with Simon standing beside it. She ran out to the yard, and into his outstretched arms.

'What happened?' she said. 'Why are you here?'

'I came back,' he said, and kissed her. 'I missed you too much, so here I am.'

'How did you know I was here?'

'I rang up Oxford, but there was no reply. I guessed you'd be here.' He kissed her again.

'The children are here with me, Simon.'

'So? I've got to meet them sometime, haven't I? What's the problem?'

Chapter Seventeen

András and Phyllida touched down in Pisa in mid-afternoon, and decided to hitchhike to San Gimignano. From there they took a slow bus to *Cappella della Vigna*, arriving in the late evening. Like Simon and Rachel before them, they walked the last few hundred metres across the narrow valley and through the olive trees. As they approached the chapel the self-important and noisy little pugs appeared, followed at once by a tall, thin, sunburned, white-haired man, whose blue eyes exactly matched the linen of his shirt.

'Is it András?' he asked.

'It is,' András replied quietly. 'Is it my grandfather, Werner Balthus?'

The elderly man came towards them, and took András's hands in his. 'I would have recognized you anywhere, my dear boy.' He smiled and shook his head. 'It's such a strange feeling to see you; it's like looking at the ghost of myself as a soldier.'

'I know.'

'How can you know?'

'My grandmother has photographs of you, taken when you were in Florizel.'

'Ah, yes! Of course!' He released András's hands and turned to Phyllida. 'I beg your pardon, my dear young lady; how impolite of me. It is Miss Turnbull, of course?'

'Phyllida, please.' She held out her hand. 'How do you do?'

Werner Balthus took her hand and, bending from the waist, kissed it. 'Welcome to *Cappella della Vigna*, both of you. Come, let us go in to Chiara.'

They found Chiara sitting on the terrace, a glass of wine in her hand. She was wearing a long, loose robe of multicoloured Indian silk, and a heavy silver necklace. A turban of golden gauze was wound round her head, and fastened with a silver and amethyst brooch. Her dark Italian eyes illuminated her long narrow face, and her skin was so deeply tanned that she might easily have passed for an Indian. She rose gracefully from her seat, screamed at the dogs to lie down, and offered wine to the travellers.

Phyllida slipped off her backpack and sank gratefully into a deep rattan chair, exhausted by the many hours of travelling, but delighted to have at last arrived in this enchanting place. She looked around her, extremely impressed by the originality of the house and the tranquil beauty of the garden. Werner brought her a glass of wine and she took it, smiling her thanks. 'What a lovely place this is,' she said. 'Have you lived here long?'

'About ten years,' he replied. 'Since my wife and I were married. It was derelict, a ruin, when we found it. It took a year to restore, but it was worth it, I think.'

'It certainly was.' Phyllida indicated the wall of sliding glass panels that separated the terrace from the interior living space. 'Are you an architect?' she asked.

'No, not at all.' He took a sip of his drink, and smiled. 'I'm afraid my working life has been one of spectacular uneventfulness,' he said. 'I was a very ordinary translator of English technical books into German until my retirement. Then I came to Tuscany and met Chiara.' He looked towards his wife, who was chatting animatedly to András. 'She has completely

312

transformed my life, I need hardly tell you. She is a most exceptional person.'

'Yes,' said Phylly. 'I can see that she is.'

Chiara got to her feet. 'Come,' she said, 'the supper will be soon ready, and I expect you'll like to have a wash and so forth. Werner, show them the guest-house, will you, *caro*?'

To the slight surprise of András and Phyllida, Werner led the way to the far end of the garden, to a stone columbarium, half-smothered by a venerable fig, and shaded by an exotic clump of tall rustling palm trees. He pushed open the creaking wooden door, and made his way in the gloom to a table, on which stood a storm lantern. He struck a match and lit the lamp, and it bloomed softly in the darkness, revealing the circular inner walls of the former dovecote. These had been fitted with tiers of shelves, which housed many hundreds, maybe thousands of books. In the middle of the floor was a large rag rug, and on it stood a sofa bed and a low table. A long wooden ladder was propped against the open trapdoor to the upper floor. 'Your bed is up there, András.' Werner pointed to the trapdoor. 'I hope you will be comfortable, both of you.'

'I'm sure we will be,' said Phyllida. 'It's lovely.'

Werner showed them the garden hose attached to a tap on the outside wall of the columbarium. 'This is for washing, you understand?' He made a deprecating little gesture with his hand. 'If you suffer the inconvenience of a call of nature in the night, it's a question of, so to say, going *à la belle étoile.*'

András and Phyllida laughed, and assured him that they would manage very well, and he left them alone to prepare for supper.

'What a dear man,' said Phylly.

'Do you really think so?'

'Yes, I do. Don't you?'

'I don't know. I think so.' András looked at her. 'It's

such an unsettling feeling, knowing that he's my mother's father and my grandfather, and at the same time seeing him so obviously attached to that extraordinary wife, Chiara. He doesn't hide his feelings in any way, does he?'

'No, he doesn't. He's a truly honest man, don't you think?'

Chiara served the dinner in the long book-lined room, originally the nave of the chapel. They sat at the round library table of limed oak, and ate a dish of *Nocciole d'Agnello*, with artichoke hearts in a herb-scented sauce, followed by some salty mountain cheese and a bowl of purple figs, exploding with ripeness, revealing their glorious pink interiors. The bread was a local country loaf, crisp on the outside, smoke-blackened from the wood-fired oven, but moist and fragrant with virgin oil within. They drank a Tuscan *classico*, mellow and full of fruit, served in blue Venetian glasses which turned the red wine into a sombre purple.

After dinner, Chiara brought a tray of coffee and two cups out to the terrace. 'Werner, *caro*,' she said, 'you and András have much to talk about, I feel sure, so why don't you have your coffee out here? Phyllida and I will clear away the dishes, and leave you two in peace.'

Feeling tired, slightly drunk but much more relaxed, András sat down on the chair next to Werner, and drank his coffee. The air was incredibly soft, sweet-smelling, the only sound the occasional thump of a moth as it blundered into the lamp. Down among the trees, tiny points of green light floated in the darkness.

'*Gluhwürmchen*,' said Werner. 'Fireflies, I think you say?'

'Tell me about the war,' said András suddenly. 'That is, if you can bear to?'

'You mean, after I left Florizel?'

'Yes.'

'It's so long ago, that sometimes I can't absolutely remember the exact sequence of events, but, of course, in the beginning we were taken back to Germany. It was January, there was a lot of snow; it took three days, maybe more, to get across France and into Germany. There, we were issued with special uniforms for the snow – white overalls with hoods, that sort of thing. Then we had a forty-eight-hour leave. I went to Dresden, my home town, to see my parents and my little sister. It was the last time I saw them. I was your age, András, just twenty-three, and my sister Ulla was sixteen. My father was a history teacher. We went for a walk together on my last night. I remember it was very cold; the sky was a mass of stars, and there was a moon. "Just the night for the bombers, *nicht*?" my father said. Then he asked me if I was being posted to the Eastern front. I said I'm not supposed to say anything, but I think so. The next day I rejoined my unit and we started the awful journey to Stalingrad. I was a driver in a transport regiment; it was our job to carry supplies to the front. There were two of us in the truck, and we did several trips, dumping the stuff at various places on the way to the front, then driving back to base as fast as we could for a fresh load, taking turns to drive. The weather was appalling, deep frozen snow everywhere. I never got really close to the fighting, but we could see the flash of the guns at night, and hear them all the time. How the Russians stood up to that terrible bombardment, I'll never know.' Werner shook his head at the recollection, and András saw in his blue eyes the pain of that memory. 'Rumours were flying everywhere. We heard that our army had been defeated at Leningrad, that the Americans had dropped fire-bombs on Germany, that the British Eighth Army had taken Tripoli. It was very frightening, it seemed that we were being destroyed from every side. On the thirty-first of January we heard that our army, what was left of it, had surrendered to the Russians at Stalingrad. We didn't wait to find out if this was true; we turned the truck round, and drove like hell, until we ran out of petrol. We decided to split up, and try to walk back to Germany across country. I was aiming for Poland, mainly because Dresden was quite near the Polish border with Germany. It was difficult to decide what to do. I had heard of the terrible acts of vengeance that the Russians were inflicting on their German prisoners, and now, of course, I know that these reprisals were a justifiable retaliation for the appalling atrocities of the Germans against the Russians.' Werner gazed steadily at András, his face gaunt. 'At that time I did not realize that the long trains one had seen from time to time, ostensibly carrying Jewish people to work in forced-labour camps, were in fact transporting those doomed, desperate families to the death-camps in Belsen, Auschwitz and Treblinka.'

'You really didn't know about the Holocaust?'

'No, not until much later on, when the British entered Belsen, and the whole world knew about it. You see, those poor families carried luggage with them, and it never occurred to me that it was all an elaborate charade, designed to encourage them to get into the railway trucks without resistance. You know, András, I thought that Germany was a civilized country, proud of its culture; it never crossed my mind that a people like us could bring themselves to commit such frightful acts of brutality against other human beings.'

'But what about the *Organisation Todt,* on Florizel? You must have known how badly the Russian and French slave labour was treated by them?'

'Yes, that's true,' said Werner quietly. 'We did know. I suppose one tried to ignore it; look the other way.'

'Just as the islanders did, for the most part, so my grandmother told me.'

Werner sighed. 'I suppose so, András. One is not proud of it.'

'No, of course not.' András shifted in his chair, not wishing to distress his grandfather more than necessary, but nonetheless anxious to hear the rest of the story. 'So, how long did it take you to walk back to Germany?'

'It must have been nearly two years. I only walked at night, and hid up during the day. I was terrified of speaking to anyone. I lived on berries and grass, and sometimes I stole root vegetables from a field, or, in summer, fruit from an orchard. I knew that the east was behind me, because that was where the sun came up, and the west was in front of me, where the sun went down. Quite early on, in the forest, I came across three corpses hanging from the branch of a tree. It was moonlight, and it was the most frightening thing I ever saw, at least I thought so at the time. I cut down the dead men, and tried to bury them under leaves and moss and branches. I took some clothes from them, trousers and a jacket, boots, everything. I buried my uniform, after I'd ripped out all the badges and marks of identity. Those men must have been dead for some time; they were quite withered and dried-up, like leather, almost skeletons, though they still smelt pretty bad, poor things. Anyway, thanks to them, I felt less conspicuous dressed as a civilian, and I got eventually to Poland, and then crossed the border to Dresden. That was at the end of February 1945.'

'So you managed to get home in the end?'

'Not exactly, András.' Werner passed a hand across his eyes. 'You see, when I got there, I found Dresden in ruins, completely burnt out, still smoking, unrecognizable. The Allies had fire-bombed the city on St Valentine's Day. Ironic, wasn't it?'

'God, how terrible. What happened to your family?'

'They were all killed; burned alive, I suppose. Not a single person I knew was left. I was twenty-four years old by then, but it was the end of the world as far as I was concerned. I just sat down in the blackened ruins of my father's house and cried like a child.'

After a short silence, András spoke quietly. 'So what did you do after that?'

'It was chaos. The Russians were advancing from the east, the Americans and the British from the west. People were doing their damnedest not to fall into Russian hands, you understand, so one kept running towards the west. When the peace was declared on the eighth of May, I had got as far as the suburbs of Munich, and there I stayed. It wasn't easy. I got several jobs as a casual labourer, with no questions asked. I was still very frightened of being picked up and shot as an army deserter, you understand. Eventually, after another year had passed, I obtained work as a freelance translator of technical books and tried to rebuild my life.'

'You never thought of going back to Florizel?'

'How could I? My happy stay there seemed as though it had never happened, after so long and ter- rible a time had passed, and in any case, I was quite sure that even if I had tried to go there, a visit would be most unwelcome. By now, the trials of the war criminals at Nuremberg had taken place, and everyone knew the truth about the Nazis. I had no reason to believe that my friends in Florizel would feel any great desire to see me again.'

'Yes, I see. So what did you do next?'

'I carried on with the translation job for forty years or so. I lived alone, spending very little money, living very simply in my small flat, where I worked, ate and slept. I saved most of my earnings, until I thought I had enough to stop working and retire. By then, the

Germans were no longer treated as moral lepers wherever they went, so I did what I had so often dreamed of in the cold northern winters; I travelled south, to Italy and the sunshine. I cashed my savings; disposed of the lease of my flat, and left Munich for ever, without leaving a forwarding address. I travelled by train, with just one small suitcase, first to Trieste, where I lived in a *pensione* for three months, and then to Venice, Bologna, Florence and in the end to San Gimignano, where I met Chiara in her bookshop. My German marks bought a lot of Italian lire, and it enabled us to buy this little chapel together. Then we did the work, and we've been here ever since.'

'How was it that you were able to disappear so completely? What about your social security pension, that kind of thing?'

Werner smiled. 'When I was living in Trieste I arranged to have the pension sent to a *fermo posta* there. I still have the box, and we go up there every three or four months to collect the cheques. It's probably rather ridiculous now, but it makes a good excuse for us to have a little touring holiday.'

It was András's turn to smile. 'But why so much secrecy?'

'I don't know. I suppose I was anxious to bury the past when I left, and it seemed like a good idea at the time. I quite liked the feeling of no-one knowing where I was; it allowed me to feel free, and I've never particularly felt like changing the arrangement.'

'But you didn't mind your picture being in that magazine article?'

Werner looked surprised, then laughed. 'No, you're right. I didn't, not at all.' He looked at András, seriously. 'It's curious, but I feel very safe here, with Chiara. It's as if I'd mentally stopped running, if you know what I mean?'

András nodded. 'I think I do, yes.' He looked at his

grandfather, who lay back against the cushions of his chair, looking tired but serene. 'I'm very glad you did agree to the article, or I'd never have found you, would I?'

'And now that you've found me, András, are you happy about it?'

'Very happy, and so is my grandmother.'

'And your mother, András? What of her feelings? She did not write to me. She is not so happy, I think?'

'No, I'm afraid she's not.' András looked at his grandfather. 'Perhaps if you came to Florizel, and went to see her, she might feel differently.'

'That's exactly what Chiara thinks. She is already making plans for us to do that.'

'Is she really? How very understanding of her.'

'When you know her better, you'll see that for her such an idea makes perfect sense.' Werner got stiffly to his feet. 'Shall we go in and join them?'

Phyllida woke at five o'clock the next morning, as the first pale light of dawn pierced the holes in the walls of the columbarium. She lay quietly, with her eyes closed, listening to the sound of rain on the roof, and the birds in the garden breaking the silence of the night, one by one. Suddenly, she was startled by the sound of the door opening, and, sitting up, saw that András had entered the room. 'Sorry if I frightened you, Phylly,' he said. 'I had to go out for a pee.'

She saw at once that he looked upset, his face red and blotchy, as though he had been weeping. 'Is anything the matter?' she asked. 'Aren't you feeling well?'

'I'm OK,' he replied. 'Just can't sleep, that's all.' He closed the door, then sat down on the foot of Phyllida's bed. 'I keep remembering all the terrible things my grandfather was telling me, about the war.' He folded his arms tightly across his chest to stop himself trembling, and looked at her, his eyes full of anguish. 'Do you know, Phylly, he actually walked across Poland wearing clothes he had stolen from the dead body of a hanged man. How could he have done that?'

'Desperation, I should think, poor guy,' said Phyllida. 'The executed man didn't need the clothes any longer, did he? Your grandfather did.'

'So you don't think that was a cowardly and evil thing to do?' András hung his head, his voice muffled, thick with tears.

'No, of course not, András. Don't be silly.'

'*Silly?* Don't treat me like a child, Phylly.' He turned away, the tears now falling unchecked down his distraught face.

Phyllida, suddenly feeling a great deal older and wiser than her eighteen years, pushed back the covers, put her arms round his cold, shaking shoulders and held him tightly. 'My poor darling,' she said. 'You're soaked and freezing. How long have you been outside, for heaven's sake? Take off those wet things, at once.'

Exhausted, obedient, András took off his T-shirt and pants.

'Now, get into bed with me, and get warm.'

'Phylly, you're bossing me,' said András, without much conviction. He got into bed and Phylly lay down beside him, pulling the coverlet over them both, then wound her arms around his chilled body, holding him close to her. They lay together, wrapped in each other's arms, until the shuddering ceased and their two enfolded bodies felt warm and relaxed.

'András,' whispered Phyllida. 'I *never* mean to treat you like child; not now, and not ever.' She lifted her hands to his face and kissed him. His arms tightened round her, and his response was immediate, urgent and total.

Much later, they slept, and when they woke, the sun was already hot.

* * *

After a late breakfast on the terrace, Chiara, sensing that Werner would appreciate more time alone with his grandson, suggested to Phyllida that she might like to accompany her to the shop in San Gimignano, and the invitation was accepted at once. Leaving Werner and András, both armed with a ferocious array of bill-hooks, machetes and curved saws, making their way down to the wildest and most overgrown part of the garden, the two women set forth in Chiara's very small and elderly Fiat, Phylly holding a rush shopping basket on her knees. The little car threaded its way along an almost imperceptible track through the olive groves, finally emerging onto the road that would take them to San Gimignano.

They left the car in the obligatory parking place outside the city walls, then threaded their way through the narrow medieval streets until they arrived in a tiny piazza encircled by a stone arcade. Within its cool shade was Chiara's shop, with *Mille Tre Libri* written in gold across its elegant glass façade in a flowing cursive script. Reading this, Phyllida smiled. '*Don Giovanni?*' she guessed, following Chiara into the sweet-smelling gloom of the shop's interior.

'*Certo!*' said Chiara, and laughed.

The little shop was narrow, though very deep, and dimly lit by pencil-points of light from concealed spots in the vaulted ceiling. When her eyes became accustomed to the dimness, Phyllida saw that she was in a treasure house of ancient leather-bound manuscripts of every description, and from many countries and centuries. 'May I look?' she asked.

'Help yourself, my dear,' said Chiara, and took herself to a desk at the rear of the shop, where a dark-haired young woman sat before a computer, working. A rattling conversation in Italian ensued, then Chiara picked up the telephone and began to work her way through a list of calls.

Slowly, Phyllida examined the shelves and cabinets, reading the titles of the volumes as she passed. Occasionally, and extremely carefully, she opened one of the beautiful old books in order to examine the contents. The soft, sensuous feel of the leather bindings, and their deeply satisfying smell, filled her with pleasure and a strange excitement. Wouldn't it be brilliant to spend one's life among such exquisite things, she said to herself. What a privilege to be able to love and care for them on a daily basis, not just as a one-off treat, she thought, and the germ of an idea began to grow in her mind.

When Chiara had dealt with her calls, and had dictated a couple of letters to her assistant, they left the shop, and made their way to a side-street where a small open-air market was doing a brisk trade. Phyllida carried the shopping basket, and Chiara bought a kilo of fat white asparagus, some knobbly tomatoes, a bunch of small-leaved sweet basil and some bell peppers. At another stall she bought pecorino cheese and a litre of buttermilk. At the fruit-seller's she chose vast yellow peaches and red-skinned nectarines. Lastly, she bought a piece of *finocchiona*, the Tuscan sausage flavoured with garlic and fennel, and, on the way back to the car, they picked up a loaf of country bread from the bakery.

They drove back to *Cappella della Vigna* through the rolling hills, passing vineyards and fields of sunflowers on the way. 'I was wondering,' said Phyllida; 'that's to say, it occurred to me, seeing all those marvellous books in your lovely shop, that it might perhaps be possible to make a living out of hand-printing and binding books, limited editions, something along those lines? What do you think?'

'It would be difficult, but I certainly don't think it would be *impossible*,' Chiara replied. 'In the first place, there are so few people willing to train for such

323

work. There are plenty of dealers, but very few artisans for restoration, even fewer with printing presses of their own. The chief drawback is, that quite apart from all the technical obstacles, such an undertaking requires serious investment. It needs real money to set up a proper workshop.'

'Yes, I see. Where could one learn the business, do you have any idea?'

'There's a monastery in Umbria that undertakes such commissions, I know, and takes students as well, but I doubt whether they would admit women. The best place, though, is in London. I could look up their prospectus for you, if you're really interested.'

'Thank you,' said Phyllida, 'I'd be very grateful.' She was quiet and thoughtful all the way home.

After tea, Chiara brought a botanical book from her private collection out to the terrace, and allowed her guests to examine the stunning hand-coloured plates concealed within the covers. The antique pages, protected by their heavy bindings from the damaging effects of sunlight, were as brilliantly vibrant as the day on which they had been painted. András seemed mesmerized by their beauty, and gazed at each picture in silence, as he carefully turned the pages, one by one. Finally he closed the book, and placed a gentle finger on the gold-embossed title. 'You know,' he said, 'this is the very first time I've really looked at a book of such age and beauty, much less held it in my hands.' He smiled at Chiara. 'Thank you for that.'

Phyllida stood up, yawning, and stretched her arms above her head. 'I need a walk,' she said. 'Come with me, András?'

'Yes, of course.' He turned to Chiara. 'Shall we take the dogs? Would they like that?'

'They *would*! They *would*! Off you go!'

* * *

The sun had disappeared behind the hill, and down in the olive-clad valley the air was cool and fresh. The only sound came from the faint rustling of the trees, and the panting of the asthmatic little dogs as they chased each other along hidden tracks, in pursuit of imaginary quarry. Phyllida and András walked slowly along the path, enjoying the silence.

'Did you have a nice time with Werner?' she asked. 'Did he tell you any more horror stories, or was it OK?'

András smiled, and took her hand in his. 'No, he didn't. But if he had, I wouldn't have minded, thanks to you, darling Phylly.'

'Why thanks to me?'

'Why do you think? Last night was the best possible cure for an attack of the jitters, wouldn't you say?'

Phyllida laughed, and, turning, put her arms round him. She lifted her face to his, and he kissed her. 'Let's sit down,' she said. 'I've got something to say to you. She led the way to a patch of soft, emerald-green grass at the foot of a gnarled olive tree, and they sat down. 'What would you say if I asked Hugo and Mum to finance us to have a press, and make books together?'

'I would say you were completely barking, Phylly. You need serious money for that sort of thing.'

Phyllida looked at him hesitantly, a little nervously. 'That's exactly what they've got.'

'What?'

'Serious money.'

'So, what's that got to do with me, Phylly?'

'Everything, if you marry me, András.'

'How could I possibly marry you, you crazy girl? I have nothing to offer you, nothing at all. Don't you understand?'

'You don't love me, then? I had the distinct impression that you did, last night, or rather, this morning?'

'I did! I do! Of course I do!'

'So, what's the problem? Is it Madeleine?'

'Certainly not. I detest her.'

'What is it, then, András? Stupid pride? Isn't that a bit old-fashioned?'

András stared at her, then looked away. 'Phylly,' he said quietly, 'if it comes down to it, I am just an islander, a fisherman's son. I left school at sixteen with five GCSEs and no ambition other than getting on with helping Dad in the boat.'

'Is that still your ambition?'

'How can you ask me that? You know it's not. But don't you see that if I married you and let your parents set me up in business with you, it would be a kind of betrayal of my own people, especially my mum?'

'But now that you've found Werner, doesn't that make an important difference? He's your family too, isn't he?' She spread her arms, indicating the beautiful surroundings in which they found themselves. 'This sort of place, and this sort of way of life, is also your heritage, isn't it?'

András said nothing. He lay down in the grass and turned onto his stomach, so that she could not see his face. Tenderly she watched him, then lay down beside him and kissed the back of his neck. He groaned, then turned over and took her in his arms, unable to resist her any longer. 'Do you always get your own way, darling Phylly?'

'Usually,' she replied, smiling, 'if it's something worth having.'

'OK, you win,' he said. 'But I should warn you. Where I'm coming from, it'll be rather a barefoot wedding.'

Phyllida laughed. 'Oh dear, that sounds a bit dire. What about the apes in hell?'

'What apes in hell?'

'It's Shakespeare. *I must dance bare-foot on her wedding day, And, for your love to her, lead apes in hell.*'

'Sounds exactly like my mother, doesn't it, Phylly? If anyone leads apes in hell, she does, poor woman.'

Chapter Eighteen

At the end of the first week in August, Phyllida and
András took their regretful leave of Werner and Chiara,
and travelled back to Florizel. Scarcely had she set foot
on the island than Phyllida took her lover by the hand
and, taking advantage of her sisters' absence at the
beach, made her parents sit down at the kitchen table,
and began to divulge to them her plans for the future,
both matrimonial and professional. Initially, Hugo and
Nelly were astonished, then wryly amused, and ultimately really rather delighted as their difficult
daughter presented her carefully thought-out prop-
osition, concluding with a request for financial
support for herself and András during their training
period in London, and the setting-up of a printing
workshop thereafter.

Hugo, doing his best to preserve the dignified and
serious demeanour befitting a prospective father-in-
law, turned to András, who had sat silently beside
Phyllida throughout her disquisition, looking embarrassed. 'What about you, András? Are you equally
keen on this idea, or have you been steamrollered into
it?'

'*Papa!*' cried Phyllida, turning red. 'What a rotten
thing to suggest!'

Hugo ignored her, and kept his eye on András.

328

'Well?' he asked quietly, belatedly realizing that he was in fact deadly serious.

András looked up, first at Hugo, and then at Nelly. 'As a matter of fact,' he said, 'I feel extremely humiliated at this whole business of Phylly asking for money on my account. It's quite alien to my nature, and I don't like it at all. It was great of you to give me the ticket to go to Italy; there's a reasonable chance of paying that back. But this is something quite other; it's a question of being set up for life, isn't it?' He glanced towards Phyllida. 'The trouble is, I'm between a rock and a hard place. I hate the money thing, but I can't bear the thought of losing her. You see, I love her.'

At these words, Phyllida burst into tears. 'I'm sorry,' she wailed. 'I didn't mean to bully you, honestly I didn't. It's just that I know it's the right thing for us, that's all.' András put his arm round her, and she wept bitter salty tears into his clean denim shirt-front.

It was Nelly, predictably, who was the first to gather her wits. She got up from her seat, came round the table, and somehow managed to embrace both the young people at once. 'Stop crying, *please*, my dearest darling Phylly,' she said. 'This is no time for tears, it's a time for celebration. *Of course*, we're terribly pleased at the news, aren't we, darling?' She glared meaningfully at Hugo, who had remained seated, thunderstruck at the dramatic outcome of his well-intentioned interrogation of his future son-in-law.

'Yes, of course we are; *absolutely*,' he said, and snatching off his spectacles, polished them furiously with the hem of his T-shirt.

Nelly, keenly aware that she was the only one not in a state of emotional instability, took what she hoped was the appropriate decision. 'Come on,' she said. 'Let's put some food and wine in a basket and have a picnic on the beach with Sophie and Gertie.' She

329

touched András's cheek lightly with her cool fingers. 'They both adore you, András, and if they can't marry you themselves, they'll be delighted to have you as a brother-in-law, I'm sure.'

The tension was broken, and Phyllida managed a shaky laugh. Hugo, galvanized into action, went to the cellar and returned with champagne, and ten minutes later they were all down in Una-Mary's cove, and swimming in the clear green sea.

The next morning, after breakfast, Phyllida and András took the four-wheeler and drove to Roc aux Chiens, intending first to deliver Werner's letter to Michèle, and then tell Rose du Toit of their plans. Hugo, anticipating her inevitable angry reaction to the news, offered to go with them, but András, after thanking him politely, refused. 'It is very kind of you, Hugo, but this one I must manage on my own, I think.'

'Yes, of course,' said Hugo. 'Won't Phylly be rather unwelcome, though?'

'I don't care if I am,' said Phyllida firmly. 'We're in this together, and if there's going to be a row, I want to be there for András.'

'OK, off you go. Take care, both of you.'

Hugo went back to the kitchen, and enquired rather half-heartedly whether Nelly needed any help. She laughed, and told him to go and get on with his own work. He retired thankfully to his study, and gave his full attention to the life of Beaumarchais.

Simon's arrival at the farm made little difference to the daily pattern already established by Rachel and her teenage children. Ciaran, charmed by Simon's humour, his gentle demeanour and eccentric clothing, very soon fell under his spell. Although both boys were initially rather reserved towards him, they were not openly hostile. After a couple of days, Adam recognized the value to be obtained from an extra set of muscles, and so the puddling of the clay lining to the pond, and the turfing of its sloping banks were finished in record time.

Having urgently discussed the question of the sleeping arrangements with Rachel immediately after his arrival, Simon set up his tent and bedroll under the lime trees behind the house, and, in order to avoid causing embarrassment or pain to the children, there he slept in considerable discomfort.

'Don't you mind?' Rachel asked, feeling guilty, but nonetheless grateful for his tact.

'I bloody do; I don't mind admitting it.' Simon, frying eggs and bacon for supper on the Dover stove, gave her a swift, hard kiss, then released her. 'I've travelled nearly a thousand miles to go to bed with you, my darling, but it's just not on, is it? We'll have to wait, that's all.'

'It's just as hard for me.'

'Is it really?' Simon turned towards her again, his pale blue eyes alight.

'Yes,' said Rachel, 'it is. You can have no idea.'

'Oh yes, I can! For two pins I'd rush you upstairs right now, while they're out of the way!'

'Simon!' exclaimed Rachel, beginning to laugh. 'The eggs are *on fire*!'

'Shit! So they are!' He snatched the pan off the fire, beating the flames with the fish-slice. 'This is entirely your fault, Rachel; you distracted me!'

'What's going on?' asked Ned, coming through the kitchen door with a load of firewood.

'Nothing's going on,' said Rachel, laughing helplessly. 'A small domestic crisis, that's all.'

'It's just your mother doing her best to sabotage my culinary efforts,' said Simon.

'Well, you know what they say, don't you?' said Ned, grinning. 'All's fair in love and war, Simon.' He gave his mother a cheeky wink and went out into the yard again, whistling.

Rachel picked up the plates from the side of the stove and put them on the table.

'Hm,' she said. 'Do you think they've guessed?'

'I hope so.' Simon began to shovel the bacon and eggs onto the plates. 'Sooner they get used to the idea, the better for all concerned, don't you think?'

'What about Stanley?'

'Bugger Stanley, Rachel. He's had his chance and he's blown it, hasn't he?'

'Very true,' said Rachel, swiftly slicing thick hunks of bread. 'You're quite right; bugger Stanley. Give the kids a shout, darling, will you?'

After supper, while Ciaran and her brothers, in a giggly mood, dealt with the dishes, Simon took Rachel out to the barn. 'I've been thinking,' he said. 'Would you be horrified if I suggested that we get planning permission to convert the barn into extra living space and a studio, and live here part of the time? We could do three days a week in London, and the rest here.'

'Would you want to make it all high tech and contemporary, like Blomfield Road?'

'What do you take me for, Rachel? An utter prat? Of course not.'

'Well, good. I'd hate that, here.'

'So would I. So, what do you think?'

'I think, great. What about water? We couldn't really manage with just the well, could we?'

'Borehole, I should imagine. This place is solid water underneath, isn't it?'

'And money? We'd need quite a lot, wouldn't we?'

'You already own the place outright. I could easily raise the wind to pay for the restoration and conversion. I only rent Blomfield Road from my grandmother, so this could be what they call our principal residence.' Simon turned towards Rachel, his face grave, unsmiling, his pale eyes fixed steadily on hers. 'I love you, Rachel. I want to spend the rest of my life with you, if you'll have me, and a lot of the time I'd like us to be living here, in this magic place.'

Rachel did not answer immediately, though her heart was nearly bursting with happiness as she listened to this declaration of love. She leaned against Simon, resting her cheek on his chest. 'There's only one thing that worries me,' she said quietly. 'If I do leave Stanley formally and choose to live here, with or without you, my darling, it's possible that Ciaran might want to be with me. How would you feel about that?'

'Fine. Should there be a problem?'

'I hope not.'

'There won't be, I promise. As far as I'm concerned, they're all three part of you, and that's all that matters, OK?'

Rachel slid her arms round Simon's narrow waist, and he held her close to him. 'OK,' she said, 'but before we go into the house, there's something else I want to say.'

'What's that, darling?'

'I want to thank you for coming here, for not despising this place, for giving me back my parents and my real roots. Without you, I might easily have allowed myself to be bullied into selling the farm for a stupid, meaningless wad of banknotes. With you, perhaps it'll be a real home again, and the place we always come back to.' Rachel raised her eyes to Simon's. 'But most of all, I want to thank you for giving me back my real self, for making me whole again.'

'Marry me, Rachel.'

She shook her head, smiling. 'I'm already married; you know that.'

'You know what I mean. Marry me when you can.'

'We don't need a piece of paper, or some grotty old

registrar to give us permission to share our lives, do we? For me, it's perfect as it is.'

'If you ever change your mind, the offer remains open.'

'Is there a time limit?'

'Rachel, please be serious. For me, it's a simple question of till death us do part. Can't you handle that?'

'Yes,' she said, 'I think I can.' She put her arms round his neck and kissed him. 'There has to be one condition, though, Simon.'

'Oh? What's that?'

'Promise not to die before me, OK?'

At the end of August, Werner and Chiara arrived in Florizel to stay with the Turnbulls. András and Phyllida met them at the harbour and drove them to the house, but that evening, after supper, András cycled back to Roc aux Chiens. He felt a certain sense of guilt towards his father, and intended to give him as much assistance as possible with the fishing until the time came for his departure to London with Phyllida.

Hugo and Nelly did not bring up the subject of either Michèle or Rose, preferring to wait for the visitors to do so themselves, when they were ready. On the third day, Nelly flew to London with Sophie and Gertrude, to settle them into their new school. With her usual efficiency, she had also arranged to see her architect about the division of the Holland Park house into two flats, in order to provide both a home for Phylly and András, and an income from the rental of the second flat, for their maintenance during their years of study. Confident that Hugo, Phylly and András would take good care of the guests, she left the island without her usual desperate feelings of regret, knowing that she would be back in a few days, and that she would only have to wind down her appointments and work out her notice before returning to her beloved island for ever.

After Nelly's departure, Werner approached Hugo and asked whether it would be possible for him to visit Roc aux Chiens.

'Of course,' said Hugo. 'Whenever you wish; Phylly will drive you over. Would you like me to telephone Mrs Langlois, and fix a time?'

'Thank you. That would be kind.'

The next morning Phyllida and Werner set off in the four-wheeler, side by side on the front bench-seat. Murphy ambled along the lanes in his usual indolent manner and Phyllida chose not to urge him into greater activity, correctly assuming that Werner was probably feeling quite nervous, and would be glad of a little extra time in which to marshal his thoughts. Equally, she said very little during the course of the drive, except to point out one or two things she thought might be of particular interest.

They arrived at Roc aux Chiens just before the appointed hour, eleven o'clock. Phyllida indicated a stone cottage on the edge of the cliff, overlooking a small stone quay. 'That's the du Toits' place,' she said. 'The Langlois farm is straight on, we'll be there in five minutes.'

'It hasn't changed at all,' said Werner quietly. 'I remember it all perfectly, as if it were yesterday.'

'Do you really?' Phyllida sounded surprised. 'Do you remember my great-grandparents, at *Les Romarins*?'

'No, not at all. Only officers visited at *Les Romarins* or *Le Manoir*, my dear.' He smiled. 'I was a very lowly soldier, you understand, and extremely glad to accept the kindness of ordinary island folk.'

'The Langlois are very nice people,' said Phyllida. 'András is lucky to have Michèle as his grandmother, and the others as his uncles and aunts.'

'Indeed, he is.'

Murphy stopped at the farm gate, and Phyllida jumped down to open it, and lead the pony through.

She drove into the yard, the kitchen door opened and Monique Langlois appeared, tall, handsome and smiling. 'Good morning and welcome, Mr Balthus,' she said. 'Let me give you a hand getting down.'

Once on the ground, Werner took her hand and shook it gently. 'You must be big Denis's daughter-in-law?'

Monique laughed. 'Certainly am. Though Dad died, a while back.'

'I'm sorry to hear it; I remember him well, of course.'

'Gran's in the orchard, waiting for you, if you want to go up. You know the way?'

'Yes, I know the way, thank you.' He gave a little bow and, turning, walked towards the small wooden door in the stone wall, and went through it.

'Come in and have a coffee, Phyllida, why don't you?'

'I'd love to, thanks.' Phyllida jumped down, tied Murphy's reins to a hitching post, and followed Monique into the house.

In the orchard, Michèle, wearing her best blue linen frock, sat on the battered garden seat in the far corner of the orchard and waited calmly for Werner to appear. She saw him as soon as he came through the green door in the high wall that surrounded the carefully nurtured orchard, and in spite of her steadiness and self-control, she was unable to prevent her heart missing a beat and the blood rushing to her cheeks. She watched him as he stood looking round, trying to locate her, and saw that his once tall and strong body had become thin and stooped, and that his blond hair, so like that of András, was now snow-white. She lifted a fluttering hand to her own head, wondering nervously whether the havoc wrought by the passage of the years had been equally devastating to herself. How strange, she thought, in the photograph I didn't think he looked so very different; I knew him at once.

Werner, having put on his spectacles, had at last spotted Michèle as she sat quietly on the seat, and at once made his way towards her with as much speed as his knees would permit. As he drew near, Michèle stood up and held out her hands. They stood facing each other, their hands tightly locked, and each looked into the blue eyes of the other, searching for the vanished lover of so many thousand yesterdays, a time out of mind, inhabited by ghosts. 'Dearest Michèle,' said Werner huskily, 'you haven't changed at all. You are as beautiful as ever.'

'You, too, Werner; you are just the same.' She smiled, and it seemed to him for a second that nothing at all had changed, that the years between were meaningless. 'Let's sit down,' she said. 'We have a lot to talk about.'

No-one ever knew what passed between them in the orchard, and no-one ever felt the need or desire to question either of them. At a quarter past one, Monique appeared in the doorway, and shouted that lunch was ready if they felt like a bite to eat, and Werner and Michèle came down from the orchard, hand in hand, and joined the family in the kitchen.

At three o'clock, Werner and Phyllida said their goodbyes, got back into the four-wheeler and drove to Roc aux Chiens, pulling up at the gate to the du Toit cottage. The two house-dogs, a pair of chained Alsatians, barked furiously from their adjacent compound. 'Do you want me to wait for you here, or come in?' Phyllida asked, eyeing the dogs nervously.

'It's probably best if I see Rose alone, I think.'

'Right; I'll wait here, then.'

Carefully, Werner put a foot on the metal step and lowered himself to the ground. 'I don't suppose I'll be long,' he said.

'I'll trot on a bit,' said Phyllida, 'and come back in a few minutes, OK?'

'Yes, fine.'

Werner walked slowly up the path and knocked on the door. After a pause, it was opened, there was a brief exchange on the threshold, then Rose stepped back and her father entered her house. 'Thank you for allowing me to visit you, Rose,' he said, sitting down uninvited on one of the three hard chairs surrounding the square, oil-cloth-covered table.

Rose remained standing, her arms crossed, staring at her father with a mixture of curiosity and resentment. 'I don't know why you've bothered to come,' she said at last, coldly. 'There's not a lot of point in it, after fifty odd years, is there? You've got here too late to make any difference to *my* bloody life.'

'It's understandable that you feel that way, Rose, and I'm very sorry about it, but I hope at least to make a small difference to András's life. He's a grandson to be proud of, my dear.'

'Yes, and he's a *son* to be proud of, and a legitimate one too, and now you've stolen him from me and handed him over body and soul to those stuck-up Turnbulls! I hate them, the whole bloody lot of them, and I hate you, too! I hope you rot in hell, you pathetic old scumbag.'

Werner, stunned by the suddenness and viciousness of his daughter's attack, took a deep breath. 'The Turnbulls are good people, Rose; they mean you no harm.'

'Why the hell should I believe that, I should like to know? How do you think it feels to be me, to have to stand by and watch my son, the only decent thing in my entire rotten life, be taken away from me?' Rose stood over Werner, leaning on the table, breathing heavily, glaring at him furiously.

Werner, bereft of speech, stared back at her, like a rabbit caught in the lights of a car. She raised an arm threateningly, and he flinched violently, then staggered to his feet, clinging to the edge of the table. Rose laughed, and going swiftly to the door, wrenched it open. 'Get out of here, before I really *do* hit you, you cringing old coward, and don't come here again, if you know what's good for you!'

Werner, really rather frightened, though doing his best not to show it, got himself through the door as quickly as he could. Once on the path, he attempted to take his leave in a civilized manner, but she cut him short, and shut the door in his face.

Phyllida, waiting at the gate in the four-wheeler, watched this exchange with some alarm. She leapt down from her seat, and ran to offer Werner a comforting arm. The door flew open again, and Rose stood before them, red-faced, her eyes blazing. 'And you, Miss, can get yourself off my private property, too! Who the hell do you think you are, prancing up my path without a by-your-leave, and letting your bloody horse shit right outside my gate?'

Phyllida looked at Murphy and saw that it was indeed true, the pony was in the ostentatious process of voiding his bowels in the road. 'I'm sorry, Mrs du Toit, I was only trying to help,' said Phyllida. 'I had no intention of annoying you, believe me. I'll clear away the mess.'

'Don't bother!' shouted Rose. 'Bugger off, the pair of you, or I'll set the dogs on you!' She went back into the house once more, slamming the door behind her, making the windows rattle.

'Come on, Werner, we'd better not hang about,' said Phyllida. They got back into the four-wheeler and drove away as fast as they could. When they had regained the road to *Les Romarins*, and Murphy was heading for home at a brisk trot, Phyllida spoke. 'I'm terribly sorry you had to endure that, Werner. I should have come in with you.'

'No, no, my dear. It was only right that Rose should feel at liberty to express her bitterness and revulsion against me, if that's how she feels. After all, her particular tragedy was my fault, wasn't it? I am entirely to blame for that, poor woman.'

'Nonsense!' said Phyllida briskly, with all the conviction of youth. 'Of course you're not. After all, you didn't even *know* that she existed, did you?'

'This is true,' said Werner in a low voice, 'but it is also true that I never made any attempt to find out what had happened to Michèle and her kind family, after the war, and for this I am ashamed and sorry.'

'You forget something, Werner.'

'Oh? What's that?'

'Michèle is not angry with you, is she?'

'No, Phylly, she is not, *Gott sie dank*.'

Alone in her empty house, Rose du Toit listened until the sound of the pony's hooves had died away. Then she sat down in the seat that her father had occupied, put her head on her folded arms, and wept as though her heart would break.

Towards the end of August, Simon returned to London and Rachel took her children back to Oxford, arriving in the late afternoon. They found Stanley and Antonia in the garden, having tea under the chestnut tree.

'Any more tea in the pot?' asked Adam. 'I'm parched, as well as ravenous.'

'There are tea bags in the kitchen, Adam,' said Antonia, smiling at him, 'and biscuits in the tin. Why don't you three go indoors and look after yourselves?'

'Oh, all right, if you say so.' Adam raised his black

340

eyebrows at his brother and sister, and they took themselves off, without having spoken a word to their father.

'Tea, Rachel?' Graciously, Antonia raised the silver teapot.

'Thank you.' Rachel sat down in a cane chair, feeling like a guest in her own house. She took the proffered cup and sipped some tea. 'That was a bit unnecessary, wasn't it?' she said, to no-one in particular.

'What was, my dear?' Unusually for him, Stanley sounded rather cheerful, even jolly.

'Oh, nothing.'

'Did you have a pleasant holiday? Good weather? Not too hot?' Though his tone was still jovial, Stanley did not sound as if he really wanted to know.

'It was lovely, thanks. We had a good time.'

'Good, good.'

Antonia stood up, elegant and assured. 'I expect you have things to talk about. I'd better supervise the unpacking, hadn't I? I imagine there's a load of laundry needs doing?'

'No, there's not much. They hardly changed their clothes at all. Rarely wore any, actually.'

'*Really?*' It was amazing how much combined disdain and disapproval Antonia managed to pack into that single word, and Rachel made a coarse gesture towards her departing figure. 'Silly cow,' she muttered, under her breath.

'Really, Rachel,' said Stanley. 'There's no call for that sort of childishness.'

'As a matter of fact, Stanley,' said Rachel, 'the same applies to you. You and Antonia make a good pair; you're a couple of hypocritical farts.'

'It's curious that you should say that we make a good couple, my dear.' Stanley fixed his small dark malicious eyes on his wife, and smiling, deeply self-conscious, he seemed to swell with self-congratulation

341

before her very eyes. 'Because I have something to tell you. Well, two things, in fact.'

Rachel laughed. 'I can guess the first thing, Stanley, you're so utterly predictable. You want to marry Antonia, right?'

'That's correct.'

'OK, what's the second thing?'

'Some time ago, my dear, I applied for a chair at Cambridge. I was short-listed for the job, and I learned recently that I had been appointed.'

'Congratulations. It's what you've always wanted, isn't it?'

'Indeed.'

'Professor Madoc. Sounds quite impressive, doesn't it? I'm pleased for you, Stanley. I expect Antonia is over the moon, isn't she?'

'Well, yes, she finds it a gratifying circumstance, my dear.'

'I bet she does,' said Rachel, and laughed. 'No wonder she's keen to marry you, Stanley. You're a pretty good catch now, aren't you?' She smiled at him, her clear grey eyes full of an amused tolerance towards his pomposity and alien values, and he could not help noticing how youthful, even pretty, she looked, as she sat there in her crumpled white shirt and worn-out jeans. He opened his mouth to express some kind of graceful regret that their marriage had failed, but before he could say anything, she asked when he would be moving to Cambridge.

'October, next year.'

'I see. I suppose you'll have to look for a house?'

'That's already in hand.'

'So what about this house? Is it already on the market?'

'That won't be necessary. My successor here seems eager to take on the house as well as the job.'

'Good heavens, you *have* been lucky!' She looked

342

steadily at Stanley. 'I guess that the luck is mostly down to Antonia's careful planning?'

'Well, yes, I suppose so.'

'And schools for the children? Has she taken care of that, too?'

'Yes, she has. It's not altogether satisfactory; it will mean that they change schools at half-term, but they'll cope very well, I feel sure.' Stanley gazed upon his discarded wife benevolently. 'Obviously,' he said smoothly, 'I have discussed the question of the divorce settlement with my legal advisers, and they are of the opinion that in fact very little needs to be done in that respect. Clearly, as I shall be taking on full responsibility for the housing, maintenance and education of our children, Rachel, you will not expect a share of our present assets. As for the question of access to the children, it goes without saying that both they and you are entirely free to see each other whenever you so wish, or is convenient. In the circumstances, it seems fair to me that I pay you a modest allowance to cover the expenses of their holidays with you, at least until they are in further education.'

'Get lost, Stanley, I don't need or want your rotten money! What sort of an idiot do you take me for? If I felt like it, I could claim half the value of this house, as I've no doubt you and Antonia are perfectly well aware.'

'But,' said Stanley, with the air of one playing his trump card, 'you already have a house of your own, haven't you, my dear?'

'Yes, I have, and I intend to live in it.'

'With your young friend, no doubt?'

'Yes, Stanley, with Simon, and with the children, whenever they feel like coming.' She rose to her feet. 'You can drive me to the station; I'm going home.' She looked at her watch. 'There's a train in twenty minutes.'

343

'Very well. Delighted to take you, of course.'

They went into the house and Rachel yelled up the stairs to the children. Three heads appeared over the banisters. 'I'm off now. Do you want to come to the station?'

The young people exchanged quick glances. 'Not really, Mum, if you don't mind,' said Adam. 'We're a bit busy helping Antonia getting our stuff sorted. Sorry.'

'It's OK; doesn't matter. See you soon.'

'See you soon, Mum,' said Ned.

'It was cool at the farm, Mum.' Ciaran blew a kiss. 'Love to Simon.'

Postlude

Nelly returned to *Les Romarins* in time for the farewell party that Hugo, Phyllida and András had arranged for Werner and Chiara. As it often is on Florizel during September, the weather that night was perfect. It was warm and balmy, and a harvest moon shed its brilliance over the island, making artificial illumination almost unnecessary. In the garden, Hugo had built a makeshift barbecue from two piles of bricks and a piece of old expanded-metal mesh he had found in the stables. Underneath this structure he lit his fire of driftwood and dried seaweed, which he hoped would give a special flavour to the langoustines, clams and spider crabs that András was providing for the feast.

Phyllida and her mother carried out a pair of wooden trestles and some planks, and Nelly spread some of Una-Mary's white linen sheets on this improvised table. As the hour of the party approached, they brought out bowls of salad and fruit, bread and cheese, and bottles of wine, as well as plates, glasses, knives and forks. As a final festive touch, Phyllida found her grandmother's many-branched silver candelabra in the cupboard under the stairs, and stuck ordinary kitchen candles into them. Their yellow flames burned steadily, tall and unwavering in the still night air.

At seven o'clock, András and Phyllida drove over to

Roc aux Chiens to bring the guests to the party, and at eight o'clock Michèle, with Denis and Monique, arrived at *Les Romarins.* They were welcomed by Hugo and Nelly, and taken to the firelit garden, where Werner and Chiara were waiting for them.

Chiara and Michèle sat together, and after a slight initial shyness on Michèle's part, were soon deep in conversation. Hugo cooked the seafood with great efficiency, though somewhat hampered by offers of assistance from Monique and Phylly, and in half an hour they all sat down to eat.

Nelly sat close to Hugo, and watched the candlelit faces of her family and new friends, and thought how beautiful and unexpected life could be. Her eyes rested on the face of her first-born, Phylly, and she gave thanks that life had given her difficult child a second chance, in the shape of András. She will dominate him, she thought, just as I did Hugo; but if they really do love each other, it won't matter. She glanced at Chiara, who sat on her right, facing Werner. Flushed and voluble, she wore a silvery organza robe with a matching turban, and a necklace of jingling Turkish coins. Listening to Chiara correcting her courteous old husband with a kind of teasing affection, Nelly smiled. Evidently, *she* bosses Werner, too, she said to herself wryly, but I don't suppose he minds very much.

Chiara then turned her attention to Denis Langlois, on her right, and Werner, putting down his fork, smiled at his hostess. 'Nelly,' he said. 'Will you come with Hugo, and visit us at *Cappella della Vigna*? In the springtime, perhaps?'

'We'd love it, Werner, thank you. Nothing would give us greater pleasure.' She reached out and covered his hand with hers. 'I should write to Rose, if I were you, Werner,' she said, gently. 'I'm sure she'll come round, given time.'

'Do you really think so?'

'Yes, I do.'

'In that case, Nelly, I will, as soon as I get home.'

After supper, they sat comfortably round the fire, talking, and András and Phyllida brought coffee and brandy. At midnight, Monique said that it was getting very late, they had to be up early for the milking, and where was András? Surprised, they all looked round, but the two young people were nowhere to be seen.

'Don't worry,' said Hugo. 'I expect they've gone for a walk, or a swim. I'll drive you home, it's no problem.'

'I'll come with you,' said Werner, getting to his feet.

When the four-wheeler had clopped off down the drive, Nelly took Chiara by the arm, and together they walked slowly across the sheep-field to the edge of the cliff, and looked down into the bay.

Far below, they could see Phyllida and András, with long trails of green phosphorescence caressing their slender young bodies as they swam together in the translucent moonlit water.

'Those two will marry,' said Chiara. 'They love each other.'

'Yes,' said Nelly, 'they do. But in their heads, they're already married, don't you think?'

The two young lovers stood up in the shallow surf and clung to each other, so that their bodies cast a single long shadow on the bright water. Nelly and Chiara turned and walked slowly back to the house together.

By the following spring, Simon and Rachel had installed a generator, a telephone and a borehole at St Cuthbert's Fen. Adam, Ned and Ciaran came to spend Easter with them, and were impressed by the rate of progress. Down in the reedbeds, deep in the fen, the bitterns were nesting, and their eerie foghorn booming could be heard, far into the night. The sound haunted all their dreams, and cast a spell around the house.

347

On Easter Saturday, it was hot and sunny. Simon and Adam got out the elderly and decrepit Flymo, oiled it and tuned the engine, then Adam mowed all the lush long grass at the rear of the house, right up to the pond. Rachel appeared with a tray of cold drinks, and sat down on the new-mown grass with Simon. Adam swallowed his drink, then carried on with the mowing, working carefully along the edge of the water, and round the great pollarded willow that reflected itself in the pool. Suddenly, the blade of the mower struck something hard and solid behind the tree, and Adam turned off the engine to check for possible damage to the blade. He saw a flat stone hidden in the grass, with some letters carved on its surface. 'Mum! Simon!' he called. 'Come and look at this!'

Simon and Rachel came to his side, hand in hand, across the grass. 'What is it?'

'Take a look, Mum.'

Rachel knelt down, brushing away the bits of grass and moss from the stone. A.N.C., she read. 'Amy Nora Cropthorne,' she said aloud. 'This must be my mother's grave. Pa must have buried her here, all by himself. How lovely of him.'

'Well,' said Adam, 'I hope she's pleased to see us.'

'I'm quite sure she is,' said Simon.

'So am I,' said Rachel, softly.

THE END

THE LOVE OF WOMEN
Elizabeth Falconer

Nelly and Hugo lived a seemingly enviable life, with their three adorable little girls, their holidays at the beautiful family home in the Channel Islands, and their large, if disorganized, London house. Why, then, did Hugo feel increasingly inadequate? He began to wonder why Nelly had married him instead of Basil, their close ally from Cambridge days. Basil had instead become an indispensable family friend, and Nelly's demanding job as a hospital doctor seemed to overshadow Hugo's own successful but unremunerative career as a writer – Hugo felt as though his only function in Nelly's life nowadays was to babysit the children and keep an eye on the erratic au pair. One day, in a fit of rebellion, he packed his bags and went to stay with Basil's mother in her peaceful Paris flat on the lovely Ile St-Louis.

Basil, meanwhile, was facing an uncertain future. Tied by loyalty to Nelly and Hugo, and with a muddled and ambivalent series of past relationships, he was at first reluctant to commit himself when he met Olivia, the self-confident young English art student living in Paris who was interested in the work of Basil's late father, a much-admired Russian painter. While Hugo discovered how hard it was to escape from family ties, Basil was to find that friendship and love do not easily mingle.

'AN UNHURRIED, LUXURIOUS STORY OF RESOLUTION AND DISCOVERY . . . THE NOVEL'S CHARM LIES IN ITS UNPRETENTIOUSNESS AND THE AUTHOR'S AFFECTION FOR CHARACTERS'

Elizabeth Buchan, *Mail on Sunday*

0 552 99623 8

BLACK SWAN

THE COUNTER-TENOR'S DAUGHTER

Elizabeth Falconer

Dido Partridge's life as the daughter of an exotic operatic soprano and her counter-tenor lover, Signor Pernice, has been a strange one. A childhood spent mainly in the dressing rooms of the great European opera houses had led naturally to her present bohemian existence in a grand old houseboat, once her mother's, moored on the Thames. This unusual home she shares with Jacob, a film director and her erratic but long-term partner, until her friends' hints of Jacob's frequent infidelities are proved true by her discovery that he had been entertaining another woman on the houseboat. Disposing of his belongings overboard and booking the first flight out of Heathrow that she could find, she ends up in Corfu, in a beautiful, unspoilt bay where she reads, swims and eats the lovely but simple food prepared for her by the local taverna keeper.

Gradually, as the peace and tranquillity of Corfu begin to work their magic on her, Dido becomes aware of Guy, an attractive lawyer who left London for the solitude of the island when his disability – the result of a childhood accident – became too much for him to bear. Guy's resentful sister Lavinia, who may know more about Guy's accident than either of them is prepared to admit, can never forgive Guy for inheriting the great family mansion in Ireland where, by coincidence, Jacob is now directing a film. As Dido and Guy start to heal the wounds which each of them has acquired through the years, they both begin to see how their lives can change.

0 552 99624 6

BLACK SWAN

WINGS OF THE MORNING
Elizabeth Falconer

Christian and his younger sister Emma, children of
a wealthy but spectacularly ill-matched couple,
had been brought up by their mother Flavia in the
hope that one of them, at least, would find a
vocation to the religious life. Their father Ludovic,
meanwhile, was absent from their lives for a great
deal of the time – an absence which, as they grew
up, became all too readily understandable. But
while Christian lived in London and
Gloucestershire with his wife Phoebe and their two
small children – a shamefully irreligious life,
according to Flavia – Emma followed her heart's
desire by training to be a fresco painter in Italy and
then, bowing to the incessant pressure from her
mother, became a nun in an enclosed order.

A tragedy in the family brought them all to crisis
point. Flavia fell apart, becoming increasingly and
fanatically religious. Phoebe and Christian had to
rebuild their family life, while Emma became
gloriously, unexpectedly free – finding love of a
more earthly kind in the glorious countryside of
Provence.

0 552 99755 2

BLACK SWAN

A SELECTED LIST OF FINE WRITING
AVAILABLE FROM BLACK SWAN

THE PRICES SHOWN BELOW WERE CORRECT AT THE TIME OF GOING TO PRESS. HOWEVER TRANSWORLD PUBLISHERS RESERVE THE RIGHT TO SHOW NEW RETAIL PRICES ON COVERS WHICH MAY DIFFER FROM THOSE PREVIOUSLY ADVERTISED IN THE TEXT OR ELSEWHERE.

All Transworld titles are available by post from:

Book Services By Post, P.O. Box 29, Douglas, Isle of Man IM99 1BQ

Credit cards accepted. Please telephone 01624 675137,
fax 01624 670923 or Internet http://www.bookpost.co.uk.
or e-mail: bookshop@enterprise.net for details

Free postage and packing in the UK. Overseas customers: allow
£1 per book (paperbacks) and £3 per book (hardbacks).